# COME THE DARK NIGHT

## DAVID TREGARTHEN

'The truth is rarely pure and never simple.'
— **Oscar Wilde**

# PROLOGUE
## OXFORD, 1998, FIRST WEEK IN TRINITY

*I look down from my vantage point high above the city, scent the early morning air and smile. It will be another of those sultry days that spring borrows from summer. On such a day, the air holds out the promise of a time beyond the teaching term that has just grudgingly begun; beyond the testing, fraught, close-knit days of Finals; beyond even those precious weeks of quiet libraries where dust motes dance as scholars snooze. On such a day, the illusory prospect of drifting on a peaceful river or browsing in bookshops along deserted lanes has not yet been shattered by the squalid reality of building works and the blind hunger of the omnipresent crowds. And on this day it is that I – or rather my Work – shall be seen.*

*I walk back across the wooden floor, carefully lift and place the head to one side, then take a moment to rest from my labours. As the young April sun rises over Oxford's spires and bell towers, my city is neither dreaming nor sleeping. Whilst darkness and quietude still prevailed – though I, of course, was busy about my Work – three dozen college porters waited patiently within the establishments they guard. Now, as the bells of Tom Tower and a hundred churches strike their conflicting chimes, these men begin to unlock the smaller wickets set inside the great iron-studded timber gateways. The more famous – or cupidinous – colleges 'fling wide their gates', knowing an influx of tourists waits to make its less than royal way. Agog to consume cultural capital, the sheep will stream inexorably in from early morning until dusk: from the grubby ring road and coach parks and railway station. Within each college, gardeners are doubtless hard at work weeding borders and mowing precious lawns still thirsty for the month's promised 'shoures soote'. Scouts and bedders begin to scrub porcelain and polish stainless steel – or so I imagine. I do not know the truth of it. Perhaps they are instead counting out linen for distribution amongst the students in their charge – most of them still dead to the world, it's safe to assume, bins outside their rooms to guard against unwanted intrusion. Excluded here, of course, the chasers of Firsts already annotating texts in quiet carpeted libraries, the earnest chapelgoers kneeling in prayer, and those Lycra-clad rowers quick-stepping it to the cold river. I see one now, cycling along the pavement, weaving between concrete bollards, almost close enough to... but, no, I must not allow myself to be distracted.*

*I hammer in the spike, muffling the sound of metal on iron with his scarf, then rest again. As I wait, silent and unseen, elsewhere cheerful shouts, ribald laughter, rise from the meat stalls in the Covered Market and the kitchens they stock. Along Catte Street and Cornmarket, Broad Street and the High, the thin light shines down alike on saints peering myopically from their niches in the church towers, and sinners, scurrying back from strange beds, rumpled-black-jacketed and pallid-faced. Loathsome in their petty deceit. Ants, all of them, waiting for one divine foot to mash them into the cobbles of Radcliffe Square.*

*My breath returns and I begin to pack away my tools. Nearby, the Old Bodleian's great quadrangle lies yet hushed, as lonely staff dribble their way past old Pembroke's statue. He stands now in shadow, impassively watching over the doorways with their neatly painted homage to the Old Schools, as he has done since his translocation in the Year of Our Lord 1723. Nearby, the sun's warming rays slide tentatively up the wall of the Sheldonian Theatre, past its encircling grotesques with their gaping mouths, till they reach the cupola's arched windows and pale-green dome, high above the waking city. My mouth waters. Soon and very soon.*

# PART I

## CHAPTER ONE

MONDAY 27 APRIL, FIRST WEEK IN TRINITY

Jonathan's eyes opened onto darkness and for a moment he did not know where he was. The air in the room was stale and there was a dark, acrid taste in his mouth. His hand groped blindly to the side of him, connecting with something cold and hard on a table by the narrow bed. As it hit the floorboards, there came the unmistakeable sound of breaking glass and splashing water. *Shit.*

Wide awake now, Jonathan shunted himself to the end of the bed and felt for the wall and the light switch. Yes, it was where it should be; he was in his own college rooms. Screwing up his eyes against the light, Jonathan stepped gingerly over the glass shards and grabbed a towel from the radiator. He threw it down over the centre of the disaster and used it to mop up as much of the water as he could, whilst sliding the debris together into a heap for Maureen, his Scout, to deal with later. He stumbled over to his tiny sink and turned on the cold tap, bending to take two great slurping draughts before splashing a handful onto his burning cheeks and brow. He stared at the mirror as water dripped down his body, making the fine hairs on his chest and abdomen stand on end. Bleary eyes, tangled, greasy hair, pallid face. What the hell had *happened* last night?

The last he could remember, he had been in the common room, chatting with Lawrence. Why had he let himself be persuaded yet again to carry on drinking after dinner? And why did it have to be port?

As he stared, the headache kicked in like a boxer's jab to the forehead and, as if by reflex, Jonathan dry-heaved into the sink. He lunged for the packet of painkillers on the bedside table and felt a sharp stabbing pain in his toe from a stray piece of glass. *Shit.*

Wrapping his bleeding foot in an odd sock he found down the side of the bed, Jonathan pushed a couple of painkillers through the foil of the packet. As he forced the chalky tablets down, he caught sight of the little clock on the wall. 9.45. *Doubleshittingbollocks.*

He had a tutorial at ten. No time for a shower now, even if he could risk crossing the hall looking like this. Stepping carefully over to the sink again, he scrubbed at his face and armpits with a flannel and lukewarm water, then tweaked a lock of hair so it hung over the scar on his forehead. He was starting to look more human, though he felt about ninety years old. He yanked up the sash window to let out the fug, then hurried into the tiny adjoining kitchenette to make a cup of coffee with one of the sachets he'd pinched from Hall. It tasted foul but he needed the caffeine hit.

Jonathan poured himself a bowl of muesli – he didn't want his stomach rumbling during the tute. A few mouthfuls in, his mistake became apparent, but by that point it was too late. He dashed for the sink in his bedroom again and vomited out the undigested mush of cereal, followed by a couple of spoonfuls' worth of dark-green liquid. Was that what bile looked like? It smelled revolting and he hastened to rinse it away, then felt something trickling from his nose. 'You've got to be kidding me,' he groaned. *Not again*. But, no, inevitably, the bright red drops fell. He stared as the water turned a beautiful translucent pink.

At that moment, there was a knock on the outside door.

'Just a minute!' he called, silently cursing himself, the college, and the universe at large.

He stuffed a bit of wadded-up tissue into his right nostril, pulled on the nearest clothes he could find, and then Dr Jonathan Reynolds, Stipendiary Lecturer in Medieval and Renaissance Literature at St Sebastian's College, Oxford, padded across his study to let in the first students of the day.

Detective Sergeant Kate Stewart nodded at the officer on duty at the tall wooden doors of the Sheldonian Theatre. They had done a good job of securing the surrounding quadrangle: the gates off Broad Street and Holywell Street were locked, and police tape blocked the access ways via the Clarendon Building and the Old Bodleian. She pushed open the heavy right-hand door and held it for her partner, Detective Constable Geoff (never Geoffrey) Simpson, six-foot-two of ginger muscle foisted on her by the Big Boss seven months ago. They both stopped short as they entered the darkened theatre. It was not somewhere Kate had been before, though she had often seen posters for concerts there and felt guilty for not making more of an effort to be cultured. As she looked around now for the first time, it was even more intimidating than she'd imagined. The cavernous space smelled of antiquity and furniture polish.

'Blow me!' Geoff said, his eyes wide. 'This is mental!'

Kate quelled him with a glance. As she began to cross the vast wooden floor of the auditorium, her footsteps echoed loudly. She was wearing what she called her sensible shoes:

designed to make her seem professional but still feminine, smart but not decorative. At the moment she just felt embarrassed by the noise they made.

They crossed past vacant rows of red seats set in a semicircle of what looked like pews beneath a huge painted ceiling, all of it loomed over by balconies and chandeliers and huge organ pipes as if from a horror film. Another set of wooden double doors with small inset windows led into a sort of backstage area, where they had to climb up an endless number of narrow steps that wound up behind the main auditorium, then up again into a smaller floor-boarded space where a man who must be the caretaker sat on a tiny wooden stool, looking wan and nauseous amongst the enormous roof beams and joists of the structure. The officer taking his statement gestured to a box of plastic shoe covers, then towards still another, yet narrower set of steps leading up to the cupola itself. Both she and Geoff were breathing heavily by the time they stepped out into the sunlight.

'Guess I won't be needing to hit the gym later,' said Geoff, rubbing his quads, but Kate ignored him, confronted by the sight of a young man's slim body slumped on a small bench, pinned against the east wall of the octagonal structure by an iron spike.

As she struggled to make sense of the scene in front of her, part of Kate's mind mechanically noted the breathtaking view of the towers, domes, and crenellations of central Oxford laid out all around, all four compass points neatly labelled beneath the appropriate windows. But the body. That mangled body, the head missing, the left arm totally severed at the shoulder, yes, down there, lying neatly to the right of the bench in a dark pool of congealed ooze. Not the death wound – not enough blood. She continued to look around the small, enclosed space, taking mental snapshots, ignoring the delicate church spires and college towers tempting her gaze as they glinted in the sun. Then she heard Geoff make a harsh gagging sound to her left and swivelled to see what he had found. Now she spotted what her eyes had initially refused to process, skipped over. The student's head, oddly small in its isolation on the floor by the north wall, encircled by burnt-out candles, its livid eyes staring blankly upwards as if in search for help that would never come. Kate clamped down on her stomach. No one would ever see her throwing up if she could help it, particularly not one of her male colleagues.

'What the *fuck*?' said Geoff, looking green.

Kate's mind worked furiously. It was already obvious this was no ordinary murder – it had been carefully staged – but why?

'Exactly,' she said. 'Thoughts, Constable?'

Geoff took a deep breath. 'Well, the immediate cause of death isn't clear but it certainly wasn't the dismemberment or decapitation. Not enough of the red stuff.'

'Right. So why go to all the trouble of taking off his arm and head?'

'I dunno – the killer's some sicko, out of his mind on psychedelics?'

'Hardly.' Kate shook her head. 'I mean, the degree of effort and thought this must have taken… not to mention time.'

'Then what?' Geoff said. 'What's this guy trying to say?'

*What indeed?* Kate thought. She turned away from the corpse and stared out of the nearest window at her adopted city. From this high angle it seemed unfamiliar, alien, full of hidden menace.

Jonathan stared at the uninspiring collection of faces across the table, four pairs of downturned eyes intent on the revision handout he'd just given them.

'Have you all reread your second-year notes and the first section of the *Canterbury Tales*, like I asked?' Four nods. Good. 'Great,' he said, trying to project enthusiasm and failing. 'We'll come to that in a minute. But first I want to get some close reading practice in as revision for the language commentaries. This extract is from the Prologue to the *Wife of Bath's Tale*.'

'Oh, we did that for A-level,' Charity piped up, looking pleased.

'Okay, great. Obviously we'll dig a little deeper today, but that should give you a good start.'

Crestfallen, Charity tucked her long, well-conditioned hair behind one ear and lowered her long lashes, accentuated with just a hint of mascara.

'Once you've all had a chance to read through it,' Jonathan continued, 'we'll discuss your ideas and then see if we can make some connections to the *General Prologue*.'

Dutifully, the four heads turned back to the handout, Timothy and Charlotte with their ever-ready pencils in hand, and Jonathan relaxed back into his chair, surreptitiously rubbing his still-throbbing foot. The *Wife*'s Prologue ought to give them something to get their teeth into. He knew he wasn't going to get through this seminar without some deft use of unseen extracts to take the pressure off him. Why were these revision seminars always so deadly?

As he looked at the students in turn, Charlotte gave a deep sigh as though troubled by what she was reading. Mousy, plump Charlotte Rudman; an unenthusiastic donation from one of the Home Counties' more minor public schools. She'd actually seemed quite promising when she first came up, he recalled – bubbly, enthusiastic, always willing to contribute to seminar discussions. She'd even got a First in Mods at the end of the year, earning Jonathan a rare word of praise from the Dean. But something had clearly happened in the summer vacation – boy trouble, Jonathan suspected – and when Charlotte came back she was like a different student. Quiet, almost timid, she now rarely ventured an opinion unless called upon and, though the comments she did make were insightful, Jonathan had to strain so hard to hear her wispy, unsupported voice he sometimes didn't bother.

Crammed up against her in the lumpy armchair they were sharing in preference to sitting on the carpet was pale and uninteresting Timothy Johnson, with his scattering of freckles, rust-red hair and nasal Midlands twang. The less said about him the better: he always sat as far away from Jonathan as he could get, his eyes firmly fixed on his notebook, scribbling down not only everything Jonathan said but everything his peers uttered too. He must have mountains of the little pads back in his room; shame none of it seemed to stick. He always stuck to the same infuriating line in essays: *This critic says this about the text, but this other critic disagrees. I think they're both somewhat right.*

Then there was Charity Davies, or Sweet Charity, as Lawrence liked to call her, showing more knowledge of popular culture than Jonathan had expected. Stunning, even Jonathan had to admit that, with her flawless complexion and those big eyes which threatened to liquify at the slightest unkind word, belying her steely nature. She was clearly set for performing stardom of some sort, and was regularly the toast of Oxford's student drama scene. Not that she was one of those thesps who trashed their studies, begging off every other essay because of a performance or an *important audition* in London. No, Charity consistently turned in her essay each fortnight, never quite brilliant but always thoughtful, and written in such a beautiful copperplate Jonathan hated to mar the page with comments.

Taking up most of the sofa with his aura as much as his robust frame was George – Sharp by name, intense by nature. He was the very image of a brooding intellectual, the shaven head only accentuating his strong northern farmer's features. A card-carrying Marxist, he'd taken to Critical Theory like Deleuze to Guattari, and during his second year Jonathan had had to struggle through reams of uncompromising essays about Chaucer and false consciousness. Now he'd browbeaten Jonathan into letting him write a longer essay about iconoclasm in *Piers Plowman* and the recovery of proletarian voices, and Jonathan could already see himself in the tutorial, trying to advise him on how to shape it into something the examiners might tolerate, whilst George's dark eyes bored into him as though he'd insulted his grandmother.

But where was Alistair? The boy had always had a loose grasp on time but he wasn't usually this late. Sporty, long-limbed Alistair Richardson came from one of the top three schools and, whilst not bearing out every trait of the entitled public schoolboy, he ticked enough of the boxes to leave the stereotype intact. Jonathan had given up hoping for even a half-decent essay from him: every time, every single time, Alistair would hand in a couple of scrawled pages ripped out from a notepad, chock-full of ridiculous generalisations juxtaposed with lines obviously ripped off from the standard critics. One particular gem from second year was seared into Jonathan's memory: '*Life in the Middle Ages was beyond awful. People died all the time, especially in the Black Death, and they were very superstitious so this made it all the more terrifying.*' Blagging, the students called it. After all, why would you bother trying when your father already had some cushy job lined up in the City? An appeal to Hacker, the Dean, for a disciplinary chat had met with point-blank refusal. 'For God's sake, Reynolds, it's your job to work out what your students need and then *give it to them*. Sort it out yourself.' And what could you give someone who made it abundantly plain you had nothing to offer that he wanted? Honestly, sometimes Jonathan wondered if the boy had a bet going to see what he could get away with. Well, as far as Jonathan was concerned, it wasn't worth sticking his neck out. Let the little twerp waste his three years. Jonathan had his eye on the prize: the renewal of his lectureship which – surely – this time would make him look like a good candidate for a permanent Fellowship. He just needed to hold on long enough. Good things came to those who waited, Lawrence always said. But how long was too long to wait? And how long could he make himself useful before people started to take him for granted?

Jonathan shook himself, realising the students had sat with the passage as long as they were prepared to. He was about to start up a discussion on the significance of the term *auctoritee* in relation to authorship when the door to his study was flung open and Alistair burst through. Jonathan could smell the ketones right across the room. Clearly the boy had had as wild a night as Jonathan supposed he himself must have had. He hoped he didn't smell as bad.

'Sorry I'm late, Dr R,' Alistair drawled. 'I overslept.'

Jonathan gave him what he hoped was a stern look. 'Well perhaps investing in an alarm clock might be a good idea,' he said, feeling like the worst hypocrite.

'Totally, yeah, totally. I totally will.'

Alistair plumped himself down in the middle of the sofa, earning himself a hard stare from George. Charity crossed her legs delicately away from him, wrinkling her nose.

'Now we're all settled then, does anyone have any ideas about the passage?'

Dead silence.

'Let me be more precise. What do you think Chaucer might be trying to say about authority in this extract?'

The silence lengthened.

'Tim? Any ideas?'

The boy flushed unattractively. 'Erm, okay, the Wife says that experience isn't authority, so I guess... er, that?'

'She does say that, it's true, but is she speaking for Chaucer, do you think?'

Timothy looked as if he'd taken an arrow to the chest. His eyes shot a mute appeal to his seat companion, who cleared her throat and said something in an undertone.

'I'm sorry, Charlotte, I didn't quite catch that. Could you repeat it?'

Wincing visibly, Charlotte leaned forward and said, 'I was just wondering if maybe he was implying the opposite. You know, that experience *can* be a form of authority?'

'That's very interesting. Can you elaborate?'

Charlotte took a deep breath. 'I've read that a lot of statements in the Prologue are from anti-feminist tracts of the time, written by men who were supposedly "authorities". So maybe Chaucer's hinting if these authoritative written texts aren't really much good, then possibly someone's lived experience might actually be worth listening to?'

'Very good, Charlotte. An astute point. What do other people think? Charity, do you agree?'

'Absolutely,' she breathed. 'That is a really good point.'

'Can you add anything to it?'

The lovely smile faltered, but she made the effort. 'The Wife of Bath's a businesswoman, isn't she, with lots of money? So maybe she's this savvy, strong-minded woman, that – as Charlotte said – is worth listening to.'

'Well, I don't agree with that at all,' came a growl from the other end of the sofa.

'No, George? Why's that?'

'She obviously represents the rising middle classes – for the first time people could inherit wealth through marriage and not just because of their birth, and that's how she got hers, and then she's making even more because of her business. And all that's fine, but what does Chaucer do? He also makes her this sex-crazed gap-toothed caricature.'

'Okay, but what's the point you're making?'

George frowned. 'It's like Engels says, "the first class oppression coincides with that of the female sex by the male". The Wife's trying to overcome institutionalised male oppression and Chaucer hates that so he makes a mockery of her.'

He sat back, arms folded, as though daring Jonathan to disagree with him.

Jonathan sighed inwardly. He didn't have the energy for this right now.

'That's an original and, er, productive approach to explore,' he temporised. 'Do beware, though, of seeming to treat the Wife as though she's real. Of course she's Chaucer's own invention, and there's a complex series of...'

'But surely she's at least partly based on a real person?' George persisted. 'I mean, this is medieval not modernist literature. Chaucer won't have just made it up out of thin air. Besides, he's in the text, too, isn't he? He's one of the pilgrims.'

'But that's a persona, remember–'

'Of course, I know that,' said George, looking insulted, 'but...'

'And probably a joke. A bit of self-mockery. He represents himself as "a popet", after all – a girlish youth or a doll – and gives himself an incredibly long, dull and boring prose piece. Why would a poet do that, other than as a kind of in-joke?'

George's frown deepened and the rest of the students were starting to look nervous, so Jonathan changed tack.

'We've shifted away somewhat from the passage on the handout but now we're all warmed up, why don't we move on to the *Tales* I asked you to prepare before the class... Alistair, you've not had much chance to speak so far.'

The boy had looked to be settling comfortably into the cushions of the sofa, his eyes heavy-lidded and unfocused. His head jerked up when he heard his name.

'Perhaps you could start us off with what you made of the *Miller's Tale*?'

'Oh, right, of course. That's the one where the guy kisses the girl's arse, isn't it?'

'It is indeed,' said Jonathan repressively. 'What else did you find significant about it?'

'Well the thing is, erm, I didn't exactly reread it in detail. All the rowers are doing these really long training sessions prepping for Eights, and I didn't really get that far into it, you know?'

'I see. What about the *Knight's Tale* then? What did you think of the way Emelye breaks up the friendship between Palamon and Arcite?'

'Oh, yeah, okay. I remember: that was really sad, wasn't it? I mean, he was his bro, right?'

Jonathan raised an eyebrow but decided to let it slide. 'So why do you think Chaucer began his series of tales with one about chivalry and courtly love and so on?'

Alistair looked blankly at him. Then, after some moments of uncomfortable silence, he said, 'Okay, the thing is that I didn't actually manage to read that one either. I totally meant to, but time just got away from me, so I'm not gonna lie I just sort of read the summary.'

The silence deepened and the air in the room became fraught with tension as the other students watched Jonathan to see what he would do. Jonathan weighed his options frantically and went for the only one that would allow him to keep both his dignity and some semblance of authority.

'That's really unfortunate, Alistair. And it's not really going to cut the mustard when you come to Finals, is it? I suggest that, rather than sit here unprepared, it would be a better use of your time to go to the library and actually read the *Tales*.'

The boy slammed to his feet in outrage. 'You're kicking me out, seriously?'

'It's not fair to the others to let you stay, I'm afraid. They're prepared, and you're not.'

'That's ridiculous! How'm I supposed to learn if you won't teach me?!' He loomed over Jonathan, his face red, and with a twinge of alarm Jonathan realised just how big he was. How much damage he could do if he felt like it. Still, it was too late to back down now.

'I've asked you to leave, Alistair. Or do I have to call the porters?' He stared the boy down, forcing his face to remain still.

'You can't do this!' Alistair yelled. 'I'm going to the Dean – it's ridiculous!' And to Jonathan's intense relief he crashed out of the room, slamming the door behind him.

'Apologies for that interruption, ladies and gentlemen,' Jonathan said with a long exhalation. 'Clearly Alistair is going through something at the moment. Let's get back to work.'

But it was no use. There was no chance for the seminar after the blow-up. Timothy looked terrified, squirming deeper into the side of the armchair, and said nothing for the rest of the hour. George at least seemed to approve of his tutor's exhibition of backbone, but he showed no interest in getting back into the discussion. Instead, Charlotte and Charity exchanged polite observations about the variety of perspectives in the text. Charlotte was just beginning to develop a promising line about Chaucer's possible imitation of medieval polyphonic music, when Jonathan realised he'd misjudged the time.

He cleared his throat. 'I'm afraid that's about all the time we have today, guys.' Crap, there was so much material he'd planned to cover. 'Charlotte's point about music is a productive one, I think. I'll photocopy some motets by Machaut for you and leave them in your pigeonholes. We can talk about them next time. I'd also like you to read the rest of the *Tales* by then.' He ignored George's barely concealed groan. 'You can leave out the prose tales, but make sure you take a look at the *Retractions* at the end. I'll want to know whether you think we should take them seriously. Is this Chaucer's real voice at last, apologising for everything he's written in fear of Judgement Day? Or is it just another game, like his comic persona within the *Tales*? Okay, thanks, guys. See you next time.'

George strode out, followed by Charity, and Timothy shuffled along after, but Charlotte hung back, fussing unnecessarily with her bag as she put away her notepad and pen. As she finally zipped it shut, she looked at Jonathan, nibbling at one fingernail.

'Dr Reynolds?'

'Yes, Charlotte?'

'I wondered if I could talk to you for a minute?'

Jonathan glanced at his watch. 'I'm afraid it's not a good time right now,' he said. 'I've got another tute about to start.'

'Oh, it's just I'm a bit worried—'

'Now, there's no need to be anxious,' Jonathan said, cutting her off. 'As always, you've done lots of reading and you've got a couple of strong angles you can develop. I'm sure you've got nothing to worry about.'

'No, it's not that – it's... Well, I'm a bit worried about one of the other students.'

She hesitated, as though unsure whether she should proceed. Jonathan debated whether he should encourage her to share her concern, then decided against it. She was probably seeing a problem where there was none, and he could already hear Nicholas and Oliver's footsteps on the staircase outside. Besides, sometimes Charlotte seemed just too sweet, too concerned for other people. He'd seen enough people spread gossip under the name of neighbourly concern to take people's motives at face value.

'I'm sure it's nothing they can't handle, Charlotte. But if you're really concerned, do pop along and have a chat with the college nurse: she should still be in her office. And I have some time tomorrow, if you'd like to come back then and talk it over, or you can drop a note in my pigeonhole.'

Charlotte bit her lip, but accepted the brush-off meekly and slipped out of the room as Nicholas and Oliver entered, deep in conversation. Jonathan shrugged. If it was important she'd get back to him. He needed his energy now. He wasn't going to be able to fob these two off with some close reading and standard discussion points. And he had a sneaking feeling that the contretemps with Alistair was going to come back to haunt him.

Kate beckoned Geoff over from where he had been debriefing the Forensics team.

'What's up, Sarge?' he said.

'What've you got?'

'Nothing much.' He sighed. 'Fingerprints everywhere, obviously – it's a tourist trap – but nothing useful... and nothing on the body.'

'Stray hairs? Fibres?'

He shook his head. 'Nope, it's clean. I mean, they've hoovered the corpse and sent the bags off to the lab, but it's not looking hopeful. You got anything?'

'Well, yeah, some basics. We've got an ID on the victim

from his wallet: a Mr Simon Beatty, banks with the Halifax, credit card, couple of store cards, and a Bodleian library card that indicates he's at St Sebastian's College, reading Classics.'

'Sebastian's... which one's that?'

'Up the road near the top of St Giles. One of the wealthy ones; owns half of Oxford apparently. I called to see if we could get one of the college authorities down here, but the twat on duty at the Porters' Lodge was having none of it. We're going to have to go over there.'

Geoff rolled his eyes. 'Great.'

'I know, right? Never ceases to amaze me how these college types seem to think they're a law unto themselves.'

So far Kate had not had many dealings with colleges, but such encounters as she'd had were profoundly frustrating experiences.

'How do they even work anyway?' said Geoff. 'It's not like any university I've ever come across. Sorry – I guess I should know this by now.' He looked faintly embarrassed.

'It's fine,' Kate said. 'It doesn't really make sense. The way I was told it, the "university" is a... concept more than anything else.' She grimaced. 'But the students are actually divided up between all the colleges and, whatchmacallum, Permanent Private Halls. That's where they live and get taught.'

'Wouldn't it be more efficient to teach them all together? I mean, my brother's uni taught them in groups of up to eighty.'

'That'd be too easy! Besides, each college has got its own weird regs and customs – you wouldn't want to squish them all together.'

'Oh, a law unto themselves across the board, eh?'

'Not just that – believe it or not, they've even got their own police force, if you can call it that!'

'What do you mean?'

'Well, nowadays it's more ceremonial than practical, I think

– but I've heard it can still cause you problems if you need to get into a college in an official capacity.'

'Are you serious?'

'Not all of them,' Kate hastened to add. 'Most of them co-operate with enquiries. But apparently a few of them get in the way of investigations. Demand warrants to enter the premises, close ranks round their members, even when they're obviously pushing drugs or harassing people. They just promise they'll deal with things "internally".'

'They can't do that, can they?'

'Theoretically no. But if you push too hard or, heaven forbid, lose your temper with them, well, then you'll get a right rollocking from the Higher Ups, cos they'll have just received a polite but deadly phone call from some QC who just happens to be an old boy or school friend of the college's Principal or President, or whatever the hell they call themselves.'

'Blimey. Is St Sebastian's one of those kind then? What're we walking into?'

'I don't know.' Kate's lips tightened. This was promising to be one of those days.

*You've got to stop looking at him,* Jonathan thought. *Look away. Look at Oliver. Look at the ceiling. Anything but him. Just do your job, for God's sake. What's the matter with you?*

But there he was... Nicholas Rivers. Twenty-one years old and such stuff as dreams are made on – dreams that left Jonathan feeling furtive and guilty, like a dog caught staring at a cake left out on the dining-room table. Taller than average; shoulder-length hair (blending thick honey and dirty-blond); intelligent eyes (one blue, one green) set off behind thin black-framed glasses; a finely drawn, delicate nose, no hint of any bump or unevenness to mar that flawless face; a plain white tee-shirt to contrast with the even tan, the fabric of the sleeves straining against the well-defined biceps; a rower's build maintained, as far as Jonathan knew, without any obeisance at the shrine that was the college weights room. Good God he was gorgeous, from his golden head to those expensively shod feet. Jonathan shook himself, pushing the illicit thoughts away.

Nicholas's tutorial partner, Oliver Black, was reading his essay this week. A slight, dark-haired boy with an indeterminate accent and clipped tones, Oliver was intelligent but with a tendency towards pedantry. His hair fell smoothly either side of his face and he periodically tucked it out of the way behind his ears. Jonathan wondered why he didn't just have it cut shorter. He tried to focus on what the boy was saying about art and preaching in *The Owl and the Nightingale* and wondered what he had been thinking, assigning such a tired topic.

'Of course,' Oliver was saying, 'some have argued for a late twelfth-century composition for the poem, identifying the two protagonists as representing Henry II and Thomas Becket, who was then Archbishop of Canterbury and later a saint in the Catholic tradition.'

Jonathan thought he detected a slight sneer in that last phrase, but ignored it. Oliver, he knew, was a paid-up member of the college's Christian Union, a group espousing a rather conservative world view, and he had learned from experience it was almost impossible to persuade such students that, historically and in practice, the whole Catholic-Protestant distinction was much less significant than they believed.

'These arguments, however, are often specious.' Oliver raised an eyebrow, as if to dismiss the hapless critics, before continuing.

'It seems much more likely – if the birds constitute allegories of historical figures at all – that the joyful but flighty

Nightingale stands in for the fun-loving Goliards of the twelfth century and the Owl for their more severe clerical counterparts.'

With his long, dark-brown hair and equally dark eyes, Oliver was a foil for Nicholas intellectually as well as visually. He was quietly spoken and slow to smile, but his quick mind and industrious preparation made him a suitable match for his brilliant peer. It certainly meant he could be relied upon to keep a tutorial flowing, even when Jonathan was distracted.

Indeed, as Oliver continued to read, Jonathan found his eyes slipping again and again towards Nicholas, his slender neck angled gracefully towards the floor, seemingly lost in thought. Jonathan, too, forced himself to adopt a pose of deep concentration, one hand under his chin, fingers splayed to conceal his overly aquiline profile, so different from Nicholas's adorably snub nose.

It wasn't Nicholas's appearance alone that prevented Jonathan from paying adequate attention to his tutorial partner. It was his looks together with his undeniable intellectual prowess. How could anyone compete with that irresistible combination? Certainly not the other Finalists. All able enough in their own way, he supposed, judging from Lawrence's reports about their progress in the later period papers. Try as he might, though, Jonathan couldn't bring himself to expend much energy on their pedestrian analyses of, as it might be, Chaucerian poetry. Not when Nicholas's readings were so persuasive, so unexpectedly perceptive, so charmingly supplemented by tossed-off references to Dante and Petrarch, gleaned no doubt not from the library alone but from that mysterious year out on which Nicholas would never be drawn – spent in Europe, Jonathan imagined, studying at La Sapienza in Rome or the Sorbonne, mixing effortlessly with the French and Italian well-to-do in a way that Jonathan could never hope to have emulated in his own unremarkable progress through his undergraduate years at Liverpool.

But Oliver had stopped speaking and was looking expectantly for a response. A jolt of adrenaline hit Jonathan low in the stomach. What had he been saying?

'Ah, yes... very good,' he managed. 'Perhaps we could start by hearing Nicholas's thoughts on that.'

He thought he detected the tiniest eye-roll from Oliver, but Nicholas began to rebut his tute partner's arguments willingly enough, directing his words to Oliver and ignoring Jonathan completely. Jonathan was surprised by a pang of hurt pride (or was it jealousy?), which he tried to dismiss. He had paired these two for separate revision sessions, as much to be fair to the other students as anything else: in group seminars the previous year they'd often been reluctant to speak, presumably anxious about being shown up by Oliver's more thorough preparation, or dazzled by a bon mot from Nicholas. Of course, he'd also had to be mindful of Hacker's strict instructions to coddle any students with potential to achieve a First in Finals. ('St Sebastian's has a reputation to maintain, Dr Reynolds! See that it does.') Still, he often felt surplus to requirements – like he had nothing much to contribute. A better tutor would have more to say, he was sure.

Nicholas was patiently countering Oliver's reading of the poem, seeming to take pleasure in the exercise.

'We have to acknowledge the poem's educational context,' he said. 'Students were rewarded for their ability to argue persuasively. *That* is what the two birds are going to be judged on, according to their dispute. The poem is clearly designed to show off the poet's skill in forensic rhetoric. To demonstrate that he deserves financial patronage, maybe even a permanent post.'

He glanced at Jonathan as he said this last, and Jonathan wondered for a second if the boy was slyly mocking his own temporary status.

'Ah, yes,' he said, mustering an unconcerned drawl. 'The poem-as-CV angle. A little derivative, perhaps, but basically sound in principle.'

With a flash of regret, Jonathan realised he'd gone too far. He had intended to deliver a gentle rebuke, reassert his authority, but had clearly only succeeded in insulting Nicholas. The word *sound* was one of the worst insults one could level at a student, currently – used around the college bar or in the junior common room to dismiss someone's ideas as pedestrian, unimaginative, ordinary. And if there was one thing you did not want to be at St Seb's, it was ordinary.

Nicholas's eyes darkened, and that beautiful face clouded over.

*Crap*, thought Jonathan, hunting for a way to salvage the situation.

'Erm, that is to say, that's another perfectly valid approach, Nicholas.' He pulled gently on the second joint of his little finger, a habit he'd developed as an awkward undergraduate and which surfaced whenever he felt under pressure. 'Although... since the poem is inconclusive, it's difficult to come down on any one side with conviction...'

He could see that this was not going down well at all. Nicholas's lip was beginning to curl, and even Oliver looked impatient.

'... and perhaps that is an alternative stance to explore,' he added, at last spotting a way out. 'Perhaps the poem was deliberately left open-ended to encourage precisely the kind of debate in its original audiences that you have been holding so articulately this morning.' He blanched inwardly at the shameless flattery and peeked at the students to see how it had gone down. A flicker of interest. Ah, this was better. 'Or indeed perhaps it is intended to suggest that no definitive answer is possible to any meaningful question.' He crossed his leg over his knee and leaned back in his armchair, affecting an expression of profound thought whilst sifting through his array of go-to texts and critical stances. 'In fact, think of Chaucer's minor poems – or even the *Canterbury Tales*, on which you did such brilliant work last year. All of these texts unfinished, inconclusive. Was that by accident, an unfortunate fluke of history? Or was it one of Chaucer's many literary jokes? Could it even be a medieval literary or hermeneutic tradition that we still don't fully understand?'

Jonathan glanced at his watch. 'But that's enough for today. For next time, guys, I'd like you to prepare something on indeterminacy in another unfinished poem: *Wynnere and Wastoure*. Here's a reading list to get you started.'

Nicholas looked like he wanted to say something more, but he took the proffered sheet. It never ceased to amaze Jonathan how willing his Oxford students were to plough through reams of turgid secondary criticism and produce a short original essay each week. He tried and failed to imagine his younger self or any of his undergraduate compatriots doing so. Yet here it was accepted as a matter of course, as though expectation bred ability. The two students left, chatting desultorily about the formal dinner due to take place in Hall that evening.

Jonathan sat back again and rubbed his eyes. He needed to get a handle on this. He was in danger of becoming obsessed with Nicholas and he could imagine no scenario in which that ended well.

~

As she parked on the double yellows at the edge of a row of parking bays outside St Sebastian's, Kate caught the eye of a traffic warden, hovering with a gleam in his eye. She held his gaze, silently daring him: *Go on, just try and ticket me when I'm "in pursuit of official duties"*! The man blanched and turned away, pretending to have seen something in the opposite direction that demanded his attention.

She and Geoff walked up to the imposing gateway to the college, a set of oak-panelled gates that must have been twelve feet high and almost as wide, surrounded by a fluted stone arch that managed to give the simultaneous impression of solidity and finesse. Above the gates a square tower rose for another two storeys, the mullioned windows of the middle storey framed by statues of saints or kings in carved niches. Craning her neck to look at the battlements against the streaky blue sky, Kate suddenly felt disorientated, as though the tower was going to fall on her.

'Woah, there,' said Geoff, putting out a hand to steady her. 'Are you all right?'

'I'm fine,' she said, twisting away from his hand. 'Let's get on with it.'

They stepped through the person-sized wicket gate, inset into the larger structure, avoiding a wooden threshold that seemed designed to trip the unwary. It led into a kind of stone hallway formed by the tower overhead. There was a set of wood-and-glass cases to the left with various notices and posters neatly pinned inside. Ahead lay a quadrangle containing a huge circular lawn, mowed to display neat stripes, surrounded by large flagstones and, around the edges, decorative cobbles. Beyond, Kate had an impression of stone arches and lots of square windows, symmetrically placed, but her attention was taken by a sharp-sounding voice to her right.

'I'm sorry, we're closed to the public today.'

The voice belonged to a thickset man in a dark suit and tie with a slight Bristolian accent. He did not look pleased to see them.

'DS Stewart and DC Simpson,' she said crisply. 'I spoke on the phone earlier to someone here. Perhaps he left a message?'

'Nope,' grunted the man. 'On his break now. No messages.'

'Well, we need to speak with the person in charge here – the Principal or whatever – on a matter of some urgency.'

The man looked unimpressed. 'You can't. The *Warden*,' he stressed the title, 'is away on business. And even if he wasn't, he wouldn't have time to see you: you have to make an appointment.'

Kate bit down on her lip. 'That's a shame,' she said, forcing her mouth into a smile. *You catch more flies with honey*, she heard her old boss saying. 'Perhaps there's someone else in authority we could see instead. It's rather important. You see, there's been an incident involving one of your students, Simon Beatty.'

The man's expression did not alter. 'Well, whatever the little twerp's done, tell them to just itemise the damage and send it in to the Dean. He'll make sure the bill gets paid.'

'You don't quite understand,' Kate said through clenched teeth. 'This isn't about vandalism, and the student in question is not going to be in a position to pay any bills. Ever again, if you catch my drift...'

The porter's face paled beneath his weathered tan and, for the first time, he looked Kate in the eye. 'Bugger me,' he breathed, 'pardon my French. What happened?'

'I'm afraid I'm not at liberty to disclose that information at this stage of the investigation,' Kate replied stiffly. 'I trust you'll be willing to put us in contact with one of the college authorities now... this Dean, perhaps?'

The man muttered something beneath his breath, but turned and shambled over to the Porters' Lodge, a small, narrow room to the side of the gateway, and picked up the telephone.

A few minutes later, a short, wiry man came hurrying out of one of the arches and across the Quad. He had a large bald section in the middle of his head, surrounded by wild wisps of long white hair, giving him the look of a monk who'd got a bit casual about his tonsure, and his half-rimmed glasses were askew on his hawk nose.

'What's all this about one of our students?' he said to Geoff, walking straight up to them without so much as a greeting and ignoring Kate completely.

'The detective sergeant here is better placed to tell you that,' said Geoff. He pointed to Kate, who put out her hand. The man inspected it as though he were looking for dirt under her nails but made no move to take it.

'How lovely,' he said. 'A female detective.'

'Yes,' replied Kate, after a brief pause. 'We've existed for some time now. Females, that is. Detectives, too.'

'And why precisely are you here, young lady?' he said, ignoring her response. 'I'm rushed off my feet with college business at the moment, so keep it as brief as you can, please. One of our students has run into some sort of difficulty, I understand?'

'Uh, not exactly. Perhaps there's somewhere more private we could talk, Mr... uh?'

'That's *professor*, or Dean, if you don't mind,' he said with an icy hauteur. 'Professor Rodney Hacker, Senior Dean of the college.'

'Well, *Dean*,' Kate replied, 'this isn't something you want made public, I think.' She gestured around the Quad, where they were starting to attract attention from a number of students.

'Oh, very well,' he snapped. 'Follow me. I suppose Governing Body will have to do without me for once.'

As they followed the little man across a section of

cobblestones towards a big black door, Kate and Geoff exchanged glances. Was this man for real?

'This way,' Hacker said, pushing open the door. 'And do wipe your feet,' he added, looking at Geoff, 'the carpets are three hundred years old.'

Catching her colleague's angry flush, Kate put her hand on his arm. 'Don't let him get to you,' she whispered. 'It's not worth it.'

They stepped into a black-and-white-tiled hallway. To the left a carpeted staircase rose to another floor beyond, but Hacker herded them into a small reception room to the right-hand side with a thick ornately decorated carpet. The room was almost filled by a large polished oval table surrounded by antique chairs.

'Sit anywhere,' Hacker said, yanking out one of the chairs and plumping himself down as if he sat in such rooms every day.

Perhaps he did, Kate reflected, sitting down carefully in a seat across from him. It was the kind of chair she'd only seen in the stately homes her mother used to drag her round in Devon and Cornwall. And the table was probably worth more than her flat.

'So...?' Hacker prompted, tapping his fingers on its shiny surface.

'So...' Kate replied, 'I'm afraid to have to tell you that one of your students, a Mr Simon Beatty, was found dead this morning in the cupola of the Sheldonian Theatre. He's been murdered.'

'Good God! That's dreadful. The boy was one of our best Classics students, and an excellent musician. Truly excellent. I don't know how the chapel will manage without him as organist.'

'Er, yes, it's a real tragedy,' said Kate as neutrally as she could manage, 'and a huge loss for the college, I'm sure. But, as I'm sure you can imagine, we're focusing on catching whoever did this, and I'm hoping you can help us out with some basic information. Contact details for the boy's family, the names of any close friends who might be able to give us a sense of his recent activities and so on.'

'Yes, yes,' Hacker said, waving his hand, 'the Domestic Bursar will be happy to deal with that kind of thing. I understand there are enquiries that must be made, and, of course, the college will pay for any... ah, counselling that may be required. There is no question about that. But you must keep this discreet, mind.' His eyes bored into Kate with an unexpected intensity. 'We cannot have this splashed all over the papers – or, dear God, the television. St Sebastian's is a venerable institution with an unblemished reputation – it must not be tainted by some sordid... investigation in the public eye.'

Kate bridled. This man was too much. 'We will, of course, act with discretion,' she said. 'But we will take whatever steps we have to in order to bring the perpetrator to justice. Might I remind you, sir, that this is a murder investigation and that failure to co-operate would be a very serious matter?'

Hacker's nostrils flared. 'I am well aware of that, madam. But might I remind *you* that, in the Warden's absence, your presence here is at my discretion.'

He stared at her, gimlet-eyed, but Kate just stared back. She wasn't going to be outfaced by this pompous fool. Then Hacker smiled, baring yellowing teeth.

'I do hope we're not going to quarrel, my dear. My concern is simply that the college's reputation not be jeopardised. It is a very old and widely esteemed foundation. Indeed, it has land interests across Oxford and much of the country.' He scratched his chin. 'Do you know, in fact, I do believe we own the land on which the police station stands – and, as I recall, the chief constable currently pays a historical peppercorn rent of only one pound per annum. It would be such a shame if that nominal sum were revised to take inflation into account.'

'What's he on about? Is that true?' Geoff whispered in Kate's ear.

'No idea,' she hissed back. 'But I've heard about stranger things in this place. Better not piss this guy off till we've talked to the Big Boss.'

Kate turned back to Hacker. 'I'm sure we'll be able to work together to solve this terrible crime whilst also protecting the college's reputation,' she said with a tight smile. 'If you could put me in touch with your Domestic Bursar, I'd be most grateful.'

Hacker met her smile with a triumphant one of his own. 'Of course, of course – I'm only too happy to help, my dear.'

For a split second, Kate felt like flashing him her boobs, just to wipe the smugness off his face.

'There is just one thing,' Geoff interjected, clearing his throat.

Kate looked at him in alarm as he slid a cardboard folder across the table.

'Could you take a look inside and tell us if it means anything to you?' he said. 'We found it at the crime scene, beneath the body.'

Hacker snorted, but flipped open the folder and took out a polythene wallet. It contained a folded-over sheet of paper on which a single, brief sentence had been typed. He scanned it, then tucked it back into the folder which he slid across the table to Geoff.

'It's quite some time since my school days,' he said. 'Eton, incidentally,' he added, smirking at Geoff. 'Might you be another alumnus? Or perhaps you're one of the Habs boys or a Winchester man?'

Geoff flushed red all up his neck, but, to Kate's relief, did not rise to the bait.

'My school's nowhere you'd have heard of,' he said. 'You were saying?'

'Ah, yes, as I say, it's many years since I've seen anything like this, but it's Anglo-Saxon: the language spoken before the Norman Conquest. Our English teacher used to recite *Caedmon's Hymn* to us – strange chap. There was some unfortunate business with the gardener, I seem to recall – or was it the maid? Anyway, I do recognise a couple of words here but I cannot tell you what it says. You should speak with Jonathan Reynolds.'

'And he would be?' Kate asked.

'Our medievalist tutor. We've had him for, oh, two years, I think – a stipendiary lecturer, don't you know,' Hacker said, still speaking to Geoff. 'The porters can show you to his rooms. How unexpected this all is. Very Dorothy Sayers, I must say. Though sadly there's no Lord Peter Wimsey on this case.'

Kate had no idea what he was talking about, but got the feeling she'd just been insulted.

'Just as well we don't have a Gaudy Night coming up!' Hacker continued with a brief snuffling laugh almost as creepy as his smile. 'Now if you don't mind – I need to plan a suitable memorial service for poor Beatty.' And he rose to usher them out of the room.

Over lunch in the senior common room, fortifying himself after an excruciatingly dull revision tutorial, Jonathan decided to broach the subject of staff-student relationships with Lawrence. Cautiously, of course, and in the guise of concern about a friend at another college.

Professor Lawrence Gresham was the English Subject Fellow at St Sebastian's, a specialist in Victorian Drama, and the closest thing to a mentor Jonathan had ever had. Jonathan had applied to study for his DPhil under the supervision of a brilliant but erratic medievalist who had promptly vanished the week Jonathan arrived, reappearing some months later in an Ivy League university in a cloud of mysterious rumours and speculation. It had been Lawrence who picked up the pieces, reassuring Jonathan that the faculty would soon appoint a suitable substitute and, when that failed to materialise, taking him on himself. ('After all,' he had said, 'you're the one who has to come up with the new ideas. Anyone with sufficient intelligence and breadth of learning can guide an able student's path effectively.')

Jonathan was intensely grateful for Lawrence's enthusiastic if vague encouragement of his thesis. Their monthly supervisions had been more often chatty than analytical, but somehow Jonathan always left feeling more confident, inspired to tackle the next section with gusto. Lawrence had then persuaded a retired professor who owed him a favour to act as the external examiner for the thesis, with the result that the viva felt like just another cosy fireside chat, and it had been no trouble to steer the old man away from that troublesome third chapter. Finally, in the long list of benefits Lawrence had bestowed, the man had arranged for Jonathan to get the teaching position he currently occupied. Still, however much time he spent with Lawrence in convivial dissipation, there was an invisible line drawn around the man's private life. All Jonathan really knew was that he was married and his wife Cynthia lived in the home in North Oxford that Lawrence maintained alongside his palatial suite of college rooms. Jonathan had never been invited to dinner, nor, as far as he knew, had any of the other Fellows. Once Jonathan had enquired politely about Cynthia's health and, although Lawrence had murmured some innocuous response, his mood had turned black for the rest of the day. Jonathan was reluctant therefore to be too explicit about his own personal troubles.

The older man shrugged off Jonathan's qualms.

'Don't trouble yourself, dear boy,' he exclaimed, one pudgy hand picking fluff off the latest in a long line of Fair Isle sweaters he liked to wear, despite the fact that they drew attention to rather than concealed his substantial belly. He looked over his half-moon glasses with an impish glint suggesting he had seen through Jonathan's ruse.

'Your *friend* would hardly be the first tutor to dip their toe into the undergraduate pool. Think of my own predecessor. His wife started out as his student, believe it or not, though you'd hardly credit her with an education at all now. Before she became entangled in that ridiculous vanity project of his, she had quite the career building.' He mock sighed.

'But such is life and love. I myself, of course, am far too much the ascetic to partake in vain worldly pleasures.' He patted his belly complacently. 'Nevertheless, in the distant days of my youth, as I recall, many's the tutor who'd on occasion call a comely lad or lass to his table to pour the divine ambrosia. And if they should retire to the tutor's rooms afterwards, why, we made little of it, so long as the affair was conducted amicably.'

The man beckoned over the SCR Steward to pour him another glass of wine and, as Jonathan covered his own glass with the excuse of an afternoon teaching session, he noted again the way Lawrence used such actions to punctuate his more controversial pronouncements. As had often been remarked around college, not always charitably, there was something innately theatrical about Lawrence Gresham.

'Naturally,' Lawrence continued, 'this is not to say that the injudicious were not punished. Elias Richardson, of infamous memory, conducted himself with such ill grace that one poor girl attempted to do away with herself. The college had to go to some pains to hush up that sorry affair and shunt Elias into a role where he could do no further damage.' He grimaced. 'Not that he needed much persuasion to forgo the glamour of teaching for the drudgery of the international conference circuit and a series of high-profile publications on so-called critical theory.'

'But isn't it all rather... unprofessional?' Jonathan persisted. 'Surely we have a duty of care, or something?'

'Well, unlike the physician, we are not required to take the Hippocratic Oath and, unlike the schoolteacher, we are hardly *in loco parentis*,' Lawrence replied in round tones. 'Of course one must always proceed with *circumspection*, but let us be realistic about these things. Oxford men and women enjoy an adult style of interaction from their first days at college: drinks parties, dinners, guided reading weeks abroad. It is only to be expected that a few lines are discreetly crossed once in a while. Doubtless it would be different if we were talking about Bristol, or Liverpool, or some such place. No offence, dear boy.'

Lawrence shuddered in what Jonathan sincerely hoped was just an imitation of outrageous snobbery, and seemed to consider the matter closed. Jonathan pushed away his dessert plate, leaving the raspberry cheesecake half-eaten.

Kate leaned back on her chair legs the way her mother always told her not to, as the last of Simon Beatty's close friends left the small, bare seminar room. The Domestic Bursar – a kindly looking if uptight older gentleman – had been persuaded to hand it over to their use for the afternoon. Apparently the college's largesse did not extend to antique furniture in the general use teaching rooms, for this one was populated with nothing more than a few cheap laminated tables and plastic chairs and a large A3 pad on an easel, still covered with some incomprehensible formulas in black marker.

'What do you make of that then?' she asked Geoff, who was scribbling down the last details in his notepad.

'Huh?' He looked up.

She gestured at the empty chair on the other side of the two rectangular tables they'd shoved together to create a makeshift interview setting.

Geoff nodded.'Oh, right. Yeah, not exactly the demonstrative sort, were they?'

There had been a few tears, but nowhere near the level of emotion she'd been expecting. Of course, she hadn't explained the precise circumstances of Beatty's death, but she would have thought just the knowledge of a friend's sudden passing would elicit some more visible signs of grief.

'I guess it came as a bit of a shock,' she said. 'They probably haven't had time to process it properly yet.' It often happened that way with emotions, she knew. She thought of how long it took her after Tom left to get really, properly angry about what he'd done.

'Yeah, probably.' Geoff shrugged. 'They've got the number for the counselling service anyway, so...' He flipped the pages of his pad. 'Okay, so what are we looking at? Student number one: out for dinner at Maxim's with her boyfriend, then stayed over in his college: I'll confirm that with him later; number two: concert at St Botolph's; unaccounted for after that, but hardly suspicious; another few confirm each other's presence at a lengthy student drama rehearsal down at the Holywell Music Rooms. Oh yeah, that posho...' He rolled his eyes. 'All night session at some twattish drinking club. We'll have to check out some of the details, but so far nothing useful.'

Kate nodded. 'None of them were with Beatty at any point yesterday; no one had any idea what his plans were.' She idly watched as a fly that had somehow made its way into the room butted its head repeatedly against the closed window. 'Where are we with the relatives?'

'The usual team's already broken the news to them, got the basics, and set up a proper interview for tomorrow.'

'Anything more from Forensics?'

'Nope. Plenty of prints and DNA evidence, obviously. None of it so far matches anything on the system.'

Kate hadn't expected anything different.

'So what's next, boss? Want to try that Reynolds guy again?'

The porters, when approached, had been adamant that the man had several tutorials and seminars scheduled that couldn't on any account be interrupted. Kate had decided there was no point creating a huge disturbance which the students would instantly spread across the college, so had agreed to come back later.

She glanced at her watch. Those sacrosanct seminars would be over by now.

'I suppose so,' she said. Then she reconsidered. 'You know what? I fancy a good strong coffee and a bite to eat. Come on, I saw a decent-looking caff across the street. My treat.'

Mr Important Professor could wait till she was good and ready.

Jonathan shut the door on his First Year practical criticism class. Only a few more of them before Mods, thank God. He'd had to keep a tight rein on his temper – he shouldn't get so irritated he knew, but honestly these kids sometimes... He didn't see why Lawrence couldn't take some of these sessions. It was far more his kind of thing, but seniority had to have some perks, he supposed. He riffled through his notes on filmic techniques in *Beowulf*, then threw them back on the desk.

He hadn't been able to get Nicholas out of his mind all through the class. What the hell was wrong with him, he wondered. Why couldn't he just concentrate on his job? Or, failing that, at least go for another tutor? More than one had made it clear they were interested at those bloody drinks parties that the Domestic Bursar organised.

Jonathan was not exactly '*out* out', as the current parlance went, so he had always ignored or politely rebuffed their advances in public. Even in Oxford's comparatively laissez-faire environment, he knew that to stand out in a personal rather than an intellectual capacity was a risky business when pursuing a Fellowship. Besides, there was something about the other tutors that put him off. Like Robin 'Cheekbones' Chalmers, known for his flashy intellect and blatant sexuality – the daring way he flouted traditional proprieties.

He'd gone for cocktails with him once at one of the City's swankier establishments. Chalmers had insisted on paying for everything. ('You're only on a stipendiary lecturer's salary, after all. Though I'm sure that will change soon.' Said with a smile that didn't quite reach his eyes.) Afterwards, Jonathan had allowed himself to be persuaded to go back to Chalmers' immaculate rooms in St Mary's College. But sitting on the expensively simple sofa, surveying the artfully dishevelled piles of the latest literary prizewinners, he'd felt something... hungry in Chalmers' gaze that made him profoundly uncomfortable, and he'd made his excuses and left.

No, that kind of thing just wasn't him. He wasn't even sure what he'd do if Nicholas himself suddenly reached out to him. Every time the thoughts came unbidden of the boy leaning over towards him, that beautiful hair falling forward, every time he dreamed of tracing with one trembling finger the smooth skin above his jaw, it felt like he was about to cross some sacred line, whatever Lawrence said. Worse still, it would take him back to that awful night in Malta... but, no, he wouldn't think about Andrew. He called to mind the advice of the counsellor he'd seen for three excruciatingly awkward sessions before he'd stopped going back. *Distract yourself. Break that cycle.* It was hard though. He still thought about him more often than he'd like. Last week he'd even thought he glimpsed him nipping into a shop off Cornmarket. That was crazy though. Why would he even be in Oxford?

Jonathan shook his head, moving over to his desk. He should really do some proper work before dinner. It was high time he finished the article he had been trying and failing to write all term. He had long given up the idea of publishing his thesis as a book: it would need too much reworking, he knew. The new article represented a fresh start. It had the working title 'The Monsters in *Beowulf*: A New Approach': a tried and tested topic and therefore, as Lawrence agreed, a fine way to make his mark in the academy, if only he could find that fresh angle. There was an increasing tendency in recent scholarship to take a sympathetic view of Grendel and his Mother, even the Dragon. Jonathan didn't have much time for that line of thinking, but he was fascinated by the moments in the poem where the action was shown from the monsters' point of view, rather than that of Beowulf or the victims.

As he ploughed his solitary doctoral furrow here at St Seb's, the poem had increasingly reminded him of the slasher videos he watched late at night, unable to sleep because of the noise from a college bop or guest night in Hall. Michael Myers in *Halloween* – gliding up the stairs to butcher his sister with a kitchen knife. Everything seen from his own inexplicable point of view. Wasn't that rather like Grendel's murderous approach to Heorot over the misty moorlands, exulting in thoughts of the flesh he was about to devour? So at least Jonathan was planning to argue now, along with identifying and exploring some other parallels to film technique in the epic poem. Vogueish, perhaps, but, as Lawrence had warned him, 'Remember the three Ps: Permanent Positions come with Publications. It's not the sixties, when a man could land a Fellowship on the basis of a strong undergraduate dissertation and a patron with the right contacts. There's only so many strings I can pull nowadays. More's the pity.'

Jonathan worked away at the article throughout the rest of the afternoon, ignoring the discomfort in his neck and back. He needed to get this done. Stopping to take tea over in the senior common room would only break his train of thought, or embroil him in one of the Dean's endless diatribes against student societies' regrettable political activism. Young Communists, Queer Rights groups, Hacker hated them all. Legend had it he'd worn full mourning for a month when women were first admitted to St Seb's in 1972. How little had changed in the intervening quarter of a century, Jonathan reflected. But even in the university's slow-moving world, Hacker was starting to seem an anachronism. He shrugged and turned back to his work.

At last the twinges of pain up Jonathan's neck could no longer be ignored, and he threw aside his pen. Stretching, he swallowed another couple of tablets, then looked at his watch. Another hour until pre-dinner drinks in the Warden's Lodgings. He pulled the two-in-one television and video-player to the front of the vast desk he'd inherited from the room's previous occupant, then moved over to the armchair, shapeless and soft from generations of use, noting that the frayed section on the right arm was looking particularly worn. Perhaps someone in Domestic Stores could come up with an antimacassar. He sank into the chair, feeling the springs shift. Picking up the remote, he fast-forwarded the VHS to the scene where sweet, skinny Tony Perkins crouched watching Janet Leigh undress through a peephole, watched over himself by stuffed birds. Could he compare the voyeurism here to the palpable sense of Grendel's looming presence – watching, waiting out on the misty moors above Heorot?

There was a knock at the door.

'I'm sorry, sir.' It was Jeffers, one of the porters who actually bothered to give Jonathan the time of day. 'I told them you'd be working, but they said it couldn't wait.' His expression managed to combine conscientious regret with disapproval for the importunate visitors.

Jonathan looked past the man's bulk to two figures silhouetted by the hall light. One had the slender shape of a woman. Jonathan put the video on pause, causing the image to flicker at the edges. The woman stepped into the room.

'I'm sorry to disturb you, Professor,' she said. 'But in the early hours of this morning a crime was committed and we've reason to believe you can help us with our enquiries. May we ask you a few questions?'

# CHAPTER TWO

MONDAY 27 APRIL, FIRST WEEK IN TRINITY

Kate stepped from the corridor into a book-lined study, sweeping the room with a swift and practised eye. A peculiar mix. Furnishings shabby but well-used rather than cheap. Bland brown carpet tiles of the replaceable kind obtainable from any wholesale retailer, partly covered by an opulent Persian rug, red and cream – whether original or fake no way to tell. A wooden door in one wall, its cream gloss chipped, might lead to a cupboard or a toilet. The study itself was already bigger than her own living room and kitchen put together. *Fuck these academics.* The one wall devoid of bookshelves was bare except for two framed pictures. One – was it a print or a painting? – depicted a haloed saint, naked except for a loincloth. He looked surprisingly calm considering the number of arrows – Kate counted six – sticking obscenely into his ivory flesh at absurd angles that surely no bowman could achieve. The other picture was too dark to make out at this distance, but it looked like a young woman in flowing robes was holding something above her head. The edges of the wall and ceiling were stained yellow with nicotine, perhaps from a previous occupant, since there was no smell of cigarettes, only the musky yet sweet scent of the occupant's aftershave. Eternity for Men, Kate recognised, waving away the thoughts it raised of Tom. She turned her attention to the man in front of her. Youngish, late twenties at most. Well-dressed, but not pretentiously so. His dark-blue jacket, velvet not tweed, set off chestnut curls, not yet thinning at the temples. He was thin, too thin even for his slight frame. Together with the worried look he now wore, it gave him an air of fragility.

The man turned off the screen of the small television he'd evidently been watching, the paused image obscured by flickering lines. It was perched incongruously on the edge of his spacious oak desk, covered in books and papers, with no computer or other sign of modern technology, except for a beige plastic office phone that would have been more in keeping in a cheap hotel. To the left of the desk lay a pile of unopened cardboard boxes, no label or clue to their contents.

'I'm very sorry to disturb you, sir,' she repeated. 'I'm Detective Sergeant Kate Stewart and this is Detective Constable Simpson.' She gestured to Geoff, who had taken his cap off and was unnecessarily smoothing his short-cropped red hair. *Vain bastard*, she thought. Turning back she thought she caught a glance of admiration from Reynolds before the man lowered his gaze. *Interesting*, she thought, careful to betray nothing on her own face.

'Do you think we could sit down?'

'Oh, of course,' Reynolds replied. 'Erm, would you like some tea?' He hovered anxiously as though unsure of the correct social etiquette for entertaining two police officers.

Kate smiled. 'That's very kind, Professor Reynolds, but I'd prefer just to get on to the questions.' She glanced at the porter still looming at the door. 'I'm sure we can find our own way out, thank you,' she said pointedly.

The burly man's face darkened. 'Just call me at the Lodge,

sir, if you need anything.' Without looking at Kate or Geoff, he turned and closed the door firmly behind him. Kate could hear his boots echoing off the stone steps as he descended to the... what was that ridiculous name again? The Buttery?

'It's Doctor, by the way,' said Reynolds.

'I'm sorry?' said Kate.

'I'm not a professor,' he explained. 'That's a more senior post. I'm a doctor – or lecturer or tutor, if you prefer, it doesn't really matter.' He smiled, evidently feeling more at ease. 'Are you sure I can't offer you some tea?'

Geoff cleared his throat. 'I'm afraid this isn't a social call, Dr Reynolds,' he said sternly.

The other man immediately deferred to him, sitting up straight in his armchair, and Kate bridled, biting back the quick-tempered response she felt like making. God, she was so tired of being treated like the subordinate in the team. People – both men and women – automatically assuming that Geoff was in charge because he was bigger, taller... and, let's face it, male. Not only was she a good ten years older, she had a damn sight more experience and better judgement. Yet she'd been mistaken for the junior officer several times already since the Big Boss had assigned Geoff to her when he was transferred up from London. What was especially galling was that Geoff often as not made no effort to disabuse people of their error. He might be easy on the eye, but he could be an annoying prick sometimes. Kate exhaled slowly. She was being unfair, she knew. Look at the way he'd corrected that idiot Hacker earlier. *Keep your cool. Do your job.*

'Well, now that we have your attention, *Dr* Reynolds, may I ask – what is your relationship to Simon Beatty?'

The tutor blanched.

'What do you mean?' he stammered. 'I've never... I mean, Simon's just the Organ Scholar here.'

Kate noted the academic's confusion without altering her facial expression. 'According to our information, Mr Beatty was an undergraduate student here at St Sebastian's – is that correct?'

'Well, yes, of course. His scholarship is to read Classics and play the organ for chapel, conduct the choir and so forth.'

Geoff interrupted. 'Sorry. You mean he got to come here for free? Just because he could play a musical instrument?'

His incredulity verged on rudeness and Kate shot him a look, but Reynolds seemed unruffled.

'Simon's a very talented musician – and a formidable Classics student, too, by all accounts.' His face fell and he halted. 'You said *was* a student here... Has something... happened to Simon?'

'I'm afraid so, Dr Reynolds,' Kate said. 'His body was found this morning in the cupola of the Sheldonian Theatre. The caretaker was making his rounds before opening up for the tourists and he got quite a shock.'

Reynolds froze. Then, 'That's terrible,' he said, shaking his head. 'Just terrible. These poor students are under such pressure, what with Finals coming up. But I would never have expected Beatty to commit suicide.'

'No, sir,' Geoff broke in. 'He couldn't have killed himself. You see...'

Kate cleared her throat abruptly and gave her colleague what her younger brothers used to call her death stare.

'Other features of the crime scene render that scenario unlikely,' she intervened, in a bland tone. 'We'll come to that in a moment. But, first, could you tell us where you were last night between the hours of 10pm and 7am?'

Reynolds looked nonplussed. 'Well, at ten we would have been finishing desserts in Hall and heading over to the SCR for coffee.'

'SCR?' Geoff prompted.

'Senior common room. Where the Fellows and tutors read the papers, have drinks before dinner, that sort of thing.'

Kate forestalled any response from Geoff with another look.

Reynolds brushed the hair away from his forehead. 'I was in the middle of a discussion about research with Lawrence – that is, my colleague Professor Gresham. He's the English Subject Fellow, the one responsible for co-ordinating the English teaching in the college. I suppose we got carried away, since I didn't get back to my rooms until the early hours.'

'And Professor Gresham can confirm that?'

'Of course. But after that I was just here. Alone.' He blushed.

'You mean you crashed out on the sofa?' Geoff asked, looking down at the shabby brown item on which he was sitting with some alarm.

'No, no. My bedroom is through there.' Reynolds gestured at the cream-coloured door Kate had noted earlier. 'It's one of the, ahem, perks of the job,' he said. 'While it lasts, I get to use this office-cum-bachelor pad.' He spread his hands, as though in self-deprecation.

'Could make achieving a work-life balance complicated,' Geoff observed, and Kate glared at him again. *So bloody unprofessional.*

But Reynolds gave a wan smile, showing even, white teeth. 'That's not really something to which we're encouraged to aspire,' he said wryly.

Then the rabbit-in-the-headlights look returned. 'So, what does all this have to do with me? And what on earth has happened to poor Simon?'

Kate's mind returned to the scene that morning. The sightless eyes staring up from the floor. The dismembered body parts, their precise placement only emphasising the chilling calculation of the act. The foul smells that rose as the Forensics boys did their painstaking work.

Now, in the quiet, comfortable surroundings of Reynolds' study, Kate gave the man a neutral account of the murder scene. As the details came, the man looked uneasy, then sickened, then, as she mentioned the severed arm, his eyes widened.

'*Þær wæs eal geador Grendles grape under geapne hrof.*'

'I'm sorry, what now?'

The words sounded German to Kate, but, although she'd taken the language at GCSE, she couldn't make out any of what Reynolds had said.

'"There it was all together: Grendel's grasp under the gaping roof." It's Old English, from *Beowulf*. I was just looking at the passage this afternoon.' Reynolds shook his head slowly as he went to his desk and started riffling through a book.

'Is this the bit you just quoted? Professor Hacker said it was in Anglo-Saxon,' said Geoff, holding up the plastic wallet with the folded-over sheet of paper.

'Anglo-Saxon and Old English are the same thing, more or less.' Reynolds took the document and glanced at it briefly, then shook his head.

'This is from *Beowulf* all right, but it's not the line I just quoted.'

He looked troubled, and Kate prompted him. 'What does it say then?'

'*Com on wanre niht, sceadugenga scriðan,*' Reynolds replied, enunciating the words carefully. 'In the dark night came the shadow-walker stalking.'

The fine hairs on Kate's neck bristled. 'And this is from where in the poem?'

'It describes the approach of Grendel, the monster that's been harassing the Danish people every night for a dozen years. It's probably the best-known passage in the poem.'

'I'm afraid I'm not familiar with it, Dr Reynolds,' said Kate, inwardly rolling her eyes. 'So I don't quite see the relevance.'

'Oh, it may not have any meaningful connection at all. But it's very strange.' He sat down. 'In the poem, Beowulf defeats Grendel by tearing off his whole arm at the shoulder.'

'Sounds like he's a bit of a monster himself,' Geoff interjected.

'Well, yes, so some scholars think.' Reynolds sounded somehow disapproving. 'Anyway, Grendel flees, mortally wounded, into the fens, and the Danes triumphantly display the arm in their mead hall. That's the bit I quoted first. It's just like what happened to poor Simon.'

'What about the severed head and the impalement of the body?' Geoff said, looking sceptical.

'Well, I'm not sure about the impaling, but, later on in the poem, Beowulf tracks Grendel to his lair. When he finds the corpse, he cuts off its head to bring back as a trophy.' Reynolds paused. 'Of course, in the poem Grendel has an equally vicious mother, but one can assume she's not relevant here.'

'I don't think we can assume anything at this stage, Dr Reynolds,' Kate said. 'Let's not jump to any conclusions.'

She continued in what she hoped was a calming tone. 'I do need to ask: did you have any personal involvement with Mr Beatty?'

'N-no,' Reynolds said, twisting his hands. 'Like I told you, he is – was – the organist in chapel. And I'd occasionally bump into him at college feasts where the choir would sing Grace. But otherwise...' He began to look almost panicky, and Kate noticed how dark his eyes were, almost black.

Kate stood up. 'You've been very helpful, Dr Reynolds. We'll have to confirm your alibi with Professor...' – she glanced at her notes – '...Gresham. But I don't think we need keep you any longer today.'

Reynolds stood up to show her to the door, his relief palpable.

'I'm sure I don't need to tell you this,' Kate said, looking him in the eye. 'But please don't discuss the details of the case with anyone else. There are certain elements we'd like to keep out of the papers. It could help our investigation further down the line.'

Reynolds nodded.

'We may get in touch about this *Beowulf* connection in due course, if that won't be a problem?'

'Of course not,' Reynolds said. 'Anything I can do to help.'

Jonathan pushed open the door to Hacker's rooms with some trepidation, the curt note still in his hands. When he'd checked his pigeonhole next to the Porters' Lodge, there it had lain atop of a pile of letters, postcards, and flyers. He recognised the spidery handwriting immediately with its sharp ascenders and violent cross-strokes: *The Dean would be grateful if Dr Reynolds would come to see him in his rooms at his earliest convenience.* Jonathan's stomach lurched. Everyone knew that a summons from Hacker meant trouble. Now Jonathan wondered just how much trouble.

'Ah, Dr Reynolds, sit down, please.' Hacker barely looked up from the immense tome he was perusing. 'I'll be with you in a moment.'

The seconds ticked by as Jonathan sat perched on the edge of Hacker's sofa, with its unyielding cushions that were somehow still as spotlessly white as the carpets, despite the amount of traffic that must come through the Dean's office during the course of his official duties. The old goat continued to read with no sign of stopping and Jonathan began to take furtive glances around the room. Rows of forbidding legal textbooks lined the walls and piled high on each side of the huge walnut-veneered desk. There was no hint of Hacker's personality, any insight into his personal life, if indeed he had any. A noticeboard hung to one side of the large bow window contained an array of lecture timetables, official college notices, the chapel termcard listing the times of Evensong and guest speakers, and, Jonathan noticed, an invitation to the Annual Bodley Dinner. It was supposed to be a very grand affair. He'd never been invited.

At last, Hacker reached for a plain blue leather bookmark, closed the book he was reading, and took off his half-glasses. As he folded them and put them carefully away in a worn black case, he fixed Jonathan with an uncompromising stare. Only when he had put the case away in one of the desk drawers and placed the book to one side at right angles to the desk did he speak.

'Alistair Richardson came to see me this morning,' he said, folding his hands over one another in front of him. 'The poor boy was most upset. Practically shaking. Apparently you threw him out of your seminar. He couldn't really say why, except that perhaps he wasn't answering your questions in the way you expected.' He fixed Jonathan with another of his snakelike stares.

'That's not exactly–' Jonathan began.

'He said he felt humiliated.'

'But–'

'I'm sure I don't need to tell you that this is not the way the college expects tutors to handle students approaching their Finals.'

'I know, Dean, but if I could just explain...'

Hacker continued as though Jonathan had said nothing, his small eyes glinting.

'Finalists need the utmost care and attention. The intellectual strain of these culminating weeks can be intense and result in their feeling somewhat, how shall we say, delicate. This is not the time to insist on formalities. Nor is harsh treatment conducive to a good performance in the exams.'

'I realise that, Professor, but–'

Hacker raised his hand, palm forward. 'Let us not speak of it any further. Just know that, if I hear of any further disturbance amongst the English set, I shall be... very unhappy.'

Jonathan's shoulders sagged in defeat. Clearly he was not going to be given the chance to put his side of the story.

'Of course, Dean,' he muttered and got up to go.

As he reached the door, however, something rebelled inside him and he swung back to face Hacker.

'Actually, do you know what? Alistair was completely out of line. He was unprepared. And insolent. I was perfectly within my rights to kick him out, and you'd realise that if you'd bothered to listen to me before making up your mind.'

Hacker looked apoplectic and his face reddened and swelled.

'Really, Dr Reynolds! Take a hold of yourself. This outburst is unbecoming.'

Jonathan forced his expression to remain defiant but already the adrenaline of standing up to the Dean was draining away and he was starting to think of the consequences. Hacker was not slow to threaten them as he recovered from his surprise.

'Dr Reynolds, it is your duty to care for the students in your charge. To nurture their budding minds, support their intellectual endeavours. It is for this that we have hired you. This is not the first time a student has complained about your questionable teaching style. So far they have been minor complaints and your results have been good enough for me to overlook them. But if your personal authority is more important to you than your students' needs, then we may have to look for another tutor with the right set of priorities. I need not remind you, I'm sure, that your term of employment will need to be renewed in September, and that renewal is not a foregone conclusion. There is a lot riding on the Finals results this summer, not least for you.'

As Jonathan closed the heavy oak door to Hacker's rooms, he knew he'd blown it. His hurriedly stammered apology just wasn't going to cut it. In however small a way, he had defied Hacker, and the man was notorious for keeping score with those foolish enough to cross him. Along with swathes of obscure case law and details of college history, his elephantine memory had room to store endless slights. No, the only thing that might assuage his wrath was if Jonathan could somehow get his students to raise their game. But how exactly to do that?

Jonathan hurried across the Quad towards the chapel passage in the direction of Lawrence's rooms. With a hand still trembling from adrenaline, Jonathan began to sort through the rest of his post. A reminder that his next optician's visit was due. An updated lecture list for the Faculty of English, with the usual insert from Modern Languages and Linguistics tucked inside. There were the Collections papers Lawrence had made him set the Second Years. He paused just outside the passage to riffle through them – yes, as he'd expected, one of them was missing. One of the First Years had had a bad time of it, barely scraping through Mods, and matters hadn't improved since. Jonathan had suspected he was suffering from stress and homesickness and sent him to the college nurse to discuss the possibility of antidepressants, but that wasn't going to stop him being sent down if he couldn't produce some decent essays soon.

Halfway across West Quad Jonathan stopped dead in his tracks. Another note. He felt another surge of adrenaline; this one more welcome. *You're so cute*, it read. *I just want to sit and look at you all day. Or run my fingers through those gorgeous curls. I bet they just look like that without you having to do anything in the morning. I'd love to get the chance to find out...* A sudden heat ran up Jonathan's body and he flushed, glancing around quickly to make sure no one was near enough to see his face.

He'd had a series of these notes over the past year, always anonymous, always on thick white card, the letters always printed in green ink, never in cursive. He'd found the first one in his pigeonhole on Valentine's Day, the message stark and simple. *I choose you*, and the outline of a heart with an arrow through it. Jonathan had dismissed this as a joke, but then another had arrived a week or two afterwards. *I really enjoyed your lecture the other day. It was so interesting. And that jacket you had on was great. Some of the others say you look untidy but I don't mind. I think a rumpled shirt is sexy. I shouldn't be writing to you, I know, but I couldn't resist. I'm a bad girl, I suppose (or maybe I'm a boy?)* Still Jonathan wrote it off as the whimsical act of a bored student who thought they had a crush. Best ignored. But the notes had kept on coming every week and he'd started to wonder if they might be from a rather dashing lecturer who sometimes flashed Jonathan a disarming smile when they bumped into each other at the Faculty Library. He hadn't thought the man was gay, but you never could tell.

If he was honest, Jonathan didn't know what to make of it all. But he'd come to feel a frisson of excitement each time he saw a hint of green ink in his pigeonhole, ridiculous though it was. Jonathan dreaded to think what the porters thought of it all – he suspected they read any post arriving that wasn't sealed before depositing it in the relevant pigeonhole. But what was there to think really? The notes could be from anyone, and it wasn't like Jonathan was responding to them. He'd even contemplated asking one of the more friendly porters about them, to see if any had been hand-delivered. After all, anyone with a key fob could access the post room. But it would just be too awkward a conversation, he felt.

Jonathan tucked the note in his jacket pocket and resumed his journey across the Quad with a light step. Then he jerked to a halt again. Another note. But this one in black handwriting and with a very different message.

*I know what you did.*

Jonathan turned the card over, but that was it, the other side was blank. His mind raced. What did it mean? What did they know – or think they knew? He felt cold all over. Was this a disaffected student trying to scare him with a random threat? For all he knew, they might have sent similar notes to a dozen other lecturers. *But what if they actually know about the thesis, or–* He shook his head. That was crazy. How would they have found out? Ridiculous. It was just some stupid prank. He balled the note in his fist, strode over to the nearest bin and tossed it inside.

Kate sighed. The interview with Professor Gresham, though it had confirmed Reynolds's alibi, could not be said to have gone well. The man had seemed offended at the very presence of the police in college, as though they were profaning some sacred ground.

Kate closed the door on him with profound relief and she and Geoff made their way back down the steps in silence. As they passed by Reynolds's staircase again, walking through the cold stone corridor towards the main quadrangle, they exchanged glances.

'So, do you think there's anything fishy going on there then, Sarge?' asked Geoff, in the overly deferential manner he employed when he suspected she was in a bad mood. 'No one seems very forthcoming.'

'Shouldn't think so. You know what it's like here. Town and Gown and whatnot. Hacker and Gresham seem like typical Oxford smart-arses.'

'And Reynolds?'

'If Reynolds was with Gresham until 2am like Gresham says, then he wouldn't have had much time to set up the murder scene. That took a whole lot of careful preparation and planning. Plus you saw him – he looked terrified.'

'But the quotation from *Beowulf*: how many people would know...'

'There must be dozens of medievalists floating around this town, I should have thought. It suggests a link to the plot of the poem, all right, but not necessarily to Reynolds. He just happens to be working on the text.'

'Right you are,' Geoff said. 'Though it's a bit weird, considering what he was watching when we came in?'

Kate looked askance.

'Didn't you recognise it?' Geoff's tone was incredulous.

'It was all flickering, and he turned it off before I got a good look,' Kate hedged.

They emerged from the dark corridor into the light of the quadrangle and turned towards the Porters' Lodge. The disapproving porter was standing there watching them with a stony gaze and, as they passed through the Lodge, Kate waggled her fingers at him, a too-sweet smile on her face. The porter looked away as though he'd seen something distasteful.

Stepping outside the gate was like stepping forward in time

from a quiet pre-industrial world to a cacophony of traffic and crowds. They turned right and walked past a large raised area in front of the college that seemed to serve no purpose other than to deny people the convenience of parking there.

'So...?' Kate pressed, as they headed for her car.

'I only got a glance, too, but I'd know that movie anywhere. It's a classic.'

Kate had forgotten her subordinate's obsession. 'Come on, then, Hollywood...' Kate stressed the nickname Geoff had within the force, referencing his good looks as much as his extra-curricular interest. 'Spill it. You know I'm not a big movie fan.'

'Anthony Perkins – Janet Leigh?' He paused, as if these names should mean something to Kate. 'He was watching the murder scene from Hitchcock's *Psycho*.'

Kate stared at him for a moment, her hand on the ignition key, nonplussed by the macabre coincidence – or *was* it that? No, the last thing she needed was to start imagining guilt where there was none. *But that's what you said about Tom*, the sneaky internal voice said. *Smoke doesn't necessarily mean fire, you told yourself, innocent till proven guilty... and look how that turned out.* She shook herself and started the car. *Let's have no nonsense.* She blew the hair out of her eyes, signalled and moved into the flow of traffic heading out down St Giles.

'It's outrageous!' Lawrence Gresham fumed. 'They think they can just come right into college, into our *home*, and start questioning us about where were you at *this* time, and what is your connection to *that* person, and... and... all manner of importunate and impertinent things.'

Jonathan nursed his glass of whisky, as the older man alternately blustered and clucked over him like a broody hen.

He had, as usual, gone to Lawrence's rooms to meet up before pre-dinner drinks. Now he was starting to regret it.

'Well, they *are* the police,' he managed weakly. 'It's their job.'

Lawrence was not to be mollified. 'That's beside the point. They have no right to question me like some common streetwalker. Where's the respect? The deference?'

'I don't think it's about lack of respect: there are procedures they have to follow. In that crim. psych. course I audited...'

But Jonathan could see the other man wasn't listening as he began to pace the floor. 'I just don't know. There was a time when officials would speak my name with reverence. *O tempora! O mores!* Once we Fellows were at the top of Fortune's Wheel, but now she grinds our faces into the mud.'

Normally Jonathan loved to listen as Lawrence went off into one of his charmingly grandiose rants against the government, the Inland Revenue, the postal service – anyone who did not accord him the respect he felt was due his position. But just now Lawrence's histrionics grated – Jonathan felt too tired to play his captivated audience.

'And what of our own university police? Are they just to be disregarded by these, these *bullies*?' Lawrence continued, referring to that lingering Oxfordian oddity which, as far as Jonathan knew, hadn't investigated a case more serious than petty vandalism or plagiarism in decades. But from the way Lawrence was talking, you would think Scotland Yard had been wantonly pushed aside like a toddler waiting in line for his turn on the slide.

'That poor gruff young woman in those unfortunate ill-cut trousers,' he said, shaking his head. 'I'll never understand why young ladies these days don't dress better. I mean, if one has to wear a uniform, one could at least ensure that it fits properly. And her shaven-headed subordinate – it has come to a pretty pass when the police are indistinguishable from roughnecks and criminals!'

Jonathan thought privately that the short haircut suited – what was his name? – Geoff. Normally he was attracted to the floppy-haired, Di Caprio type. He made a mental note to go and see *Romeo + Juliet* again, maybe this time at the little cinema on Walton Street. Then he felt guilty. How could he contemplate something so trivial when Beatty was lying on a cold slab somewhere across town? His body and its contents probed and dissected by pathologists; police officers prying into every aspect of his life.

'It's all very difficult, isn't it?' he said. 'But think how much more difficult it must be for the poor boy's family and friends.' *I wonder if I should ask the chaplain to look in on them*, he thought. *No, I'm sure he's already on it.*

'Oh yes,' said Lawrence. 'Tragic. Simply tragic for them. But they will come in time to accept and bear the losses which fate brings to us all eventually.' He sipped his sherry. 'You know,' he remarked, 'I've always felt that we make too much of death in our culture. The Asians take a much more sensible approach. In Japan, for instance, they educate kiddies about death from a very young age. They see it as an inevitable part of the cycle of life, not as something to fear. That's not to say they don't feel grief. But it's observed in a much more moderate way without all the wailing and angst we indulge in here. Of course, it's all much less of a worry if you believe in reincarnation. Each transformation brings you that one step closer to nirvana. For the Chinese, now, there's much more of a taboo. It's not discussed. Upsets the inner harmony, don't you know? All the same, they have these elaborate funeral ceremonies and long mourning periods, but it's kept civilised. No broadcasting your private grief to all and sundry. We Westerners could really learn something from them, you know.

Though I wouldn't go so far as to eat dog. There are limits!' He gave a short laugh.

Jonathan shifted uncomfortably in his seat. 'Er, I had no idea you were so interested in, er, Asian culture.'

'Oh yes,' Lawrence said airily. 'I had to look into it as part of the Tome.'

The Tome – always audibly capitalised – was Lawrence's way of referring to the research project he'd been working on since before Jonathan was born: it was always on the point of completion but always needed one more round of revisions. From what Jonathan had heard, it sounded fascinating – a detailed comparison of nineteenth-century European drama and opera.

'But you're not looking into Chinese opera, surely?'

Lawrence looked appalled. 'Good God, no. Lot of dissonance and noise.' He shook his head. 'No, my dear boy. *Turandot*, by that showman Puccini. Always ready to pinch a melody or two from Catalani and improve upon it. Or, in this case, pinch a few Asian pentatonic harmonies and file off the edges. Some very enjoyable sections, in fact, if a little overblown in the riddle scene. Of course, Puccini's late work is a *little* outside the purview of the Tome, but one must be thorough!'

A considered look came over his face. 'You know, the plot of *Turandot* is predicated on the threat of beheading.'

Jonathan stared at him.

'Oh yes, before that fat grandstander started butchering *Nessun Dorma* for the masses, the aria was a declaration of confidence in Prince Calaf's ability to win the princess and *not* lose his head. You know,' he continued meditatively as Jonathan looked on with increasing unease, 'I once saw a quite wonderful performance at *La Fenice* – before that dreadful fire, of course – in which the *mise en scène* throughout was dominated by an enormous, terrifying blood moon. And, following the execution of the Persian Prince in Act One, his severed head – along with those of the previous unsuccessful suitors – remained in the background on a spike, subtly picked out with a red spotlight. Macabre, of course. Several of the critics complained about the way it undercut the love scene. Which, of course, it did. But I thought myself it grounded the opera. Usually Turandot's abrupt switch from hatred to love is tough to swallow. One minute she's haughty and cruel: the next she's melting with desire. In this version, one sensed the violent passion pulsing beneath the surface. Blood lust. Something quite beautiful about it, actually. Blood in the moonlight. A fatal love.' He downed the rest of his sherry. 'Quite beautiful,' he repeated.

Jonathan was still attempting to formulate a coherent response when Lawrence's eyes went wide.

'Good gracious, look at the time!'

Lawrence indicated the grandfather clock which stood proudly between the two windows overlooking West Quad. 'With all this fuss, I'd forgotten all about High Table. Hacker will throw a fit if we traipse in late, especially for an undergraduate guest dinner. You know how he likes us to show a good example for the blessed kiddies.'

He darted over to the chaise longue by the window, a lurid slash of crimson velvet against the white sofas and plush white carpet, and grabbed up his gown in a flurry of charcoal-black folds. 'No time to run and get yours, I'm afraid. You'll just have to risk the displeasure of la Hacker.'

Fortunately, they reached the SCR just as the Senior Dean was giving the signal to head over to Hall and Jonathan found an unattended MA gown hanging from the hooks in the entranceway. He slipped it on over his clothes, hoping its owner was dining out for the evening, then made his way to the back of the small gathering of Fellows and Tutors waiting to process through the narrow passageway to the college's dining hall. St Sebastian's was one of a number of colleges which observed precedence at High Table, so the Fellows processed in in order of their accession to the institution. Lawrence, being a member of long-standing, was one of the first in line, whereas Jonathan made up the rear with two Modern Languages tutors and a Visiting Fellow from the States. Jonathan wasn't against rules per se, but this one seemed particularly pointless, unless the point was to let people know their place.

They all stood behind their chairs, looking down at the long polished table, dark with decades of wood stain and lacquer, lovingly applied by generations of college servants. The students, who were already halfway through their first course, rose dutifully as Hacker banged his gavel on the table.

'Thank you, ladies and gentlemen,' he said in his customary unctuous tones. 'As some of you will know, there was, yesterday, an unfortunate accident in which one of our junior members, Mr Beatty, lost his life.'

At the word *accident*, Jonathan looked up, startled. He caught Lawrence's eye and the older man frowned as if warning him not to react to this alternative version of events.

'I shall not go into the details of this tragic incident,' Hacker continued smoothly, 'but it goes without saying that our thoughts and prayers are with the young man's family and friends at this difficult time. I know that you will all respect his memory and refrain from unseemly speculation or gossip. A memorial service will follow in due course, but in the meantime, let us bow our heads for a moment of reflection.'

The rustle and whispers in the Hall stilled, leaving a pool of silence which deepened until, at last, the Senior Dean spoke again.

'And now, as is customary, before we enjoy the bounty of the oceans and fields, let us remember the sacrifice of St Sebastian, illustrious namesake of our great college, and those founders and benefactors who gave so generously that this oasis of knowledge might be preserved. Just as Sebastian did not shrink before those fatal slings and arrows of the Roman soldiers, so let us not baulk at the sacrifices we must make every day in the pursuit of Lady Wisdom. *Benedictus, benedicat.*'

As soon as Hacker had intoned the Latin words of the short form of the college Grace, Jonathan's neighbouring colleagues began to gabble away to each other in Italian. The Visiting Fellow turned out to be a Mathematician and ran true to stereotype, yielding only monosyllabic answers to Jonathan's polite questions about his work and how he was finding life in Oxford. By the time the soup plates had been cleared and replaced with the fish course, Jonathan had no more energy or patience for drawing the man out, and they lapsed into an awkward silence.

Kate had gone through the preliminary survey report again, trying to spot some detail they'd missed, but nothing was jumping out at her. The physical evidence summary wasn't much help either: all the protocols had been observed meticulously – no problems with the body being moved, or evidence improperly stored – but there had just been nothing much up there in the tiny cupola. And, of course, the weapon was still missing.

'The only thing that's unusual here is the lack of evidence,' she said.

Geoff looked up, startled, from the blown-up photographs he'd been comparing with the crime-scene sketches. 'What?'

'I mean there's usually at least something to go on. At least some signs of a struggle, a torn bit of clothing or something. But nada.'

'Yeah, it sucks. But what can you do?' He shrugged.

'No, I'm saying that the lack of evidence is evidence in itself.'

'How d'you mean? Like he's a ghost?' Geoff waved his hands dramatically in the air like a magician performing a disappearing act.

Kate snorted. 'Don't be dumb.'

'It's a joke. You're saying he was in control, careful, methodical.'

'Right. But more than that. If there's no signs of a struggle then the victim didn't struggle.'

'Obviously – oh. Which means either he wanted to die – which seems unlikely for a twenty-year-old kid – or he had no idea what was coming until it had already happened.'

'Which suggests…'

'Which suggests maybe he got the victim so drunk that he couldn't even tell what was going on.' Kate paused. 'But if he was that drunk then he'd never have got up all those stairs.'

'Maybe they took the booze up with them and sat there downing vodka or whatever, and afterwards the killer took the bottle away with him.'

'But the victim smelled normal. I mean, apart from the blood, obviously. We'd have noticed if the corpse stank of alcohol.'

'Right. I can't even go in the break room at the same time as Gordo on a Saturday morning.'

Kate wrinkled her nose. 'I know what you mean. The guy's got a problem.'

'So if the vic wasn't drunk, then what? Drugs?'

'Maybe. Pass me over those pics of the body…'

She flipped through the grisly images until she found the close-up of the head. The muscles and sinews of the jaw and neck were stiff in rigor mortis, making it look like the victim was straining for something. She bent closer to look at the eyes. There was an odd dark red-brown stripe across them and beneath the opacity the pupils were definitely dilated.

'Look at this.' She passed the image over to Geoff.

'What am I supposed to be seeing?'

'The pupils are dilated. Couldn't that suggest the presence of drugs: voluntary or involuntary?'

Geoff said nothing, but shifted uncomfortably in his seat.

'What? What did I say?'

It almost looked like the man was embarrassed.

'Okay, clearly I've said something stupid. Out with it.'

'Erm, so I spent quite a while dealing with drug overdose cases back in London. And pupil dilation obviously can be a sign of drug use. But it doesn't mean anything when the vic's already dead.'

'Why not?'

'I mean, I don't know all the technical terms, but you see how all the muscles are stiff – and the eyelids as well?'

'Yeah, of course. That always happens after death. For a few hours anyway.'

'Right. And the muscles of the face and neck are the first to be affected, including the eye muscles. But the muscle that closes the iris stops doing that, so the pupils remain dilated – that's why people usually close the eyes of the dead. Because otherwise they look like they're staring and it's creepy.'

Kate flushed hot with embarrassment. Of course she knew that.

'But what about that weird stripe across the eyes? I've not seen that before.'

Geoff looked embarrassed again to be schooling his superior.

'Yeah, that's pretty normal, too, I'm afraid. You wouldn't necessarily see it a lot, because, as I said, it's customary to close the eyes after someone dies. But if for whatever reason that doesn't happen, then the eyes dry out and that stripe appears. I don't know why. It's called something French that sounds like moustache.'

Kate attempted to laugh it off, though inside she was cringing. 'Clearly I need to retake that part of the training,' she said, smacking her forehead. 'Oh well. I guess that leaves us nowhere.'

'I don't know,' said Geoff. 'The drug angle seems a fair assumption. But we'll just have to wait for the autopsy report to find out.'

He looked back at the sheaf of photos, but Kate felt the need to break the tension.

'Must be dinner time,' she said, giving an exaggerated yawn. 'Fancy a takeaway? I can get it: I need some fresh air.'

'Sure, food sounds good. My eyes are swimming...' Geoff began. Then, realising what he'd said, he recovered with 'Too much paperwork. But I'm off the takeaways at the minute: not good for the gut.'

It didn't look to Kate like he had any trouble in that area. In fact, his stomach looked admirably flat. But who was she to argue with a man wanting to keep in shape? It was a welcome relief from the rest of her flabby male colleagues.

'Salad from the Co-op then?' she said.

'I don't think we need to go crazy. But a turkey sandwich on brown would be nice.'

'Coming right up.'

~

Kate watched with envy as Geoff tucked into the anaemic-looking triangle of beige on beige at the other end of the break room. It wasn't the sandwich she envied – obviously – but the way he seemed to fit in so effortlessly with the other officers. Gordo and Bill munching on their supersized burgers and fries; old Dougie with his stinking pile of cod and chips. Not that she couldn't hold her own in terms of the crude jokes and mindless banter. But there was still that unspoken barrier between her and the rest of them – even from David Samuels with his own very visible difference. Sammy – as the boys had immediately christened him, as in Sammy Davis Jr, because, hey, they're both black, geddit? – certainly had his own share of crap to deal with, she knew that. The rest of the force was frighteningly white and most of its members made the usual assumptions. But fundamentally Sammy was still one of the lads. And there was nothing she could do about that. It had been all she could do to get herself included in the after-work drinks crowd. When she'd first started, the guys had 'just assumed' she'd want to hang out with 'the girls'.

Kate took another bite out of her pasty, still scalding hot from the microwave, and fixed her eyes on the break room's little TV like she didn't care what the rest of them were up to. Sadly, it was tuned to the BBC and *Birds of a Feather* was on. Dorian was parading around in her usual leopard print with some boy a third of her age and, as the canned laughter exploded, Dougie shuffled over to her, trailing chips from his fat greasy fingers as he did so.

'Hey, that bird's pretty fit for her age, you know.'

'I suppose so,' Kate said.

'Always got a skinny kid on her arm though.'

'Usually.'

'You got anyone at home?'

'Nope.' She carried on staring at the TV and hoped he'd take the hint.

No such luck.

'So if you was to go with someone, what would he be like then?'

'Haven't thought about it much lately.'

'But say you did,' Dougie persisted. 'Would you want someone your age or someone younger?'

Kate tried to give him her patented death stare, but by now the other officers had taken an interest.

'Yeah, Stewart,' said Gordo. 'Old or young?'

'Do you fancy them poofy-looking types with the fancy hair?' asked Bill.

'Or real men like me?' added Gordo, attempting to puff out his chest and suck in his gut.

'Or me?' added Bill.

Kate sighed. 'None of your business, guys. And breathe out, Gordo, before you burst a blood vessel. Besides, if I was going to pick a man, it wouldn't be another officer... and definitely not any of you losers.'

'Oooh,' came the chorus.

'Oh grow up!'

'What about Hollywood here, then?' said Dougie, pointing to Geoff. 'He's not that much younger than you and he's got some muscles on him.'

The other officers smirked as Geoff's face reddened. To her horror, Kate found herself blushing too and hastened to rescue the situation.

'When I want a ginger toy boy,' she said, 'I'll place an ad in the *Oxfordshire Times*, all right? Now, if you don't mind, I've got work to do.'

She scraped her chair back, chucking the remnants of her pasty in the break-room bin, and pushed through the door. Too late, she remembered its loose hinges, and winced as it slammed against the wall with a loud crash.

As the door closed, she heard the other men snigger and wondered if Geoff had joined in.

Jonathan picked at the fish, a piece of turbot so bland the chef had – evidently in desperation – smothered it with a spicy, garlicky sauce. Leaving most of the dish untouched, he gulped down his glass of Sauvignon and waited patiently for the SCR butler to notice and refill it. He sat back in his massive walnut chair and tried to find a more tenable position. Opulence without comfort. That was the effect the Governing Body must have been going for when the Hall was last remodelled in the late nineteenth century. He took a sip of metallic-tasting water from one of the huge tankards Hacker insisted they still use, wondering if silver particles built up in one's system and, if so, how many years he would have to eat and drink here before being poisoned. Smiling, he looked out across High Table into the vast elongated rectangle of the Hall, banks of candles on the long tables turning its darkness into dusk. Here and there faces he vaguely recognised were illuminated by their flickering light, animated, chatting faces that betrayed no hint of the gnawing anxiety Jonathan himself increasingly felt in this place.

He remembered the first time he had dined in college, his nervousness over what to wear, aware that to ask was social death. As he'd been warned many times, *in Oxford, if you need to ask, then you don't deserve to know*. He settled on his smartest suit – better to be too smart than too scruffy – a tailored grey number originally from Italy which he'd unearthed in a vintage shop on Little Clarendon Street. He'd worn an open collar – ties were so constricting – and felt he looked both refined and dashing. As a new tutor, he was seated next to the Senior Dean, for this occasion only treated as a guest. He recalled watching out of one eye which knife and fork his neighbour selected first and copying his every move down to positioning his linen napkin (never a serviette) in the same way. Acutely aware of his lack of history in the city, his inability to make sparkling yet inoffensive small talk, Jonathan's mortification became complete when Hacker leaned over and interrupted his conversation with the pleasant young bespectacled Physics Fellow to his right, his blond hair a mop of untameable curls, gown squeezed over the enormous and quite dirty woollen jumper he sported despite the heat in Hall.

'Now, Dr Reynolds, you will notice that beneath the scruffy monstrosity that Dr Miller has chosen to sport, there is nevertheless a shirt and tie.' Hacker looked Jonathan directly in the eye. '*We wear ties to dinner.*'

Jonathan had no idea what to say to that, so stammered, 'Yes, of course, yes, sorry,' as Hacker's regal gaze swept on to his next victim, and he and the Physics Fellow (now, mercifully, moved on to a position at Yale), in mutual embarrassment, avoided eye contact for the rest of the meal. In want of anything else to do, and too self-conscious to do nothing, Jonathan had consumed so much wine that afterwards he had staggered back to his rooms and thrown up the whole meal.

Now, as his gaze moved back down the crammed undergraduate benches, the students revelling in the excitement of the termly Guest Dinner, but not yet drunk enough to become inappropriately boisterous, Jonathan spotted Nicholas's unmistakeable profile with a sudden intake of breath. His skin looked even more flawless in the candlelight which glinted on his teeth as he smiled at something said by his dinner companion, a dark-haired girl Jonathan didn't recognise but instantly resented for the ease with which she could talk to

Nicholas. Their relaxed demeanour betrayed a level of familiarity and shared history Jonathan envied. He watched them for a few minutes, then, with a prickling of the hairs at the back of his neck, became aware that he himself was the object of someone's attention. Glancing to Nicholas's right, he saw a few places further up the table another face he recognised: Charlotte was staring at him, an unreadable look on her face. Did she know? Jonathan's heart lurched, but he knew that to acknowledge the potentially compromising situation would be fatal for any vestiges of authority he might still have. With careful indifference, he affected not to see his student, continuing to glance around the Hall as though lost in contemplation of the paintings of former Wardens that watched over their old college in serried ranks. Then, as though recalling something amusing, he turned back to the Visiting Fellow and asked him if he thought any dimensions existed beyond the fourth. All he had to do then was pretend to listen and nod periodically until Hacker stood to indicate it was time to move back to the SCR.

As they processed out of the side door, Jonathan risked a glance down the tables, but Charlotte now appeared to be engrossed in a serious conversation with her companions who now included, he noticed, Oliver. He hadn't realised the two students socialised with each other. It made sense, though, since they were both members of the Christian Union. A close-knit group whose members tended to socialise with each other or with their counterparts from other colleges, Jonathan had not encountered the CU much in his time at St Seb's, although he'd noted the flyers for the talks they put on every so often in the Southcote Room, giving their take on the Bible and a range of social issues.

Jonathan was not a believer himself. At least he didn't think so. Neither of his parents had been churchgoers, and the accounts of Christianity he'd had at school RE lessons had seemed to have nothing to do with his life. Every year at Christmas, though – right up until she became too weak to go out – his mum had always taken him to the Christingle service down at the local parish church. They always gave out candles stuck into oranges to all the kids, presumably to make them safer to hold, and for some reason they were also studded with delicious sweets on little cocktail sticks. These had been the main attraction, but there had also been a kind of magic in the moment when they turned out all the lights to sing a carol. Somehow in the darkness of the old building, the congregation's pale faces made strange and unearthly by the flickering candles, Jonathan had felt a sense of something more, something numinous even.

But those days were long gone. The Christingle visits had stopped with his mother's passing and Jonathan had never been interested in attending church in his student days. Since taking up his lectureship at St Seb's, though, he occasionally went to Evensong in the college chapel. He liked the low-key approach to religion taken by the chaplain, a short, jolly man who always gave Jonathan a warm welcome whenever he attended, but never asked awkward questions about his personal life. They tended to chat instead about choral anthems and organ music, which Jonathan had been surprised to discover he quite enjoyed. With a pang of guilt, Jonathan realised he had momentarily forgotten the organ scholar's tragic fate. He wondered if many of the students in the Hall knew exactly what had happened yet, or if they just believed the accident story. Hacker had certainly clamped down on the situation hard enough, telephoning a police contact of his to ensure the investigation proceeded with due sensitivity to the college's all-important reputation. The police interviews had therefore been discreet, and Beatty's close friends had been urged to honour his memory by not spreading the details of his gruesome death.

Jonathan was, of course, one of the last SCR members to exit Hall and, as he did so, just ahead of the Modern Languages tutors, a good-natured cheer went up from the students. Now their feasting could continue without the restraining influence of their pedagogues. As he passed through the corridor to the back entrance of the SCR, Jonathan idly wondered how many of the students would make it to lectures and tutorials the next day.

Not that anything much would happen if they didn't. When he had first begun to teach for St Seb's, Jonathan had diligently reported absences to the Senior Dean, but had soon discovered that, despite Hacker's commitment to academic success, his unwritten rule was that, so long as students passed their Collections – brief exams at the start of each term – they were not to be unduly badgered. In rivalry with another wealthy college nearby, St Seb's prided itself on its number of Firsts, but it was not at all the done thing to be seen to be working hard for one. As Lawrence had pointed out in his patrician way, St Seb's was possibly the only place where a student might self-consciously conceal a scholarly edition of *Paradise Lost* inside a copy of *Playboy*. And, on the scale of cool, Jonathan imagined, he himself ranked pretty low, in anyone's book.

Inside the SCR, Jonathan made his way through the milling Fellows towards Lawrence, who had laid claim to a small sofa near the drinks cabinet and was sipping on a glass of claret. Jonathan took the seat next to him. He wanted to discuss Beatty's case further and since Lawrence had also been questioned, he assumed even the stern Detective Stewart wouldn't mind.

'Such a tragic example of life cut short in its prime – a subject worthy of Henry Wallis,' Lawrence said, evidently still delighting in the dramatic circumstances.

'But why would anyone want to kill him?' Jonathan wondered.

Lawrence leaned towards him, his eyes shining. 'Young Beatty, it seems, had more than a few ill-wishers within the college community – and doubtless around the university as well.'

'But he seemed such a quiet, timid sort whenever I saw him in chapel.'

'Not so timid with a few drinks inside him, apparently.' Lawrence lowered his voice to a conspiratorial throaty whisper. 'From what I've heard, Beatty didn't just like to fiddle around on the college Organ-with-a-capital-O. He went through the choir like a pickpocket through a St Giles Fair crowd, then moved on to the rowing crew. He'd throw a few glasses back at one of the drinks parties he always wangled his way into, then make his move. He'd start by complimenting his chosen one: their voice, their skill, their physique as it might be. He'd keep bringing them and himself more drinks until the supply ran out, and then he'd invite them back to his rooms.' As if reminded by his story, Lawrence broke off to top up his glass. 'You know how impressive that set they give the organ scholars is. So there they'd be, cosily drinking until at last his guest would yawn and say it was time for him to be making a move. And that's when young Beatty would suggest a little sleepover – I heard this directly from one of the graduate students. Nothing sleazy or overt, of course. "Why don't you take my bed", he'd say, "and I'll take the couch. It's more comfortable anyway". He may even have believed himself at the time. But a couple of hours later, he'd creep in beside his guest, complaining of the cold, and then would begin a little game of *Where can I put my hand now?*' Lawrence paused to take another sip of claret. 'Nothing wrong with that, of course. Plenty of students enjoy some late-night shenanigans after a couple too many, then part ways in the morning without troubling to sing an *aubade.*'

Jonathan wasn't particularly surprised. He had heard similar tales about a certain type of ostensibly straight but less than particular male undergraduate. *How wasted was I last night?!* they'd joke. Or, from the more anxious, *I've never done anything like that before: let's just keep it between ourselves, okay?* As an undergrad, some of his friends had been the recipient of such clichés and were vocal in their irritation afterwards.

'No, the problem was the morning after,' Lawrence continued, 'when he'd turn stone cold and kick them out before breakfast without so much as a cup of coffee. Worse than that, he'd act like they'd never met, blanking them in the Quads, even going out of his way to be unpleasant – spreading rumours about them, or talking down their abilities and intelligence. Sad, really.' He leaned back into the sofa, his eyes taking on a slightly unfocused cast as he drained his glass. 'In my day, we knew how to conduct our little *liaisons* with some dignity, some understanding. We were mature enough to stay friends when the candles of desire inevitably guttered. But Mr Beatty had built up quite the reputation for himself: arrogant, manipulative, irresponsible. I hear he was even thinking of transferring to another college to make things less awkward, but the chaplain wouldn't hear of it. Told him he had a duty to the college and that, if he wanted to keep his scholarship, he'd have to lie in the bed he'd made for himself. Though, of course, that's what caused all the trouble in the first place!' He chuckled at his own joke, then rose unsteadily to his feet.

The crowd of Fellows had dispersed and Jonathan and Lawrence headed for the door. The empty room looked rather shabby, its furnishings in disarray, its tabletops filled with smeared glasses drained to their dregs. As he walked back through the cool night to his rooms, Jonathan couldn't stop thinking about about Beatty. How unhappy and lonely the boy must have been, to behave the way he had. And now he knew that final loneliness of death, lying somewhere on a cold metal table.

Haunted by the image as he lay in bed waiting for sleep to come, after an hour of tossing and turning Jonathan admitted defeat. He got up and went to the kitchen to fetch a mug of water – less risk of breakage than a glass, he hoped. Sipping at it, he forced down one of the sleeping pills his friend Lucia had donated to him last year when he'd had a particularly bad bout of insomnia. A good night's sleep would set things right.

## Thames Valley Police Document D0137 in The Dark Knight case:

### Handwritten diary entry

*In the sunset years of a dying millennium, the world teeters and the end is surely near. A sick world it is, full of corruption and ugliness. I see it. I see it all.*

*I see selfishness. Greed. Lies. The worship of Mammon and the desire for pelf and a cenotaph.*

*I see young women arrogating masculine power to themselves, and men relinquishing their birthright for a mess of pottage. They embrace confusion and call it liberation.*

*There are wars and rumours of wars, but the time is not yet.*

*I see men dying of the sickness they have brought upon themselves and called heroes for it.*

*I see children growing up not knowing which path to follow.*

*Venal politicians speak of education but repeat the most basic errors of history. Scientists transgress the laws of Nature and manufacture abominations in the name of progress.*

*The deserts are riven by infidels and the armies of the corrupt West as they fight over liquid as black as men's hearts. But still, the time is not yet.*

*A golden princess tramples matrimony's sacred bond, flaunting her shame in public, and she is adored for it.*

*A global network arises with the potential to facilitate greatness, and men use it to satisfy their basest desires.*

*How long, O Lord? How long must I endure it? Why do you not act?*

*For I... I see it all for the hollow sham it is.*

*In this august seat of learning, a monument to Man's highest aspirations, its denizens display only pretension and hypocrisy. Charlatans and rogues dwell in the House of the Lord, flanked by Professors of Pedantry and Lecturers in Lewdness and Lies.*

*I remain silent. For now.*

*But all that is hidden shall come one day into the light, and the Truth shall be known.*

# CHAPTER THREE

## MONDAY 4 MAY, SECOND WEEK IN TRINITY

Kate awoke with a start to a loud thumping noise coming from just outside her flat. She sat up in bed, the adrenaline coursing through her, ready to fight off whatever threat this might be, then groaned as she realised it was Maureen Jones's kids kicking their football against the outside wall. At 6.30am. Again.

She flopped back down on the mattress and covered her face with the pillow. Shaun and Declan Jones had been the bane of her life ever since she moved into her tiny flat on the Blackbird Leys estate. If they weren't playing football at the most inopportune times, they were pumping Reel 2 Reel and The Prodigy out of their knocked-off speakers. Their mother was never around to sort them out, since she left for some job across town well before Kate's alarm went off in the morning, and, as far as Kate could tell, spent most evenings at the local with a crowd of dubious types.

The banging continued and she hauled herself out of bed with a curse. Stomping through the living-room-cum-kitchen, she slammed open the casement window and stuck her head out.

'Knock it off, you little shits! It's not even seven o'clock yet.'

'Make us, bitch!' yelled back Shaun, the elder boy at eight years old.

'Don't make me come down there, or we'll see how you like being handcuffed to the bike racks!' She tried to inject as much threat into her tone as she could before her first coffee of the day.

Both boys gave her the middle finger, but moved away and started kicking the ball against another flat.

*Good enough*, Kate thought, slamming the window shut again and heading for the kettle. She longed to move out of this dump, but the divorce and relocation had not been good for her finances, even if she could find the time and energy. As she sipped her coffee, she looked around the flat. Threadbare beige carpet with some unidentified stain left in one corner by the previous tenant. Saggy sofa across from the TV beneath the window. Tiny galley kitchen with a microwave; the remnants of last night's pizza still piled up by the sink. A few paperbacks stacked against one wall. Everything else was still in the cardboard boxes she'd stashed under her bed upon arrival and never got round to unpacking. This wasn't where she'd hoped she'd be at this stage in her life.

Draining her mug, she shuffled back to the kettle for a refill and fixed herself some breakfast. She still had half an hour before she needed to get ready for work, so she took her cornflakes back over to the settee and resumed watching the video she'd fallen asleep over last night. Mulder was being his usual ridiculous self. If she were Dana (*fat chance*, she thought with a sigh), she'd have just left him to it. Still, for better or worse, she was hooked.

As the credits rolled, she walked into the bedroom just in time to hit the off button on her alarm clock.

The unexpected warmth of the morning made Jonathan feel fractious and he cursed himself for not having closed the curtains of his study the previous night, allowing the hot sun free rein to invade the room and no doubt bleach and dessicate his books and papers. He was about to walk over and open the window when there was a knock at the door.

'Come in,' Jonathan said, trying to sound nonchalant – as though he had not been nervously anticipating his next tutorial with Nicholas; agonising over what to wear in his bedroom next door. What combined professionalism with a sense of fun – intellectual but at the same time modest? Or did he want to try for absent-minded yet brilliant? How, then, to avoid just seeming like a crazy old coot? He needed to come across as young and vibrant, but not lose the air of authority he cultivated for his students' benefit. *Damn it.* No, what he needed was to get a life. Take a leaf out of Matt Williams's book – he didn't give a shit about what the students thought of him, did he? Just turned up, gave a dazzling lecture on A. E. Housman's fondness for rustic youths and various parodies thereof, then disappeared off up the Headington Road to his lovely boyfriend, lucky sod.

Nicholas breezed into the room as usual. No doubt clouded that smooth brow. He threw his books carelessly onto the small glass-topped coffee table in front of the sofa and sat. Oliver followed, his painfully thin frame seeming to squeeze itself into the cushions opposite, as though to keep as far away from physical contact as he could. Digging into his leather satchel, he drew out his essay – another thick sheaf of typed pages, Jonathan saw with dismay – and prepared himself to read.

'Er, what's going on, guys?' he said. 'It's Nicholas's turn to read, remember?'

'Oh, I'm really sorry, Dr Reynolds,' said Nicholas. 'The

director called some extra rehearsals for *Titus* over the weekend, so I didn't get a chance to write up my notes. I hope that's okay. Oliver said he didn't mind.' He gave Jonathan the full puppy-dog eyes treatment: the picture of contrition.

'Well, if you'd started your essay earlier–' Jonathan frowned, determined to resist the obvious attempt to manipulate him. '–then I expect you wouldn't have run out of time, rehearsals or not.' He sighed. 'But I suppose it can't be helped now. Just make sure you write something for next week – this is invaluable practice for Finals, you know. You don't want to waste it.'

Nicholas looked as if the Final exams were the last thing on his mind, but promised to deliver next time and Jonathan felt it would be unwise to push the matter. He gestured to Oliver to begin reading.

Without much conviction, he hoped to be spared some of the student's over-compensatory erudition. His First Year Old English seminars had been blighted (for Jonathan as well as the other students) by Oliver's insistence on following up every minute point of grammar, every obscure linguistic or etymological nuance. And Jonathan knew he was not alone. Even Lawrence had expostulated about what he called the boy's almost provocative pretension, after he had quoted in a single essay both lengthy comments from a German critic and a short passage of Ancient Greek verse, in the original language, no translation provided. As Oliver dismissed a half-dozen literary critics with airy contempt in his introductory paragraphs, Jonathan surreptitiously stole glances at his tutorial partner.

Dressed in a simple grey tee-shirt that showed off his tanned, muscular arms, Nicholas lolled on the sofa in a manner that somehow exuded complete confidence. His light-coloured chinos bunched around the crotch and Jonathan forced himself not to stare. As Oliver's voice droned on about pageantry and what for some reason he was calling the intellectual fraudulence of allegorical personifications, Jonathan stifled a yawn, then, casually, looked back at Nicholas. To his dismay, Nicholas had evidently seen the yawn and now made eye contact, a sly smile curving his lips. Jonathan immediately looked away, setting his expression into a studious frown. He was not going to expose himself to mockery.

The minutes ticked by. When he dared to glance back, he saw that Nicholas had closed his eyes, still in the same relaxed pose. As Jonathan watched, Nicholas's hand shifted from where it had rested on his chest and began to stray downwards. The young man started to pick idly at the hem of his tee-shirt, then pulled it up to expose an inch of smooth, brown stomach. A jolt of adrenaline flooded through Jonathan's body. He turned his head towards the oblivious Oliver but continued to watch out of the corner of his eye as Nicholas's slender fingers gently stroked his belly. What the hell was the boy doing?! Did he realise Jonathan could see him? Did he *want* him to watch? Time seemed suspended, Jonathan caught between fear and desire. Then, to his horror, Nicholas's eyes snapped open and he stared straight at Jonathan.

Jerking back as though he had been punched in the chest, Jonathan leapt from his chair and walked over to the window, wrenching up the sash and letting a cool breeze into the room. With it came a scent of jasmine from the bush outside the window.

Oliver stopped reading with a frown.

'Apologies, Oliver. It seems the room is too warm and stuffy for your tutorial partner.' He cleared his throat.

'Mr Rivers, perhaps now that the room is cooling down, you could dress with some decorum and sit up and pay rather more attention to what Mr Black is saying.'

He injected the words with as much asperity as he could muster and was gratified to see Nicholas immediately sit bolt upright and adjust his tee-shirt. Was that a hint of hurt feelings in his eyes? Jonathan did not dare dwell on the possibility.

He conducted the remainder of the tutorial with cool formality, taking care to praise Oliver's undeniably perceptive contributions without too obviously ignoring Nicholas. Too little attention would be as much of a giveaway as too much, he thought, and, certainly, allowing his feelings to be known could only result in ridicule. Nevertheless, as he closed the door on the pair of them, his relief was allayed with dismay. He could feel the twinges of pain at the back of his head and neck that were familiar harbingers of the migraines he'd suffered since his early teens.

Jonathan managed to swallow a couple of painkillers before his next tutorial with Charlotte and Timothy, but by the end of the hour the sight in his left eye was occluded by bruise-coloured smudges. Hastily, he scribbled a note cancelling his tutorial with George and Alistair and pinned it to the outside of his door. He retired to his bedroom with an ice pack from the tiny fridge that had come with the room, hoping it would cool the blood throbbing at his temples. He drew the curtains, lay gingerly on the bed, and waited for the pain to stop.

Kate slammed the phone back into its receiver.

'Nothing!' she said, scowling across at Geoff. 'A week of door-to-doors... interviews... intel. Nothing. No one saw anything. No one knows anything useful. Forensics has got zilch that we could actually link to the killer. No prints from the body or clothing, not even partials. The Home Office pathologist can't tell us anything we didn't already know.' She swore viciously. It made her feel a little better.

Geoff looked up from the typewriter in the cramped office

they shared at the station on St Aldate's. 'Language!' he said amiably. 'Still nothing on the security camera?'

'Nope. Dodgy cassette,' Kate said with an eye-roll. 'And it only covered the main entrance to the building anyway.'

'I know the university likes to spend its money on books and statues and whatnot,' said Geoff, frowning. 'But it's like they think crime doesn't exist – or only affects the hoi polloi. I can't believe there's only one security guard for that whole area. And hardly any cameras, even when they're working. It's enough to make you wish you were on follow-up duty for May morning. At least that only involves chasing up drunk and disorderlies and the odd shopping trolley chucked off Magdalen Bridge.'

'So we're still at square one. The Big Boss is not going to be happy.'

Kate said this last phrase quietly. The last thing she wanted was for DCI John Cooper to hear her calling him that, though everyone at the station used the nickname. Cooper was a corpulent man and surprisingly sensitive about his bulk for someone to whom other people's feelings were so foreign. Kate had no intention of alienating the man who'd begrudgingly handed her her promotion and who held the keys to her future career. At thirty-seven and single again, she didn't have much else to hold on to, as her mother kept reminding her.

'Cooper's never happy,' Geoff observed. 'Not now his wife's got him on that veg-only diet. I sometimes catch him looking at me like he'd like to take a bite out of my arm.'

'Well it is quite meaty. Maybe we should have a whip-round and buy him a bucket of burgers to get you off the hook.'

'Truckload, more like.'

Kate laughed guiltily, then turned her attention back to the case. She didn't want to encourage too informal an atmosphere at work. Not while she was still trying to establish the right working relationship with her colleague. Simpson had been moved to the force in Oxford in mysterious circumstances, then assigned to her with instructions to keep him on a short leash but no specifics. Over six months later she still didn't know that much about him. Was he gay, straight, bi? Did he live alone or with a partner? No wedding ring, but that meant nothing nowadays. She'd made a couple of discreet enquiries around the force, but no one knew anything much. He was well-liked, as far as that went, stood his round at the pub the police officers frequented. But he wasn't forthcoming about his home life or hobbies, didn't get involved in office politics.

'Just what's this killer up to?' she wondered out loud. 'We've established from Beatty's friends that he'd rubbed a lot of people up the wrong way, but a few one-night stands gone bad doesn't seem like a major motivation to kill someone. Give them a good punch on the nose, maybe,' she added, thinking of Tom, her ex. 'And why do it in so bizarre a way? Why go to so much trouble?'

'What gets me,' said Geoff, 'is why the victim went with him. I mean it's not as if you just break into the Sheldonian and climb up all those steps just to enjoy the night view.'

'We've got to assume a romantic or sexual scenario, surely.'

'What – come up twenty flights of stairs with me and then I'll show you a good time?'

'You know what students are like when they're drunk,' Kate said, irritated by Geoff's dismissive tone. 'Three doors down, they've got reports as long as your arm of students breaking into the botanical gardens after hours, "borrowing" priceless silverware, sticking traffic cones on the heads of statues.'

'So this started as a drunken date that went wrong? It seems too elaborate for that.'

'I know,' Kate persisted. 'But I think that's how the killer got Beatty up there in the first place. He may have pretended to be drunker than he was – manoeuvred Beatty into place, then made his move. According to the autopsy report the victim had received a blow to the head prior to decapitation. That must have knocked him out, then the killer could get to work.'

'That's a pretty hefty job, you know,' said Geoff, looking down at the muscles straining the sleeves of his crisp white shirt. 'You can't just cut off someone's arm and head with a couple of swipes with a kitchen knife. It takes strength or a really sharp blade, preferably both.'

'Right. But from the way the blood had pooled at the bottom of the torso it looks like the death blow was that small incision to the femoral artery. Once he'd incapacitated his victim, he drained the upper body of as much blood as possible before beginning on the decapitation.' Kate consulted her notes, grimacing at the gory pictures included in the folder. 'That's consistent with the precise, careful cuts he made around the neck and at the shoulder. The killer took his time, knew what he was doing: exactly where to slice.'

'I don't get it,' said Geoff. 'I would have thought you'd need, like, an axe or sword or something to cut through someone's neck.' He massaged the muscles at the back of his skull with one hand. 'I mean, it's pretty thick back here.'

'As I understand it, it's not that hard as long as you're not hacking away at random or trying to cut through the bone itself. Apparently, there's some joint where you can slice right through, with a sharp-enough blade... I can't remember the name. Something to do with the ocean, I think.'

'How the hell do you know that?' said Geoff, looking disturbed. 'And how would the perp?'

'Some Path guy once cornered me at the office party back at the place I used to work. Think he thought he was impressing me. Anyway, once the victim was dead, our killer had as long as he needed to neatly sever the head and arm, and the rest of the night to finish the set-up.'

Geoff shook his head. 'What, so now we're looking for a student who works part-time as a butcher?'

'I'm thinking more like a medical student – someone with a knowledge of anatomy. That's if it is a student at all, and not someone older.'

'So, a medical tutor, or a surgeon?'

Kate groaned. 'I don't know, Geoff, all right? It could even be an actual butcher, for all we know. Or anyone who could buy or steal a scalpel. We have no idea how they met, where or when. The IT team is going through Beatty's emails and they've promised to try to hack his profile on some internet dating thing called Oxford Romantics, but no leads so far – and you know how backed up they are.'

A sombre mood pervaded the room. They sat in silence for a few minutes, then Kate jumped as the phone rang again. Geoff picked it up. He listened intently, interrupting the caller twice to ask 'where?' and 'how long?' then carefully replaced the receiver into its cradle before looking at Kate, his eyes shining.

'Well...?' she said. 'Don't make me drag it out of you.'

'There's been another,' Geoff replied.

Jonathan awoke forty minutes later, feeling no pain, just mild nausea and a frigid sense of emptiness. He drew the curtains and looked out on the grey pavement and drab stone walls of Friars Passage. It had rained while he slept and the air from the partially opened window smelled at once clean and musty. Somehow the rainfall had not reduced the heat or the closeness. The scent of jasmine was now particularly strong.

A wave of tiredness came over him and he sat on the wide windowsill and rested his head against the side of the window. What was he doing? Twenty-seven years old and still only a temporary tutor at St Seb's – a post he'd secured, he knew, only because Lawrence had pulled strings for his former doctoral student. A loner even during his years at Liverpool, the few friends he'd made had drifted away following his move to Oxford, and the twin demands of his thesis and regular trips up the A1M to visit his dying father in Newcastle had left little space to develop a new social circle. Once his dad's beleagured liver had finally packed up, he'd already been into the writing-up stage: too late to start joining clubs and meeting people.

So research and teaching it had been, the former a dispiriting process of sending out judiciously selected chunks of his thesis to academic journals to be met with tepid responses or outright rejection, the latter blighted by waves of anxiety brought on by having to grapple with students who, despite being only a few years younger than him, seemed precociously brilliant, socially confident, or both together in one intimidating package. He sometimes despaired of ever securing a Fellowship, even with Lawrence's backing. Time after time he would muster his energies at interviews in order to present himself as witty, charming, urbane: the kind of person anyone would want as a colleague. *Give them your best self*, he would repeat like a mantra. *Don't just answer the question they ask – tell them what you want them to know. Surprise them. Entertain them. Play the game.* And yet every time he got into the interview room, he could feel himself freeze, a layer of wool settling over his mind and emotions. He came across as intelligent enough, he knew. But flat. No depth. No spark. And that spark was what made all the difference. Always had; always would. Unless you had the right connections, of course, like good old Lawrence.

Jonathan looked at the bottle of Lagavulin which was somehow unaccountably in his hand. Had he really been about to pour himself a glass? A surge of nausea threatened to overwhelm him. *No use turning into your dad.* He put down the bottle and reached for the phone.

As they approached Radcliffe Square, a uniformed officer raised the wooden barrier that blocked the entrance off Catte Street and waved them through. Kate parked the car on the cobbles near the Radcliffe Camera, the black metal gate to its surrounding grounds now cordoned off. Huddles of students, ousted from their morning research, stood by the encircling fence, staring at the domed stone building with curious eyes. One particularly bold individual, a floppy-haired blond boy with an eminently smackable face, caught Kate's arm as she passed.

'What's going on here, then, love?'

'Nothing you need to know about, *love*,' she snapped, ducking under the perimeter tape. Pleasingly, Geoff made no comment.

A short flagstone path then a dozen stone steps led up to double wooden doors in an arched doorway. To Kate's surprise, as soon as she got inside she was confronted with a small stone landing and yet more steps, curving up to the left and down to the right. She glanced up. Elegant black balustrades spiralled towards a pale-green-and-cream ceiling fussy with plaster ornamentation. It was like a huge eye staring down at her.

'Basement, right?' she said to the officer standing by the door, who confirmed it with a nod.

She and Geoff followed the curve of the steps down to another pair of wooden doors with inset glass panes through which she could see a large circular room surrounded by bookcases and set out with long tables and reading lights.

'Down here,' came a voice behind her to her left.

Beneath the staircase she had just descended, three more steps led to another wooden door, propped open by the owner of the voice. Behind him Kate could see yet another flight of steps leading downwards.

'James Bude,' said a smiling dark-haired man. 'One of the SOCOs. Forensics have already processed the scene, so you're good to come on down.'

At the bottom of the stairs, a door to the right bore the legend 'Gentlemen.'

'Nothing's been moved. Smell's not great, I'm afraid.'

'You surprise me,' Kate said, pushing past Bude, bracing herself for what she might encounter.

The small toilet area contained the characteristic mix of foul odours, stale urine dominant amongst them, aided and abetted by the cloying scent from a wedge-shaped plastic air-freshener. The floor was covered in dirty footprints from a succession of shoes and near the sink lay a pool of liquid that Kate hoped was just water. She turned to the stalls, three of them in a neat row, the doors to the two on the left lay open, revealing toilets in municipal black and white and circular dispensers of a thin, shiny paper Kate remembered from her school days and had hoped never to encounter again. She walked over to the right-hand stall and gingerly pushed the door open, stopping as soon as it encountered resistance, then poked her head round.

The figure slumped back against the cistern might have been an ordinary heart-attack victim, caught mid-strain – something Kate had seen often enough in her time – if it were not for the gory mess where its head should be. And that head was perched incongruously on the figure's bare thighs, eyes closed, short blond hair somehow miraculously unbloodied, the skin of the face pallid and waxy. Like the other victim, a candle stood near to the corpse, burnt to a half-inch stub.

Kate stepped back, allowing Geoff to take a look.

'Any details yet?' she asked Bude.

'Cards in the wallet confirm him as one Travis Greene,' the man said. 'A twenty-two-year-old Master's student at St Oswald Hall.'

He held up the victim's library card. The picture on it, a headshot, showed a fresh-faced blond man; his blue eyes were serious and unsmiling.

'Another student,' said Geoff. 'English this time.'

'Okay, got it,' Kate said to the SOCO. 'Anything else?'

'Just this,' he said, holding out a folded sheet of paper.

Kate took it, unfolded it and read the contents.

'You're going to want to see this,' she said, turning to Geoff.

Her colleague took the paper and scanned the short sentence it contained, then looked up. 'I guess we'll be needing to visit Dr Reynolds again.'

Jonathan stretched his feet out under the table in St Giles Café, nursing a hot cup of builders' tea across from Lucia. He listened as his friend talked, her slender hands conjuring meaning from the air, imposing sense and order on a wayward world by sheer force of will.

Dr Lucia Brodie, tutor in seventeenth-century literature – and the only one of Jonathan's peers that he fully trusted – had once been described by Lawrence as 'that vivacious Scot'. ('That's code for *opinionated, female foreigner*', Lucia had said when Jonathan told her later.) She was certainly living up to her reputation this afternoon, her black hair swinging across her face as she tilted her head in staccato movements, fixing her sharp gaze first on one of the café's occupants, then another. She looked for all the world like a sparrow keeping an eye out for worms or crumbs, except that, for Lucia, knowledge was her sustenance. Of people present or ages past, she made no distinction. She was currently regaling Jonathan with an excoriating account of her recent experience at an interview for a permanent post at Grayling Hall, a small but beautiful college near the railway station.

'And so he said, "Dr Brodie, how would you account for the paucity and poor quality of women's writing in your period?" And I said to him, "Professor Ravenstone, I'm not quite sure of the *agenda* behind your question. However, what I will say is that Dryden would probably *concur* with your opinion and this is not at all to his credit." Then I lectured him on literary misogyny for ten minutes. Needless to say, I didn't get the job: She Who Must Not Be Named did.'

Jonathan was quick with his sympathy. 'But you're clearly the best qualified person for the post,' he said. 'I mean, the other internals don't even specialise in the right period and, from what you told me, the outside candidate couldn't wipe his nose without assistance.'

'Thanks, dahling,' she replied, giving a credible impression of Zsa Zsa Gabor.

Lucia generally adopted the precise and genteel brogue of her literary namesake, but she possessed an incredible talent for accents, slipping in and out of them as the whim took her. Jonathan generally struggled to keep up with her mercurial shifts of mood and subject, but he had noted that, in moments of high emotion, even her base Edinburghian accent shifted and hints of a childhood further north slipped through.

'I've only myself to blame, I know,' she continued. 'As my mother used to say, I should bite my tongue like a good girl, then play merry havoc once I get what I want. Of course, even then, I couldn't have competed with the Nameless One. I mean, I've had myself some lowlights.' She patted her bob in a grotesque imitation of Mae West. 'But there are limits!'

'You're not blonde, it's true.' Jonathan sighed. 'Maybe you should have invested in some peroxide.'

'Still wouldn't give me the fortitude to stroke JR's ego... or whatever else he had in mind.'

Professor Jerry Ravenstone had a notorious penchant for young blondes with a keen intelligence and a willingness to do whatever it took to secure their career. Since the English Faculty was impoverished, it generally relied on colleges to pay the salaries of new Fellows for the first few years. As a corollary, that meant the final say in who got hired went to the college. Or, in this case, Jerry.

'Pretentious hack,' Jonathan said. Lucia still didn't look her customary cheerful self, and he searched for words that might lend her moral support. 'With that ridiculous leather jacket. Not to mention those painfully cool lectures on Derrida. *Il n'y a pas de hors-texte*, my ass. Wonder what his wife thinks about that procession of blondes.'

He stopped short, feeling slightly ashamed of himself. For all he knew, in private, Ravenstone might be an old sweetie and devoted husband. Perhaps he felt the need to cultivate a persona for the benefit of his Faculty rivals and students, like so many others around here. Like...

'Penny for them, love?' Lucia was looking at him with concern. 'You were staring off into the distance like you didn't even know I was here. Are you all right?'

'I'm fine. Just... tired. Let's change the subject,' he said.

'Well, what's new in your neck of the woods?' Lucia asked. 'I've been jabbering on about my job hunt. How's yours going?'

He shrugged. 'Same old,' he said. 'Send off for the further particulars, fill in the forms–'

'All of them slightly different,' Lucia interjected, 'so you can't just copy from one to the next.'

'Exactly. Send off the forms in the college post, hoping no

one asks why you're posting so many large brown envelopes. Wait to hear back for a month, then give up hope and embark on the next cycle.'

'God, don't!' said Lucia. 'Makes you wonder why we bother.'

'Well, what else would we do?'

'I don't know...' she said, gazing over his shoulder. 'Publishing? Archival work? Something in the City? You know, sometimes I feel quite like jacking it all in and going to work as a housemaid in some crumbling Gothic castle in the Highlands.'

'I can just see that,' said Jonathan, smiling. 'You – in the middle of nowhere, no concert hall, no cinema. You'd go mad in a matter of weeks!'

'That *is* the point of a Gothic castle, is it not?' Lucia laughed, and poured herself some more tea. 'But back to you, sweetie. If there's nothing going on in the job hunt, how about *l'amour*?'

Jonathan rolled his eyes. 'The less said about that, the better.'

'No, come on. I may have sworn off romance while Keneva and I try to work things out, but that doesn't mean I'm not interested in what you're up to. Spill it.'

Keneva was Lucia's long-time partner. Things had hit a rocky patch when Keneva without warning accepted a three-year job in Bergen, Norway. But the two of them had a long history together and, after some acrimonious conversations in which too many things had been said, they'd resolved to try a long-distance relationship for the duration of Keneva's post and see where things went. When all was said and done, they made a good couple, and Jonathan hoped it worked out. He cleared his throat.

'Well, there are a couple of things going on,' he said reluctantly.

'I knew it! So...?'

'You're not going to like it.'

'Who says? Try me.'

'So, I've been getting these notes in my pigeonhole for the last few months.'

'Ooh, intriguing! Very *84 Charing Cross Road*. Except hopefully neither of you is old and crusty. So who is this guy?'

'That's the thing. I don't know. I don't even know if it is a guy: they don't sign their name.'

'Curiouser and curiouser. So more like *The Shop Around the Corner...*'

'Er, maybe. I haven't seen that.'

'It doesn't matter. Go on: what's this anonymous writer been saying?'

Jonathan quickly ran through the content of the one-sided correspondence. Lucia scrunched up her face.

'I was hoping for something a little less PG-rated, if I'm honest,' she said. 'So far that sounds like the kind of stuff a schoolgirl writes to the gym teacher. *Ooh, you're so handsome. I'd climb a rope for you any day.*' She grimaced.

'I guess so,' said Jonathan. 'I've kind of been hoping it might be one of the other lecturers. Or maybe a postdoc or something. But it could be a student obviously...'

'Ugh, imagine. How creepy would that be?'

There was an awkward pause, then Jonathan thought he'd better come clean.

'That's the other thing,' he said. 'I've kind of developed a bit of a crush on one of my undergrads.'

Lucia's face fell. 'Jonathan, no!'

'I know, I know, it's stupid. But he's just so... I don't know. He's gorgeous, and charming – and really smart. And I think he's been giving me these signals that he likes me too. Like just this morning.'

He described what had happened during the tutorial. As he did so Lucia's face hardened.

'Jonathan, I love you, but that is bullshit. You know perfectly well that students are off-limits. They're adults, yes, but you're not equals... you're in a position of power. You get to decide how much support they get in college. You might even end up marking their Finals papers. A relationship would be totally unethical!'

Jonathan quailed under his friend's fierce gaze.

'You're right. You're totally right,' he said. 'I'm stupid to even think about it. And I am in a position of authority – even if I feel completely powerless most of the time. I'm sorry. I shouldn't even have mentioned it. You must think I'm an utter fool.'

Lucia's expression softened.

'Well maybe not an *utter* fool,' she said. 'Just an eensy-weensy tiny one.' She smiled. 'I know you wouldn't do anything about it anyway. You're much too much of a Cautious Cathy for that.'

'Hey!' said Jonathan, stung.

'Oh, you know what I mean.'

'No. No, I don't. Just because I don't throw myself into a relationship with someone I've met twice at a lesbian cat-fancying party doesn't mean I'm pathetic.'

As soon as he said it, Jonathan regretted the words. Lucia's eyes darkened.

'I'm going to let that slide for now, because I can see you're having a tough time of it.' She fixed him with one of the intense looks Jonathan knew had more than once reduced a hapless student to tears. 'But if you say anything like that to me again...' She let the silence develop.

'Lucia, I'm so sorry, I don't know why I said that. It just

came out. I don't know what's the matter with me at the moment.'

'Apology accepted,' she said in clipped tones.

'No, I really mean it. You're my best friend here and I don't know what I'd do without you.' His eyes pleaded with her to understand. 'Can you forgive me? Really?'

'Well, just this once,' she said, with a hint of warmth creeping back into her voice. 'And, for the record, Keneva's the lesbian; I'm bi... and I don't think you're pathetic.'

'I don't know. It feels that way sometimes. I'm in my mid-twenties with no boyfriend and, after this summer, probably no job either.'

'I can't do much about the job, honey. But I'll keep my eyes peeled for a suitable man. We can't have you wasting your time on anonymous pen pals and whatnot.'

Jonathan smiled. 'Don't knock it – it's the best offer I've had all year!'

'Right, that's it. I'm taking you to the Tower the next time they do karaoke. That always gets people chatting.'

'As long as you don't make me get up and sing...'

'Hah, no fear of that. You couldn't carry a tune in a bucket, love. In all seriousness, though, it's about time you let yourself meet someone who deserves you. Who knows? Maybe this letter-writer will turn out to be a hidden gem. Someone who's sweet, and decent, and who'll value you for who you are.'

'Well you'll be the first to know when I find out who that is!' Jonathan cracked.

Lucia rolled her eyes and ordered another tea.

*You cannot imagine the exquisite tedium of severing a man's head. You believe, of course – addicted as you are to the foolishness*

*of the media – that I must derive pleasure from the act, some sort of sexual frisson, compensating, no doubt, for the inadequate childhood I must have had. Daddy's absent love. Mother's cloying embrace. Others may find their release in such a way, but not I. For they are weak and I am strong. When I raise my blade, gleaming in the candlelight, to make my first incision; when I carefully penetrate the layers of flesh and fat; when I feel out the atlanto-occipital joint, making no more of a cut than is strictly necessary, it is not an erotic act but simply a job that must be done. There may be pleasure in a job well done, efficiently achieved, but, in the end, it is simply my Work. And that is enough.*

*You judge me, do you not? You sit back in your tasteful armchair or propped up against your carefully selected pillows and you presume to judge me, snug in the hypocrisies of your middle-class existence. But I answer to a higher Judge than you. And I have no time or cause to trouble myself with your cant or your delicate qualms – for the days are rushing on and the hour approaches. I must keep the wick of my lamp well trimmed and my jar filled with oil. And I must be about my father's business. Indeed, I must.*

*No, you cannot understand my Work – the full immensity of its purpose. How could you? But still you watch. You look on, compelled, unable to turn away, for something within you recognises the justice and the truth of what I do. It is yet but a poor worm, a fledgling bird inside your consciousness, a narrow stream – a trickle, even – of pure water, almost swamped by the muddied turbulence of your confusion, but nourishing, cleansing, salvific. Turn towards it, nurture it, I counsel you. For the storm approaches and when its righteous winds blow how else will you stand?*

*And so it is that I share with you my Work. That you may learn from my example. From the discipline and control it necessitates. For I am not come to punish – not you – not yet. I am come that you may have life.*

*Watch now, therefore, as I proceed. Take notes. Read, mark, learn, and inwardly digest. Like old Cædmon, chew the cud and bring forth sweetness.*

*Are you watching?*

# CHAPTER FOUR

## MONDAY 4 MAY, SECOND WEEK IN TRINITY

Jonathan darted across St Giles, dodging cars and buses, feeling lighter than he had in days. He always felt better after he'd spent time with Lucia, even when they quarrelled. She somehow managed to inspire him with renewed confidence. In his research, his prospects. In himself. All the same, his mind returned to the start of their conversation. It had raised familiar question marks over what it was he wanted out of his career. Sometimes he didn't think he even wanted to be in Oxford, job or no job. He loved the city, he really did. The stately, ancient buildings and spectacular gardens bursting with colour. Visiting speakers of the highest calibre, some of whom made him feel like a gushing fangirl. The musical and artistic prowess on display in every college chapel and high street coffee shop. The sun on the river. The exquisite loneliness of the Taylorian's deserted stacks. At times it was even possible to squint and see that Brideshead myth alive and thriving.

Yet, at the same time, the place was not remotely conducive to happiness and stability. Jonathan had heard the rumours about attempted suicide and self-harm by desperate students, working themselves to the point of exhaustion. The rumoured wing of the Warneford Psychiatric Hospital dedicated to Finalists on the edge. All hushed up and minimised in the press, of course: no use tarnishing the university's shiny image. And when those students who survived became tutors and Fellows, as some of them did, they seemed to internalise its peculiar ethos of exceptionalism ('the brightest and the best') coupled with a fierce loyalty to the system and a distrust of outsiders. The traditions and shibboleths unique to each college, like tripwires to catch the unwary. *If you need to ask, you don't deserve to know.* The arrogant complacency about other scholars' specialisms: like the feminist postcolonialist whose work spanned all of two decades, but who dismissed the work of queer theorists for its 'lack of range'. The poses of eccentricity that sometimes approached the pathological: like that Restoration Drama expert – Lancashire, born and bred – whose accent was now so clipped and refined as to be almost incomprehensible. Or that sober, tweed-wearing Romanticist once spotted through a chink in the curtains dancing a naked bacchanal to Stravinsky's *Rite of Spring*.

*Ugh, you're getting as bad as Lawrence,* Jonathan thought. *If you don't watch out, you'll turn into just another bitter old queen, gossiping about others to make up for the lack of anything interesting going on in your own life.* He shook himself as he stepped into the Lodge, then headed with purpose across the Quad towards the SCR and lunch.

'I'm sorry, ma'am,' the porter said, 'I just don't know where Dr Reynolds might be at the moment.' He seemed genuinely regretful not to be able to help Kate, a far cry from the officious idiot who'd been on duty the first time she and Geoff had visited the college.

'He doesn't have a lecture or seminar timetabled or something?'

'I wouldn't know, I'm afraid. We don't have access to the tutors' schedules unless they've booked out one of the college teaching rooms.'

'But last time,' Geoff interjected, 'the guy told us we couldn't see Reynolds because he had tutorials all day...' He stopped as realisation dawned. 'Oh. Right. He didn't actually know that. He was just stonewalling us.'

The porter looked embarrassed. 'I couldn't rightly say, sir. But sometimes our lads do get a bit overprotective. And some of the Fellows can get' – he glanced around, lowering his voice – 'downright nasty with us if we let them be disturbed. I'm sure whoever it was didn't mean any harm by it.'

*I'm not so sure about that*, thought Kate.

'Can't you give us any idea where he might be?' she asked.

The man pondered for a moment. 'Well it might be as he's giving a lecture, right enough. That'd be up at the Faculty Building along Manor Road. Maybe you could try there?'

Thanking the porter for his help, Kate turned to exit the Lodge. She stepped carefully over the wooden threshold, then heard an agonised groan behind her. She turned to find her colleague clutching his head, beet-red in the face and using language that would give a nun palpitations.

'You all right there, buddy?'

'No, I'm bloody not. Cracked my head on that stupid bloody low lintel, didn't I.'

Geoff looked so outraged, Kate had to fight back a smile.

'Walk it off, man. You're a big boy now and we've got work to do.'

She strode off in the direction of the squad car, Geoff trailing behind her, swearing all the way.

Jonathan hauled open the heavy wooden door of the college library and nodded at the graduate student manning the reception desk as he crossed to the stairs. Once on the landing, he elected not to turn right and walk down the long, carpeted corridor to the English section, which would risk bumping into one of the Finalists who tended to stake out the desks at this time of year, piling books up around them like they were making a fort. Instead, he stepped forward onto the long timber floorboards of the Old Library, their wood stained so dark as to be almost black and polished to a glossy sheen.

As he passed the seventeenth-century globes, he trod with extra care. In the past he'd lost his footing on the slippery floor and almost reached out to grab one of them. He shuddered to think of the embarrassment, not to mention the obscene expense, if he'd not caught himself. It was a mystery to him that the college librarian, a cantankerous man almost as fat as the globes, had not gated off this section of the library. No doubt that would come in time, but for now Jonathan loved to take advantage of his privileged access to the sixteenth-century bookcases with their long wooden benches and huge leather-bound tomes, some of them still chained to the shelves. Occasionally, when he was sure no one could see him, he amused himself by pulling a volume off the shelves: an early edition of Milton, or a copy of Johnson's dictionary with scribbled annotations by some unknown hand. At such times he would wonder how many previous scholars and students had handled the same books, reverently stroking the stiff yellowing pages, avoiding any contamination of the crisp black lettering of the double columns in their centre.

Today, however, Jonathan merely spread out the materials of his article-in-progress across one of the long desks at the back of the high-ceilinged room, along with a couple of reference books and set to work, taking a perverse pleasure in the discomfort of the hard bench on which he was sitting. He began by scanning through some of his earlier notes, looking for a stray idea he might have jotted down and then forgotten about. He came across a list of questions scrawled over one page. *Why is Grendel never described in detail? What is the significance of his beheading?*

The unwanted image of Simon Beatty flashed into Jonathan's mind and he pushed it away. He mustn't think about that. *Why does Grendel have no father? Is Beowulf less justified in killing Grendel's mother, as Rogers suggests?* There were so many angles he could pursue, Jonathan quickly realised he was in danger of losing himself in a hopeless maze of speculation. He needed to shift the research on to firmer ground. He flipped to another page of his notebook which dealt with the poem's contexts and began to cross-check them with the relevant reference works.

As he continued to read, Jonathan became more and more interested in the connections between *Beowulf* and some Old Norse sagas. He nipped downstairs to the card catalogue that some grad students were transferring on to an electronic system, but there was nothing useful in the college's collection. He'd have to head over to the Faculty library. *I'll need to be there later anyway*, he thought. As Jonathan put his notes away, he had to shake himself as Beatty's image again crept into his mind.

The porter on reception at the Manor Road Faculty building was nice enough when Kate and Geoff questioned him.

'Sure, we've got all the lecture lists pinned up over here,' he said in response to Kate's query.

He led the way to a long series of cork noticeboards lined with blue felt affixed to one of the pale brick walls.

'What subject?'

'Huh?'

'Will you be wanting Law? Economics, English, Linguistics?'

'Oh, right, we're looking for lectures by a Dr Jonathan Reynolds in Medieval Literature.'

'English it is then. Let's see.'

He unpinned one of the lecture lists and handed it to Kate. It was made up of perhaps a dozen thick white sheets of paper folded over and stapled at one edge to create a slim booklet. Each page was filled with tightly printed lines of small type, divided into different italicised sections – *History of the English Language, Special Authors: Tennyson and Browning* – unfamiliar jargon like *Honour Moderations, Course II, Schools,* and a confusing assortment of letters and numbers.

'Looks like you'd need at least an undergraduate degree to keep track of what's what,' Kate remarked to Geoff.

'Reynolds on it?'

'Give me a sec.'

She scanned the first couple of pages. 'Yup, right here.'

Geoff looked over her shoulder and read. '"*Beowulf* and the Modern Horror Film". Well that makes sense of a lot of things.'

Kate thought back to the film Reynolds had been watching when they first met. She nodded. 'Let's check it out.'

She turned back to the porter. 'Can you point us towards, er...' She glanced back down at the list. 'Seminar Room 2?'

The man frowned. 'I can show you where it is, yeah. But you can't go in while he's giving a lecture. There's some benches nearby. You'll have to wait there for a bit till he's done.'

'We'll see,' said Kate non-committally.

She and Geoff followed the man down two broad flights of

stairs with polished wooden banisters to a mezzanine level. All the floors were covered in panels of a mellow, chestnut-coloured cork which made sticky noises as the three pairs of shoes made contact and then lifted from it.

The man paused outside a heavy, dark-brown door. A long metal handle ran from top to bottom next to a slit window made of safety glass.

'That's odd,' he said.

'What's that?'

'The light's on, but there don't seem to be any students in there.'

He stepped back to let Kate see.

Peering through the narrow window Kate saw seven or eight rows of long dark-brown benches. *What is it with the colour scheme of this place?* All the benches were empty.

'Do you mind if we take a look?'

In answer, the porter pushed at the heavy door, which opened slowly. Cautiously he poked his head round, then stepped into the room, gesturing for Kate and Geoff to follow. A wooden table with a lectern atop stood near a large whiteboard, overhead projector and screen. But otherwise the room was empty.

'You're sure this is when Dr Reynolds' lecture is scheduled?'

'Yes. I don't know how to account for it. Unless...'

'Unless?'

'Lecturers have to attend all their timetabled lectures. But, if no students turn up, then obviously they can cancel them.'

'What, the lectures aren't compulsory?' Geoff looked askance.

'No. The academics tend to offer lecture series on whatever topic they're researching at the moment. If that doesn't fit what the students are interested in writing essays on, they don't have to attend.'

Geoff scowled. 'Seems like a stupid system to me,' he muttered.

'Geoff!' Kate admonished her colleague.

'No, it's fine,' said the porter. 'No skin off my nose. You know,' he said, leaning forward and adopting a confidential tone. 'Sometimes lecturers use it to their own advantage. There was this one guy – a real dick he could be when he wanted to be. Anyway, this one year he deliberately offered a series of lectures on this obscure sixth-century Celtic text, assuming no one'd be interested so he'd get to cancel.'

'Ha!' Kate grinned. 'That's quite funny.'

The porter raised an eyebrow. 'Not if you're interested in Celtic literature.'

'There can't be that many people who are, surely?'

'Well I am, as it happens.'

Too late, Kate noticed the light brogue underlying the man's speech.

'Oh, sorry, I didn't think...'

'What – that just because I'm on reception here that I wouldn't be interested in literature?'

'No, I mean... Crap, forget I said anything, okay?'

The man smiled broadly. 'I'm just kidding, it's fine. You're right, there aren't that many of us into that stuff, I guess.'

'So what happened then?' Geoff wanted to know. 'Did you kick this guy's arse?'

'Nah. I wouldn't keep my job long if I let the academics get to me. To be honest, I wouldn't expect anything more off the guy. But there were a few students and other academics who got pretty ticked off. Felt he was disrespecting their area of expertise or their heritage or whatever. They got together and decided to turn up to his first lecture and confront him. See if he had the balls to try and bullshit his way through it.'

'And did he?'

''Course not. The guy can bullshit for England – and does, most of the time – but I guess twenty pissed-off faces put him off his stride. At least temporarily. He mumbled something weaselly about needing some more time to prepare and slunk off.'

'So did the others complain about him?' Kate asked.

'Nope. Think they thought they'd made their point and he wasn't worth it.'

Geoff frowned. 'So he got out of doing his job and didn't face any consequences?'

'You don't know much about academics here, do you?' the other man said, laughing. 'Do you really think there are consequences?' He walked off back towards reception, still laughing.

'What now then, boss?'

'Let me think,' said Kate, rubbing her temples in an attempt to massage away the tiredness. 'What would I do if I was an academic who'd come all the way over here to find I didn't have to give my lecture after all?'

'I don't know – head for the nearest café or pub?'

'Maybe. But there aren't any around here, are there?'

'No idea. Not a part of town I'm familiar with.'

'I think it's mainly playing fields and different Faculty buildings with lecture halls and libraries.'

'Are you thinking maybe he's gone to the library to do some research?'

'It's worth a shot. Come on.'

They walked out past reception and turned right down some concrete steps that led towards the car park. Halfway down there was another door marked 'English Faculty Library'. Geoff hauled it open and they found themselves confronted with yet another set of stairs. Kate sighed, then headed up towards some glass double doors beyond which there were some electronic barriers and another reception desk to their left.

'Can I help you?' said a pleasant-looking plump blonde holding a barcode scanner, a pile of books in front of her.

After the preliminaries had been exchanged, she swiped them through the barriers and into the main library, another expanse of cork-tiled floors, long tables with reading lights, and a set of towering bookstacks along the left and front ends of the room.

The librarian got up from her chair and came around the table to meet them, revealing a large pregnancy bump.

'You're welcome to walk round the room,' she whispered. 'But please be as quiet as possible: we've got Finalists working here.' She indicated a dozen or so figures dotted around the tables, some scribbling assiduously away in large notebooks, others slumped in their chairs with an assortment of books and journals piled around them. One hapless individual had fallen asleep and a tiny amount of drool had dripped onto the table from his open mouth.

'I'd come with you myself, but...' She indicated her stomach. 'This is like carrying one of those army rucksacks. One more week, then it's maternity leave, thank goodness.'

As she sank back into her chair and picked up the scanner again, Kate and Geoff walked further into the room, edging past the tables looking for a familiar face. That yielded nothing, so they split up, each tackling one of the bookstacks.

When they met back at the reception desk, Kate spread her hands in a mute query. Geoff shook his head. Still nothing.

Kate turned to the librarian. 'Is there anywhere else Dr Reynolds could be? A Faculty coffee room or something?'

'Yes, there's one downstairs next to the photocopier room. You're welcome to check either of them; they're not locked.'

As they turned to go, she hesitated, then said, 'There's

always the Special Collections rooms as well. I'm not supposed to hand over the keys to non-members, but I guess since you're the police...'

She handed over a bunch of keys. 'All the rooms are along the same corridor, so you can't get lost.'

Kate and Geoff descended the stairs again which dog-legged left in front of the outside door down a final flight to the basement. Another noticeboard lay dead ahead, crammed with a disorderly array of notices, flyers for drinks nights, for sale ads offering second-hand bicycles and used textbooks, and posters advertising plays and music recitals. The corridor then led left and abruptly right to reveal a series of yellow-brown doors stretching into the distance. Kate and Geoff tried them one by one, encountering the promised photocopier and coffee room, both of which were empty. At the end of the corridor there were two doors with inset glass. When Geoff tried the handles they were locked, so they peered through the windows to find medium-sized rooms with floor-to-ceiling bookshelves behind grilles. Again, there was no one inside.

'I'm beginning to think no one actually does any work around here,' Kate observed.

'No kidding.'

There was one last door, this one without a window panel. Affixed to it was a metal label bearing some guy's weird unpronounceable name. Kate jiggled the handle, preparing to try one of the keys, but the door was unlocked. She swung open the heavy door and stepped inside.

Jonathan jumped as the door opened behind him.

'Dr Reynolds?'

It was the two detectives, the woman – Stewart, wasn't it? –

standing in front, her expression serious. She'd recently washed her hair, Jonathan noticed, and conditioner had smoothed out her severe black bob, though not enough to mitigate its harshening effect on her jawline, accentuated by the crisp, pressed collar of her jacket. *Is she a formidable woman, or merely trying to appear so?* he wondered.

'The porter told us we might find you here.'

The woman's tone was sharp. Her handsome colleague, Simpson, stood behind her to her left, avoiding eye contact for some reason. Jonathan traced with appreciation the outline of hard pectorals and well-defined biceps beneath his thin shirt. He did not ordinarily find redheads attractive, but this one had an unusual colouring that in a woman might be called Titian-blonde.

'What can I do for you, officers?' Jonathan began. 'I'm not sure I can add much to my previous statement.'

'If I may, Dr Reynolds?' Stewart took a step closer, followed by Simpson. 'There's been a development in the case, and I'm afraid we need to ask you some more questions. Do you know a student named Travis Greene?'

A flash of heat went through Jonathan's body, followed by a feeling of icy cold. This was all he needed after the lecture debacle earlier.

'Erm, I'm not sure,' he hedged. 'I see so many students, what with lectures and out-teaching for other colleges.'

Simpson frowned. 'Do think carefully, sir. We're talking about Travis Greene of St Oswald Hall, studying for the English Master's programme. Originally from Texas.'

Stewart broke in. 'Our records indicate that you taught him for an optional paper on medieval romance.'

'Ah yes,' said Jonathan, controlling his breathing and putting on a look of vague recognition. *This could be bad.* 'Travis Greene from Ozzie Hall. I did indeed teach him as an "out" student last year as a favour to the Fellow in Charge.' He deliberately affected an air of urbanity. 'Pleasant chap. He's all right, I hope?' *Please don't let them know*, he thought desperately.

'I'm afraid he's not, sir,' the redhead said. 'He was found dead earlier today in the basement of the Radcliffe Camera.'

Jonathan's knees began to shake, and he dropped his pen with a clatter.

'I'm sorry, Dr Reynolds,' Stewart said. 'This must come as a great shock.'

Jonathan demurred. 'Oh, I didn't know Travis well. But of course, something as sudden and violent as this, whomever it involves...'

'That's odd, sir,' said Simpson, his tone chilly.

'What do you mean, Detective?'

'As with the first victim, a piece of paper was found on the body–'

'Not another quotation from *Beowulf*, surely?' Jonathan interrupted.

'Not this time, sir.'

Was it Jonathan's imagination, or had the temperature in the room actually dropped?

The man continued. 'It's another note typed on a word processor.' He took a sheet of paper out of a clear plastic wallet and handed it to Reynolds. 'Go on – take it. It's already been dusted for prints.'

Jonathan accepted the sheet with trembling fingers and looked down. The paper contained a single sentence, along with an ink drawing of what looked like a sprig of holly next to an axe and a spear. It read: `Jonathan Reynolds taught me my fleshly fault.`

Jonathan recoiled, nearly falling off his chair, as the events of the previous year flooded back. 'Oh God!' he breathed.

Stewart cleared her throat. 'Would you like to reconsider your earlier statement?' she said, adding 'sir' in a tone that was more menacing than polite.

Jonathan put his head in his hands. There was nothing for it but to explain the whole situation and hope it didn't get into the papers. He knew he'd done nothing wrong really, but it didn't reflect well on his ability to handle troubled students. Besides, Hacker had made it crystal clear in that supremely embarrassing meeting that, if any details became public, the college would take an extremely dim view. 'St Sebastian's has a reputation to uphold,' the wizened little man had said through those thin, pursed lips. 'Our students' parents count on us to safeguard the well-being of their children.' *And you count on them to keep the college endowment healthy through donations and bequests,* Jonathan had thought sourly.

'Could we do this back in my rooms?' he said, hoping to buy himself some time. 'I don't want to take the chance of anyone overhearing.'

Stewart looked annoyed but agreed, and the three of them filed back through the corridor and up the stairs towards the exit.

Back in his rooms, Jonathan adopted as calm and open a tone as he could muster. 'Travis was a sweet young man and very gifted,' he said, spreading his hands. 'But you must understand that he was troubled. He'd come over to England to do his Master's, following his undergraduate degree at Austin. He'd never left the Deep South before, still less been abroad, and he'd had quite a strict upbringing. He was beginning to, ah... discover himself at Oxford.'

'You mean he was gay,' Simpson said matter-of-factly.

'Exactly, yes,' Jonathan replied. 'Though I'm not sure he'd quite realised that for himself when he first arrived. He was very much trying to figure out who he was.'

'I understand he was a keen rower and weightlifter,' Stewart interjected. 'Perhaps that very macho environment made it difficult to explore his sexuality.'

'Not precisely,' Jonathan said. 'It's strange, but these kinds of all-male, *macho* as you say, groups tend to adopt a surprising latitude when it comes to sex. Any sign of effeminacy is quickly stamped on to be sure but, beyond that, once the beer or Pimms starts flowing, pretty much anything goes.'

On an impulse, he turned toward Simpson. 'Boys will be boys, as they say.'

He had hoped to make Simpson uncomfortable with this remark, drawing the focus off his own embarrassment, but the man met his eye with a frank, untroubled gaze.

'And how would you account for the statement about you?' Simpson said simply.

'Well, that's where it becomes a little awkward. I had to promise to keep quiet about what happened. But I don't suppose that matters now.'

'We'd encourage you not to hold anything back, Dr Reynolds,' said Stewart.

'As I said, he was a troubled young man. He came from a place where he wasn't exactly encouraged to be open, and he struggled with his identity, even somewhere as comparatively liberal as Oxford.' Jonathan cleared his throat. 'I try to encourage a friendly relationship with my graduate students, and we tended to go for a drink after our supervisions. At the King's Arms, usually, since it's between our two colleges. One afternoon he seemed preoccupied about something. When I asked if anything was wrong, Travis confided in me. I tried to be supportive – you know, whilst remaining professional.' *Ha!*

*More like terrified of what might happen if he knew you were gay too*, he thought. 'Unfortunately, I'm afraid Travis became more than a little interested in me. Started turning up after all my lectures, wanting to have in-depth discussions. Began dressing like me, dropping into my office unannounced, that kind of thing. I discouraged him as sensitively as I could, but eventually I had to report him to the Dean at his college. Of course, he was immediately reallocated to a different tutor and instructed to keep away from me.'

Jonathan broke off to pour himself a shot of whisky and downed it in one.

'And how did Mr Greene take all this?' Stewart wanted to know.

'Not well. There were, you know, pills. And a note. He had quite a well-developed sense of guilt, apparently, coupled with a somewhat dramatic, reckless streak. The college hushed it all up, of course – no need to embarrass him or anyone else. But it seems the poor boy must have struggled to let it go.'

'Or someone else found out about it, and wanted to make it look so,' Stewart said.

'How do you mean?'

'It wasn't suicide, after all.'

'It wasn't?'

'I'm afraid not. He had been decapitated.'

Jonathan felt sick. 'Just like Beatty.'

'That's right, though his arm was left attached this time.'

'So, then, this is the same killer – he's...'

'We're trying not to jump to conclusions at this stage, but that seems a likely scenario.'

Jonathan's mind raced. 'But, then, why would the killer... why would anyone other than Travis want to bring up what happened between us after all this time?'

'I don't know, Dr Reynolds,' Stewart said. 'But that's what

we're trying to find out. We'd like you to spend some time writing up a more detailed account of your, ah, experience of Mr Greene, if you would. Then we'll interview you again – tomorrow at 4pm, if that's convenient?'

'I'll have to rearrange a class, but, of course, of course,' said Jonathan, eager to seem co-operative. The last thing he needed was to fall afoul of the police.

As the officers turned to leave, something struck Jonathan. He called them back from the corridor.

'You said Travis had been decapitated?' He shuddered at the image.

'That's right, sir,' Simpson replied. 'The same MO as the first killing.'

'Not precisely,' Jonathan observed mechanically. 'This time the quotation wasn't from *Beowulf*, and his arm was still intact.'

Stewart looked at him with interest. 'Meaning?'

'I'm not sure,' Jonathan said slowly. 'But he *was* beheaded, and the note talked about being taught of his "fleshly fault". That's a very peculiar turn of phrase.'

'I thought so too,' said Simpson. 'Does it mean anything to you?'

'I'm afraid it does,' Jonathan said, stepping over to his bookshelves and pulling down a slim volume. He thumbed through the pages until he found the passage he wanted.

'I want to read you a section from the climax of *Sir Gawain and the Green Knight*.' He saw their blank faces. 'It's a fourteenth-century medieval poem set in the days of King Arthur. The Tolkien translation is better, but this one's closer to the original in the literal sense.' He caught the look of impatience in Kate's eyes and checked his nervous babbling. 'Anyway, at this point in the poem, Gawain realises that he's, well, screwed up and let himself and the Arthurian court down. He's furious with himself and talks about "the fault and the frailty of the crabbed flesh", saying "How tender it is to entice teachings of filth!".' He flipped the page. 'And there's another bit soon after where the narrator describes how he wore a green girdle – sort of like a belt – "In tokenyng he watz tane in tech of a faute". That is, as a token that he was taken, or caught, in a fault.'

He looked up from the book. 'It's not precisely the same phraseology, but those key words are clearly there: fault, and flesh, and the idea of teaching.'

Stewart gave him a dubious look. 'Sure, the words are similar, but that's quite a stretch, isn't it?'

'The words alone wouldn't carry much weight, I agree, but consider the manner of dispatch.'

The detectives looked blank.

'Beheading... The whole premise of *Gawain* rests on the eponymous hero accepting a challenge to behead the Green Knight, who of course magically survives, and then go on a journey to receive a similar blow a year and a day later. The story is set at Christmas – hence the holly on the piece of paper, which is also what the Knight was carrying along with his axe.'

He riffled back through the book. 'Let's see, it says "But in his one hand he had a holly-twig, that is most green when the groves are bare, and an axe in the other, huge and ugly". He doesn't actually carry a spear here, but I think what's important is the juxtaposition of the weapons and the holly, which is a symbol of fertility, or the power of nature, or of peace, depending on which line you take. Anyway, the Knight kicks off this exchange of blows game, which Gawain later tries to get out of by trickery. In fact...' – Jonathan's conviction grew – 'Maybe the killer sees this all as some kind of game. The poem's structure is built around games that turn out to have serious moral implications and consequences.'

The detectives were beginning to be swayed by Jonathan's

logic, he could see.

'But why connect the victim to this particular poem?' Simpson persisted, but Stewart was there ahead of him.

'It's his surname,' she said slowly. '*Sir Gawain and the Green Knight*... Travis Greene.'

'Exactly. But there's something else,' Jonathan said. 'The first murder was based on the Old English poem *Beowulf*. This second one alludes to a Middle English romance.'

'What are you saying?' Stewart asked.

'These texts are major works of medieval literature. The killer may be inspired in his actions by famous killings of the Middle Ages.'

'What, like in *Se7en*?' Simpson asked. 'With the Deadly Sins and so on?'

'Maybe,' Jonathan replied, thinking over the lurid plot of the film made famous only a couple of years before. 'Those killings were certainly highly staged too. But there's no explicit connection here to deadly sins or anything like that. I think what we're looking at is perhaps more general than that: the medieval period, the literature. I don't know. But, believe me,' he continued, his heart sinking, 'if that's the case, there's a lot more where these two came from. Whoever this killer is, it's possible he's just getting started.'

~

## Thames Valley Police Document D0137 in The Dark Knight case:

### Handwritten diary entry

*We live, we are told, in the caring decade. The last before a new millennium more hopeful than the last. We inhabit a classless society built on glowing ideals of choice and personal autonomy. On promises of global alliances. Of peace and prosperity.*

*Lies, all of it. Blatant lies from self-serving grey men, feathering their nests, concealing their bedizened whores and backroom deals.*

*No. If this is the era of equality, then sleaze is its only common denominator. Filth its only currency.*

*Foetid hippies and the nouveau riche splash around in the muck together with dissolute pop stars and depraved newspaper magnates.*

*Everywhere I look, the people disgust me. The very air I breathe is tainted.*

*Sometimes I walk down the street, imagining I carry a gun. In my mind's eye I point it at the heads of those who come towards me. Gluttonous fools stuffing maw and belly. Profligates dragging around bags stuffed with worthless trifles and cheaply made goods, flaunting their tasteless mediocrity. There are not enough bullets in the world.*

*I cannot hope to stem this nation's slide into an abyss of ignorance, where culture has become synonymous with elitism; where television networks parade footage of enseamed sheets, revelling in life's most foetid realities. All for the mindless consumption of the wretched masses.*

*No, all I can hope to do is to make a personal stand. To make one small change in hope of sparking a chain reaction. Maybe even a revolution.*

*For change must come. The very earth cries out for it.*

*And God will do nothing: I realise that. He is deaf and blind. It is up to us to remake this fallen world. To be a conduit for truth. A transformation that begins with one man, but is greater than any one man.*

# PART II

# CHAPTER ONE



## KATE

'Are you kidding me?'

The Big Boss did not look happy, his wide face displaying several shades of red that made Kate fear for the state of his heart.

'Well if you'll just let me–'

'You want me to authorise bringing a civilian in on a multiple murder investigation, not to mention...'

'He's really a very–'

But he would not be diverted, the words coming inexorably like blows to a punching bag. 'Not to *mention* that he has links to both cases.'

'Sir, I know, sir, but he's been ruled out as a suspect. His alibis check out and there's no reason at all to think he's capable of something like this. I really think he could be an invaluable source–'

'You've said. Don't start that again. There must be plenty of other medieval experts who could keep us up to speed on notorious killings from a thousand years ago, surely.'

'Absolutely, sir. And if you really want me to find someone else I will. Though it will mean more time,' she added slyly.

'You know, getting a list of experts, giving them all background checks.' She knew the pressure her superior was under to solve such cases quickly, and sure enough, DCI Cooper's face began to lose some of its redness. She pressed her advantage.

'And his links to the victims actually make him a good person to keep on board,' she suggested. 'Keep it simple. The fewer civilians who know all the details the better. Even if he is somehow mixed up in it, all the more reason to keep him close.'

'Hmph. Muddies the waters, more like. But the tighter we can keep this the better, right enough. I've had not just the wardens of St Seb's and St Oswald's but the VC himself on the phone telling me to keep this discreet and wrap it up as soon as. They've instituted safeguarding procedures at the libraries and colleges, obviously – reduced opening hours, locked any unmanned gates, sign-in books at the Lodge, and so on – but they're not best pleased at the prospect of the university being associated with seedy gay stuff. But nor do we want the force seeming like a hotbed of homophobia. Not a good look nowadays.'

'Er, absolutely, sir,' Kate deadpanned. 'Not a good look... So we *are* taking the line that it's about sexuality?'

'Not necessarily, but we've got to cover our bases. What do you and Simpson think?'

'Too early to say for sure, but both victims were definitely gay, so...'

'Notified the LGB community, or whatever they call themselves now?'

'Yup. No details, of course, just put out a warning to the club nights and pubs that a gay-basher's on the prowl. Be on the alert, take precautions, don't walk home alone, the usual.'

'Good. We don't need Stonewall on our backs, complaining about police prejudice again. I'm having enough trouble keeping this out of the press as it is.'

'How's that been going?'

The big man sighed. 'Just this morning I've had to squash a story about "Oxford's Queer-Killer". So just you and Simpson be careful who you talk to. This could be some journo's big payday if he gets the scoop.'

'No worries about that, sir. And the request for access to the online dating site? I haven't heard anything from Legal.'

'I put it through soon as you filed the paperwork, but the smart-ass CEO – some American kid on a mission – is yammering on about the right to privacy, all that shit. We'll get it, right enough, but could take a while. I'd chase it up for you, but I'm up to my balls dealing with the rail enquiry.'

Kate had almost forgotten the rail crash that had occurred the previous month when an overtired driver passed a signal on red and collided head-on with another train. The identification of the bodies, notification of next of kin, and subsequent investigation had taken most of the Big Boss's attention and the force's resources for the last few weeks.

The man looked at his watch. 'I'm late for lunch,' he said, and Kate wondered how much of his bad mood stemmed from the pressures of his workload and how much from his being 'hangry', as Geoff put it.

'Move it along then, Stewart,' Cooper said. 'But I'll be expecting regular updates. And keep your pet academic on a short leash. Anything goes wrong, it'll be your guts not mine for garters.' He dabbed at the bald section in the middle of his head with pudgy fingers. 'You'd better catch this bastard and damn quick.'

*Great*, she thought. *First really big case and it could be my last.*

'Are you sure about this, Sarge?'

Just what she needed, Geoff badgering her too.

'Sure about what?'

'You know, Reynolds.'

'Reynolds what?' She wasn't going to help him.

'No offence, Sarge, but it's not exactly procedure, is it? Letting him in on the case.'

'Don't see why not. Plenty of times we bring in a consultant. You know that.'

'I know, but...'

'But?'

'He's not just a consultant, is he? He's connected to the victims. Named in the note we found on Greene.'

'And?'

'Doesn't it complicate things unnecessarily? I mean, what if there's another one and he's linked to that one too? And is he going to be able to stay detached? The last thing we need is to have to pussyfoot around his emotions.'

She decided to relent on him.

'I know, Geoff. Point taken. Reynolds is a risk. But my instinct tells me that he's going to be worth it. He's not turned into an emotional wreck so far, he knows the literature, and, more importantly, he's not an uncooperative arse like the other academics we've interviewed. If this is a killer fixated on medieval deaths or whatever, then Reynolds is our best chance of understanding what's going on. Maybe even getting the march on our guy.'

'Maybe. But I'm not comfortable about this.'

'I'm not asking you to be.' Kate injected a note of chill into her tone. 'But in my view, he's the best lead we've got at the minute. Besides, it's in his interests to get this case solved too. If the press learns about the note found on Greene...'

'Right you are, Sarge.'

'And stop calling me Sarge,' Kate said, rising to pull down another file from the mountain on the shelf by her desk. 'My name will do fine.'

After introducing Reynolds to a few of the team down the hallway and ushering him into the office, Kate asked Geoff to get them all coffee. He returned from the machine at the end of the floor with three plastic cups of sludgy liquid and some Hobnobs he'd unearthed from somewhere. Reynolds nibbled at one gingerly as though he'd never had a biscuit before and didn't quite know what to do with it.

Kate looked at the man, sitting alert in his chair, his eyes darting around the room, taking in the filing cabinets and whiteboards, the victims' photographs blown up on the wall, and, she was sure, the threadbare coffee-stained carpet and faint musty smell of the windowless room.

'So, we need to start building a profile,' she said. 'The kind of person the killer's likely to be, his concerns and interests, potential blindspots, anything that might help us narrow down the pool of suspects – which is, let's face it, massive at the moment.'

'Right. Like Hannibal Lector helped Jodie Foster's character do in *The Silence of the Lambs*,' Reynolds said, with a hint of excitement that made Kate's heart sink.

*Oh crap*, she thought, *what have I done?*

'Not exactly,' she said, as politely as she could. 'Profiling's not really like you see it in Hollywood films, where some brilliant mind builds an elaborate description from the moon's position on a given Tuesday. It's a much blunter tool than that. But when HOLMES – the police database – doesn't come up with anything, it can help us decide where to concentrate our resources.'

Reynolds looked disgruntled. 'I'm well aware that films don't represent reality, any more than literature does,' he said. 'And I've read Canter's book – and Keppel's.' He looked at Kate, a hint of truculence in his eyes.

*Good God*, she thought, *you're one up on me then.*

'You've got some interest in criminology then?' she probed.

'Yes, I audited a course on the history of criminal psychology during the second year of my D.Phil. – my doctorate – I thought it might throw up some useful angles for the thesis.'

'And did it?'

'Not really – it just distracted me from writing and left me with lots of catching up to do in my third year. Still, it was fascinating: we went through the various theorists from the early ones like Lombroso and Bowlby through Eysenck and Skinner and up to Kohlberg and Cornish and Clarke.'

'Riiight,' said Geoff. 'Because what we need's more theories rather than more prisons...'

'Well, the jury's out on that, I suppose,' said Reynolds. 'I'm just saying I'm not a complete ignoramus: I do know a bit about this stuff. I also know,' he continued, looking mutinous, 'about the drawbacks of profiling techniques as they've been developed so far.'

'And those would be?' Geoff's tone was sharp. This was his bag.

Reynolds swallowed, his Adam's apple bobbing up and down in his scrawny neck. 'Well, if investigators rely too much on the profile they've drawn up, it can lead to them ignoring suspects who don't quite fit it – as happened early on in the Bundy case. Or, as with the Yorkshire Ripper, the police can get overly fixated on hoax information. They might even be dragged off the right track because of their own unexamined biases.'

'Our biases?' Kate said mildly, quieting Geoff with a gesture. She was interested to know what Reynolds thought he knew about this.

'You must be familiar, surely, about the criticisms of the Yorkshire police force at the time?'

Kate said nothing, but motioned for him to continue.

'The Ripper was interviewed nine times over the course of the investigation, but he was a middle-aged white man – like the police officers involved – so they couldn't believe he was capable of such horrific acts. Besides, they didn't take the killings seriously at first, because the victims were only prostitutes, hardly worth bothering about.'

Kate could see Geoff's knuckles turning white as he gripped the arm of his chair.

'Those officers also had to sift manually through tens of thousands of paper documents,' she observed dryly. 'There were no computers then – not even the shit ones we're reliant on here now,' she added. Only that morning, she reflected, they'd had yet another promise that their current fleet of antiquated machines was about to be replaced. 'And then as now,' she continued, 'the officers were still waiting for a proper national agency to be set up and resourced. But, absolutely, Geoff and I will try to take our *biases* into account as we go.'

She wondered again if she had made a mistake, asking Reynolds to assist on the case. Was he going to be antagonistic? Geoff was pissed off enough already. And if this didn't work, the Big Boss would bring in an outside team as quick as grease through a goose, she just knew it.

But the academic was looking apologetic.

'I didn't mean to imply that you...' he stammered. 'I mean, I just wanted–' He spread his hands. 'I suppose I wanted to show you that I'm not a complete idiot about this kind of thing. I'm not an expert like you and Detective Simpson, of course, but I think I can be helpful here.'

The man's unexpected humility, whether affected or not, was disarming – to Geoff as well as Kate, she could see. The atmosphere in the room thawed.

'So,' she said, with a measured exhalation. 'Now that we've clarified that none of us is an idiot, what else can we establish?'

She pointed to the long wall of the office and the two whiteboards, on which Geoff had noted the key information about the case so far.

'All the stats indicate that the killer is likely to be a man, almost certainly white, possibly young. Serial killers normally don't start on human victims until later in life, of course, but that's not always the case, and both the victims here were young, gay men, both had social hang-ups, and it seems likely there was a sexual element to both killings, judging from what Intel's turned up on their backgrounds along with the circumstances of their deaths.'

Geoff was making notes on an A3 flipchart. He'd transfer material to the whiteboards later, once they'd decided what was important.

'But is it about sex, or jealousy, or hate?' he said, cocking his head.

'Right,' said Kate. 'Is this a case of the killer feeling guilty about his sexual needs and taking it out on his conquests?'

'Or is he some sort of extreme homophobe, posing as a potential lover in order to punish the men for their supposed sins? Forensics found no DNA evidence on the corpses, so presumably no sex actually took place, before or after the deaths.'

Kate glanced at Reynolds, who was shifting uncomfortably in his seat. *Keep it plain and simple*, she thought. 'It seems likely the offender was acting alone,' she said. 'And clearly these murders were well planned. This is no spontaneous crime of passion.'

She thought for a moment. 'What about the killer's background? This is where you come in, Dr Reynolds. With the medieval literature and such. We're assuming this man was a student or other member of the university, since he'd need to be able to gain access to the Radcliffe Camera.'

She consulted her notes. 'That building currently houses part of the Bodleian's collection of books and journals in English, Modern Languages, and Theology. So does that mean we can narrow our search to students and scholars in those areas?'

'I'm afraid not,' said Reynolds, shaking his head. 'Anyone with a Bod card can enter that building. It's not restricted to members of a specific discipline.'

'Could we maybe consult the lending records?' Kate asked. 'You know, see who's been borrowing what?'

Reynolds smiled. 'The Bodleian is not a lending library. Quite the reverse, in fact. It's a Copyright Library, which means that, by law, it's entitled to a copy of any book published in the British Isles. But it doesn't lend any of them out.'

'Seriously?' Geoff said. 'It's got, like, thousands of books and no one can borrow them – not even students and specialists?'

'Millions of books,' Reynolds corrected him. 'And not even royalty can take them home. King Charles the First tried to borrow a book back in 1645 and got short shrift. Though I guess, given that he was executed four years later, maybe his authority was on the wane at the time.'

Geoff rolled his eyes. 'What about a sign-in book then?'

'There isn't one,' Reynolds replied. 'And it'll be no use relying on the porter's recollections. Hundreds of readers stream in and out all day. Besides, when I've used it, the man on duty has barely glanced at my Bod card. Pretty much anyone could get in there with a stolen card if they wanted to.'

'But the poems he used as his model,' Geoff persisted. 'Not everyone knows them. They must be significant?'

'Possibly,' Reynolds said. 'Though they are major literary works,' he added with a touch of primness. 'Anyone might potentially know them. But if the murderer is, shall we say, inspired by medieval killings from literature, that might suggest he is a current or former tutor or student in that area. That really would start to narrow things down.'

He paused, a peculiar look on his face. 'You know, it hadn't occurred to me,' he said. 'But it could be one of my own colleagues in the Faculty.' His skin took on a greenish cast.

'Let's not jump to any conclusions just yet,' Kate cautioned. 'We're just laying out the possibilities at this stage.'

'But the literary connections... and the links to me... You don't think...?' A tremor ran through his voice. 'Am I a target?'

'We can't rule that out, Dr Reynolds,' Kate said, knowing it was best to be honest. Then, in what she hoped was a reassuring tone, she added, 'But it's far too early to suggest that with any conviction. There's a lot of other potential explanations to consider.'

She could see that Reynolds was not comforted.

'But perhaps you could tell us about a few other medieval murders,' she suggested. 'Let us know what we might be in for.'

'Well...' Reynolds rubbed his eyebrow with two fingers. 'Where to start? There's *Judith*, obviously. In the same manuscript as *Beowulf*, another monster beheaded, though this time it's a would-be rapist.' As he spoke, he stared at the wall, his tone subdued. '*Judith*'s a religious text, so there's a difference there, I suppose.'

'*Beowulf* and the other one are pagan poems?' Geoff asked.

'It's not as simple as that. *Gawain* contains a lot of religious elements – the hero prays to Mary and goes to confession and so on – and some scholars would say it encapsulates a theological point: that you should trust God more than your own strength, or magic, or whatever. But it's not a religious text in the sense that it's not a sermon or about a saint. Like *Beowulf*, where the hero might mention God, but he's not a holy man battling a demon – though come to think of it, some critics do think Grendel is demonic, so–' He broke off, looking frustrated.

They were getting off track, thought Kate. 'So there are maybe religious aspects to the other poems, but this *Judith* poem is actually about a saint?'

'Not exactly,' Reynolds said again, with a helpless shrug. 'But it's based on a book of the Bible – well, the Catholic Bible.'

'There's a difference?'

'Oh yes,' said Geoff unexpectedly. 'Council of Trent, right? They decided some books were in and some were out.'

Kate looked at him.

'Watched a documentary,' he clarified.

*Why?* she thought, but turned to Reynolds. '"Not exactly", I'm guessing?'

He gave a wan smile. 'It's certainly where the division was made official, in a way. But the differences go back at least as far as the fourth century, when Jerome and Augustine fell out over whether to accept the Hebrew or the Greek translations of the Old Testament. Some books were in one version but not in the other, like *Judith*. So Jerome, and later the Protestant tradition, decided that the ones that weren't in the Hebrew version weren't authentic, weren't inspired.'

'Like *Judith*,' Kate said.

'Exactly.'

'So it's *not* actually a Biblical book and she's not actually a saint.'

'Well, it depends who you ask, I guess, but some of the Anglo-Saxons certainly thought it was and she was.'

*Good grief*, Kate thought. 'So where does that leave us?' she said, trying not to grind her teeth.

'I'm not sure. If we start thinking about explicitly religious texts, though, there's all the martyrdoms. Saints getting, well, terminated in ever more spectacular ways.'

Kate motioned for him to continue.

'Lawrence on his griddle; Catherine on her wheel...'

'Like the firework,' Geoff interjected.

'Joan of Arc,' said Reynolds, ignoring him. 'Burnt at the stake. Thomas à Becket, murdered in the cathedral; Stephen, stoned to death; Sebastian, shot at with arrows; Lucy with her eyes gouged out. Agatha had her breasts cut off; Bartholomew was skinned alive; Hippolytus, ironically, was torn apart by horses.' He took a breath.

'Pretty barbaric,' Geoff said, with a glint in his eyes.

*Are you enjoying this?* Kate wondered.

'I suppose so,' Reynolds said, raising an eyebrow at Geoff. 'I mean, yes, absolutely those deaths are barbaric. But no more so than what's going on in wars around the world as we speak. And, of course, a lot of these martyrdoms probably never happened in reality, or at least not in the way the texts describe. They're hagiographies, holy biographies if you like, designed to inspire and teach. Maybe even to entertain... stop people falling asleep in church.'

'People can't seriously have enjoyed hearing about that stuff,' Kate objected. 'Those stories sound gross: all about people being tortured and dying in agony.'

'How many million copies has *The Silence of the Lambs* sold? And Stephen King and Dean Koontz are doing pretty well out of horror and torture.'

They sat in silence for a while. Then Geoff got up and went over to the whiteboard.

'So, how many of these saints got their heads chopped off?'

'Good idea,' said Kate. 'Let's make a list.' She turned to Reynolds.

'Judith, obviously, carries out a beheading. Edmund, king and saint – in his legend he refused to bow to a Viking leader and was shot full of arrows, then beheaded. His head got separated from the body but, miraculously, a ravenous wolf protected it until the English people came looking for it. It's quite a cute story, actually.' Reynolds smiled. 'The people call out, "Where are you?" and the head keeps shouting out, "Here! Here! Here!" Like a child fed up of playing hide 'n' seek.'

'Let's not get sidetracked,' Kate said firmly, pointing to the whiteboard. 'What else?'

They continued for another half an hour, drawing up lists of medieval killings, dividing them into beheadings and other violent acts, until the whiteboard started to look like a profile of the sickest killer a Hollywood screenwriter could ever have invented.

After Reynolds had left to deliver a seminar paper at the Faculty on a topic that sounded so unlikely Kate wondered momentarily if he had made it up, she and Geoff continued to pore over the evidence and various hypotheses. Documents were still streaming in from the wider team: chemical analyses, witness statements from the students and staff who'd been in the Radcliffe Camera when the body was found. It was all depressingly routine though. Kate was still pissed off at the lack of respect Geoff had shown earlier in the day, but made an effort to be civil. After all, she had no choice but to work with the man. And, if he didn't help her solve this case, she might end up with a lot worse wherever she was seconded next. The Big Boss was not known for his capacity to forgive and forget.

Ironically, Geoff now seemed to have changed his tune where Reynolds was concerned. Whatever his earlier objections, he kept coming back to how intelligent the other man must be, to have secured a job at the university.

'Temporary job,' she reminded him.

'Still, to be teaching at Oxford at his age,' Geoff persisted. 'How impressive is that? Furthest I got in school was GCSEs – and even then I just scraped it. English especially. My teacher used to say I had a "natural inaptitude" for the subject. I hated her.'

Kate made sympathetic noises, but couldn't really relate. She'd liked English. Not the poetry so much. Or Shakespeare. But they'd done *Lord of the Flies*, which was pretty readable, and *To Kill a Mockingbird*. Most of her class had a crush on Gregory Peck when they watched the film. She smiled dreamily, then awkwardly had to explain why to Geoff. He looked strangely at her for a moment, then started nattering about Peck's other films. Typically he was really into two films she'd never heard of called *The Keys to the Kingdom* and *The Yearling*. The last one sounded to her more like the title of a Jackie Collins romp. *What was that look?* she wondered. *Did he think I was a lesbian or something?* Some of the other guys on the force did, she knew. Typical. *Just because I don't want to touch your dick doesn't mean I've sworn off them completely.* She'd often thought it but never said. So far. *Just push me though. Just try it.*

'You listening, Sarge?' Geoff said suddenly.

'Er, yeah, sorry,' she replied, mentally castigating herself. She didn't need to antagonise him any further. 'I was just thinking: are there any film versions of those poems? You know,

*Beowulf* and *Gawain*, or whatever?'

'Not that I know of,' the man said. 'Maybe some arthouse version or something. Nothing I've come across. Why?'

'Just thought they might be worth watching. You know, see if we can work out how the killer's thinking.'

'Well I guess I could try and find some… But that's what Reynolds is for, isn't it? To cover the medieval angle.'

'You're right,' Kate conceded. 'I guess I was just hoping for an excuse to take a break from all these bits of paper for a couple of hours.'

'Tell me about it. Is it me, or are they breeding? Every time I look round it seems like there's another stack of forms or reports to go through.'

'And none of it useful.'

They lapsed into companionable silence.

Geoff broke it. 'So, how did you get into this line of work then, Sarge?' he said. 'I mean, why, I guess.' His demeanour was diffident but it was evident the answer was important to him.

*At last, the million-dollar question*, Kate thought. *Wondered when that'd come.* There came a point in every work relationship in the force where colleagues sized each other up. Worked out those who were in it for the long haul, and those who saw each post as a rung on a ladder towards upper management or consultancy. Who wanted as easy a life as possible till they could retire and collect their pension, and who wanted to do the right thing come what may. Who was a hobby-horse crusader for justice and who was on the take. She picked her words carefully.

'It was to spite my parents, at first,' she admitted. 'They were pretty strict, and really keen on education. Typical aspirational lower-middle-class, I guess. The salt of Sidmouth. Pushed me to do well at school. "No TV until you've done your homework", no late nights. That kind of thing. Kept talking about my future like it was some concrete thing that was already set up in the distance ahead of me. Not like I had a choice or anything. You know?'

Geoff shrugged and said nothing, but she could see he was listening.

'Well, anyway, I did what they told me. Studied hard and got pretty good grades: enough to get into uni to do Law. They were so happy. My dad actually hugged me. He hadn't done that since I was ten. They're not a demonstrative lot. My mum rang round all the neighbours, showing off: "My daughter's got into university. First in the family!" Putting on airs and graces – I mean, God, her idea of sophistication is a bottle of Blue Nun and a tray of defrosted vol-au-vents. The parties she planned! Then they found out I'd chosen to go to Birmingham: two hundred-odd miles away. "But we'd have to get the train from Exeter", I remember my mum said, like it was going abroad. Complaining they'd hardly get to see me. Like that wasn't the idea in the first place.'

She paused, recalling the guilt-trips and recriminations.

'And then when I got there I knew by the end of the first term that it wasn't for me: full of clever-clever types and pseuds droning on about their gap years. So I did what I should have done in the first place – put in an application to join the force, where I might actually be able to do some good.'

'How did your parents take that?' Geoff asked.

'They were really supportive and told me to follow my heart, what do you think?'

'Hey, no need for the claws!' Geoff said, holding up his hands and laughing.

'Well, ask a stupid question.' She sipped her coffee, which was stone cold. 'Yurgh.'

When she came back from the machine with two fresh cups, Geoff prompted her.

'So, you were saying?'

'So I was saying my parents were less than delighted. Especially when I had to move back in with them during the application process – you know how long that takes. There's only so long you can sleep on friends' couches. Anyway, after an excruciating year, I got in. Met my ex-husband Tom the first day on the job. Married within the year, divorced in three. Did my job, *became* the job, and after a while, bibbidi-bobbidi-boo, here I am.'

'Yeah, simple as that,' Geoff said, sounding unconvinced.

'Well you don't want to hear about all the people I had to sleep with to get to this position,' she said, knowing that was precisely what a lot of the men on the force thought lay behind her career progression.

'Huh,' was Geoff's only rejoinder, his expression unreadable.

'What about you then? What's your tale of family trauma and unmet expectations?'

Geoff's face darkened, and he recoiled like Kate had slapped him. 'I don't want to talk about it.'

Kate kicked herself, as she recalled what Charlie, the station gossip, had said when Geoff had been transferred. Something about a cloud on his record, low-level violence, some sort of family connection. At the time she'd dismissed it as being none of her business, but now she realised she'd inadvertently struck a nerve.

'Shit, sorry, Geoff, I didn't mean to say the wrong thing. I wasn't even thinking about you, really, just my own stupid family.'

The man's shoulders relaxed. 'It's okay. I know you didn't mean anything by it. It's just...' He took a deep breath and held it.

'Look, you don't have to tell me anything,' Kate hastened to reassure him. 'Seriously, you don't. But if you want to, well, I'm not a gossip. It goes no further than these four walls.'

Geoff remained silent for several moments, and Kate thought he wasn't going to say anything more. Then, quietly, he began to talk.

'I wasn't good at school. Like I said before. I mean, now dyslexic kids've got extra help and stuff, but when I was at school hardly anyone in my area had even heard of it. So I really struggled with my homework, fell behind. The teachers just thought I was thick. Or lazy. Or both. And how was I supposed to know any better, if they didn't? So I pretended I didn't care. Wagged off school when I got the chance, along with some other lads who weren't up for wearing a uniform and pretending to be good.'

Kate noticed the man's accent got stronger when he talked about his past. She tried to pinpoint it – *Hackney? Enfield?* – then gave up.

'So,' she said. 'Smoking behind the bike sheds. Chatting up girls. That kind of thing?'

He gave her a funny look. 'Something like that. Along with a bit of petty theft and vandalism. I was so busy fitting in, trying to make sure no one called me out for being thick, or different. Never noticed what was happening to my own brother further down the school.'

He paused, as if the memory still pained him.

'Gary was always quiet, liked to play on his own. Didn't like football. Preferred reading and wasting hours on these comic strips he drew with all these superhero characters he made up. I just thought he was boring. He was just my little brother, you know: a pain-in-the-neck rival for my parents' attention. But he was getting more than enough attention of the wrong sort at school, as I found out later. Not surprising, I guess, a nerdy weak kid, bit of a loner, and every school has its bullies.

Anyway, somehow they found out his weakness – a note to another boy in his bag or something, I don't remember. And that was it. They wouldn't leave him alone. *Gary the Gay Boy*. They just kept on at him like they were sharks in the deep water and he had an open wound. And I didn't see it.'

He exhaled loudly. 'My own brother, and I didn't notice anything. Until it was too late. It happened at the end of July, the last day of term. I remember how sweltering it was. I'd just finished my GCSEs and I was looking forward to doing nothing all summer. I'd gone home to change out of my uniform before heading into town to join my friends, but as soon as I got home I knew there was something wrong.'

Geoff's breathing had become shallow and laboured. 'My mum was still out at work, wasn't due back till dinner time, but the front door was unlocked. I called for Gary, but there was no reply, so I went upstairs. I don't know what it was, but something made me go into his room. Normally we kept out of each other's way. But that day I knocked on the door and went in. And there he was on his bed, a bottle of Mum's pills by his side, and a neat note.'

'Like Travis Greene,' Kate said. 'God, that's awful.' She reached out to touch Geoff's arm, then thought better of it.

'I don't know what the note said, I didn't even read it, I just ran to the phone and called an ambulance, the police, Mum, Dad, everyone I could think of.'

Geoff's voice was calm and unemotional, but Kate could see a flicker at the corner of his eye as he stared at the wall, away from her.

'Did he–?' She held her breath.

'No, they got to him in time. Pumped his stomach. Within a few days he was right as rain, at least physically. Mum and Dad moved him to a different school. The creeps who'd been harassing him got expelled and our headmaster gave an assembly at the start of the next term all about bullying. You know the kind of thing. But me? I just knew I'd failed. Failed as a big brother – as a decent human being, even. I should have been there for him. Should have noticed something was wrong.'

'How could you have done?' Kate said. 'You were just a kid yourself.' She looked at the man's slumped posture and contemplated reaching out to pat him on the shoulder but didn't.

'Anyway,' Geoff said in a brisker tone. 'After that, I decided that I was going to do something good with my life. Some job where I could help people, protect them, that kind of thing. And becoming a policeman seemed like a good start. Except that it turned out not to be a great idea to do it where I grew up.'

'You ended up running into those guys that bullied your brother?' Kate said.

'No,' Geoff replied. 'They were long gone by then. Clogging up the system in some other borough, probably. But the... memories were still there. And when I came across some teenage thugs gay-bashing some kid behind a nightclub, towards the end of my shift, well, let's just say that the words "excessive force" came into the official report.'

'You beat them up?'

'Kicked the living shit out of them,' Geoff said, looking at Kate defiantly as though daring her to disapprove.

'Well, that's just fantastic,' she said wryly. 'Just what I wanted in my life: a dyslexic ginger with anger management issues.'

She deadpanned for a beat, enjoying the look of outrage on Geoff's face, then winked at him. The explosive laughter that followed was all the reward she needed that day.

*I tie the final knot to fasten the feet securely to the stage light, carefully reposition the bowl beneath the body, the head swinging gently as it hangs down, then I make the cut. Not to the throat – see how I thwart your expectations: you shall not get a gush of blood from me – but much higher up, at the ankles. The exsanguination begins. Quietly, subtly. The dark trickle is tentative at first, pausing on the edge of the leg hair like a reluctant mouse on the border of the wheatfields, then it musters courage, flows more evenly. But not hastily. No, there is no lack of control here. Like raspberry syrup dripping down an ice-cream cone the flow continues, parting momentarily at the knees, then joining together again down the thighs, pooling around the shrivelled flaps of meat surrounded with dark moss, then on again to caress the abdominals, the sternum, the pectoralis major and minor, over the clavicles and down the strong, thick trunk of the neck. Beneath lies the seduction of the sternothyroid, the longus colli, the omohyoid, the sternocleidomastoid. Stop. I must forgo those delights today. On the ruby treacle flows, and now, from the protrusion of the chin, some drops – too early – to the waiting bowl. But enough continues, ventures across the lower lip, quests inside. It looks even darker and more lustrous against the whiteness of the teeth. A stir, as the tongue tastes the tang of iron, hoping perhaps for sustenance, for some eleventh-hour reprieve. But it is a dying impulse, instinctive, primeval. And the red ink of correction continues to flow, filling the nostrils, the eye sockets. At last it reaches the hair, smooth, soft, dark, dangling down. A final leap of faith, through nothingness, and the flow reaches its goal, as we all must. Rest, containment, inanimation. But what is this? The bowl is overflowing. It is insufficient. Not a leaky vessel, like Woman, just limited, like Man. Who would have thought the old man to have had so much blood in him? The old man, the flesh, the new wine. Stop. You know, do you not, that the human body contains nine or ten pints of blood. You have certainly been told so in school. And so it is in truth, give or take, in the maddeningly imprecise way of humans. But have you ever considered what that would look like, gathered into one place, complete of itself? Nine and a half pints – let us reason, you and I together – a little over five litres; one gallon – let us not split hairs. A large washing-up bowl. The blood that makes clean. Though your sins are as scarlet. And now it seeps across the floorboards, following the rake of the stage, and I must step back lest my shoes be painted. For, though Art is being created today, I am not part of it. That is the eternal sorrow of the Creator. Forever outside, looking on. But the stark reality of life and death. The truth of their relation. That is the consolation. For it will be seen.*

# CHAPTER TWO



## JONATHAN

The starter was Cornish scallops with roast fennel. Jonathan picked at it without much enthusiasm. He hadn't really been hungry lately. Not for the over-rich fare the college provided anyway. He looked around the Hall at the portraits of college presidents past, looming over the high, oak-panelled space. Some sported stiff Elizabethan ruffs, others more modern dark suits under the folds of their black gowns. *And not a single woman among them,* he thought. Of course, there were female Fellows at colleges like St Genevieve's and St Elizabeth's, but still.

He realised he had been staring at nothing, picking at his starter, and rudely ignoring his neighbour at the table. Turning to engage him in conversation, he found him to be a bearded, trim-looking man in what looked to be his late thirties, presumably a guest of the chaplain two to Jonathan's left. He was handsome in a low-key kind of way, and as Jonathan introduced himself, his smile revealed even white teeth and crinkled the corners of his eyes in a way that was quite attractive.

'Good to meet you, Jonathan,' the man said in smooth,

rounded tones. He reached out a hand and gripped Jonathan's in a firm handshake.

'Robert Little, rector of St Wulfram's Church, but, please, call me Bob.'

Jonathan's heart sank. St Wulfram's was well-known as a bastion of hard-line conservative Anglicanism in Oxford.

'So, Bob,' he said, searching for a suitably anodyne conversation starter, 'what brings you to High Table tonight?'

'Oh, I like to keep in regular contact with the chaplains, where I can. You know, find out what's going on at college level, what's exercising the students lately. Exchange professional courtesies. That sort of thing. A good number of the congregation at St Wulfram's are undergraduate students, don't you know?'

Jonathan did know. St Wulfram's seemed to attract the sporty, public-school-educated students with whom Jonathan had always felt uncomfortable. With their uniform of brightly coloured jeans and soft leather filofaxes, these students radiated confidence in themselves and the narrow world views they espoused. Jonathan always had a hard time persuading the English students among them to take medieval and Renaissance texts seriously. It was exhausting, though part of him understood their reluctance to accept that many of the institutions they revered had developed their 'traditional' form relatively recently and as a result of complex social changes.

In talking to Reverend Little, however, Jonathan was pleasantly surprised to find the man well informed about the church's chequered history and quite open to the viability of other hermeneutic perspectives, if a little keen to emphasise his interest in manly pursuits like squash and rugby.

The man's charm was undeniable – just the right side of smarmy – but Jonathan refused to be swayed by his apparent sincerity or the warmth in those blue eyes. He was not in the mood tonight. Instead, he pressed him on some comments he had made to the press recently on gay clergy and the ordination of women.

'How can you justify that kind of hard-line stance?' Jonathan said. He was conscious even as he spoke of the faux pas he was committing in challenging a guest, but that old reckless feeling had come back. *What was anyone going to do about it anyway?* 'It's totally inconsistent,' he said. 'We've just been talking about how all of that stuff is peripheral to what's at the centre of the historic faith.'

'You're right, of course, that one's sexuality is not strictly speaking a salvation issue. However, it's important to be clear about what behaviours can and cannot be tolerated in those called to the priesthood. We are held to a higher standard, and that is as it should be. For, as the Apostle says, *the overseer must be beyond reproach.*'

'Well, Paul had a lot of harsh things to say about all sorts of activities and lifestyles that the church has no problem with now. And you know who had nothing to say about gay people at all? The founder of your religion. I've checked and he doesn't mention homosexuality once. And what's more' – Jonathan heard his voice rising and forced himself to adopt a calmer tone – 'he was pretty happy to let the disciple he loved rest on his bosom, or whatever the phrase is. That doesn't sound like someone who was overly anxious about male intimacy.'

'I know, I know,' the other man said, smiling. 'You've made your point eloquently and, to an extent, I agree with much of what you've said. Several of my most treasured colleagues are gay, and yet do a fine job shepherding their congregations. And I would certainly never want any of my parishioners, whatever their struggles, to feel excluded from the congregation. But you have to understand, I have a duty not just to those in my charge but also to my position.' He fingered his collar. 'I must represent faithfully the views of Synod – that is my job,' he said. 'I have to take a clear and firm line on these things when speaking in an official capacity. Even if my personal views are a little more... nuanced. Do you see?'

Jonathan didn't, but he saw no use in arguing the point. In his experience, these conservative types could rationalise their prejudices till the cows came home. And he'd already been the recipient of a few baleful glances from Hacker, who somehow always seemed to sense when someone at High Table was treading on dangerous ground. He muttered something polite and changed the subject to the safer topic of music. A few preliminary sallies revealed that the reverend, like Jonathan, was a fan of choral music, especially Elgar.

'I would have thought *Gerontius* would be a bit "High Church" for your tastes,' Jonathan ventured.

'We can't let the Devil have all the best music, can we?' His table companion winked. 'The melodies Elgar gives the Angel are just gorgeous. I don't think anyone's ever written better for mezzo-soprano, especially if you include his *Sea Pictures*. I went to a performance of them in the Holywell Music Room last term that was absolutely stunning.'

The man looked enraptured, but then his face fell. 'The pianist was Simon Beatty, actually. I was so sorry to hear about his loss. Terrible thing. Just terrible. And the way he died... so macabre.'

'I didn't know the... the manner of his death had been made public,' stammered Jonathan, not sure how much knowledge he should admit.

'Oh, one of my congregation knew him a bit and came to talk to me about it. He was quite upset, poor chap. Come to think of it, he's one of yours, I believe...'

But at this point the chaplain leaned over and commandeered the vicar's attention, and Jonathan had to turn to the Fellow on his other side, a crusty geographer who immediately tried to enlist Jonathan in his long-running campaign to draw on the college endowment to commission a new set of silver candelabra to be used in Hall on special occasions. He was very glad when the warden rose to signal that dinner was at an end and he could escape detailed discussions of gilt and filigree.

As he left Hall, Reverend Little caught him up and took his hand in a surprisingly warm grasp.

'I do hope we'll see you at St Wulfram's some time,' he said, holding Jonathan's gaze with clear and seemingly guileless eyes. 'And I must introduce you to my curate. He took his BA in English Literature before he began his training, so I'm sure you'd have a lot in common.'

The man smiled and for a moment Jonathan had the impression of a more than vicarly interest. Then he dismissed the idea. *That's just wishful thinking*, he chided himself. *You're starting to see gays everywhere, like that awful queen, Chalmers. The man just wants to recruit you for his church. More people, more money, more power, right?* Again, though, the cynicism he'd developed over the past few years left him feeling cheated somehow. As if he'd missed an opportunity for a meaningful connection. Maybe he would go along to one of Little's services. What could be the harm in that?

As he reached his rooms and unlocked the heavy door, Jonathan felt the unmistakeable warning signs of another migraine. They were becoming more frequent. When he'd first come up to Oxford, they'd tended to occur when he overexerted himself: pulling an all-nighter, or carrying heavy-laden shopping bags back from the supermarket over on the other side of town.

'You're like *The Princess and the Pea!*' Lawrence had mocked, with just a hint of approval for what he evidently saw as a pose of hypersensitivity. 'Next you'll be languishing with consumption, like Violetta.'

But lately the headaches, with the concomitant nausea and visual disturbances, had become more frequent and devastating. He massaged his scalp and temples with his fingers and wondered what to do. Should he go back to the GP, as Lucia kept urging him? The previous year he had gone along to the surgery on Beaumont Street, but his assigned GP – a balding malcontent with an apparent distaste for patients – had dismissed his concerns. 'Too much sitting and studying, Mr Reynolds,' he'd said, and Jonathan had bristled at the omission of his correct title. All too common in the medical profession, he'd found, as though they resented the existence of academic doctorates. 'You need to take up a sport; get out into the fresh air. Find a nice young lady to take your mind off things.' The fat fool had died just a few months later, Jonathan had heard, of an apparent heart attack. *So much for sports and fresh air*, had been his first thought, before the inevitable guilt at his lack of compassion had kicked in. He wondered who his GP was now.

Jonathan pulled the curtains in his room resignedly and took another couple of the full-strength painkillers he saved for the worst of his attacks. He'd been prescribed them by the sympathetic college nurse retained by St Seb's – though did the ability to prescribe imply she was actually a doctor? he wondered momentarily – but Jonathan preferred not to take them too regularly. He had no intention of becoming an addict, however glamorous Coleridge and Byron had made it look. He'd heard of too many Oxford dons succumbing to liver or kidney disease, weak and stick-thin. He'd even overheard the students gossiping mean-spiritedly about Fellows who reputedly stashed sherry or whisky bottles behind the books on their shelves.

*Little shits*, he thought, with a sudden rush of loathing for students in general. They came here with their stuck-up arrogance, their firm opinions about everything and everyone, yet what did they know? Most of them had horizons no larger than a career at Price Waterhouse in the City or a stint with Slaughter and May. What sacrifices had they made to get here? And what possible insight could they have into the great works of the past? The age-old questions of human value and selfhood? He calmed himself with an effort. He was being unfair, he knew. A lot of the arrogance was fear-based bluster. And not just amongst the students. He recalled complaining to Lawrence after a celebratory dinner in Hall at which his table companions had seemed especially well-heeled and intimidating. His mentor had laughed, knocking back his umpteenth glass of port.

'Oxford is a city of masks, you know. That same distinguished professor with the double-barrelled surname who talks of fine wine and skiing in Biarritz is the son of a shit-shoveller in Epping whose pedigree goes back as far as a cripple attempting the limbo.'

Not all the students were braying careerists either. Many of them were hard-working. Studious. Genuine. Personable. Students like Nicholas.

Jonathan lay back on the soft wool coverlet of his bed, the painkillers taking effect at last, wrapping him in a welcome haze. He pictured Nicholas's tawny locks in his mind, the way they fell forward over his forehead. That finely chiselled jaw and sensitive mouth. The intense look he got in his eyes when he was pursuing a point in tutorials. Jonathan allowed a smile to turn up the corners of his mouth as he drowsed contentedly into oblivion.

～

He awoke to an insistent drumming outside his room with no idea how much time had elapsed. He stumbled to the door, rubbing his forehead, clear now of pain. Nicholas stood in the corridor, a look of distress written large on his face. Jonathan automatically stepped back from the door, his face reddening, hoping the boy couldn't somehow tell what he had been thinking earlier, but Nicholas evidently had something else on his mind.

'Oh, Dr Reynolds,' he stammered, taking in Jonathan's dishevelled state. 'I'm sorry to disturb you. I d-didn't know who else to talk to.' His usual confident demeanour was gone.

'Whatever's the matter, Nicholas?' Jonathan said, ushering him to the sofa and sitting beside the shaking student.

'It's H-Harry – he's...' Nicholas broke off, a wild look in his eyes.

'What?' Jonathan said, but he had an awful feeling he knew what was to come.

'He's d-dead. We didn't... we thought... Oh God, it was horrible!' Nicholas's breath came in great gulps, and it was obvious he was fighting to hold back tears. 'There was so much b-blood... on the stage, all over the stairs.' He shuddered and buried his face in his hands.

'Slow down now,' Jonathan soothed, whilst his mind raced. 'Take a deep breath. That's it. And another. Let's get you a cup of tea.'

It felt a ridiculously inadequate response, but, like all the distressed students Jonathan had dealt with in the past – dumped by their boyfriends or girlfriends, failing their exams – Nicholas seemed grateful for any show of support, however small. He busied himself about the preparation of the hot drink, thinking about what could possibly have happened. Was it more of the killer's handiwork?

As Nicholas sipped the tea, his shoulders lowered and his

face cleared. Jonathan listened as he laid out the upsetting events.

'So I'm playing Saturninus in Dan's production of *Titus Andronicus*, you know?' he began.

Jonathan did indeed. The production had encountered a certain amount of resistance amongst Faculty members, concerned at the possible controversy that might be stirred up by the play, with its themes of cannibalism, rape, mutilation, and bloody violence. The director, a brilliant but erratic tutor at Goldacre College named Daniel Collins, had nevertheless insisted on pressing ahead. For Jonathan the production had all the marks of a classic train wreck in the making, but a colleague who'd seen one of the rehearsals had actually given it measured approval.

'Things have been going pretty well,' Nicholas continued. 'There were a few fluffed lines in the rehearsal today, but no major snags in Act One. Then Harry – he was playing Demetrius, you know – had this huge argument about how he should deliver one of his lines. You know he and Dan were...' He broke off, looking awkward. 'Well, a bit of an item. I mean, everybody knew.'

Jonathan had heard the rumours that his colleague took more than a directorial interest in some of his leading men. 'Bloody thesps!' Lawrence had snorted. 'In and out of each other's beds like Brando and Dean went in and out of the closet.'

Collins's latest muse, Harry Berkeley, was a beautiful Modern Languages student at St Margaret's. He came from a famous family and had his eye set firmly on the West End.

'Anyway,' Nicholas continued. 'Harry stormed off, saying he wished he'd never left Julian, and that he was "done".'

Julian Jeffries was a well-known theatrical producer, in whose Earls Court flat Harry Berkeley had reputedly been living when he met and took up with Collins. 'Not the wisest career move for one pursuing the parasitic lifestyle,' Lawrence had snickered, when regaling Jonathan with the scandal. 'One should never trade down.'

'So what happened then?' Jonathan asked gently, pouring Nicholas another cup.

'We all assumed he'd just flown off the handle as usual and that he'd walk back in again after a few minutes with a joke. I mean, they fought all the time. Harry was so... volatile, at times. But he never came back. Then, this morning, when Dan unlocked the theatre before the run-through, we found...' He choked.

'We...?' Jonathan prompted.

'Me, Joe, and the actor playing Tamora,' Nicholas said. 'Dan wasn't happy with the scene where Tamora persuades Saturninus to forgive Titus. We were going to run it again, when we got to the Burton Taylor, it was obvious at once that something was wrong. We climbed up the stairs to the performance space and saw something hanging from one of the stage lights in the ceiling. I thought it was just a dummy in a costume at first – someone's idea of a sick joke. Then I saw all the blood...'

He began to weep quietly, his lip quivering as the tears streaked across his cheeks and down the line of his jaw, and Jonathan's heart ached.

'It was like a horror film,' Nicholas continued, gulping for air between words. 'Harry had been hanged upside down and... bled like... like a pig. I nearly threw up. Dan was beside himself. It was awful. He tried to cut the ropes, but he was slipping around in the blood, and, when he finally got him down, he just sat there hugging Harry's body and rocking it from side to side.'

'Good God,' Jonathan said, 'that's... appalling.'

But now Nicholas had told the worst, the words came rushing

out of him. 'And then the police came and they were asking us questions for ages, going over and over it. It was horrible. I ran all the way back to college afterwards. I just wanted to get away from it. But I couldn't stop thinking about it. And I couldn't talk to any of my friends about what happened. The police were very strict about not talking to the press or anyone who wasn't involved. But then I thought of you. You've been helping the police, haven't you? So it's all right to talk to you.'

Jonathan hadn't realised anyone knew of his contact with Stewart and Simpson, but it was hardly surprising, college gossip being what it was. He was about to ask Nicholas how he'd found out, but the student had begun to cry again.

'None of it makes any sense,' he said, his voice rising in pitch. 'Harry was chatting to me just a couple of days ago, excited about an audition he'd gone to in London for some show. He was so full of plans, of life, and now...'

He broke down completely and Jonathan instinctively put his arm around his shoulder. Nicholas's body stiffened momentarily, then released as he burrowed his head into Jonathan's side, his chest heaving. At length, his breathing took on a more regular rhythm and he drew back and looked up at Jonathan, his eyelashes moist with tears. His eyes seemed huge in their proximity. Jonathan froze, his mouth inches from Nicholas's, for what felt like an eternity. Then Nicholas leaned forward and kissed him. Soft lips, a lingering kiss. An electric shudder ran throughout Jonathan's body. *Can this really be happening?* he thought. For a blissful moment he returned the kiss. Then, regretfully, he pulled away.

'You're overwrought, Nicky,' he said in a gentle but firm tone, for the first time using the diminutive form most of the other students adopted. 'You don't know what you're doing, and I... well, I think you need to go back to your own room and lie down for a while... or at least call one of your friends to look after you.'

As he saw the hurt look in Nicholas's eyes, something small inside Jonathan died.

As he closed the door, Jonathan knew he'd done the right thing. But the encounter had left him feeling unsettled and a few minutes later, he grabbed up his coat and headed downstairs, intending to go for a walk around Southwark Quad to clear his head. The elegant, clean lines of the Italianate columns below the Old Library always had a soothing effect on his mind, and they did not fail him now. The entrance to the Gardens was locked, and, although Jonathan had a key to the side gate that could be reached through an adjoining building, after a few slow circuits of the quadrangle, he made his way out of the north entrance and back through the stone arches and corridors to his rooms.

He sat at his desk, staring at his notes for the *Beowulf* article but couldn't bring himself even to pick them up. Lately his interest in the topic had waned, as a new idea had begun to emerge. Reading *Grettir's Saga* where the hero, like Beowulf, confronted a mysterious monster had made him curious about not the similarities but the differences between the two narratives. Beowulf had gone on to kill two other monsters, apparently confident in his heroic status. Grettir's fight with his monsters had left him afraid of the dark, cursed with bad luck, doomed to die alone. One man ended his life as a hunted man, outlawed from society; the other celebrated for his deeds, mourned by his people. Jonathan couldn't help wondering whether the saga author had ultimately understood more about the human condition. Perhaps Grettir's confrontation symbolised the truth that, in the end, humans are always alone. No one can ever really know another person – what's in their heart. They are always irredeemably other. Grettir's tragedy was that he understood this when it was too late. Beowulf's tragedy was that he never did. His fame was built on heroic deeds that turned out to be futile. He might have gained the dragon's treasure before he died but, without him, his people were going to be wiped out by the invading Swedish armies. And, worst of all, his men – his *heorðgeneatas*; his hearth-companions and intimates – clearly never really knew who he was. Not really. They mourned him as a merciful king and a gentle lord, when what he really was was a fame-hungry braggart more focused on his legacy than his people's welfare.

Jonathan sighed and pushed his notes aside. Who was going to want to hear any of that? He contemplated picking up the phone to call Lucia, get her to talk him out of his funk, but she'd just bollock him for what had happened with Nicholas. No, the saga author had it right. Fundamentally, humans were alone in the world. And whatever Lucia said, Jonathan was never going to find the right man, someone he could trust with his whole self, both the good and the ugly. If relationships were about taking a leap of faith, as she put it, about being open and honest and vulnerable, then he was better off without them. He moved over to the armchair and slumped into it feeling sorry for himself.

As he glanced despondently around the room, his gaze fell on the stack of cardboard boxes heaped in one corner. They contained one of the new PCs and keyboards that Governing Body, seeking to spend a surplus or offset tax before the end of the financial year, had bought for each of the tutors and fellows. It was part of some scheme to bring the college up to date with current technology – Hacker had droned on about it at a meeting the previous term – but Jonathan had no intention of joining the digital revolution if he could help it. He didn't even use a typewriter, still less a word processor or computer. He took pride, when communicating with tutors or students at other colleges, in using elegant postcards which he selected at the little shop at the entrance to the Bodleian or at the bookbinder's on Turl Street. *The personal touch*, he thought with satisfaction. But more and more of his colleagues were switching to computers, and even some of his students would present, instead of handwritten sheafs of paper – the swirls and flourishes of their writing giving such a valuable insight into their personalities – bland, printed-out essays, typed, no doubt, in some sweaty, crowded undergraduate computer room.

Maybe he was missing something, though, Jonathan worried. Maybe typing up his article would help him marshal his thoughts better, structure his argument more clearly. He scooted his chair across the carpet to the boxes and reached out to open the nearest one, drawing his fingernail under the masking tape on the lid. Then he let his hand drop back. He just couldn't bring himself to wrestle with the equipment, the prospect of trying to decipher the incomprehensible instructions to work out what went where. He should have allowed the computing officer to set it up months ago when he'd offered.

Jonathan sat back in defeat. Then, on an impulse, he reached over for the telephone and dialled the number DS Stewart had given him at their first meeting. It was answered at the third ring.

'Simpson here,' came a male voice.

'Ah, Detective Simpson. I was hoping to speak to your partner.'

'She's not here at the minute, I'm afraid. There's been another murder and she's following up some statements. We were going to call you, actually. It looks like we were wrong about the medieval angle. This latest one happened to an actor in a Shakespeare play: I'm ploughing my way through a summary of it now. Anyway, can I help with something?'

Jonathan hesitated. 'Well, it can probably wait till the morning if you're busy. I just had a distressed young man here earlier, Nicholas Rivers, one of the students who witnessed the scene, actually. I'm sure your team took his statement down at the theatre, but he gave me an account too and I thought it might be worth comparing notes. In case there were any details he forgot the first time round, you know?'

'Of course,' Simpson replied. 'That's very sensible. And I can certainly take down the details and pass them on to Detective Sergeant Stewart when she gets back.'

There was a silence, and then Jonathan found himself asking, 'I don't suppose... you'd care to do it over a drink somewhere?'

As the silence lengthened, he kicked himself. What was he thinking? He must still be discombobulated from the encounter with Nicholas earlier. Then the other man's voice came back cheerily.

'Sure. I don't see why not. Given we're working together, I guess we should get to know each other a bit better. Let's see, you're at St Seb's... Meet you at the Arrow and Quiver in fifteen minutes?'

Jonathan managed an astonished acceptance before he put the phone back into its cradle.

If Jonathan had entertained any hopes of Simpson's extra-curricular interest in him, he was soon disabused of them. After the preliminaries and some good-natured arguing about who was going to buy the beers, they had sat down on some stools next to a small table in the long corridor near the bar. Then Simpson had just come straight out with it.

'Just so there's no confusion, Dr R – this is just a friendly drink. In the interests of collegiality. If you're looking for a date, I can give you my brother's phone number. You're exactly his type. But I'm straight.'

Jonathan had immediately flushed beet-red, but the other man seemed completely unfazed by the interaction, moving easily on to a discussion of Nicholas's account of the scene at the Holywell Music Room, which matched up in all details with the accounts officers had taken. That done, Jonathan had expected Simpson to take his leave, but instead he ordered another round, returning from the bar with a couple of brimming pint glasses and a packet of salted peanuts between his teeth.

'So,' he said. 'I take it you're into films then?'

'Er, yes, I suppose so,' said Jonathan. 'How did you know?'

'*Psycho*,' came the unexpected response.

'What?!'

'You'd been watching Hitchcock's *Psycho* when we first interviewed you.'

'Oh yes – that must have seemed a bit suspicious!'

'Not really. If everyone who watched a horror film turned into a killer, we'd be inundated at the station. Besides, it's a classic. Love Hitchcock.'

'Me too,' said Jonathan. '*Psycho*'s not my favourite, actually – that's *Rope*. But I was trying to make some connections between *Psycho* and some of the texts I'm working on.'

'*Rope*'s your favourite? Really? I mean, it's interesting technically, with all those long takes and so on, but I've always thought it's a bit stagey. I'd have expected you to like something more literary, like *Rebecca*.'

'I mean, that's great too. You've got to love the young

Olivier. But there's something about the way Hitchcock slowly builds the tension in *Rope* – and you can see poor Farley Granger getting more and more stressed as the dinner party goes along.' *Not to mention the erotic subtext*, Jonathan thought.

'Fair enough. I'm more of a *North by Northwest* man, myself.'

'I would have thought you'd like *Rope* – you know, being based on a real-life murder.'

'Yeah, Leopold and Loeb. Intellectual superiority and all that. But, funnily enough, we detectives don't tend to want to spend too much time off-duty thinking about murder.'

'No, of course. Sorry.'

Simpson brushed it away. 'It's fine. I guess it's like my assuming you'd like literary adaptations.'

'I do, actually. Though, predictably, I'm not always impressed by what they've done with the book.'

After an hour of amiable disagreement about a whole range of films, Simpson left, pleading paperwork. Jonathan elected to stay on in the pub. The termly English Drinks was due to start shortly in St Sebastian's Lodge, an eighteenth-century former Judge's Lodgings adjoining the college and used for formal functions and social events. It didn't make sense to traipse back to his rooms before returning. So Jonathan nursed his beer whilst he debated whether to buy a bag of peanuts to soak up the wine with which he was about to be plied. Part of him was shocked that Simpson was so sure of his sexuality – was it really that obvious? *And isn't it a bit insulting to assume that his brother and I will like each other, just because we're both gay?* Then he grinned. *Don't take yourself so seriously*, he thought. *Besides, maybe Simpson's brother is as good-looking as he is.*

As Jonathan climbed the broad but steep stairs up to St Seb's Lodge, he could see the drinks party was already in full swing. The front of the mansion was all gables, symmetrical corniced windows, architraves, and stone urns. Inside, the huge central hall boasted more cornicing, moulded panelling, an immense marble fireplace, and a dramatic crimson-carpeted staircase with twisted balusters in dark wood. The latter was cordoned off, as it always was. Jonathan had no idea what lay beyond it on the second storey of the house. He'd always been confined to the main hall. That was currently thronged with the expensively clad *literati* Lawrence somehow always gathered together for these occasions. He pretended it was to round out the students' education and enable them to make connections, but really it was so he could hang out with his friends at the college's expense. Sadly, the numbers involved meant the quality of the wine suffered, but the students never seemed to care. He could see them dotted around the room in small clumps, all too obviously staring at and whispering about the famous names around them. Jonathan grabbed a red wine from the many glasses lined up on the long linen-covered sideboard, surreptitiously downed it, grimacing at the sharp aftertaste. He picked up another glass before heading into the mêlée. Just in time, he spotted Alistair glaring at him from one corner and swerved in a different direction. There was no sign at all of Nicholas, thank God. This thing was bound to be awkward enough without having that to deal with.

Half an hour later, though, Jonathan found he was enjoying himself. The third and fourth glasses had given him a pleasant buzz and he'd accidentally bumped into one of the *important people*, which had led to a fascinating conversation about the remnants of Old English vocabulary in Northern Irish dialect and the promise of an inscribed copy of the author's latest novel. Then, with a sinking heart, he saw Charlotte Rudman weaving her way past gesticulating arms and dangerously full wine glasses.

'Hullo, Charlotte,' he said, putting on his game face. 'Good to see you. Are you having a nice time?'

'Yes, thanks, Dr Reynolds. How about you?'

'Oh yes. It's a lovely evening for it.'

An excruciatingly polite conversation ensued, as Jonathan fought to navigate the twin dangers of 'tutor' talk and oversharing of personal information.

'How are things?' Jonathan said. 'Not too stressed about Finals, I hope? It's so important to take some time to relax at occasions like this. Can do one the world of good.'

Charlotte nodded nervously. 'I'm sure you're right, Dr Reynolds. It's difficult to feel it's not wasting useful library time though. There's so much I still need to read.'

'Oh, I'm sure there's nothing to worry about,' Jonathan said vaguely. He really didn't feel like bucking someone else up at the moment and searched for a way to steer the conversation on to another topic.

'What about the rest of the gang?' he said. 'They seem to be enjoying themselves, from what I can see. I notice, though,' he said carefully, 'that Nicholas isn't here. Oliver too. Perhaps they'll pop along later.'

'I don't think so,' said Charlotte. 'Nicky said something about an emergency meeting to discuss *Titus*. Last-minute rehearsal stuff, I guess. The performance will be coming up soon.'

So word about the murder hadn't reached Seb's yet, Jonathan thought. Made sense. Although Beatty and Greene's killings had been passed off as an unfortunate accident and suicide respectively, pending the investigations, it was going to be impossible to conceal what had happened to Berkeley: not least because clearly several people had witnessed the scene of the crime.

'It's Olly that I wanted to talk to you about though,' Charlotte continued.

'Oh, has something happened? Has he had an accident? Is that why he's not here?'

'No, no, nothing like that. He said he had one of his shifts at the Shelter tonight.'

'The Shelter?'

'Oh, didn't you know? He's been volunteering at the homeless shelter one night a week: been doing it for the last year or so. It's really sweet actually.'

'I'd no idea. How... charitable.' Jonathan tried not to sound surprised and failed. It just showed you, people had hidden depths. Who would have thought the boy would take time away from his studies to devote to the poor and needy?

'I know. He's really modest about it too; hasn't told anyone. I only found out because it clashed with a CU meeting once.'

'Oh, right, yes, you two... yes.' Jonathan put down his wine glass on a nearby ledge and tried to focus. 'But what's the problem then?'

Charlotte glanced around. 'Er, it's not really something I should say where other people might overhear.'

'Let's just pop through there for a moment then,' said Jonathan, pointing to an adjoining room.

Once next door, with the hubbub of the party muted, Charlotte unburdened herself.

'I'm a bit worried about Olly, to tell you the truth. He's stopped coming to CU so regularly and he never used to miss a meeting.'

'Well, that's not something to worry too much about, surely, what with Finals coming up and everything?'

'I know, but it means he's losing contact with his support

group, you know? And with the stress of Finals and everything...'

She trailed off.

'What are you trying to say?'

'Well it might be nothing, but I know he had a really difficult time of it when he came up, and I'm worried that stress might bring stuff up again; make things worse.'

What on earth was the girl talking about: a difficult time?

'You're going to have to spell it out.'

'Oh, I really wasn't supposed to tell anyone. He's a very private person, you know. But when my mum... passed away in the Summer Vac before Second Year, he was so lovely and supportive. He told me that his mum had died, too, in an accident in the year before he came up. He was still really cut up about it. We didn't really talk about any of that stuff after that, but I always felt there was a bit of a bond there. And grief doesn't... well it doesn't ever really go away.' A large tear gathered at the corner of the student's eye and Jonathan found himself hoping he wouldn't have to comfort her.

'So,' he said smoothly, 'you're concerned he may be struggling to cope with the aftermath of his mother's loss as well as the stress of impending exams?'

'Yes. Yes, I suppose so.'

'Well you've done the right thing in telling me. It's best to catch these things early.' *You can say that again*, he thought. *Last thing we need is a suicidal Finalist on our hands. Hacker would kill me.*

He thought quickly. 'It's a little tricky, since Oliver hasn't told me about this himself. But, in the circumstances, I think I'm justified in alerting the college nurse and Student Welfare. They'll make contact and offer him support, counselling, antidepressants, whatever he needs to get him through this.'

Charlotte's smile in response lit up her face, almost making her look pretty.

'Oh thank you, Dr Reynolds! That's such a relief.'

And before Jonathan realised it, she'd thrown open her arms and given him a quick but fierce hug.

'Er, okay, yes, well, that's no trouble,' he said. 'We'd better get back to the party though. Don't want to seem rude.'

As he made his excuses and wandered over to talk to one of the postgrads, Jonathan gave a wry smile. *What is going on today?* he wondered. *That's the second close encounter of the student kind. If I'm not careful, George or Charity will be crying on my shoulder before midnight!* Still, he supposed a bit of erratic student behaviour was to be expected at this stage in term, particularly given the recent violent and troubling events. All of a sudden, the alcohol turned sour in Jonathan's stomach as he wondered where it would all end.

# CHAPTER THREE



## KATE

'So, your theory seems to be a bit off, Dr Reynolds,' said Kate, riffling through the photos of the previous day's crime scene spread out on her desk. *Blood. It looked unreal; dark red, almost purple, clotting thickly under the stage lights.* She shuddered and glanced up at the tutor and Geoff, sitting next to one another, looking awfully chummy as they chatted about yet another film she hadn't heard of. Geoff had told her about their pub meeting when he arrived that morning. *What's going on there?* she wondered, then dismissed it from her mind. He was probably just trying to suss out their consultant. Geoff was one of the most open guys she'd yet encountered in the force. He'd even rebuked colleagues when they'd slipped into the kind of unthinkingly homophobic and sexist language that tended to be bandied about the station. And now she knew about his brother, it made even more sense that he had no qualms about being seen having a drink with a gay guy. Shame there weren't more like him around really. Attitudes were slow to change, and plenty of colleagues seemed stuck in the eighties when it came to sexuality, not to mention gender and race. Turning her attention back to the case, she began to review what they knew so far.

'The victim is one Harry Berkeley: twenty years old, student, actor – and the director's lover. The killing was based on this play by Shakespeare they were doing called *Titus Andronicus* – pretty gory and disgusting all round I'd say, from the synopsis, but for some reason the murderer selected the deaths of Chiron and Demetrius as his inspiration. He hung the victim upside down...'

'Hanged.'

'What?' She looked at Reynolds.

'It's hanged – a picture can be hung, but not a person. Well, not in polite company.' He blushed.

Kate stared at him, lost for words, then shook her head. 'Okay. He *hanged* the victim upside down and collected his blood in a large bowl placed beneath the corpse. From what I gather about this play, I guess we're lucky he didn't stick it in a pie and make someone eat it. Of course, you get more than a bowlful out of a human body, so there's also blood on the stage, including on some soldiers' helmets and bows and arrows that had been left out. The props mistress was *not* best pleased about that, I can tell you. Somehow, despite all the blood, the team's not found any useful footprints and only some partial fingerprints.'

'That confirms that the killer is careful and aware of the dangers inherent in his occupation then, as well as highly literate,' Reynolds interjected.

'Yep, and, again, well-prepared – in one of the victim's pockets, we found a quotation from the play. It just says "Villain, what hast thou done?" So, not much to go on there.'

'I don't know,' said Reynolds, 'that's a line from Demetrius to Aaron the Moor, so is the killer representing himself as Aaron – a notoriously evil villain? And is he putting words of blame in his victim's mouth? Doesn't seem right.'

'No, that doesn't seem likely in view of his previous MO,' Kate said.

'Absolutely,' said Reynolds. 'He normally places the blame elsewhere – but where? In the play, it's Titus who kills Demetrius, in revenge for what he and his brother did to Titus's daughter, Lavinia. Horrifically, they rape her and cut off her tongue and hands. But that doesn't seem to have any relevance to what's going on here.'

'From what I gathered,' said Geoff, 'this Demetrius guy is angry with the Aaron character because he's shagged his mother and she's had a baby.'

'So, a sexual motive again?' wondered Kate. 'The victim was well-known in the theatrical community and, shall we say, well-connected. He was estranged from his family, like the other two victims, and, like Beatty, he had made some enemies in his social circle. Do we think the killer might have been a former lover, jealous of his relationship with the director?'

'But then how do we account for the other two killings?' Geoff wanted to know. 'They can't all have been former lovers, surely.'

'Maybe not,' Kate conceded. 'But the victims were all gay, so there's presumably *some* sort of sexual connection.'

'It might not be as simple as that.' Reynolds cleared his throat. 'I think the literature angle is still key.'

'What do you mean?'

'Well, as I was discussing with Geoff last night,' he began, 'it's clear that this isn't a series of medieval murders anymore. Shakespeare might have found a lot of his source material in medieval history and literature, but he's scarcely a medieval type himself. It could be, of course, that the killer is obsessed with both the Middle Ages and the Renaissance, but I wonder whether we might not need to expand our horizons still farther.'

'I'm not sure I follow,' said Kate, controlling her irritation.

*Why is it that academics can never seem to get to the point?* she thought.

'Jonathan – erm, Dr Reynolds – was explaining to me that our perp might be working his way through the English canon chronologically,' Geoff said, going over to the flipchart and picking up a black marker.

*English 'canon'? You* have *been talking to Reynolds*, thought Kate, saying aloud, 'And that would be?'

'The books and poems that are accepted as the classics of their day,' Geoff said smoothly, beginning to write. 'So, *Beowulf* is the key text from the Anglo-Saxon period, then *Gawain* is a major poem from the period after the Norman Conquest. So, if this play by Shakespeare represents the Renaissance period...'

But Kate had caught on. 'Then we could still be at the start of a series of murders following the chronology of English literature right up to the present day,' she said, her heart sinking. 'How many more could there be then?' she said, looking at Reynolds. 'And can we use this to predict what might come next?'

'I don't see how,' said Reynolds with a shrug of apology. 'English literature is a vast field, and it's full of murders and gruesome violence.'

Kate motioned him to go on.

'Well, it's not just the twentieth century that has a fascination with violence and atrocity: the darker side of human nature. Thinking backwards, as well as *Dracula*, which inspired all those shlocky films, Dickens' novels are chock-full of deaths: the Victorians were obsessed with it, especially if it was happening to cute kids like Little Nell. In the broadsides they could read detailed accounts of executions and murders almost every day. Their drama was full of Fallen Women, who always had to die by the end of the play to redeem themselves: like *The Second Mrs Tanqueray*. And before that? Well, as my A-level teacher used to say: "if you're not sure what a text's about, go for sex or death – you've got a fifty–fifty chance of being right". The Gothic novel is built around mortality – of a rather melodramatic form for my taste. You know, *Frankenstein, The Monk, The Castle of Otranto* – morbid melodrama.' Reynolds looked almost personally offended by the idea. 'The Romantics were also obsessed with everything from suicide to violent madness and monstrosity. When they weren't shagging each other, naturally. And, as for medieval and Renaissance culture – it was utterly pervaded by the memento mori. The idea that in the midst of life we are in death, as the Book of Common Prayer puts it. Shakespeare wasn't the only writer who capitalised on his audience's appetite for dismemberment and bloodshed.'

'So,' Kate said, as Reynolds concluded his impromptu lecture. 'We've no way of knowing what play or novel or poem the killer is going to work with next. And no way of getting ahead of him.' She tossed her notebook back onto her desk and shot a disgusted glance at Geoff, who'd written the list of three texts on the flipchart, followed by a question mark. *State the bloody obvious.*

'Unless...' said Reynolds, leaning back in his chair, 'maybe we can use his psychology against him. From what I've read in the profiling literature – and bear with me,' he added, catching Kate and Geoff's sceptical look, 'I know I'm not an expert. However, I understand that, despite limitations, profiling studies have been pretty consistent in showing certain traits that serial killers have in common. Chief amongst them, it seems, is arrogance: a sense of themselves as somehow better, cleverer than others, especially the police. It's this... hubris, I suppose, that often leads to their being apprehended.'

'That's right,' Geoff contributed. 'They're so confident they'll never get caught that they slip up.'

'That's the ones that actually do slip up, of course,' said

Reynolds, suddenly taking on that look of myopic concentration Kate associated with academics. 'It's always struck me as a weakness in the studies that we've no way of knowing how many serial killers are out there, either too clever or too careful to be caught. We'll just have to hope our killer isn't one of them.'

'You were talking about using his psychology against him,' said Kate, hoping to get Reynolds back on track. 'Did you have something in mind?'

'Well, so far you've issued a summary statement to the press, concealing key details of the crimes, obviously, and refusing to confirm any connection. Correct me if I'm wrong...'

'No, that's right. Standard procedure at this stage.' She shrugged.

'So I gathered from Geoff,' Reynolds said. 'I don't mean to imply any criticism. What I was wondering, though, was what if you placed a new story in the newspapers, saying that there had been a couple of murders, but claiming that the police are in fact closing in on the killer. That he's made all sorts of stupid errors and it's just a matter of time before he's picked up.'

'He'd hate that,' Kate said, seeing where Reynolds was going with this.

'Absolutely. You could even plant a fake interview with a psychologist, claiming the killer is likely to be – I don't know – an impotent, repressed loser. Below average intelligence, that kind of thing.'

'Which is exactly the kind of thing that would make him feel humiliated, furious even,' Geoff said, catching on too, his enthusiasm obvious.

'Precisely. So furious, perhaps, that he'll be driven to some unwise act in an attempt to disprove the unflattering characterisation.'

'Which might be enough to give us the lead we've been looking for,' Geoff finished, his eyes shining.

'I don't know,' said Kate, shifting in her seat. 'There's a lot of things could go wrong with this. And the press is already raring to blow this all up.' It was all very well Reynolds getting all gung-ho – and for a cautious man, he seemed to be all for other people taking risks – but this wasn't about him. She thought of what the Big Boss would say if things went tits-up.

'Hmm, no,' she said. 'I don't think so.' She saw both men open their mouths to argue and spoke over them. 'It's too much of a risk at this stage. We're going to follow protocol. Geoff, you and I will step up the one-to-ones with friends and family, check back over statements, fill in some of the details.'

She ignored the man's look of impatience, and turned to Reynolds. 'The team's slowly been building up profiles of the victims, but there may be things they've missed. We'll get in touch if there's anything else you can help us with, but for now Simpson and I have a lot of work to do.'

As she showed the man to the door, she thought she caught a wry glance between him and Geoff. It caught her like a blow to the kidneys.

The next day was filled with telephone and in-person interviews, a long laborious process of checking and rechecking details with the victims' frustrated friends and family members, most of whom did not see why they should have to go over exactly the same information they had already given to other officers, sometimes more than once. Kate was so used to repeating the words 'I'm just trying to get the facts clear' that more than once she found herself saying them to an interviewee who hadn't objected in the first place.

The night was filled with the resulting paperwork and snatched half hours on the disgusting break-room couch. By ten o'clock the next morning Kate had drunk so much coffee and eaten so many packets of salt-and-vinegar crisps that she felt bloated and antsy. Geoff was looking flushed and irritated. He had rolled up his shirtsleeves to his elbows and the tiepin that normally clipped his dusky red tie to his shirt had gone askew.

DCI Cooper poked his head around the door. 'A word, Stewart?'

'Of course, sir. Er, come in?'

He hovered in the doorway, a pile of newspapers under his arm. 'Perhaps you could give us a minute, Simpson?'

Geoff looked quizzical, but closed the file he was reviewing and exited the room. The Big Boss closed it on his heels, then sighed deeply.

'Something wrong, sir?' Kate said.

'You tell me, Stewart,' he replied, tossing the newspapers down on her desk.

'OXFORD DEVASTATED BY TRIPLE MURDER!' one screamed.

'INCOMPETENT COPS STUMPED BY COLLEGE KILLINGS!' ranted another.

A third went with the more picturesque, 'DEATH STRIKES THE DREAMING SPIRES'.

'Crap,' said Kate.

'Crap doesn't even begin to cover it, Stewart. The phones have been ringing off the hook. Slavering journalists, human rights groups, anxious mothers wanting to know if their precious student baby is safe. Front line have managed to fob most of them off, but this has blown up big now and no mistake. I've got those college nobs on the phone complaining about potential disruption to the student experience, whatever that's supposed to be, if they have to lock everything down, and not so delicately hinting at their connections to His Grace, the Duke of fuck-knows, and I've got the Chief Constable breathing down my neck and fretting about his budget. Where are you with this damn investigation?'

She sighed. 'No firm leads, I'm afraid, sir. Not yet. We've been reinterviewing like crazy. Following up everything. But this killer's really careful. It's not your usual man stabs lover and then regrets it. We managed to get partial prints in the Berkeley case but they don't match anything in the database. We're doing everything we can, but there's just so little to work with.'

'I was afraid you'd say something like that.' DCI Cooper broke eye contact and looked away at the wall.

'Sir?'

'I need some results right quick. And a triple set of interviews telling us just about nowt isn't going to cut it.'

'That's not fair, sir,' Kate objected. 'You know as well as I do that this stuff takes time. And we've still not been given access to the dating site.'

'Well time's running out,' the man replied, still not looking at her. 'For you and for me. If you don't come up with something soon, I'm going to have to bring in someone from outside. And that won't look good for you...'

Kate bit down on the fiery response that came to her lips. 'Don't do that, sir,' she managed. 'Not yet. I'll find something soon, I promise. Killers always slip up somewhere, you know that. This is my case, and I'll solve it.'

'You'd certainly better hope so.' He opened the door to find Geoff immediately outside, a guilty look on his face. 'And I don't expect my officers to eavesdrop in corridors, Simpson. Out of my way before I put you on a triple shift.' He swept past him, forcing Geoff to squeeze himself against the wall.

Geoff waited till the sounds of the Big Boss's departure faded into the distance, then looked at Kate.

'So we're screwed then?'

'Like a hooker up the Cowley Road on a Saturday night.'

After a sleepless night and more badgering from an increasingly impatient Geoff, Kate decided to try the tactic Reynolds had suggested, strong-arming the cute but weak-chinned temp in Legal, for the necessary clearances to run the story. She had decided to place slightly different versions in the twin student newspapers, *The Thames* and the *Oxford Scholar*, and a third on the front page of the *Oxfordshire Times*. If the killer read the papers at all, he'd see the story, no doubt about that.

She just hoped this worked. Cooper's bringing in some out-of-towner would put paid to her hopes of securing another promotion in the next couple of years. And she needed it. Her parents still treated her job like some sort of unusual hobby, to be cast aside when she inevitably met the right man. ('I still don't see what was so wrong with poor Tom', was her mother's infuriating refrain, even though she knew exactly what was wrong with him.) Maybe if she made DI they'd finally start to take her career more seriously.

They did not have long to wait. Early on Sunday morning Kate received a call from the First Response Team, reporting a suspicious death at the Radcliffe Infirmary. Feeling a bit sick at the thought of what her actions might have prompted, she called Geoff to meet her there and hotfooted it across town and up the Woodstock Road.

After flashing their identification at the reception staff and being directed down a maze of identical shiny corridors, pervaded by the cloying smell of disinfectant, Kate and Geoff eventually found their way to a small room guarded by a bored-looking officer. Inside there was a hospital bed with both side rails down and an inactive IV drip and monitor at its head. In it lay an inert figure covered completely with a thin white bedsheet.

'What are we dealing with?' Kate demanded of the SOCO on duty, a young South Indian woman with a striking profile, a pristine uniform, and exquisitely painted turquoise fingernails.

'Victim is Michael Tudor, Mike to his friends,' the woman said. 'Also known as Michaela when he performed his drag act at the Tower.' The Tower was one of the city's two gay pubs, Kate recalled, down by the river off Eden Square.

'He was quite good apparently,' the officer continued. 'Lip-synched to Barbra Streisand. "People"… "Enough is Enough"… that kind of thing. Victim's day job was working as a server at St Sebastian's College, waiting on the Fellows at High Table and such. Good worker, no major complaints, no known enemies.'

'Close family nearby?'

'Nope. Single child, dad pissed off long ago, mother recently deceased.'

Another isolated gay man, Kate thought. What else might link the victims?

As the officer continued to brief them, she revealed that Tudor had been found in a guest room occasionally used by staff when they had a particularly late shift. The college Scout assigned to clean it had gone in to empty the bin and change the bedlinen and had come across Tudor, apparently passed out drunk on the floor. When she was unsuccessful in her attempts to wake him up, she raised the alarm. Tudor was rushed to the infirmary in hopes of reviving him, but all the doctors' efforts had been unsuccessful.

'So, when they first found him, he had these purplish spots and patches all over his skin,' the SOCO continued, distaste written on her face. 'And it looked like pus and blood had oozed out of him. They'd cleaned him up before we got here, so there are no photos, but they wouldn't be much use anyway.'

'Let me guess,' Kate said. 'The bodily fluids weren't genuine.'

The other officer looked surprised. 'How did you know?'

'Call it woman's intuition,' Kate replied grimly. 'Go on.'

'So, yeah, the dark marks and whatever had been produced using make-up and paint and so on. They're still working up a full analysis. But take a look at this.' She peeled back the sheet.

The pale, slim body held no horrors for Kate, but, as always, the sight of youth extinguished too early by death caused a pang.

'What am I looking at?' she asked.

'These marks,' said the officer, wincing as she pointed to a profusion of small red dots all over the victim's torso. 'It's like the perp used him as a pincushion. Completely sick. Of course, the docs had removed the pins, but they kept them for us and we've sent them off for processing too. Maybe they can work out where they came from.'

'I guess it was designed to accentuate the impression of sickness?' Kate ventured. 'Anything else we should know about?'

'So, yeah, when they lifted the body, a note was revealed on the floor underneath, purporting to be from the victim. In it, he apologised to his family and friends; said that his diagnosis was too much to live with, and that he hoped they'd understand.'

'Diagnosis?' Geoff asked.

'HIV,' came the inevitable reply, and Kate's heart sank. Great strides had been made since the crisis that had blighted the eighties, she knew, but HIV and AIDS still carried the weight of stigma from an ignorant and frightened public, and inconsistent results from the drug regime currently favoured by healthcare professionals. *The poor bastard,* she thought.

'But that's the odd thing,' the SOCO continued. 'Our preliminary enquiries confirmed that Mike had confided in his next of kin about the diagnosis, but blood tests have revealed no evidence of infection. He was an entirely healthy young man.'

'But why would anyone lie about something like that?' Kate wondered.

'Who knows?' the other woman replied. 'The doctors called us in once they'd realised there was something off about the victim. We managed to rush an initial tox screen, and, although they'll do more tests once they've had a chance to transfer him over to the morgue, it indicated that his system contains significant amounts of anticoagulants and zinc phosphide.'

'Meaning?'

'Rat poison,' the woman answered with a shudder.

'But why the fake body stuff?' Geoff's normally imperturbable face telegraphed shock and revulsion.

'I don't know,' Kate replied, shaking her head. 'But we know someone who might.'

'Daniel Defoe's *A Journal of the Plague Year*,' Reynolds pronounced without hesitation when they consulted him about it, after hurrying across from the infirmary, dodging the busy traffic on St Giles, to St Seb's, working their way through the college's new secure but time-consuming sign-in process and up to his college rooms. He looked tired, as though he'd not slept, but seemed alert enough. 'At least, we're not sure it was actually Defoe who wrote it, since it's written like an eyewitness account and may be heavily based on journals by Defoe's uncle. But still, it's an important work, providing a much more detailed account of the bubonic plague – the Great Plague – than even Samuel Pepys does in the Diary.'

He paced around his study. 'Presumably the plague is intended to link to the AIDS epidemic – often dubbed the "gay plague" by the more rabid elements of the tabloid press.'

'But that's where our killer made a mistake,' said Geoff. 'The victim wasn't actually HIV-positive.'

'No,' Reynolds mused. 'That seems to have been another of Mr Tudor's colourful inventions.'

Kate raised an eyebrow.

'He was a very experienced server,' Reynolds hastened to add. 'Always efficient and courteous at High Table. But I had heard things on the college grapevine.' *Did Lawrence count as a whole vine,* he wondered, *or just a slightly malicious tendril?* 'If we're to be frank, the boy was a bit of a fantasist, a pathological liar. He could be quite manipulative, in fact. And, sad to say, that probably stemmed from embarrassment at his actual circumstances.'

'Which were?'

'In a word: pathetic,' Reynolds said sadly. 'Far from the glamorous life he claimed to enjoy in his time off – meeting this famous person in a London club, going on some fabulous holiday paid for by a wealthy lover – the nearest Tudor got to glamour were the cheap wigs and body glitter he wore for his lip-synch performances. The rest of the time he lived in a caravan which he'd inherited from his mother on the edge of some farmland out near Binsey. Just him, two dogs and a parakeet. Straight out of a Charles Aznavour song.'

The reference was lost on Kate and she looked at Geoff for help, but got only a helpless shrug. She pressed on.

'And this plague journal – that explains the brown patches and the fake blood?'

'More or less,' Reynolds said. 'The killer may have been intending to allude to the lesions characteristic of Kaposi's sarcoma. As I understand it, they can appear anywhere on

AIDS patients' bodies, but often occur on the limbs or face. I mean, thankfully, it's now much less of an inevitability than in the eighties, with antiretroviral treatments and whatnot.' He picked up an old book, with tattered gilt edges. 'But listen to how Defoe describes the Plague as characterised by "buboes", or swellings in the armpit and groin. They would grow hard and were incredibly painful.'

He read a short section which described victims being infected with gangrene, and people cutting their bodies open to try and flush out the disease with the flow of blood and pus.

Kate grimaced. 'Well that's certainly graphic enough.'

'Certainly is,' said Geoff. 'But what gets me is this: why suggest it was a suicide? The killer must have known that tests would reveal the presence of the toxins, even if, as he presumably thought, Tudor *had* been infected too.'

'Is he suggesting Tudor brought it on himself?' Reynolds offered diffidently. 'I mean, you know, a lot of these religious conservatives took that line in the eighties.'

'Still do, some of them,' Kate confirmed, thinking of her brother's nutjob wife. Her ostensibly liberal parents had welcomed her into the family bosom, despite her right-wing opinions on those she dismissed as immigrants, queers, and Jews.

'Perhaps,' Reynolds said. 'There's a punitive element in the previous cases too. He could have been punishing Beatty for his promiscuity, and there's an, erm, erotic element to the Greene and Berkeley cases too.' He coloured.

It was odd, reflected Kate. The guy was such a prude at times, yet at others he seemed more cavalier in his attitude to social mores: almost excited by people's flouting of the conventional rules. What was that about? And again, he apparently had nothing much going on at his college – he never mentioned any friends other than this Lawrence fellow – but he seemed perfectly at ease chatting with her and Geoff. Decidedly odd.

'But this *is* different from the killer's usual practice,' Reynolds was continuing. 'All the other murders have been obviously that – murders. There's no way they could be confused with suicide, even momentarily. So why is this one different?'

'You think he's been nudged onto a different trajectory by the stories we planted in the papers?' asked Geoff.

'I don't know,' said Reynolds. 'But something's changed, and it's not just the timing.'

The three of them sat in silence, staring at the books on Reynolds' shelves, as though the answer might leap out from one of them. Eventually, Kate sighed.

'Okay, it's no use sitting around worrying. We've been at this for hours. We should all go home, rest, think about something else, like protocol dictates. We're not going to do anyone any good if we get stale and exhausted. Let's meet back here tomorrow morning – if that's okay?' She turned to Reynolds, who nodded. 'Maybe then we'll have a fresh perspective on all this.'

Still, the energy in the room seemed low. *We need a break,* she thought. *And I... I need to get it together. My career's on the line here. And that newspaper stunt hasn't achieved anything, other than maybe hastening that poor sod's death.*

At home that night, Kate opened a bottle of wine, screwed in a couple of earplugs to drown out the noise from next door, and pored over her notes, reading and rereading every report, every detail. What tied these killings together? Was it the victims' sexuality? Their isolation? The links to English literature? Or was it something else entirely, something they'd all missed? *Assume nothing... Believe no one... Check everything.* That was her old mentor's mantra, repeated ad nauseam to her and anyone else who would listen back in the Serious Crime training unit ...*What have I missed?* In the end, she fell asleep on the couch, still dressed.

# CHAPTER FOUR



## JONATHAN

Jonathan crossed off his name on the SCR list with a frisson of excitement. Not that he was going to tell any of his colleagues why he wouldn't be at High Table that evening. If Lawrence asked, he'd say he had a queasy stomach so was just going to have some dry toast. But the fact was, Jonathan Reynolds finally had a date. And not only that, he was finally going to meet his secret admirer.

As he changed his jacket back in his room, he couldn't resist opening the locked bottom drawer in his desk for another quick peek at the notes. They'd continued to come every few days, in the same handwriting, the same green ink. Jonathan had a fleeting moment of disquiet as he remembered the other note that he'd received that first week, but fortunately nothing of that nature had arrived since. No, the green writer, as he liked to think of him, was something quite different. Of course, Jonathan hadn't known what to make of them at first. *Morning, handsome. Hope you have a great day.* Or *Saw you in the Library the other day. Love that blue shirt on you.* Should he be creeped out or flattered? But as the notes kept coming, he'd relaxed about them. They never said anything alarming and if someone fancied him but was too shy to tell him in person, what was the harm in that? In fact, he'd come to anticipate their arrival on a Monday morning with a smile. Then last week's had suggested meeting up. *I hope I'm not making a fool of myself*, it read, the writing cramped and small to fit on the notecard. *But I feel like I have to see you and explain myself. Hiding beyond anonymity like this makes me feel like I'm lying somehow. Anyway, you don't have to come, but if you'd like to meet me then I'll be at Browns at 7pm. I'll book one of the booths and leave your name with reception. I'll wait till 7.30, then if you haven't come, I'll stop bothering you and this will be the last of these notes. But I hope you'll come.*

Jonathan hadn't been sure till today whether he would go or not. It felt callous to even think about romance with everything else that had been happening. But life had to go on, after all. And it seemed most of the city agreed with him. After the initial alarm and hysteria had died down, people had adjusted to the situation surprisingly quickly. The gay pubs had shut down temporarily, of course, but everywhere else it was more or less business as usual but with a few more bouncers and security guards.

The deciding factor had been when he'd walked through West Quad that morning. He'd caught sight of a tattered poster for *Trainspotting* in a student's window. 'Choose Life' it admonished him. So that's what he was going to do. There was no danger, after all, meeting in a public place, and he could always walk away if he felt like it. Lucia kept telling him he deserved someone who appreciated him, and just maybe this would be the one. He certainly wasn't getting anywhere with the guys he met in the Faculty and at drinks parties. And, of course, at seminars... He pushed down thoughts of Nicholas – and the gnawing worry that he might tell someone what had happened. No. This was exactly what he needed. A distraction.

A meet-cute. And that Blake Edwards movie had ended up with Basinger and Willis together, right, despite the ridiculous shenanigans beforehand? He smiled at the memory. He'd been watching too many horror films lately. Maybe it was time for a romcom.

~

Jonathan rearranged the cutlery in front of him so it sat at right angles to the table edge. The waiter who'd shown him to his booth had winked as he took his drinks order, a small Pinot Grigio. 'Coming right away, sir. And I'll leave you the drinks menu in case you want to order a bottle when your companion arrives.' Now, twenty uncomfortable minutes later, Jonathan wondered whether to order a third glass or just go. He picked up his cream-coloured napkin and tried to fold it into a mitre. The soft linen just drooped.

'Would you like to order an appetiser while you wait, sir?' It was the waiter again.

Unable to take the pity in his eyes, Jonathan drained the remaining inch of liquid in his glass. 'Ah no. I think my companion must have got detained. I'd better go back home and telephone to see if everything's okay.'

'Of course, sir. We do have a telephone at reception if you'd like to call from here?'

'Thank you, but no.' Jonathan shrugged on his jacket. 'I'll just have the bill, please.'

Outside in the cool air, Jonathan paused a few yards down from the restaurant, silently kicking himself for getting into this embarrassing situation. Had the green writer ever even intended to turn up? he wondered now. Or had the notes and the date just been part of some elaborate joke at his expense? Well, it served him right for getting his hopes up. Stupid. Feeling too restless to go back to college yet, Jonathan set off down Little Clarendon Street past the rows of bars and restaurants and shops. The brightly lit interiors were inviting, but Jonathan wasn't about to sit somewhere else on his own like a lemon. He reached the end of the street and stopped. If he turned right on Walton Street, he could walk up past the art cinema and into Jericho. Left would take him past Winchester College and further into the city centre. He decided he'd head down Hythe Bridge Street as far as the station, then loop round and back up to the High, maybe even as far as the Botanic Gardens. By the time he got back to college then, he'd probably be exhausted enough to fall asleep and forget this stupid evening had ever happened.

As he passed Winchester College, he stuck two fingers up in the general direction of the patronising English tutor there. *Probably isn't even in though*, he thought. *Probably at home pretending to play happy families with his poor unsuspecting wife.* He felt a momentary temptation to pop into the Chinese on Hythe Bridge Street for some of their delicious dim sum, but fought it. *Only winners deserve Chinese dinners*, he thought, taking pleasure in the childish rhyme along with the self-pitying sentiment. *Hey, you get to wallow for a couple of hours*, he told himself. *You can pick yourself up tomorrow.*

He reached the rows of cycle racks that bordered the station. There were always hundreds tied up there, whatever the time of day. Maybe half of them were abandoned, or maybe there were just that many commuters, Jonathan didn't know. In the past, apparently, students and academics had just left bikes unlocked wherever they left them, and people used them whenever they needed to in a take-one-pass-it-on kind of system. No one was that trusting anymore though.

On an impulse, he decided to go inside the station itself. The vestibule was deserted and his footsteps echoed on the hard floor. Just a single attendant sat behind one of the ticket counters. Feeling self-conscious, Jonathan wandered over to the big paper timetables pinned to boards behind glass and pretended to be checking some details for an imaginary journey. There was one last train to London tonight, he noticed. *Maybe I should just get on it. Lose myself in the crowds where no one knows me or cares what I get up to.* Someone braver would do that, he knew. But that someone wasn't him. *Where would I stay? And I don't have a change of clothes or a toothbrush...* He shook his head. *Lawrence of Arabia, you're not. Or even Michael Palin.*

He exited the station via the other door and, turning a sharp right, almost tripped over a homeless man who was set up there with his sleeping bag and a small cardboard sign that read 'Please give.'

'I'm so sorry,' he said. 'I didn't see you there.'

'Spare some change?' came the inevitable response. The voice was raspy and of an indeterminate age.

Jonathan shook his head and apologised again. There were dozens of these people around Oxford, he knew, all wanting a handout. Some of them were probably genuine, he supposed, but of course, it was impossible to tell. He'd been told soon after he arrived that there was a syndicate of beggars who were dropped off in vans every morning and who made quite a healthy living off gullible tourists and bleeding hearts. 'Can you spare some change, please?' they all said, in exactly the same nasal tone and cadence. *And even if this guy is genuine, he'll probably just spend the money on booze*, he justified to himself as he turned away.

'I know you,' he heard from behind him. 'You're Jonathan Reynolds.'

Jonathan froze. How did this guy know his name? What should he do? He wanted to just ignore him and walk away, but that might make the beggar angry. He might even attack him.

'I think you must have mistaken me for someone else. Have a good night,' Jonathan said over his shoulder, then silently swore as he realised how tactless that must sound.

'No, you are,' the man persisted. 'I know you are. The other one's told me about you. He talks to me sometimes. Buys me the odd sandwich and sits a while. Tells me things.'

'Oh, that's nice,' said Jonathan weakly. 'I must get on though.'

But the man either wasn't listening or didn't care. 'I used to be like you, you know.'

Jonathan turned around to face him. 'I'm not sure what you mean.'

'Oh yes, I was just like you. Bit the worse for wear now, but I knew a lot of things. Didn't do me any good though. The colleges are mean, you know. They don't care about you. You do your best and then when you just need a little bit of help they kick you out.'

There was a plaintive tone to the man's voice. Jonathan wondered if he'd once been a student who'd got into the wrong company, been rusticated, as the colleges put it, and gone rapidly downhill. Or maybe he was a former tutor even. Jonathan hazily recalled being told once, late at night during a drinks party, about an up-and-coming academic, took a starred First as an undergraduate, golden boy of the Faculty, brilliant doctoral thesis, tipped for the next open Fellowship. Then something had snapped, tipped him over the edge. 'No one knows if it was drink or drugs or just the pressure,' his interlocutor had breathed in gossipy tones. 'But now he just traipses around the city, mumbling to himself. It's such a tragedy,' he'd said with barely concealed glee. 'Such a waste.'

He took one awkward step towards the man, feeling in his

pockets for any coins, but came up short. 'Erm, I'm so sorry,' he said, spreading his hands helplessly.

'You want to be careful, young man,' said the beggar. 'He's got plans for you. He didn't say what, but you want to be nice to him or there'll be trouble.'

'Right, right, of course,' Jonathan said, backing away.

But the man yelled after him, 'Remember – he's watching you!' Then he began to sing in a cracked macabre voice. *'There's a somebody I'm longing to see. I hope that he, turns out to be, someone who'll watch over–'* He broke off in a fit of coughing.

Jonathan fled. Behind him he could hear fading into the distance the wretched sounds of racked lungs gasping for air. Jonathan ran up Park End Street towards New Road and the High. But he didn't care where he was going now so long as it was away from that horrific interchange. His skin felt like it was crawling, and the snatches of melody kept replaying in his ears. At some point he turned right at random, running blindly, narrowly missing curious passers-by and bus stop signs. Then without warning the pavement suddenly changed to cobblestones and his foot twisted beneath him and he fell sprawling onto the ground.

A woman ran up to him. 'Are you okay?' she asked with concern in her voice.

Grasping his throbbing ankle in one hand, Jonathan exhaled shakily. 'Yeah, I'm fine, I'm fine, thanks.'

'Well, if you're sure.'

The woman seemed reluctant to leave him there, but Jonathan brushed off her offer to help him to a nearby café for a cup of tea.

'That's so kind, thanks. Honestly, I'm all right though.'

But he wasn't. After she left him, Jonathan sat gingerly on a low wall and stared at the cars going back and forth along the street. He felt moisture at the corners of his eyes and blinked furiously. What was the matter with him? He wasn't some child to be upset over a hurt foot!

When eventually the pain had dulled into an ache, Jonathan tried his weight on it. Not broken or sprained, it seemed. So far so good. He walked slowly down a nearby lane, trying to stretch it out, but couldn't manage more than a slow limp. He wasn't going to get back to St Sebastian's like this. He'd need to find a phone booth and call a taxi. Jonathan had been hobbling down the lane, concentrating on where he was putting his feet, but at the end of the path he looked up to see the stone façade of a church with narrow mullioned windows. He'd found his way to St Wulfram's, he realised, recognising the old, restored Norman door at one end. There was a light on in a small building annexed to the church and he walked towards it, not sure quite what he was hoping for. He knocked on the door.

'Dr Reynolds! What an unexpected pleasure!'

'I'm so sorry to just barge in like this, Reverend Little,' Jonathan stammered. 'You must be very busy and I–'

'Not at all,' the other man interrupted. 'And please call me Bob. Were you just in the neighbourhood, or – no, I can see that you're favouring your ankle. Have you had an accident? Please, come and sit down over here.'

He ushered Jonathan towards an old wooden pew, presumably reclaimed from the church. It was covered in what looked like a handmade knitted cushion.

'Let me make you a cup of tea. Or would you prefer something stronger?'

'No, really, please don't fuss. I'm fine. I just tripped on the cobbles.'

'I insist. I was just about to put the kettle on anyway.' He looked conspiratorial. 'I know the Apostle says a little wine is good for the stomach, but to be frank I much prefer tea. I probably drink far too much of it.'

Jonathan allowed himself to relax as Little busied himself in an adjoining kitchenette. A sudden lassitude came over him and he felt his eyes become heavy.

'Here we are then!'

Jonathan's eyes snapped open and he reached out to take the steaming cup proffered towards him.

The vicar moved a pile of photocopied sheet music from the other end of the pew and sat down, placing his own cup and a plate of chocolate digestives between them.

'Have a couple of these. It's always good to have a bit of sugar when you've had a shock.'

As if sensing Jonathan's unease in his unfamiliar surroundings, Little took the lion's share of the conversation, talking easily about an upcoming event for which he was finalising preparations. After several minutes, he paused.

'But here I am, chattering on about church affairs. Tell me a bit more about yourself. Do you have faith?'

Startled at the unexpectedly direct question, Jonathan stammered, 'Oh, you know, I'm not sure, really. Well, no, I guess. That is, not a firm belief in God like you.'

'We all have doubts from time to time,' the other man said, smiling. 'But what is it that presents the barrier for you, if you don't mind me asking?'

'Oh, well, it's just it all doesn't seem quite real... no offence.'

'None taken. But why is that?'

'It's a few things,' Jonathan said, flustered at being put on the spot. 'I mean, I've read most of the Bible in relation to my work.'

'Ah yes – medieval history, isn't it? A time when the Christian warriors of the Light fought back the shadows of the Dark Ages. Such courage.'

'Er, not exactly,' Jonathan said. 'I study medieval literature rather than history. But those texts are certainly steeped in religious issues, and influenced by the Bible.' He decided to leave it at that.

'So your difficulty is with the Bible then?' Little persisted.

'I suppose so. It's purportedly this text inspired by God, but it's so inconsistent. For instance, there's the Ten Commandments on the one hand, telling people, "Thou shalt not kill". And then, on the other, God's ordering the Israelites to exterminate the nations living around them.'

Little leaned against the hard wood of the back of the pew. 'That's an interesting one,' he said. 'One thing very few people realise is that the original text doesn't actually forbid killing. In the Hebrew it means "Thou shalt not murder".'

'But isn't that the same thing really?'

'Not for some groups of Christians, who'd draw a firm distinction between, for instance, a murder motivated by greed, or lust, versus an execution for heinous crimes that threaten the fabric of society.'

Jonathan said nothing at first as he tried to process what Little was saying. Then, 'Doesn't it trouble you?' he said. 'The countless lives taken in the name of your religion over the centuries?'

'I prefer to call it my faith,' said Little. 'But yes, I have had long nights of the soul over the troubled history of my forebears, and the terrible acts perpetrated even today by those who claim to work under the banner of Christ.' He sighed. 'What you must remember, though, is that unlike our Father in Heaven, none of us is perfect. None of us has access to the truth of things. All of us are groping blindly in the dark night of a fallen world. *Now we see as in a glass, darkly.*'

'So, in the meantime, people can just carry on doing whatever they think is right according to their own reading of a random translation of an ancient text?'

'I don't have all the answers, I'm afraid,' Little said quietly. 'Nobody does. But that is why we must have faith.'

'You people bandy that word around all the time, but what does it even mean?'

Jonathan's temper was beginning to rise, but the other man spread his hands in a concessive gesture. 'As the writer to the Hebrews says, *Now faith is the substance of things hoped for, the evidence of things not seen.* I appreciate that's not a wholly satisfying answer,' he said, his calm expression unbroken. 'But, ultimately, can we be totally sure about anything? The philosophers tell us that Man is as one who lives in a cave, knowing nothing but the flickering shadows on the wall, unaware of the bright world outside. Your postmodern writers tell us there is no Truth, merely contingent smaller truths that may collide or intersect. How, then, do you know that I exist in reality and am not some figment of your mind, lost in solipsism and a world of its own projection?'

Jonathan's head began to spin, but the man still went on. 'But, for me, this is the benefit of my faith. We are told that there is an Answer to these unfathomable questions, and it is the Man who is God. For He said, "*I* am the Way, the Truth, and the Life". And that is what I believe, and what gives me the strength to continue my work. As the French might say, *je ne sais pas la vérité, mais je la connais...* But enough theology and philosophy.' He chuckled. 'You must be wanting to get back to college.'

Jonathan hesitated as he thought about stepping into the dark night outside once more, making his way back to his empty rooms. 'If you don't mind,' he said weakly, 'could I have one more cup of tea before I go? I'm feeling just a little bit dizzy.'

'Oh dear.' Little clucked. 'Perhaps the fall was more of a shock to the system than you realised. Let me get you some more biscuits as well.'

When he returned, it was with a whole tin of assorted biscuits which he placed on the table in front of them.

'You seem troubled, Jonathan,' he said kindly. 'Is there something else the matter at the moment?'

'I don't know. I think I'm just a bit out of sorts.'

'That's quite understandable with all that's been going on lately. It's so shocking, to think that there's a killer at large in Oxford. He must be a terribly sick, confused man.'

*You don't know the half of it.* Slowly, fumbling over the details as he tried to avoid telling Little anything he oughtn't to, Jonathan related what had been happening to him over the past few days and weeks. The other man made sympathetic noises, refilling Jonathan's cup when he finished his tea.

'I cannot imagine what you must be going through,' he said. 'But I can promise you that I will pray for you – and that the police might have the wisdom and the discernment to catch this killer and give him the help he needs.'

'Help?' snorted Jonathan. 'Sounds more like he needs one of those Christian executions we were talking about!'

'Ah, we all deserve at least one chance to repent and be forgiven. Let us judge not, lest we be judged.'

'That's very holy of you, reverend. But I don't find it so easy to contemplate forgiveness for someone who's done such evil things. And not only snuffed out the lives of his victims but robbed their families and all who knew them.'

Little nodded calmly. 'I quite understand. I do. And you are not the only one to be deeply disturbed by these tragedies: one of my parishioners–' He broke off as the door from the main church opened and a tall figure stepped through.

'Oh, this is good timing,' said Little. 'Jonathan, let me introduce you to my curate...'

But Jonathan had already leapt to his feet.

'Andrew?!'

As the other man's face dropped in horrified recognition, Jonathan let his cup slip and shatter on the tiled floor.

~

*Miserere mei, Deus: secundum magnam misericordiam tuam.*

Jonathan let Allegri's timeless strains cascade over him, the sepulchral echo of the cloister accompanied by the comforting hiss of stylus on vinyl. He rarely took the time to listen to records nowadays, but receiving the note and thinking about its implications had left him feeling agitated; in need of soothing.

*Have mercy upon me, O God: according to Thy great mercy.*

*According to the multitude of Thy mercies, do away mine offences.*

Jonathan was not normally someone who permitted emotion to affect him, but for some reason today the clarity and innocence of the solo trebles – hitting that achingly beautiful high C and descending in smooth cadence – brought tears to his eyes. He grimaced. *Ridiculous.* But his mind kept returning to Andrew... Andrew Morris. The one that got away.

*Wash me thoroughly from my wickedness: and cleanse me from my sin.*

The memories flooded back. The aquamarine of the bay bleeding into purple where rocks lay hidden beneath the choppy waters. The cloudy skies, sullen late-winter light, riven by unexpected shafts of tawny warmth from the persistent sun. Their hotel room, his own neatly stacked clothes and minimal belongings amongst Andrew's trail of discarded items.

Jonathan had joined Andrew in Malta at his friend's request. They'd had a particularly gruelling term, suffering together through Professor Beddoes's excruciatingly earnest lectures on Darwin's impact on Victorian literature and Dr Callow's series on deservedly minor American novelists.

Andrew often took off to Europe outside term time for a few days off season: 'to clear the head and banish the winter blues', as he put it. He'd found a cheap deal in a newspaper a few days before and phoned to book it on the spot. As he read out the description of the resort, with its golden sands and uninterrupted sea views, Jonathan had expressed envy and wished he could just take off like that. Andrew, his handsome face flushed with wine, had invited Jonathan to join him, pointing out the deal was for the room, not per person, so 'why not?' To his own surprise, Jonathan had found himself accepting the invitation.

Of course, the resort hadn't quite turned out as expected. After a long and bumpy ride to the north of the island in a bus so antiquated its yellow paint had turned to orange where it had not already flaked off, they had checked into the hotel to find it was next to a building site. Their uninterrupted sea view was, in fact, of a half-completed minimart and a sky-hoist. What was worse, the sands turned out to be more grey than golden, and the pavements around the shops and bars were covered in litter and dog excrement. Most of the businesses were closed for the season or under refurbishment, and Jonathan succumbed to a stomach bug, after making the mistake of drinking the local water.

Still, none of that had seemed to matter. Andrew never let anything get him down, and his infectious joy transmitted itself to Jonathan, lending him an uncharacteristic sense of positivity and lightness.

*Thou shalt make me hear of joy and gladness: that the bones which Thou hast broken may rejoice.*

He remembered how Andrew had mimicked the mannerisms of the other tourists staying in the hotel, and the painfully amateurish performances of the hotel's year-round entertainer, who alternated renditions of local popular songs with overenthusiastic versions of Sinatra and Dean Martin. Andrew's imitations were uncanny. He had every eye-roll and gesture down pat, and often back in their room, he had Jonathan in fits of helpless laughter, clutching his pillow as his stomach cramped.

At other times they had lain back on one of the beds, watching old movies on the hotel television. Andrew was particularly fond of Sophia Loren, Jonathan recalled, though he also had a soft spot for Vivien Leigh and Elizabeth Taylor. He remembered how they'd once watched *Streetcar* and *A Place in the Sun* back to back, chatting about how gorgeous the female stars were, whilst Jonathan secretly lusted after Marlon Brando and Montgomery Clift.

They had never discussed matters of a romantic nature. Jonathan had nothing to tell, never having dared to date anyone, and Andrew's girlfriends never seemed to last more than a couple of weeks. Still, as the days wore on, Jonathan felt increasingly close to his friend, as though something special was growing between them. The shared jokes, the easy tactile familiarity. Surely they meant something.

On the final night of their stay, they had shared a couple of the hotel restaurant's cheap bottles of wine in celebration, and when they returned to their room, Jonathan's head was swimming. He had never felt as relaxed and carefree as he had with Andrew, and told his friend so. Andrew had seemed pleased, even flattered, but had passed it off with a joke as usual. Soon they were engaged in one of the bouts of rough and tumble Andrew had initiated several times on the trip, sometimes tickling Jonathan until he had to scream for mercy, or simply hurling all his weight on him until he could barely breathe. A joyful suffocation.

*Cast me not away from Thy presence.*

Jonathan knew that Andrew had several older brothers and

sisters and assumed this was the kind of activity siblings engaged in. He had just enjoyed the human contact and sense of closeness. But that night it had felt different, some kind of indefinable tension had filled the room. It was as though a palpable connection existed between them – a bond that tied them, invited Jonathan to move closer. And so he had.

*Thou shalt open my lips, O Lord: and my mouth shall shew Thy praise.*

The kiss had seemed to last for hours – time held in suspension as Andrew's soft lips met his, yielding as Jonathan's excitement rose. He had not been wrong, he knew it. His long-suppressed feelings were reciprocated, after all.

Then, suddenly, Andrew was on the other side of the room, his face a snarling mask. The jagged, vile words that came out of his mouth struck Jonathan like a blow to the gut. He had stumbled out of the room, hot tears threatening to fall from his averted eyes. He managed to get across the hotel lobby without occasioning more than an odd look or two, then fled into the street, the cool air welcome on his burning cheeks.

He walked quickly along the road and down towards the beach. It was dusk and from the overgrown, barren olive trees that studded the pavement, the thronging wagtails shrieked at the sunset. In a confusion of rage and despair Jonathan walked along the deserted beach for what seemed like hours, a knot inside his body where his heart should be. At last he stopped and sat on a rocky outcropping, staring into the ocean's blackness, listening to its insatiable roar. Just the other day, he had sat on the nearby pier with Andrew, their feet swinging just above the cold water. He had pointed out a curious illusion created by the waves near the shore. The water's swell drifted in and out over a group of large, pinkish boulders, making them seem to be heaving deep breaths, their chests rising and falling with the tide. Indeed, to Jonathan, the whole world had seemed alive, land and sea, animated by his sense of joy, the happiest he'd felt for a long, long time.

That evening, though, as Jonathan sat at the sea's edge, everything seemed lifeless, dull. A wind whipped up from the ocean, sending a fine layer of gritty sand scattering across his footsteps, as though to scrub away any sign of Jonathan's presence.

He sighed and walked back to the hotel, knowing he had no alternative but to brave Andrew's anger and disdain, to apologise for crossing the line, and hope to salvage something of their friendship. But, when he gingerly pushed the door to the room, it opened onto darkness, and Andrew's inert form did not respond to his whispered enquiry.

The next morning Andrew had been all business, hurriedly packing and paying their bar tab. On the ride to the airport and on the plane he had claimed to be exhausted and kept his eyes closed all the way, though Jonathan was sure he wasn't sleeping.

By the time they got back to central London, where Jonathan was going to catch a train back to Oxford and Andrew another to his parents' house in Woking, Jonathan knew that the friendship was over, even before the awkward goodbye when Andrew refused to make eye contact as he perfunctorily shook his hand.

*Bury the anger, the guilt, the shame. Bury it deep inside.* The experience had made Jonathan determined not to expose himself to that kind of risk ever again, and he had lived accordingly, never making the first move, always keeping a firm lid on his emotions, the way he expressed himself. He'd sometimes been called cold, even boring. But if that was the price of avoiding such pain, surely it was well worth it.

And now Andrew was back in his life. Out of nowhere. And apparently now he was part of the church he'd always bad-mouthed in the past. And married too. Jonathan had spotted the ring glinting gold on Andrew's hand before he turned on his heel, yanked open the door and ran.

*The sacrifice of God is a troubled spirit: a broken and contrite heart, O God, shalt Thou not despise.*

As the music died away, Jonathan felt no calmer. The resolution and comfort promised by the words intoned with such purity, such calm strength by the choir seemed hollow. The past held nothing but shame and sorrow, and the future felt precarious. He would have to see Andrew again. He knew that. There were some things that had to be confronted. Things that needed to be said. But not now. He couldn't face that just now.

In need of a distraction, Jonathan glanced at his watch and saw he just had time to catch Evensong before dinner. He turned off the record-player and hurried out.

Slipping discreetly into the little rectangular chapel, with its rows of unexceptional stained-glass windows and pale flagstones, Jonathan stepped into one of the rear pews. He saw he was one of only a handful of members of the congregation outside of the choir. Out of the corner of his eye as he took his seat, he noticed Oliver shoot him an odd look from his place amongst the tenors and thought, *That's right, we have lives too.* Most students, he knew, assumed their tutors retired into a cupboard whenever they weren't teaching, just waiting for their next seminar to come along. For some it was almost true. Certainly not many bothered to turn up for Evensong anymore, except the die-hard C of E faithful and music lovers who wanted to hear a particular anthem.

Jonathan cleared his mind, letting his thoughts settle into the familiar rhythms of the liturgy. Normally, the rigid back and forth of invitation and response bored him, but today the formulas comforted him with a sense of stability. These rituals had survived greater vicissitudes than the ones he faced: through regicide and regime change, fire and flood.

*The Lord is my Shepherd, I shall not want.*

As he mouthed the words of the responsorial psalm, he watched the choristers' faces in turn as they sang. When he came to Oliver he was astonished to see a look of pure joy on the boy's face, transforming its usual sullen expression as though transported by the secure faith and trust embodied in the Biblical passage. Moved, Jonathan silently castigated himself for misjudging the boy. *Everyone has hidden depths*, his mother used to say. *Never judge a book by its cover. How would you like it if someone jumped to conclusions about you on first impressions?*

Jonathan thought back to the first time he had sat in these pews, alongside a terrified-looking Fresher with a mullet cut and questionable taste in clothes. Neither of them had had any idea when to sit or stand, what responses to make, and this had seemed to reflect the world outside the chapel, too, with its unspoken rules and inexplicable traditions. He didn't know what had happened to the undergraduate student, but he himself had learned quickly enough. He had swiftly assimilated what he needed to know during those first months at Oxford: how to speak, how to dress, without occasioning either mockery or undue scrutiny. But still sometimes when he emerged from his rooms in the morning, he felt like he was stepping out into a theatre where everyone else was off-book already and he hadn't been provided with even a character outline.

The chaplain stepped up to the understated wooden lectern to begin his address on the assigned reading for the day from the Letter to the Hebrews: 'Now faith is the assurance of things hoped for, the conviction of things not seen.' The man launched into a somewhat disjointed set of points connected by a couple of rambling anecdotes, but Jonathan's mind stayed on the familiar text. What did that even mean: *the assurance of things hoped for?* Surely the whole point of faith and hope was that you *couldn't* be sure about them? Assurance. Conviction. Certainty. Well what did you do when there was no certainty?

Jonathan felt he had never been certain of anything in his life. Certainly not his career path. And now he was a tutor here, rubbing shoulders at college and Faculty parties with academic superstars and minor celebrities. But still every so often there came that nagging doubt, that sickening certainty that someone somehow was going to pull the mask from his face and expose him as a fraud.

'Smoke and mirrors, my dear boy,' Lawrence always said, if ever Jonathan hinted at any insecurity. 'It's all smoke and mirrors – and a little behind-the-scenes prep. That's all any of us need. Keep one step ahead of the little fuckers.' Jonathan envied the man's confidence in his own self-worth, that arrogant certainty that brains and breeding would carry him through life with panache. Lawrence had never been exposed to the ugliness of the real world, Jonathan felt sure. Never had to worry about how to pay the bills, like Jonathan's mother, after his father was fired for drinking on the job. Never had to endure spiteful laughter from other schoolchildren because of his unfashionable clothes and off-brand trainers. But it was that laughter and worry that had made Jonathan determined to achieve something with his life. Made him study harder than any of the others and, against all the teacher's expectations, had carried him all the way to the University of Liverpool and beyond that to St Sebastian's College, Oxford.

*Where's that fighting spirit now?* he scolded himself. Was he just going to let some crazy stalker bring down his career by enmeshing him in a scandal? As the junior organist stumbled his way through a Buxtehude voluntary, Jonathan set his jaw, hoping to convey confidence, even defiance. He nodded briefly at Oliver and another student he dimly recognised as he made his way to the chapel exit, then strode down the stone corridor towards Hall.

*A baby was born once – if you can call it being born... birthed, perhaps, like a dumb beast. A baby once was birthed then: a conjoined head with no body. It – for what else can one call it? – had eyes that could blink and a mouth that could smile. An abomination.*

*But this is the truth that we must confront – man lives in a fallen world. A world full of abominations, of monstrosities. And man is himself monstrous.*

*Consider: the small intestine is twenty-two feet long; it coils, feculent, within you. The colon contains over four hundred different species of bacteria; they teem, legion, within you. The salivary glands produce over a pint of saliva every day; it pools, putrid, within you.*

*But none of this – none of this compares to the foetid stench, the rotting pustulence of man's inner being. His rancid thoughts and rank desires – all hidden within, hoarded as a miser hoards treasure. But what is hidden must and shall come into the light to be seen.*

# CHAPTER FIVE

TUESDAY 19 MAY, FOURTH WEEK IN TRINITY

JONATHAN

The air had been close and sultry all of Monday, but the weather shifted during the night and there was a chilly breeze the next morning. From the window, Jonathan could see traffic backed up all the way down St Giles. No doubt that explained why Stewart looked so frazzled as she sat there fidgeting on his sofa. It looked like she and her partner had slept as little as Jonathan had, so he made the filter coffee extra strong. Just as well he'd popped across the road to buy cinnamon rolls and pains au chocolat from Maison Blanc. Simpson certainly seemed to appreciate them.

They reviewed the details of the cases once more, Simpson supplying the details where Stewart's memory failed her, but none of it made any more sense than before. After finishing another coffee, they were all sitting in silence, the prevailing mood gloomy.

'Another morning and nothing to show for it but...' Geoff started.

Then Stewart's pager buzzed.

'Can I use your phone?' she asked.

After dialling the station, she listened to what the officer on the other end had to say, expressionless.

As she put the phone down, she turned round with an odd look on her face, whether of disturbance or excitement Jonathan couldn't say.

'That was a SOCO calling from the Radcliffe Infirmary,' she said. 'The killer's already struck again. But this time it really is different... The victim's alive and conscious.'

A few hours later, Jonathan turned left off the Woodstock Road and walked into the entrance quadrangle of the Radcliffe Infirmary. As he did so, the noise from the buses and cars mercifully died away. Housed in an improbably beautiful building, the Radcliffe had been built in the late eighteenth century to honour some aristocratic physician. The frontage had a symmetrical grandeur, heightened by a stone fountain that the architect had placed in the middle of the quadrangle that hospital staff now used as a car park. Within a stone circle, a semi-naked figure appeared to be drinking from a large stone bowl he held over his head with muscular arms, and from which a thin stream spurted into the pool below. Jonathan had visited the hospital several times for physio the previous winter after sustaining a minor knee injury. On one occasion there had been a cold snap the night before and snow coated the roofs and windowsills and blanketed the ground. The fountain itself had iced over and the stark beauty of the frozen figure had taken his breath away. Today the water was a dank green, giving off a brackish odour, and the stone figure was discoloured with algae.

Once inside, Jonathan met Stewart and Simpson at reception. They'd phoned to invite him to join them, having completed the formalities. He was astonished at the ease with which the police officers seemed to have breezed through the hospital bureaucracy. It seemed if you possessed a uniform and a warrant card, you could get past anyone, even an NHS ward sister. As they approached the curtained-off bed of the latest would-be victim, he wasn't sure what to expect. Whatever it was, it certainly wasn't the tiny, well-groomed figure of Samir Bhatia.

A second-year undergraduate at St Seb's, Jonathan had had occasion to reprimand Bhatia more than once during a stint as Junior Dean, a rotating disciplinary post none of the Fellows wanted. Bhatia was a political hack, ever-present at the Oxford Union's Debating Chamber, and with an unerring talent for rubbing people up the wrong way. Against all the rules, he would hang around the Porters' Lodge, canvassing votes in the student elections, and harangue members over lunch in Hall. Jonathan had had to deal with several complaints of harassment and intimidation from rival candidates, who claimed Bhatia's dirty tricks campaigns strayed far outside the walls of the debating chamber. He might have been small, but he was fiery and clearly not to be messed with. Interviewing him, Jonathan had found Bhatia to be a superficially charming individual, his words as slick as his hair, but with a political ambition far exceeding any discernible talent. Most unpleasant was the complete lack of empathy he showed for any of the victims of his campaigning.

Now, Bhatia lay supine and still under thin white sheets, and his dark-brown skin had taken on an unhealthy yellowish tinge. Two close-set red marks in his neck looked angry and swollen. A single *Get Well Soon* card on the bedside cabinet spoke eloquently of the political bridges he had burned, though, oddly, a childish drawing of a house with an oversized teddy bear outside had been Blu-tacked to the side of the cabinet. Perhaps sent from some young relative, Jonathan speculated. As

Bhatia confirmed his identity and details to Stewart and Simpson, he seemed to Jonathan a pitiable figure, his voice and demeanour defeated, far from the loud, entitled bray Jonathan remembered. Even his accent was not as 'RP' as it usually was.

'Uh, hi, Dr Reynolds,' the boy said weakly. 'What are you doing here?'

'Just checking in on you,' Jonathan replied, not sure if Stewart would want their connection to be known. 'Do you remember anything of what happened to you last night?' he added, catching an approving nod from Stewart across the bed.

Bhatia hesitated, an embarrassed look stealing across his face.

'It's all right,' Jonathan reassured him. 'Anything you say will remain confidential.' He had no idea whether that was true, but this was no time to be worrying about that. They needed to find out what the boy knew while they still could.

'It's just a bit...' Bhatia began. 'If my parents found out, I'd be disinherited. I don't see them much during term time – I pretend I'm too busy. They've no idea I'm...'

'Gay?' Jonathan supplied, with what he hoped was an air of sympathetic understanding.

'Yeah, I guess,' the boy said, squirming a little. 'No one does, really. In my community it's not accepted, and the Union's not much better. If my rivals knew, they'd use it against me in the hustings.'

'Really?' Simpson interjected, looking up from his notebook.

Bhatia turned his head towards him, even that small movement clearly costing him some effort. 'You'd be surprised how conservative some students can be,' he said, a weary look on his face. 'Some of them barely tolerate women and northerners, never mind gay Indians.' He sipped water through a straw from a glass by his bed.

'Anyway, I'm not sure how much help I can be. I'd gone to a

club night at BaNaNas to see if I could meet someone, you know, for a… hook-up or whatever. I'd normally do that via the message boards – for the anonymity – but sometimes I just have to… you know, get out. Besides, there was a costume theme, so I knew I could go without much risk of being recognised. The face mask I was wearing meant I couldn't see people that clearly, but this guy in a vampire outfit came up to me and we started talking. He kept holding his cape over the bottom half of his face and I couldn't really tell how fit he was, but I'd had quite a few beers, and he seemed interested, so I thought, what the hell? I took him back to my room in college and he offered me a pill. He said it was E, but I've taken that before and it's just made me high and, you know, horny, I guess.' He shifted uncomfortably, avoiding Jonathan's eye.

'Anyway, I guess this must have been from a bad batch, or maybe it was Rohypnol or something, 'cause I started to pass out. I kept drifting in and out of consciousness – at times it was like I was floating above myself. I could feel him doing things to me, nothing… sexual, you know, but he seemed to be trying to move me off the bed and into the middle of the floor. I've no idea why. I was panicking, 'cause I could barely move. Then he leant over me like he was going to bite me but he was holding his head oddly, then he moved back and he got something sharp in his hands. He started jabbing it into my neck. My arms weren't responding properly – it was like they were moving through treacle – but I got my mobile out of my jacket pocket. I'd just got one to help with co-ordinating my election campaign. Anyway, I managed to dial 999, but before I could say anything, the guy saw and grabbed it off me and threw it across the room. It must have spooked him, though, 'cause he ran off. Then I passed out again and, when I woke up, here I was.' He spread his arms to the hospital room, then let them drop to the mattress as though they were too heavy to lift. His face sagged and he looked appalled, as though just realising how close he'd come to death.

'We'll let you get your rest,' Stewart stepped in. 'You must be exhausted from your ordeal. Don't worry,' she added, 'you've been very helpful.' But the expression on her face belied her encouraging words.

As they walked away across the shiny blue floor, something was nagging at Jonathan.

'I'll catch you up,' he said to Stewart and Simpson, and went back over to Bhatia.

'Did you notice whether the other man was short or tall?' he asked.

'Not really,' Bhatia replied. 'He was average height, like you.'

'So, bigger than you.'

'Of course, most guys are.'

'But you said he had trouble moving you off the bed and across the floor?'

'Sort of. He was holding his head at a funny angle away from me the whole time, like maybe he was struggling with the weight. I don't know. I guess he was a bit of a weakling,' Bhatia said, with a hint of humour returning to his brown eyes.

Jonathan thanked him again and hurried to rejoin the detectives, waiting impatiently for him in the corridor.

'Something you'd like to share?' Stewart asked with asperity.

'I'm not sure,' said Jonathan. 'Just something that doesn't make sense to me. Let me think about it.'

In the cramped office at the station on St Aldate's, Stewart shuffled the mounting piles of papers on her desk. She looked tired, Jonathan thought. As they'd walked through the station past various offices, he'd noticed how the woman had tensed up as they passed the door with DCI Cooper's name on it. He recalled that there was some question as to whether Stewart and Simpson would be permitted to retain the case.

'Looks like the killer's getting sloppy,' he said aloud. 'Maybe our plan to irritate him worked after all. We've got two murder attempts in pretty quick succession, and one of them was botched.'

'Let's hope so,' replied Stewart, 'and it's not that he's shifting up a gear. There's still very little physical evidence – fluids, hairs. He knows what to avoid. Though we did get full fingerprints off Bhatia's phone.' She sighed. 'But you may be right. He clearly didn't intend for Bhatia to survive their encounter. And just what was he going for with that unsubtle costume?'

'Even I know this one,' Simpson interrupted. 'It's Bram Stoker's *Dracula*, right? Like the Gary Oldman film. Fangs and bats and all that?'

'Of course,' Stewart said. 'Or the Christopher Lee ones. Only here it's not virginal white girls getting the Count's attention.'

But something didn't gel for Jonathan. He shook his head. 'I'm not so sure.'

'What?' exclaimed Stewart. 'I mean, come *on* – vampire costume. And Bhatia had certainly bled a lot.'

'I'm not saying the vampire myth isn't relevant here,' Jonathan said. 'I'm just not sure it's Stoker's novel that's being referenced.' He tried to sit back in the plastic chair he'd been offered, then thought better of it. 'Obviously Stoker is famous for popularising the myth of the undead monster, preying on the living. But he's not the originator, even in English literature. I know there's a story that Stoker drew on for his novel...' He shook his head. 'I just wish I could remember what it was.'

'The brainy Dr Reynolds comes up short,' said Simpson with a grin. 'Who would have thought it?'

Jonathan knew he was being teased, but it still rankled. 'Come on,' he said. 'It's years since I studied the Victorian era. It's not like I have an eidetic memory for the entirety of English literature.'

'Oh I know,' said Simpson, still grinning. '*Not my period* – that's what you guys say, isn't it?'

*Fight fire with fire*, thought Jonathan. 'No, you're quite right,' he said, adopting a belligerent tone. 'I mean, you know everything there is to know about detection, don't you? After all, you're the one who worked out what the link was between Beatty and Greene, and Berkeley and Tudor, aren't you? Oh no, wait, that was *me*.'

'Careful or you'll cut someone with those claws!' said Simpson.

'Now, now, boys,' said Stewart. 'Let's play nicely.' She rose to her feet. 'Dr Reynolds, perhaps you could do some research into what this other book might be? And Geoff,' she said, turning to her colleague, 'maybe you could check out where we are with collecting statements from Tudor and Bhatia's extended family and acquaintances. I've got a lot of work to do here and I'd quite like some peace and quiet to do it in.'

As Jonathan left the room, still bantering cheerfully with Simpson, he looked back at Stewart. She looked as though she felt a bit left out, he thought.

After a quick chat with Lawrence, in which his colleague tried and failed to suppress his disapproval at Jonathan's ignorance of his period of expertise, Jonathan was ready to update Stewart and Simpson. They came to his room just after five o'clock. His offers of tea and sherry were declined, and, once seated on his sofa, Stewart crossed her legs and jiggled her foot up and down.

'What've you got for us?' she said.

'As I thought, there's a short story by John William Polidori which predates *Dracula* by nearly seventy years. Polidori was a bit of an unfortunate figure. He was the son of an English governess and an Italian scholar – hence the surname – and he qualified as a doctor aged nineteen. He immediately entered Lord Byron's service – you know, the poet who was "mad, bad, and dangerous to know" – and travelled with him to the Villa Diodati at Lake Geneva for that famous holiday in which Mary Shelley came up with the story of *Frankenstein*.'

'Oh, *that* famous holiday... And this helps us how?'

Catching Stewart's look of impatience, Jonathan hurried on. 'Well, Byron also started writing a spooky story on the trip. He abandoned it, but Polidori sort of stole Byron's main character and wrote his own story about a vampire, which was published a couple of years later in 1819. The poor man seems to have suffered from depression, partly because of a lot of gambling debts, and he died shortly afterwards, possibly by his own hand, but it's Polidori's late Romantic story that sparked off the Victorian obsession with vampires. And it's his story that first brought together the various staple elements of the genre, along with other tales like Sheridan Le Fanu's *Carmilla*. Stoker may be the most famous vampire guy – the name everyone knows, but he's just the populariser, if you like. Polidori's the real inventor. I just skimmed the story again, and it's not bad at all.'

'Okay,' said Stewart, sounding faintly irritated. 'But where does that get us? Surely it's not important *which* vampire story the guy was alluding to – we're not writing an academic paper.'

'It's *important*,' Jonathan replied, repressing his annoyance at Stewart's flippancy, 'because it helps us know where we are in the killer's personal chronology. If the allusion is to Stoker, then he's jumped all the way to the very end of the nineteenth century. That would mean the next murder should be from Modern literature. If not, and it's Polidori, well, we may still have the Victorian period to go. It's not much, I know, but at this point surely you need all the leads you can muster.'

He could see from Stewart's face that he was not wrong. Clearly time was running out on this case.

'So what do we do next?' Simpson wanted to know.

'We go back over the evidence in Bhatia's room,' Stewart said with resolution. 'Maybe the killer left something to confirm the allusion he was making. Maybe he even forgot something in his haste to get away and the team overlooked it.'

They obtained the spare key for Bhatia's room from the Lodge with a minimum of trouble, though Jonathan had to promise to return it the minute they were done. Clearly even the usually phlegmatic porters were rattled by the mysterious deaths. As they made their way through college towards the ugly seventies building in which he was housed, Jonathan saw the students they passed in dribs and drabs watching him and the detectives with eyes alternately curious and fearful.

The student's set, a small sitting room with a tiny area off to the right hardly big enough for the bed and sink it housed, had a musty smell, redolent of unwashed sheets and inadequately laundered clothes. The latter still lay in heaps on the carpet, though Jonathan assumed the police would have been through them all.

'It's true what they say,' Stewart noted. 'Some people are too posh to wash.'

Jonathan forbore to comment.

The three of them pored over the room's contents, Jonathan

concentrating on the books and papers, and the detectives taking the rest. After half an hour, Stewart called a halt to the search.

'We're not going to find anything,' she said with disgust. 'We've been through every item twice at least. Let's just call it a day.'

Simpson and Jonathan acquiesced, and they walked back through the college towards the Lodge again. As Stewart and Simpson prepared to take their leave, they were interrupted by the cheery voice of one of the porters, a big bluff man with a stiff, upright bearing. Most of the porters were ex-military, Jonathan knew, now seeking a comfortable gig after years of toil in the army or navy.

'Dr Reynolds?' the man called, a strong Oxfordshire accent in evidence.

'Oh, hello, Will,' Jonathan said, turning to face him. 'How are you?' The man was not one of his favourite people, but Jonathan had learned when he first arrived that it was best to be polite to the college staff. If they chose, they could make one's life difficult in small ways and big.

'Telephone message for you, sir,' the man said. He handed him a piece of thin green paper, the row of perforations still visible where it had been torn off a phone pad.

Jonathan glanced at it, and the blood drained from his face. 'When did you get this?' he asked.

'Someone phoned to the Lodge last night,' the porter said. 'But with all the commotion after the... incident' – he lowered his voice – 'I forgot all about it. I'm sorry, sir, I hope it wasn't urgent. I couldn't make any sense of the message.'

'Don't worry, Will, no harm done,' Jonathan reassured him. But when he stepped outside the college gate with Stewart and Simpson he urgently beckoned them closer.

'Look at this,' he said, holding out the sheet with shaking hands.

On the piece of paper was a single sentence, written in the porter's laborious scrawl.

*Oh, do not touch him – ... do not go near him!*

The detectives looked at Jonathan blankly.

'It's from Polidori's *The Vampyre*,' he confirmed. 'But that's not all – look at the time.'

At the top of the note were the figures 23:13.

'That's just *before* the emergency services were called last night,' Stewart observed.

'Exactly,' said Jonathan, feeling sick. 'At the same time poor Bhatia was semi-conscious and in danger of his life, the killer phoned the Porters' Lodge and left this message for me.'

'He knows you're helping us,' said Simpson, looking dismayed. 'And he's in control enough to do something like this to taunt us, even when something went wrong with his attempt to kill Bhatia.'

'There's something else too,' Jonathan said, tugging on his little finger as his mind whirled. 'I've been wondering about this for some time now, and the Polidori reference kind of clinches it. These killings aren't just in a loose chronological order – they fit into the period divisions of the English literature course here at Oxford.'

'How do you mean?' asked Stewart.

'All English students start with Old English, of course, but then they go on to study for a series of papers denoted by dates.' As he rattled off the titles, Jonathan could see the officer's eyes glazing over at the list of numbers, so he hurried on. 'The students don't take them in that order – they study Victorian and Modern literature together with Old English in the First

Year – but if you rearrange them in chronological order, the killings fit the pattern.' He ticked them off in his head. 'If that's true, it means the next killing is indeed going to be drawn from Victorian literature. Maybe Dickens or George Eliot or even Wilkie Collins. No way to be sure which, of course.' Then realisation dawned. 'But it also suggests that the killer is teaching or studying English here at Oxford – or wants to appear to be doing so. Good God – it must be one of my Faculty colleagues after all.' He fought down the feelings of nausea.

'It's worse than that.' Stewart's words came slowly. 'Think about it. More than one of the victims studied at St Seb's, which suggests the killer is at least familiar with the college, its entrances and exits and so on. More than one of the killings – including that of Travis Greene, who was *not* at St Seb's – is connected to you, Dr Reynolds, in some way. This is not some crazed killer targeting random gay men around Oxford.' She paused to think how to phrase what she had to say next. 'Dr Reynolds, I think he's using these victims to communicate with you personally, and, I'm sorry to say this, but I think it's not just one of your colleagues. I think it's someone who knows you very well, who may even be quite close to you.'

Jonathan leaned against the towering stone wall of the college for support, as his world came crashing down around him.

Jonathan brushed off the detectives' concern and their offer to assign someone to accompany him everywhere. There was an officer stationed in the Porters' Lodge now, just a Quad away, and the whole college was on lockdown, no one in or out without signing the porters' register. Hacker had been irritated enough by having to accept a police presence in the college he saw as his own domain, and Jonathan wasn't going to draw his wrath down on him personally by flaunting a personal bodyguard. Alistair had whinged to Hacker again after the cancelled tutorial and, although Jonathan had explained and attempted to reschedule, the little shit hadn't even turned up. In the event, an hour alone with George hadn't been as painful as he'd feared. Without the other students around, George had seemed to relax and their conversation about medieval estates satire had actually been quite pleasant. Not that that was going to help him with Hacker. Jonathan knew he was hanging on by a thread. The old snake was really too much. He'd even been reluctant to tell the student body what was really going on, feigning an unwillingness to cause alarm, though the press had not just let the cat out of the bag but thrown it over the wall there. Unusually, the warden himself had stepped in to issue a warning that students should be vigilant at all times and go around in pairs for their own protection. But that was as far as it went. At any rate, Jonathan didn't feel it was right for him to get special treatment. Still, once the three of them had parted ways, he felt suddenly vulnerable and in need of a friendly face.

He walked over to West Quad in search of Lawrence but, when he approached his mentor's set and knocked on the heavy wooden door, he received no answer. He could hear from within the overwhelming strains of the 'Liebestod' from 'Tristan und Isolde' through the thick timbers. Jonathan was not himself a fan of Wagner – he was of Rossini's opinion that the operas contained lovely moments but some ugly half hours. However, he knew Lawrence was an aficionado. Assuming Lawrence hadn't heard his initial rap, Jonathan used his fist to thump on the door. Nothing.

He waited while Jessye Norman and the London Symphony Orchestra descended from their mutual climax and knocked again, calling Lawrence's name. Still nothing.

As the mellow voice began to sing again of how softly and gently her dead lover was smiling, Jonathan, sensing something was wrong, pulled on the heavy iron handle and cautiously advanced through the little corridor beyond into Lawrence's sitting room.

Inside, the music was an auditory assault. The room reeked of alcohol. An empty bottle lay on its side next to one of the sofas, its white covers stained with something Jonathan hoped was red wine. Lawrence was nowhere to be seen. Fearing the worst, Jonathan turned down the volume on Lawrence's state-of-the-art CD player, and went over to the small side-room in which he knew Lawrence often took catnaps on a daybed heaped with luxurious cushions and pillows. The door was ajar. He held his breath as he pushed it further open, afraid of what he might see.

To his intense relief, no bloody corpse greeted his gaze, but what he saw was almost as traumatic: the sight of his respected mentor and peer, weeping uncontrollably and clutching an empty wine bottle like it was his only friend. The smell of wine and stale sweat mingled unpleasantly in Jonathan's nostrils.

'Lawrence,' he stammered. 'What's going on? Are you okay?'

'Leave me alone,' came the slurred reply. 'I don't want to see you.'

'But you're upset,' Jonathan said.

'What's it to you?' the old man said.

Taken aback by his belligerence, Jonathan forced himself to try again.

'Maybe if you talk about it, you'll feel better. Let me help you.'

Lawrence looked up at him from under heavy, red-rimmed lids. 'You don't care about me,' he snarled. Then he lay his head on a silk-covered cushion again. In a small voice disturbingly like that of a child he whined, 'Nobody cares about me.'

'That's not true,' Jonathan persisted, ignoring the manipulative tone. 'I do care about you. Lots of people do. Your wife, the other Fellows here.'

'Those fraudulent shits,' Lawrence spat, abruptly furious again. 'They don't care about anything other than their next review in the TLS and what's for dinner. And my wife.... *my wife.*' His voice rose. 'Cynthia hasn't cared about me for thirty years. Not since...' He broke off.

'Not since what?' Jonathan said, trying to keep the old man talking, hoping to draw him out of himself.

'None of your damn business, is what!' Lawrence shouted the words with unexpected venom and Jonathan had to duck as he hurled the wine bottle at his head. It struck the doorpost behind him and shattered in pieces.

Alarmed at Lawrence's erratic behaviour and volatile mood, but more concerned for the other man's welfare than his own safety, Jonathan gingerly stepped over the glass shards and reached out his hand to touch him gently on the shoulder.

'Get off me!' Lawrence bellowed. 'You're not my son. You're not Edward.'

'I know I'm not your son,' said Jonathan, bewildered. 'You don't have a son. You don't have any children. You must be confused. Come on now,' he soothed, 'lie down properly and try to sleep.'

But Lawrence would not be pacified. 'You think I don't know?' he said. 'You think I can't tell what you're trying to do?'

'I don't know what you mean. Honestly.'

'Oh yes, you don' know anythin'. You're so innocent, so needy. "Help me write my thesis. Help me get a job. I'm so helpless, I need someone to look after me". You know exac'ly what you're doing. Wormin' your way into my affections, tryin' to replace Edward, tryin' to replace my son. Well, you can't,' he hissed. 'Because he's *dead*. And no one can bring him back!'

Stunned, Jonathan kept silent. Lawrence had never spoken of the early days of his marriage to him, of any plans for a family, of the tragedy at which his words hinted. What could he say? How could he persuade the man of his genuine concern?

Lawrence, however, had reached beneath a pillow and extracted another bottle of wine, which he attempted to decork with clumsy hands. As Jonathan looked on, not knowing what to do, what to say, Lawrence's hand slipped and the sharp end of the corkscrew plunged into the fleshy part of his other hand. With a cry of pain, Lawrence held out his hand, palm upward as a bright-red pool began to gather. At that moment he looked utterly helpless.

Spurred into action, Jonathan ripped off a strip of silk from one of the cushions and wadded it up, pressing it into Lawrence's hand. Thinking quickly, he tore off several more strips and bound them round the makeshift dressing, hoping it would staunch the blood long enough for one of the first-aid-trained porters to come and bandage it properly. Stepping back over the broken glass in the doorway, he walked over to Lawrence's desk and placed a call to the Lodge. 'You'd better get over to Professor Gresham's rooms. There's been an accident.'

After Jonathan hung up he looked in on Lawrence again, but the man was curled up on the daybed once more, pathetically repeating, 'I'm sorry, I'm sorry' over and over again. *I don't want to see him like this*, thought Jonathan, repelled at the now abject figure. As the duty porter entered the set, carrying a bulky first aid kit, Jonathan made a quick excuse and left, hurrying back to his own rooms, where he poured himself a large slug of whisky.

The smoky liquid felt good as it burned its way down Jonathan's throat and he poured another drink. Sipping at this one, he realised for the first time that he was truly alone. In the past he had always been able to rely on Lawrence for sage counsel and moral support, but his mentor very clearly had his own problems to deal with, and, with Lucia away at the big Dryden conference at UCLA, there was no one else. Stewart and Simpson, whilst sympathetic, barely knew him. No, Jonathan Reynolds was on his own and the target of some sick killer's unfathomable plan.

~

Thames Valley Police Document D0241 in *The Dark Knight* case: Handwritten diary entry.

*I have read the runes. Cast the bones. Consulted the oracle. And I have come to the inescapable conclusion: I do not exist.*

*I do not mean that I have no physical presence. That would be foolish. My body is as real as yours. I feel pain like any other man. If you prick me, I do bleed: if I pluck a hair, it stings. Action and reaction. When I say that I do not exist, it would be more accurate to say that there is no 'I': no circumscribing, limiting identity.*

*I look back through my life in search of what makes me who and what I am – what guides my actions – and I see nothing, no unifying force, no centre to govern my days.*

· · ·

*I look inside – gaze within – searching for a kernel of self: a soul, if you will, and I come up empty-handed. I can discern no goal, no noble end for which to strive, no purpose to inspire my passion.*

*I have tried to look beyond myself – to look for meaning in my fellow man. But no matter how far I go, how deep or wide I search, I find nothing of value. Wherever I gaze I find petty envy, obscene greed, self-serving lies. Man enacts cruelty upon cruelty to man in a never-ending river of treachery. And God remains silent, impotent.*

*I could seek refuge in the grave, but something within forbids me to court my own demise. Perhaps I lack the courage.*

*I glance back upon the sands of life and see no footprints: not even mine. I see only an endless blank surface, continually erased by an indifferent ocean and the cold winds of time.*

*There is no true self: I have come to see that. Only an illusion of unity created by language and custom. That which we call 'I' is merely the random misfiring of synapses and chemical interactions within the brain of a naked ape. Yes, a mere upright ape, convinced of its own genius as it capers in the squalid cave of its own delusion, entranced by flickering shadows cast by the bone-fire. Whilst outside, the darkness waits for it, as it waits for us all.*

# CHAPTER SIX



Kate tried to distract herself, flicking through from *Judge Judy* to an episode of *Changing Rooms*, but the music from next door was way too loud to ignore. *Why the hell aren't those kids at school?* She contemplated shopping Maureen to social services, but knew it would be taken as a declaration of all-out war on the estate. Just not worth it. But the thudding impact of plastic ball on brick started up again. *The little shits aren't even inside listening to this crap*, she realised. *Right. Enough. I'm not having this ruining my one late start this week.*

She pulled her long coat on over her pyjamas and stomped downstairs in her slippers. Shaun and Declan took one look at her as she slammed through the double doors to the courtyard and scarpered, leaving their football behind them.

'Where do you think you're...?' she began, then gave up. Like as not, they were off to hang around the shopping centre, on the lookout for anything good (meaning dodgy) that was going. The music was still blaring out from their flat, proclaiming something about a gangster's paradise. Well maybe their mother was home. Kate had a few choice things she wanted to say about her parenting style.

Kate took the concrete steps two at a time, then wove her way between the laundry spread out along the corridor to dry. She spotted a *Peter Rabbit* duvet but couldn't imagine either Shaun or Declan being happy to snuggle up under that. *Would have thought hookers and sports cars would be more their style,* she thought, as she rapped loudly on the door to their flat. Nothing. She peered in the window but couldn't see any signs of life. To her surprise the place was neat as a pin. She thumped on the door again, then swore as she had to concede there was no one home. She might as well just get ready for work.

As she swung round to go back to her own place, she was startled to find Maureen just a couple of feet away, a worried expression on her face.

'Detective Stewart, Miss – is there something wrong? Has anything happened to Shaunie and D?'

'Damn right there's something wrong – do you hear this crap? I could have you up on a noise pollution charge!'

'I'm so sorry. Just a minute.' The other woman fumbled with an improbably large set of keys, eventually locating the right one, opening the door and disappearing inside.

After thirty seconds, the music shut off, creating a silence that Kate could almost breathe in. Maureen emerged into the corridor again.

'I'm so sorry,' she repeated. 'They must have forgotten to turn it off before they left for school.'

'What do you mean?' Kate snapped. 'They were here until, like, about five minutes ago, and last I saw of them they were heading for the Arcade. Don't think there'll be much school for them today – like last week.'

The woman's face crumpled and Kate was embarrassed to see that she was on the edge of tears. For the first time, Kate noticed the dark circles under her neighbour's eyes and her unhealthy-looking, sallow skin.

'You mean they's been skipping school again?' she asked in a low monotone. 'They *promised*. And the headteacher was supposed to let me know if there were any problems.'

She reached out towards the door frame to support herself. 'I just don't know what to do anymore. Ever since Stan left...'

The tears at the corners of her eyes began to overflow, making a thin trickle down her weathered cheek, and Kate didn't know where to look.

'I'm sorry,' she mumbled. 'I should let you–'

'No, please, miss, come in for a minute. Let me make you a cup of tea.' Maureen dashed the tears away with the base of her palm. 'I'm so sorry the boys have been disturbing you. I know your work with the police is very important, and they should know better. They're good boys, really.'

But even as she said it, she didn't sound convinced. Kate felt a sudden rush of sympathy for the clearly exhausted woman and so awkwardly accepted the offer of tea, sitting gingerly on the edge of a couch that had definitely seen better days.

'I'm sorry about the mess,' Maureen said, gesturing at the living room. 'I don't get time to clear up properly no more.'

*What mess?* Kate thought. *It's a lot tidier than my place.*

As she sipped her mug of builder's tea with milk that should probably have been used up the day before, Kate cast around for something to say.

'So you've been living here a while then?' she said eventually.

Not a stunning conversation starter, but the woman seemed almost grateful for it. 'Oh yes, we moved in here when Shaunie was on the way. Wouldn't have got such a big place otherwise. Nearly nine now, he is. Starting to look more and more like his dad.'

She looked both proud and sad as she said it.

'Your husband's not around anymore?' Kate asked cautiously, unsure if she was treading on delicate territory, but Maureen seemed unperturbed, speaking as though she were just idly chatting about the weather.

'No, Stan headed back to Lithuania a while back now.'

'Oh?' Kate kept her expression neutral.

'He couldn't stay after the divorce. He tried to persuade me to keep him, but I just couldn't. Not after what he did.' Her eyes flicked towards the bedroom. 'And the kids are better off without him,' she continued. 'Much better. He'd only let them down like he did me. It's just, you know, they don't understand yet. They're not old enough. They know I kicked him out but they don't know why.'

'That must be hard.' Kate couldn't think what else to say.

Maureen sighed. 'Well, you know, it is what it is. But what about you? A woman as clever and pretty as you must have her choice of men.'

Kate was surprised to hear what sounded like envy in the other woman's voice. 'I was married too,' she said reluctantly. 'Divorced now.'

'Oh dear.' Maureen sounded genuinely concerned. 'That's a real shame.'

'I guess so,' said Kate, fighting the urge to set down the tea and run out of the room. This woman was clearly a sharer.

'No children of your own then?' Maureen said.

'No, thank goodness!' Kate replied without thinking. 'Oh, sorry...'

'Don't worry.' Maureen smiled, seeming to take Kate's reaction in good part. 'I knows as my two can be a handful. It's difficult without Stan around to lend a hand – not that he did much around the house, but at least he brought in some extra money and could drop the kids at school on his way to work. I has to start so early at St Sebastian's that I can't take them myself, and I don't get free from my other job up at the JR until after they're due home again.'

'Wait, you work at St Sebastian's College as well as the John Radcliffe Hospital? What do you do?'

'I'm a Scout – I've worked there almost as long as I's lived here.'

'A Scout... that's posh for "cleaner", right?'

'Yes, I does a few hours at the college, working on one of the Fellows' and then one of the student staircases, then sometimes I nips back here before I catch the X13 up to the hospital. It makes for a long day, but it's not so bad as long as my gentlemen are behaving themselves and not throwing too many parties. Oh, the tales I could tell!' It was like the woman hadn't talked to anyone for a week, the way she chattered on – and maybe she hadn't, Kate thought.

'You don't happen to have come across a Dr Reynolds, have you?' she asked.

'Oh yes, Dr Jonathan is one of my gentlemen. How do you know him?'

Kate thought rapidly. 'I just had to consult him recently for one of my cases,' she said, feigning nonchalance. 'Seemed an all right guy.'

'Yes, he's a lovely man. Very quiet, but no trouble at all. Not like some of them. The things I could tell you! It's like Piccadilly Circus in some of those staircases... And some of them students are so rude too... leaving their rooms in all sorts of a state, and just expecting me to clean it all up for them... I mean, not all of them, of course – there's this lovely lad I does for who's always chatting to me about this and that, helping me with my cleaning buckets... really takes an interest in me, he does, asking me about what I do up at the hospital, worrying about my shift patterns, telling me I works too hard. Lovely boy.' She smiled, and topped up Kate's tea before she could stop her. 'I does worry about Dr Jonathan though.'

'What do you mean?'

'Well, I says it as shouldn't, but I don't think he's very well, poor man.'

'What makes you think that?'

The woman leaned forward conspiratorially. 'I empties all the bins, don't I? So I sees what gets thrown away. And some of it is downright disgusting, let me tell you...'

Kate could see that Maureen was about to launch into some lurid anecdote, so cut her off. 'And you've seen something unusual in Dr Reynolds' bin?'

'Not so much unusual. But there's so many empty packets of pills. And quite a few bottles.' A guilty look stole across the woman's face. 'You don't know him, do you? Don't say anything. We're not supposed to talk about the Fellows. I could get in trouble.'

Kate reassured her and swiftly moved the conversation on to another topic before saying she had to go and get ready for work. But her mind kept coming back to this new insight into Reynolds' private life and what it might mean.

Later at work, Kate decided not to tell Geoff about what she'd gleaned about their consultant. The two men seemed to have been getting on like a house on fire, bonding over their love of movies and whatnot, and anyway, Geoff didn't seem the type to be interested in gossip. It wasn't like Maureen really knew anything, after all. Kate's own parents got through buckets of aspirins, having heard somewhere that they were good for your heart. And plenty of people had a little tipple at the end of the day. Didn't mean they were alcoholics or whatever.

She spent most of the morning debriefing the various officers who had been collecting witness and next-of-kin statements, following up on missing details and cross-checking related accounts.

It was tedious but necessary work, and normally Kate was able to lose herself in the minutiae, taking pleasure in crossing every 't' and dotting every 'i'. But today she kept finding herself coming back to the image of Maureen, pale and tired, stuck looking after two kids who didn't even understand why their deadbeat father had left them and probably blamed their mum for it. It certainly explained a lot. She couldn't imagine what the guy had done, but it had to have been bad, or why else would the woman bother to dump him? Kate found herself clenching her fists as she thought about Maureen's situation. *I guess you're softer than you realised*, she thought. Or maybe she just felt guilty for the unkind things she'd thought about the woman before she'd actually bothered to get to know her.

'Got a minute, Sarge?'

Geoff toed his swivel chair over towards Kate's desk, a thick folder of papers in his hands.

'What's up?'

'I wanted to run some of this info by you on the staff and students at St Sebastian's. The team's drawn up lists of names by subject. I didn't get them to go too deep in terms of background for every single tutor and student – we'd be here till next Christmas – but I told them to do a bit of digging on the ones in English, just in case.'

'Anything interesting?'

'Not much. There's just a couple of discrepancies I thought you might want to take a look at.'

Kate riffled through the papers in dismay. 'You don't want me to check through all of this right now, do you?'

'God, no.' Geoff winked. 'Got to leave me with something to keep me busy! Just turn to page twenty-three and twenty-six. We've got two different parental names recorded for Oliver Black and Charlotte Rudman, two of the undergrads, and a conflicting date of birth for another named Nicholas Rivers. Thought I'd better flag them.'

'Thanks, Geoff. I'll give the Domestic Bursar a call, see what's going on.'

~

'St Sebastian's College, Domestic Bursary. May I help you?' said a crisp, cultured voice.

'I'd like to speak to the Bursar, please. This is DS Kate Stewart.'

'I'm afraid he's unavailable at present, Miss Stewart. May I take a message?'

'It's DS Stewart, and this can't wait: I need information on two of your students as part of a police enquiry. Can you locate the Bursar for me?'

'I'm sorry, that won't be possible.' The voice was a little sharper now. 'But I can put you through to the College Secretary. She can help you with any student information you need.'

After an interminable wait, another crisp voice came on the line.

'Detective Stewart? This is Sarah Cottingham, College Secretary. I understand you require information about two of our students.'

Ignoring the other woman's discouraging tone, Kate told her what she needed to know. She had been bracing herself for a lecture on protecting students' privacy, but apparently this was not the Secretary's main concern. After a long wait, she returned to the phone with news.

'So, Detective, according to our files, Oliver Black changed his name by deed poll during his first year here at college. It's a sad story, actually. His parents, Owen and Ilsa Truman, had brought him up in Germany, where his mother was born and his father worked as an English teacher. Tragically, they died, and Oliver moved to England to stay with his paternal aunt. Once he came up to Oxford, he adopted the Anglicised form of his mother's maiden-name, Schwartz, presumably in her honour. Charlotte Rudman's story is just as sad. Her mother died of cancer a couple of weeks into Michaelmas Term – Charlotte had to take several weeks off that year, and she failed her Spring Collection the first time round.'

'Sorry – Collection?'

'Oh yes, you wouldn't know – it's what we call the short exams students must take at the start of certain terms. Just two hours or so. It's to make sure they carry on working during the vacations, I suppose. If they fail a Collection they are sent down. But in this case Dr Reynolds argued we should allow Charlotte to retake her Collection on compassionate grounds.'

*How gracious.* Kate swallowed the series of further questions that sprang to mind. 'And the name change?'

'Oh, her father remarried...' She paused. 'Well, what do you know? Looking at the dates, it must have been quite quickly after his first wife passed. Some people...'

Rivers' date of birth proved to be more of a poser, and the Secretary promised to 'look into it', though her acerbic tone suggested Kate shouldn't hold her breath for a speedy response.

'And, in future,' the woman added as a parting shot, 'please direct any questions to me and my staff. Should they be within our power to answer we shall, of course, do so. The Domestic

Bursar is a very busy man, so please don't trouble him with your enquiries.'

'It's like women barely exist at that college!' Kate continued, with a heat she hadn't realised she felt. 'Oh, I know there's female undergraduates – at least since the seventies when St Sebastian's caught up with women's lib. But the whole thing is set up for men to thrive,' she continued. 'And women are either handmaidens and secretaries to the men, or inconvenient add-ons. Including me, from the moment I come through that barred wooden gate and the porters call me "Miss" and think I must be your girlfriend.'

'God forbid!' Geoff quipped with a wink. He'd been listening patiently as she listed all the things she didn't like about the university and its colleges, but was clearly not taking her too seriously. Kate scowled at him; she was not going to be derailed from her tirade.

'And despite all the female students and ancillary staff, where are the women Fellows? I was looking on the board in the Lodge, and you could put all the ones I spotted in a room and not have enough for a netball team.'

'Well there are in the women's colleges,' Geoff objected.

'Yeah, women's colleges,' Kate spat. 'That's it, segregate us so we don't ruin your old boys' club!' She shook her head. 'But I wouldn't expect you or your precious Dr Reynolds to understand.'

'What, because we're men?' Geoff said, his face flushing.

The mood in the room shifted abruptly. Kate had never seen her partner look so angry; he was visibly having to control his emotion.

'I know you face struggles as a woman in the force,' he

continued. 'I've seen the looks and heard the comments. But I'll tell you something else for free: I've called guys out for it, more than once. And it hasn't made me popular.'

'Well pardon me if I don't feel sorry for you,' Kate said, her eyes flashing.

'I wasn't asking you to feel sorry for me,' Geoff growled. 'But don't make out I don't get it – like Jonathan and I are some sort of misogynistic monsters. Because we're not.'

Taken aback by her partner's passion, Kate muttered an ungracious apology. But now she looked at her colleague's turned back with new eyes. Where did the violence of this reaction come from? And was the fury directed at the injustice or at Kate herself? She knew he'd had outbursts of anger before – he'd admitted as much. Should she be worrying about being around him? She knew she could take care of herself physically. No concerns there. But she wasn't sure she wanted to spend large amounts of time with someone who might blow up at her at any moment. She'd had enough of that with Tom. Her ex-husband came across as the easiest-going man in the world – that had been part of what attracted her to him. But, it was true what they said, you never knew what went on behind closed doors.

*You feel I have not been forthcoming with you. You are wondering how it is I gull these unsuspecting fools – or lure them, or beguile them, or whatever else it is you believe I do. In short, how I achieve the necessary preconditions of my Work. You feel perhaps that I am concealing things from you. But the truth is that you know already. It is no secret, the chthonic evil at the root of human existence. You have been told since your earliest days that the heart of Man is deceitful above all things, and*

desperately wicked. And that it is not what goes into a man that defiles him, but rather what proceeds out of a man.

So there it is. It is almost comically easy. All I must do is look and see what is there and then work with it. Play upon it like a musical instrument.

I play on the rebellious spirit of one, his desire to transgress. He lies about others, and breaks petty rules and regulations, and it is a cry for attention, though he does not know it, a need to be seen. And I see him.

I fan the flames of another's secret lust. He hides in the shadows, yet truly longs to be fully known, to be seen for what he is. And I see him.

The third, I flatter. I admire his performance, both on and off the stage, giving his craven ego what it craves. His affectation of wealth, his jealousy of his peers, his weak-minded self-absorption, his self-serving actorly tricks, all prevent him from attaining credibility, never mind greatness in any role. But he yearns for an audience. Is all too willing to strut one final hour upon the stage. And I see him.

The lies of another are a disease, they riddle his soul with pustulence and render the very air around him foetid. He says whatever he must, does whatever he dares, to avoid being seen for who he is. But I, at least, see him.

The fifth likewise cloaks his deeds in darkness, fearing to be known. But he exacerbates his deception with the hypocrisy of politics. Like his counterparts in Westminster, his credo is exitus acta probat, the end justifies the means, in that most deceptive of systems. And I see the truth. I see them all, as I see him.

And the next... with the clumsy façade he has erected... I see him too...

But you... you must surely now be wondering if I see you... Is it possible? Could it be?

But that is not the fear you should be entertaining. No, your *danger lies in how closely you yourself are watching... how well you see* me. *As the old charlatan himself warned:* wenn du lange in einen Abgrund blickst, blickt der Abgrund auch in dich hinein. *If you gaze long into an abyss, the abyss also gazes into you.*

Look away now.

# CHAPTER SEVEN



## JONATHAN

Feeling bilious from the rich fare at High Table, Jonathan walked slowly towards Back Quad and the Domestic Bursar's rooms, to which he'd been invited for his twice termly drinks party. It was his third invitation in a row, and, whilst he had cried off the previous two occasions, pleading pressure of work, it was not advisable to refuse a third time. Jonathan couldn't afford to alienate anyone, he knew, still less one of the college's stalwarts. Not with his temporary post inexorably approaching its end.

Stephen Granville-Smith was not an academic, Jonathan knew. He'd been made an honorary member of Governing Body at St Seb's two decades previously, after crafty real-estate speculation on his part had increased the college endowment fivefold and cemented the college's position as one of the richest in Oxford. Now in his sixties, Granville-Smith cultivated the image of a gentlemanly eccentric, though everyone knew he was only two generations away from a fish stall in the Covered Market, a connection he had done his best to bury by distancing himself from his family. Another thing everyone knew, but never discussed, was his sexual orientation. The former

Domestic Bursar – or DB, as the students now affectionately dubbed him – had been devoted to his partner, Hugh, a London solicitor for the past three decades. They shared custody of a Yorkshire terrier named Rocky – not after Sylvester Stallone's character but in allusion to the (ironically, closeted) heart-throb of the fifties and sixties, Rock Hudson. Nonetheless, any hints that they were anything more than friends, or impertinent questions about their home life, were met with feigned incomprehension.

Jonathan liked the old man, despite his pretension and his tendency to interpret any random comment as a personal attack. It was hard to hold a grudge when he took such delight in the formalities and traditions of the college, such patent pride in his belonging to an august institution. He quickened his step. If there was one thing sure to offend DB and occasion an acerbic comment, it was arriving late to one of his drinks parties. And the man would have no compunction, he knew, about complaining to Hacker of Jonathan's lack of collegiality. That was the kind of thing that could sink a man's career.

He made his way up the flagstoned staircase to the third storey attic rooms in which DB lived and entertained, and, sure enough, the old man greeted him with a thin smile.

'So glad you could join us, Dr Reynolds.'

Jonathan did his best to ignore the barely veiled criticism and accepted the glass of port he was offered with what he hoped was gracious thanks. The large carpeted sitting room was already filled with people, all of them men, he noted. He flinched inwardly as he realised this was going to be another of DB's set-em-up occasions. Unlike the notorious annual Gay Dinners hosted by the gregarious Music Fellow at one of the grander colleges on the High Street, to which the great and the good of a certain persuasion were invited, DB's gatherings were informal, low-key affairs. Periodically, he would invite eligible bachelors amongst his acquaintance – who were either known to be gay, or thought to be persuadable, or even just gay-friendly – to intermingle over drinks. Nothing was ever explicitly said about the nature of these parties, but Jonathan knew that DB took pleasure in brokering what he called 'special friendships'. What made Jonathan uncomfortable was that DB included both graduates and the more able undergraduate scholars, speaking airily and, to Jonathan's mind disingenuously, of the importance of mentoring and the pedagogic principles of Ancient Greece. No one was fooled, of course, and the parties were widely referred to as the Gay Gatherings to distinguish them from their more formal counterparts across the city. They were a source of much amusement to those members of Governing Body who did not actively disapprove, like Hacker, especially when DB made one of his many identification errors and propositioned a camp but irredeemably straight scholar, often to his hapless confusion or alarm.

Jonathan pushed his way through the knots of invitees deep in animated conversation. He nearly had his glass knocked from his hand by a gesticulating young man whom Jonathan did not recognise but who appeared already well along the road to inebriation. Drunkenness and lack of decorum were two of DB's other bugbears, and Jonathan was not surprised to find DB hovering behind him with an ominous expression on his lined face. Sure enough, when Jonathan had fought his way to the mantlepiece at the other end of the room and placed his back to the fireplace with relief at having survived the throng, he saw the intoxicated young man being guided politely but firmly to the exit.

Jonathan caught his breath for a couple of minutes, before looking around for a small group he could join, hoping there would be at least a few people he already knew and could talk to without having to go through the torture of introductions and 'do you know so and sos'. Then, he heard his name called.

'Jonathan! It's so nice to see you again.'

He looked to his left and saw a middle-aged man he didn't recognise approaching him. Average height, greying hair at the temples, glasses, an old-fashioned pale-brown suit. No, nothing. *Crap.*

'It's nice to see you too,' he managed. 'Remind me, sorry, it's...?'

Evidently crestfallen, the other man nevertheless maintained a polite smile. 'Dominic,' he said. 'Dominic O'Clery. We met at the drinks after the last graduate seminar. You know, after that woeful paper on Anglo-Saxon medicine.'

Jonathan murmured something non-committal. He really had no recollection of this man at all.

Dominic laughed. 'Do you remember, it was so dull Francis Werner started picking bits of fluff out of his jacket pockets and dropping them on the floor, and old Ernest Stanton was so outraged he kept looking round with those huge owl eyes to see if anyone else had noticed and was going to do something!'

The paper at least was starting to ring a bell. 'Oh yes,' Jonathan said. 'And then Francis dozed off and slumped there in the corner, snoring ever so softly.'

The discussion turned to rumours of intrigue and infighting amongst the Faculty and Jonathan relaxed as he realised he'd got away with it. It was always so awkward when you forgot meeting someone who evidently remembered you. As Dominic moved off for a refill, Jonathan castigated himself, resolving to pay more attention to the man next time they met.

His gaze drifted across the throng and was arrested by the huge chintz-covered couch to the far right of the room. Three people sat there, deep in conversation, and with a jolt Jonathan saw that one of them was Nicholas, whom he'd not seen since their emotional encounter. They had had a tutorial scheduled, but Oliver had turned up alone, explaining that Nicholas was feeling unwell. Jonathan knew he would have to see Nicholas again eventually but had been planning how best to achieve that with a minimum of awkwardness. It looked like the decision had been taken out of his hands.

He approached the sofa and raised his glass when the three young men noticed his presence, breaking off their intense chat.

'Good evening,' Jonathan said, in as nonchalant a manner as he could manage. 'Hullo, Nicholas.'

The student's expression was unreadable as he introduced Jonathan to his friends as 'one of the tutors here'. It transpired they were graduates from a nearby college, rowers whom DB had met at Summer Eights and invited along with the promise of introducing them to a former rowing legend he boasted amongst his acquaintance. That friend was not in fact in evidence, it seemed, and the graduates were thinking of taking their leave to attend another party back in their own college. They invited Nicholas to join them, but to Jonathan's mingled anxiety and relief, he elected to remain. As the other men left, Jonathan searched for something to say.

'I hope you didn't stay on my account,' he began awkwardly.

'Nah, too far to walk at this time of night,' Nicholas replied, though Jonathan knew the other college was a scant three hundred yards away across Museum Street.

'Besides,' the student continued, 'the drinks are better here.'

As if to underscore his point, a cork popped in the little kitchenette adjoining the sitting room, and DB re-emerged with a bottle of champagne in each hand.

Jonathan hastily swapped his unfinished port for a fresh glass of the bubbling amber liquid and sipped it nervously. Was Nicholas going to bring up their last meeting? Did he hold a grudge for the way Jonathan handled it?

It seemed that, if he did, Nicholas was not going to address it now. Indeed, cheeks flushed, he embarked on a long anecdote about his time skiing in the Alps the previous winter. Jonathan could not tell what the point of the story was. The closest he'd got to skiing was watching *The Heroes of Telemark* with his dad, and the vocabulary of *couloirs* and *moguls* meant nothing to him. He just nodded and smiled, making non-committal noises that could have signified either approval or sympathy. He was further dismayed when DB came up behind him and, evidently having caught part of Nicholas's monologue, exclaimed, 'Oh, do you ski? How marvellous. Do you prefer Val d'Isere or St Moritz?'

*Of course*, thought Jonathan, *trust DB to know all about the sport of the aristos.*

The man didn't wait for a response. 'I find the French Alps a little touristy nowadays, don't you? But I never can resist the fondue in Switzerland.'

He tapped his paunch regretfully.

Nicholas seemed charmed. '*FIGUGEGL*,' he replied incomprehensibly, but this apparently delighted DB and the two went off into a voluble discussion of various resorts and skiers that left Jonathan feeling more excluded than ever. He had just made up his mind to present his excuses and go back to his own rooms, when DB turned to him and clasped his arm.

'But here I am, running my mouth, when we should be quizzing you about your close encounter with the law.' He giggled self-deprecatingly. 'It must be so exciting, getting first-hand experience of a murder hunt.' He turned to Nicholas. 'Did you know,' he said in a throaty whisper, 'that Dr Reynolds has been aiding two detectives in their investigations? Quite a coup for the college, even if the circumstances of the deaths are a trifle... vulgar.'

'How so?' said Nicholas, frowning.

'Oh you know, such dreadful violence – and the seedy way he must have met them. It's all a little déclassé, don't you think?'

Jonathan was impressed anew at DB's ability to combine gossipy prurience with judgemental prudery. Nicholas, however, seemed less than enamoured of the man's hypocrisy.

'The only thing I think is vulgar,' he said, getting to his feet and drawing himself up to his full height, 'is talking about those murders in so cavalier a fashion. It's repugnant.'

He span on his heel and Jonathan looked on in bemused admiration as he pushed his way to the door. Not many dared insult DB at his own party. Jonathan spotted a momentary look of – was it fear? – on the man's face, but then he harrumphed loudly: the epitome of outrage.

'It's always the same,' DB declared to the room at large. 'You give people an inch... I've spent so much time and money on these young ingrates and they're never grateful, not one little bit... I don't know why I bother, I really don't. No one sees what I do, no one cares.'

He was at once surrounded by a coterie of friends, smoothing his ruffled feathers and replenishing his glass. 'Do you know what? I think I'm going to go as well.' Jonathan seized his opportunity and slipped out of the room, intending to catch Nicholas up and try to straighten things out between them. But when he reached the bottom of the stairwell and stepped into the chilly outside air, it was as if Nicholas had simply been swallowed by the blackness. Jonathan shrugged and picked his way unsteadily past the dim nightlights fixed at intervals along the path back to his rooms and bed.

At first Jonathan thought the figure huddled in his doorway, head on knees, must be a booze-sozzled student who'd got the wrong staircase and slumped in puzzlement against a door that wouldn't unlock. But as he approached, ready to shoo the hapless drunk away again, the figure raised its blond head and fixed Jonathan with a pleading look from those chocolate-brown eyes he knew so well.

'Can we talk? Please?'

A shiver ran all the way down Jonathan's spine. His first impulse was to run. But then he forced his panicked feelings down. It was time, he resolved. Time to confront his past.

As he poured the drinks, Jonathan glanced over at Andrew, folding and unfolding his hands, perched on the very edge of the sofa. *Good, he's nervous, the shit.* The man was as handsome as ever, damn him, even if he'd thickened a little around the waist in the intervening years. Jonathan walked over and proffered the glass of whisky, projecting an air of confidence he did not feel.

'Thanks.' The other's voice was small and subdued.

'You're welcome. It's Lagavulin. Single malt.'

'Oh. Right.'

'Aged eight years.'

'Okay.'

They sipped the golden liquid in silence that became increasingly uncomfortable.

'Er, you'll be able to taste the peatiness,' Jonathan said. 'But there's this hint of spice and sweetness at the end.'

The comment seemed to galvanise Andrew out of his nervous passivity.

'I didn't come here to talk about whisky,' he said, with an edge to his tone.

'What did you come here to talk about then?'

'I don't know. Us, I guess.'

'What do you mean, "us"? There's never been an "us" – not even before you freaked out in Malta and then ghosted me.'

Andrew's shoulders slumped. 'I know. I'm so sorry. You can't imagine how much I've regretted that. The way I acted. What I said.'

'You're right. I can't imagine. Because you never got in touch. Not so much as a note.'

The other man's expression became even more tormented and his hands started shaking. Somewhat to his surprise, Jonathan found that he was enjoying his position of power. Being able to affect someone else like this. And why shouldn't he? He deserved a bit of revenge after what Andrew had done to him.

'I wanted to. You have to believe me. But you have to understand what I was going through back then. I'd never felt like that towards a guy before. And you know what my family was like. Is like.'

'*I* have to understand...' Jonathan said incredulously. 'You think things were any easier for me?'

'I know, I know, coming to terms with your sexuality is always difficult. But at least you hadn't been brought up to go every Sunday to a church where at best people thought being gay was an affliction or a test, and at worst that it meant there was something intrinsically wrong and evil about you. And you didn't have a mum who scrutinised your every act and gesture in case you did anything that might embarrass her in front of the Fellowship.'

'Yeah, you're right. I was *so* lucky to have a dead mum. Really saved my teenage years.'

Andrew looked aghast. 'I didn't mean. Oh God, I'm getting everything all wrong.'

Jonathan watched the other man squirm for several

heartbeats, then suddenly the anger drained out of him and he just felt tired.

'You've got ten minutes to explain yourself. I'm curious to see how you ended up back in Oxford as Bob Little's curate.'

Talking quickly, Andrew summarised the events of the intervening years. His lacklustre Finals performance; his lack of direction; the pressure from his mother to pick a respectable career; the ever more frequent questions about when he was going to settle down; the application and acceptance for training at the conservative Bible college in Cambridge.

'And that's where I met Clara again.'

'Clara Gates?!'

'Yes. She was visiting one of my fellow ordinands. It was like a sign from God. We went for a walk along the Backs in the sunshine to catch up. It was so easy to talk to her and we kept in touch by letter and after a while I just knew we were meant to get married.'

Jonathan couldn't believe what he was hearing. At college, Clara Gates had been known as one of the nicey-nice girls Andrew had never had time for: all Laura Ashley print dresses, heavy fringes and no make-up.

He forced himself to be polite. 'And how is Clara these days?'

Andrew smiled a tight smile. 'She's well. We both are.'

Jonathan waited. There was clearly something he wanted to say.

'It's just...'

As the silence lengthened and he realised Jonathan wasn't going to help make it easier for him, Andrew took a deep breath, his eyes fixed on the carpet.

'Well, it's just we had so much to talk about before we were married. And the engagement was so exciting: telling our parents and all our friends.' *Not all of them*, Jonathan thought.

'Planning the wedding. It was great. And then, afterwards, we gradually realised that talking was all we were good at.'

Andrew's speech trailed off awkwardly. He was still avoiding Jonathan's gaze, but as if compelled to, he took another gasping breath and the words came tumbling out of his mouth.

'In the end we realised we were both gay and that marriage wasn't going to fix things. We'd hoped against hope, both of us, that it would. Prayed that it would. But eventually we had to face the fact that nothing was going to change. And it hasn't. Oh, we've made the best of it. We make a good team, actually, we really do. I assist Bob and lead study groups and preach the odd sermon, and Clara runs Bible studies with the ladies and helps with the teas... But I'd be lying if I said I hadn't thought about you from time to time over the years. What we had between us and how it ended. I never thought I'd get the chance to see you again. To apologise for what I said. But then I opened the door at the parish centre and there you were. I was so shocked I didn't come after you when you ran off. But I should have done. So here I am now. To apologise and to try to make amends. But if you still hate me, I'll go. I'll go and I won't bother you again.'

For the first time since they'd entered the room, Andrew met Jonathan's gaze, a pleading look in his eyes and, against his will, Jonathan's heart melted. In the knowledge of the misery the other must have put himself through, all the bitterness and rancour faded away, and the good memories came to the fore, those golden moments of their friendship.

'I don't hate you, Andrew,' he said. 'I never did. Not really. What you did back then killed me; it hurt me so, so deeply. But I could never truly hate the first person I ever loved.'

As he said the words he'd never dared or had the chance to say, Jonathan felt the cathartic release of finally telling the simple truth. He'd loved him. It was that simple.

The other man's body went rigid and the veins in his neck stood out as if he were trying to contain some intense emotion, and Jonathan wasn't certain for a moment whether Andrew was about to explode with anger again. Then, slowly, Andrew got to his feet and stepped across to where Jonathan was sitting. He reached out with one trembling hand and laid it on Jonathan's cheek, touching it so lightly and tenderly it made Jonathan shiver. And then he leaned forward, his full lips parted, and kissed him.

Some time later, Jonathan drifted out of sleep again, his mind still hazy. The space in the bed beside him was still warm but the body that had occupied it was no longer there. Jonathan smiled as he remembered how good it had felt to hold Andrew in his arms at last, their shared love restoring what those lost years had taken. He stumbled barefoot through into the study.

'Hey, come back to bed. It must be, like, 2am or something.'

But the naked figure huddled with knees drawn up into the armchair was silent.

'Andrew?'

He went closer, peering to see in the dim room. Andrew held his head in his hands, covering his face, and his shoulders were trembling.

'You must be freezing. Come back to bed,' he repeated. Then, as there was still no response. 'What's wrong?' he said. But really he knew what Andrew was going to say before he opened his mouth.

'Everything's wrong. Me. You. This. I shouldn't have come here. A moment of weakness and now I've betrayed everything I believe in. God. My marriage. And for what?'

Jonathan felt sick. 'I thought it was for love. But I guess I was kidding myself.'

'Love! How can this be love? We haven't spoken to each other in years. We barely know each other anymore.'

'I don't think that's true. You haven't changed that much since that summer in Malta. We had so much fun, watching movies, drinking wine, laughing at the other hotel guests. You know we had something. You said it yourself just a couple of hours ago – I'm the first person you ever loved. And it's obvious you still care for me: you're just hung up on the ridiculous rules of your stodgy old-fashioned church.'

'They're not ridiculous. And they're not the church's rules: they're God's. The Bible's perfectly clear...'

'I'm no expert,' Jonathan interjected. 'But I've read enough of it to know that that's not true. And there's plenty of Christians who'd agree with me. You've just been listening to the wrong people.'

But Andrew's face was still wracked with self-loathing.

'Oh God, what have I done? What will Clara say if she finds out? She'll leave me! What will Bob do? I'll get kicked out of the ministry.'

Jonathan rolled his eyes. 'Don't be so melodramatic. If what you've told me about Clara is true, this won't exactly come as a shock to her. And if the C of E kicked out all the gay clergy, half the pulpits in the country would be empty.'

'You just don't get it. St Wulfram's isn't like that. Bob would never understand.'

'I think he might surprise you.'

'Oh what's the use of listening to you? How could you comprehend any of this? You're not a believer. None of this means anything to you.'

Any sympathy Jonathan had had for the other man evaporated in the heat of his anger. 'How fucking dare you?!

Just because I don't believe the crap you do, doesn't mean I don't believe in anything. And at least I don't pretend to have all the answers to life. At least I don't preach to people and lie about who I am, you... you hypocrite!'

By now Andrew was shaking all over.

'I'm sorry, I'm sorry. Please just don't tell anyone. It'd ruin my life and I couldn't bear it. I don't know what I'd do if Clara and Bob found out.'

'Get out,' Jonathan said quietly and coldly. 'Put your clothes on and get out. I don't even want to look at you anymore.'

He walked over to the window and stared out, seeing nothing, his back turned until he heard the outer door click shut. *And so it ends not with a bang but with a whimper.*

There was no chance of further sleep after that, and Jonathan's rooms seemed somehow cramped, the air stifling. After enough time had elapsed for Andrew to be well away, Jonathan pulled on a jumper and trousers and headed down the Buttery staircase. Halfway down he suddenly felt dizzy and had to sit on one of the broad steps, the blood pounding at his temples. *That's what too much champagne and too little sleep gets you.*

He had planned to take a short restorative walk, but when he emerged into the cool night air he padded in his slippered feet over to the huge oak tree that stood in the centre of the Quad. A semicircular bench had been constructed around its thick trunk and he sat for a moment, looking up into the overhanging branches that reached up as if groping for the stars. He listened to the intermittent hooting of owls in the still night, then became aware of other noises in the far distance. Was that the sound of voices shouting? *Probably some drunken undergrads*, he thought, picturing an acrimonious break-up. But something made him get up and walk across the Quad in the direction of the disturbance.

As Jonathan exited the short wood-panelled corridor that led through to Back Quad, his gaze was drawn upwards to DB's third-floor rooms and, above them, the neo-Gothic crenellations of Fools Tower, so-called because it had no external windows and no apparent purpose beyond the decorative. It was always lit up at night by tasteful spotlights concealed behind the faux battlements, but tonight the beams exposed wreaths of black smoke, streaming up from the cross-hatched windows of the floor below. Jonathan's stomach lurched at the thought of the damage that could result if the fire spread through the ancient timbers and beams. It was like the burning of Manderley in *Rebecca*. As he approached in fascinated horror, he passed knots of students gathering in the Quad below in varying states of undress and alertness, and scanned the faces, hoping to find DB somewhere amongst them. But all he found was Lawrence, his face ashen and more lined and drawn than Jonathan had ever seen him, no trace now of his former self-absorption.

'Has someone gone to help Stephen?' Jonathan shouted over the hubbub of voices.

'The door to his lodgings is locked,' Lawrence replied. 'No other way to get in. Someone's rung the porters, but with the smoke...' He shook his head.

'Good God!' Jonathan took an involuntary step backwards. 'You don't mean he's still in there?'

'I'm afraid so,' said Lawrence. 'Everyone says he seemed fine at drinks. Didn't seem to have a care in the world. But I guess you just never know...'

At this point their shouted conversation was interrupted by the arrival of the fire engines in the street behind Back Quad, presumably alerted by one of the automatic alarms that were set up all over Oxford to guard against just such a hazardous eventuality amongst the old timber-filled buildings that thronged the city.

Jonathan watched as the men expertly directed streams of water into the conflagration, exchanging mute glances with Lawrence as if to confirm that this was really happening. After what seemed an agonising length of time, but must have been less than an hour, Jonathan and the other bystanders looked upon a blackened and gaping mess, a far cry from the stately architecture that had once graced the building's upper storeys. An ambulance crew hastened up the staircase and emerged minutes later carrying an inert figure on a stretcher, a small towel covering the occupant's face; at his feet a curious heap of charred wood and a small metal spike. *Poor DB*, thought Jonathan, *he didn't deserve to die like this.*

Jonathan was still standing there in stunned disbelief, when he heard a voice behind him unexpectedly calling his name. He was about to turn around when he felt something cold and hard slip around his wrists and heard a distinct metallic click. He stared at the uniformed officer uncomprehendingly as he said, 'Dr Reynolds, I'm placing you under arrest on suspicion of murder.'

# PART III

---





In the close air of the dark corridor outside DCI Cooper's office, Kate took a deep breath as she prepared to confront the Big Boss. *Calm yourself. Control the anger. Plan what you have to say.* The first she had heard of Reynolds' arrest was a whispered phone call early that morning from Sue, one of the friendlier secretaries. Kate had paced around her tiny apartment, ready to spit with rage at the lack of respect it implied. The Big Boss had come good on his threat and brought in outside help without so much as a heads-up. But why? Why hadn't he talked to her first? Why had he let whoever it was start crashing around making arrests? Was she off the case? Well, she wasn't going to let it drop without a fight. *Not on your life.* She had been psyching herself up all the way in to work along the eastern bypass and up the Abingdon Road, and once inside the station, she'd set her jaw and stalked through the main office, ignoring the looks that came her way, some of pity, some of *Schadenfreude.*

With one last long exhalation, she rapped smartly on the door to Cooper's room, turned the handle and pushed it open, not waiting for a reply.

She stood in the doorway and glared at the corpulent man behind the desk. 'What the hell's going on, Cooper?' *So much for calm*, she thought, as all she'd meant to say flew out of the window.

DCI Cooper looked up from the report he had in his hand. 'First of all, DS Stewart,' he said, 'watch your tone. You're not on *Law & Order*. Second of all, you know exactly what's going on.'

He leaned back in his swivel chair, one arm draped across his paunch. He was dressed in his usual ill-fitting dark-blue suit, and, although it was only ten in the morning, Kate could already see dark patches spreading from his armpits.

Cooper sighed. 'You screwed up, Stewart. Do I have to list the ways?' He held up his podgy fingers. 'I trusted you with this. I had to, with all the other crap on my plate. But what did you do? Cut corners with paperwork, disregarded protocol... and that effing stunt with the papers... You're lucky you're not up on a charge of reckless and unethical conduct.'

Kate's stomach roiled, and she was glad she'd had nothing but coffee for breakfast.

'And to top it all off,' the man continued, 'you let Reynolds in on all the details of the case and even let him visit one of the victims, completely compromising that part of the investigation. You know better than that. And to have missed that stuff in his study...'

His look managed to convey both frustration and disappointment. Kate was put on the back foot. What stuff? What had she missed?

'But to bring in some outside guy who starts making arrests without even a word to me?' she stammered. 'How do you expect me to work with someone like that? Who is he anyway?'

For the first time, the big man looked uncomfortable and he looked to his left without saying anything. Kate stepped further into the room and froze as she saw the other man sitting there.

'That would be me.'

Kate could barely hear the words over the pounding of the blood in her head. She clutched at the door frame for support, as the man continued speaking.

'Nice to see you again, wifey dear.'

Quickly, Kate marshalled her wits. 'That would be *ex*-wife. And it's good to see you, too, *Francis*.'

A cheap but palpable hit, she saw, as a flush spread up his neck, and she suppressed a grin. He hated anyone knowing his real first name, feeling it came across as less manly than the alliterating monosyllable he'd adopted at the start of his career.

Tom Turner: the Golden Boy of policing; determined and, in the eyes of many, dreamy. Except that, for Kate, the dream had turned into a nightmare three months into their marriage when, coming back early from a shift, she caught him shagging her best friend. Acrimonious was not the word for the subsequent divorce.

She took a deep breath and forced herself to look at her ex-husband. He was still infuriatingly handsome, though his curtained hair made him look more like an ageing member of a boy band than the man widely tipped to become the youngest chief inspector in the history of the Metropolitan Police, as Kate's mother never tired of reminding her. Unlike Kate, Tom's rise through the ranks had been meteoric, smoothed by his confident charm and ability to say whatever his immediate superior wanted to hear. His blond hair and blue eyes could be used to devastating effect on susceptible women, as Kate well knew, and his prowess on the squash court and football field went down a treat with his male colleagues. How could a man that handsome and sporty be anything other than a good guy? Maybe he dissed his girlfriends behind their backs, but that was just lad's talk, right? He must be, what, forty by now, but he could pass for ten years younger – no doubt aided by regular applications of *Just for Men*, she thought sourly, recalling how he'd hogged the bathroom and the hairdryer in their shared home in Gloucester. *Best thing I ever did, walking out on that self-absorbed man-child*, she thought.

'So,' she said. 'It wasn't enough to steal my house and my dog. You thought you'd better start taking over my cases too?'

'Yes, it seems there's no end to the number of your responsibilities I have to take care of,' he replied with a smile that showed all of his perfect white teeth. 'I guess the Detective Chief Inspector felt it would be more useful to bring in someone with a perfect track record of convictions... as opposed to someone who's, quite frankly, out of her depth.'

Kate took a step forward.

'Right, okay.' The Big Boss coughed. 'I didn't want you to find out like this, Stewart. I'd meant to call you last night, but I never got the chance. Obviously this is a bit awkward...'

'Whatever gave you that idea, boss?' said Kate, narrowing her eyes at him.

'Erm, yes, well. DI Turner has expertise in this area, as I'm sure you're aware. He's highly trained in the Reid Technique, and he's very kindly offered to step in till we've got all this nonsense under control.'

'This *nonsense* would be my case, that I've been working overtime on for weeks now, and which you suddenly just decided to give to this... this fucking toerag.' The fury roiling inside Kate suddenly exploded. 'I mean, I knew you'd been all over the place lately, what with the rail enquiry and everything. But this is bloody ridiculous. There's no way Reynolds did these murders, whatever Tom Tit here thinks he's found, and you'd realise that if you weren't so starved by the stupid diet your wife's got you on that you can't even think straight.'

There was a stunned silence in the room. At last, DCI Cooper cleared his throat.

'I told you I'd call in outside help if you didn't wrap this case up quick smart, and you didn't. And I don't have to justify management decisions to you. You got too close to Reynolds. You missed the clues – hell, you didn't even look for them. You screwed up. And now it's over.'

He heaved himself to his feet and came round the desk, forcing Kate to back towards the door.

'And one more thing,' he said. 'I do *not* tolerate insubordination. From anyone. I'm suspending you – with pay – for forty-eight hours. You need to calm down and get some perspective. You're lucky you've been a model officer until now, or it'd be more. Go home, DS Stewart.'

The last thing Kate saw as she backed into the corridor was her ex-husband smiling, with the same smug expression he'd had on his face when Kate left their house for the last time. The closing door seemed to shut on all her hopes for her career.

Back in her apartment, Kate continued to seethe. It wasn't just the indignity of having the case taken away from her, or even seeing Tom's satisfaction. From what Geoff had told her in a whispered conversation on the way out of the station, he'd immediately targeted Reynolds as a prime suspect – on what grounds, Geoff didn't know – insisting on a full search of his study in a dramatic night raid authorised at the last minute by the College Dean. Typical Tom: always getting results. Quickly, and by any means necessary. But what made this rankle more than anything else, Kate realised, was the thought that she'd been wrong about Reynolds.

She'd had little time for the few academics she'd met, with their obsession over pointless trivia like grammar and titles, and Reynolds had initially confirmed her prejudices. How he'd irritated her with his prissy precision and inability to let a point go in conversations. But, as they had spent time together, Kate had come to appreciate the man's concern – even impatience – to puzzle out the truth, not to remain content with easy answers. She'd come to trust him, to like him, even. And she knew that Geoff felt the same. It had started to feel like a meeting of the Film Club when the two of them got together. Geoff had even bought Jonathan a copy of an easy listening LP that Anthony Perkins had once unaccountably cut. How could they both have been so wrong about him? How had he fooled them? And what crucial clues had they missed?

On her way out of the station, she had demanded a copy of the evidence against Reynolds and, reluctantly, one of the secretaries had agreed, slipping her a folder of photocopies under the desk. It certainly seemed damning.

A series of undated diary entries in Reynolds' handwriting raged melodramatically against the evils of the age: diatribes against politicians, disturbing fantasies about shooting people in the street. As the entries progressed, it seemed as if the man's grasp on reality was deteriorating, like he was having a mental breakdown.

Underneath the photocopied diary pages, Kate found photographs of the art prints on the walls of Reynolds' study, identified in some officer's neat writing as Botticelli's version of St Sebastian's martyrdom and a depiction of a Jewish heroine called Judith, carrying the head of her enemy. Why would any sane person want such pictures on their walls? she wondered. It didn't look good.

Finally, and most damning of all, there was a letter, unambiguously taking credit for the murders, the sickening words typed on thick creamy paper headed with the college crest of two black arrows crossed on a background of silver – or argent, as Reynolds had corrected her, soon after they met.

**And so the game comes to an end**, the letter ran, after quoting a passage from *Jane Eyre* detailing Bertha's maniacal leap to her death, as the flames rose around her.

```
I do not expect to be lauded for my
work, for this world seldom recognises
genius in its own time. But future
generations will see me for who I am,
and praise my name. For the present age
is dark and full of falsehoods and lies.
Yea, the liars and the whoremongers
prosper, and mediocrity thrives in the
halls of learning. Yet it shall not
always be so. For I have set out the
path of righteousness and I have shown
forth the strait gate. Those with ears
to hear: they shall hear. And those with
eyes to see: they shall bear witness.
And my work shall continue unto the End
of Days, which shall surely be not long
delayed.
   O, come, thou redeeming Death! O,
come, thou cleansing Fire! Amen and
amen.
```

Could it actually be by Reynolds? If so, the guy really was nuts.

Kate placed a discreet call to one of the more sympathetic

members of the investigative team and discovered that the signature had already been analysed by handwriting experts and, leaving allowance for natural variations, it was judged to match Reynolds' known signature in 'multiple significant aspects'. Wow, the new guy's been busy, she thought bitterly.

Apparently, the team was still checking details of Reynolds' whereabouts during crucial time periods, but, since all the murders occurred at night, and Reynolds' crucial alibis involved his colleague and mentor, Lawrence Gresham who might conceivably be trying to protect his mentee... Well, it didn't look good. Especially if they eventually turned up some DNA evidence, as the team was confident they would. Particularly damning was the confirmation from one of Reynolds' own students that the tutor had been seen engaging in an altercation with the last victim, Granville-Smith, at a drinks party the night before the murder.

No, it looked bad for Reynolds right enough. She turned the case over and over in her mind. Something just wasn't right. She knew she was probably being unduly influenced by the rapport she had built up with the guy, but she couldn't help feeling that they had missed something. Some crucial piece of evidence. Some factor that could prove Reynolds wasn't guilty, despite the mounting evidence against him.

At a loss, she called Geoff, hoping at least to vent her feelings about how the case had been snatched away from them. Her partner sounded guarded on the phone, but agreed to meet her during his lunch break at the Royal Beaumont, a tiny pub off St Wulfram's Street. Off-shift police officers normally frequented the Head of the River where St Aldate's met the Abingdon Road, but she didn't feel like being around colleagues right now.

～

As Kate crossed the tiled floor to the booth Geoff had secured for them, she noticed her ordinarily relaxed partner seemed tense.

'How's it going, Sarge?' he said, sipping on his craft ale as he flipped a coaster round and round with his fingers.

'How do you think it's going?' she said, and took a long draught of her beer, savouring the bitter tang at the back of her throat. Then she apologised.

'Didn't mean to snap. I just keep going over it all in my mind and I can't believe Reynolds did it. Call me crazy.'

'No,' Geoff said, sitting up. 'I'm glad you said that. I don't believe it either. I mean, I've met a lot of dodgy types over the years and I pride myself on being a pretty good judge of character, and with Reynolds I just don't see it. We were with him for days and I didn't get the slightest hint that something was off. All right, the guy was a bit messed up, right? But no more so than some of those other dons we've talked to. And as for being a killer? No way.' He sat back, his arms crossed tightly.

'I know. The degree of mess alone would freak him out. I mean, he's the kind of guy who puts a protective layer of paper over his own toilet seat...'

Geoff grinned. 'But what about what they're saying at the station?' he said. 'You know, a psychotic break or split personality, or whatever. If that's true...'

'Wait, what?' Kate said.

'Oh, right,' said Geoff, 'you wouldn't have heard. Current thinking is that Reynolds developed some sort of dissociative personality disorder – maybe stress-induced, maybe biological. Apparently there's plenty of other cases, though the only time I ever came across it was in that TV thing, *Sybil*, with Sally Field gurning her way to a Primetime Emmy. Seemed pretty dubious to me.'

'It's dissociative identity disorder,' Kate said. 'And it's not common, but childhood trauma can trigger it, apparently.'

She'd covered the basics during a course on abnormal psychology she'd attended as part of her professional development, and she tried to remember the symptoms. Headaches, anxiety and depression, loss of time or memories, self-sabotage, uncharacteristic or compulsive behaviours. Did they fit what she'd seen of Reynolds?

'I don't know,' she said. 'I mean, like you say, Reynolds was a bit messed up. But plenty of people are depressed, or get headaches when they're anxious – and he's had good reason to feel like that recently! And he's not engaged in odd behaviour as far as I know. Has he?'

'Well, if he wrote those diary entries, then that's pretty odd, if you ask me.'

'But even if that's true, it's not like most people with problems start killing people. They might go a bit doolally on medication, or if they've had a brain injury or something, but they don't start planning and executing convoluted murders.'

'Right. But what if he did?'

Kate paused. 'Well, I guess it'd be up to a judge or jury to decide whether Reynolds could legitimately be considered in command of his own faculties when he committed the murders – you know, *mens rea* and all that. If not, a barrister could push a defence of temporary insanity.'

She considered the possibility, then shook her head.

'I don't buy it though,' she said. 'It's too far-fetched. What, the guy's totally normal half the time, works hard to help us understand what's going on, then the dark night comes and he suddenly goes all Jekyll and Hyde and becomes a vicious killer? I don't think so.'

'What about the letter though?' Geoff said. 'How do we explain that? And the report of him fighting with the victim the evening before the murder?'

'I don't know.' Kate sighed.

They sipped their drinks glumly for a few minutes, staring at the varnished surface of the table. Then Geoff looked up.

'There's something about that letter that bothers me,' he said. 'It just doesn't seem like the kind of thing he'd write, despite the signature. And the fight? Well, academics start feuds all the time, don't they? Doesn't mean they actually want to kill each other.'

'What did you say?' Kate interrupted.

'What, academics feud a lot?'

'No, about the letter.'

'Erm, I just said it didn't seem like the sort of stuff Reynolds would say. It's not his phraseology.'

'No, you said *write*,' Kate persisted, the fine hairs on her arms rising. 'It's not the kind of thing Reynolds would *write*.'

'So?' Geoff looked baffled.

'So you're right... Reynolds didn't *write* it at all. He typed it out on a computer or word processor, printed it, then signed it. Or, rather, the killer did. Reynolds would never have done that. You know as well as I do that Reynolds didn't type his work – the computer the college gave him was still in the box, for God's sake!'

'That's right!' Geoff said, his eyes shining. 'He never even checked his college email account. He told me once he had no intention of using it till he was forced to. But that means...'

'Yup. Someone typed that letter and somehow got him to sign it, or maybe even forged his name. Whatever, he didn't do the killings.'

'And the real killer is still on the loose,' Geoff replied, realisation dawning. 'Shit, he's been playing us...'

'And the sooner we work out who he is, the better... preferably before he's claimed another victim.'

# CHAPTER TWO



## JONATHAN

Jonathan's hands and legs refused to stop shaking. He didn't know whether it was the adrenaline of fury or of fear. The fury came from the indignities he'd suffered before being unceremoniously slung into the six-by-eight holding cell he currently occupied. The fear was because he had no idea what was coming next, and he could neither fight nor flee. He tried to nurture the anger, cultivating it like a kindling blaze, hoping to obliterate his terror in a holocaust of wrath. How dare they treat him like this? Without dignity or decency. He was a university tutor, for God's sake, he told himself, trying to channel Lawrence's patrician self-assurance. Surely he deserved a modicum of respect. Instead, two bored-looking guards had got him to strip off right in front of them, then searched through his clothes as though expecting him to be carrying contraband or a gun. Thankfully they'd returned his shirt and trousers, minus his belt for some reason. They'd asked to take a swab of his saliva for DNA testing and he'd felt unable to refuse. In a brief telephone conversation, a bored-sounding duty solicitor had advised him to comply with whatever the police wanted.

The holding cell contained a hard bed and, in the corner, a metal toilet which Jonathan had no intention of using if he could help it. It didn't look too dirty from his present vantage point, sitting gingerly on the edge of the unyielding mattress, but he was not going to go close enough to be sure. Who knew who'd used it before him?

Try as he might to keep the spark of his fury alive, the fear of uncertainty won out and Jonathan's shoulders slumped. *I'm so tired.* He got up and paced around the cell, then sat down heavily again, then paced once more. The minutes ticked inexorably by. *So hungry.* Jonathan tried to hold himself in a state of suspension, the way prisoners of war and hostages did, at least according to the interviews that seemed to be all over the television in the last few years. *If Keenan, Waite, and McCarthy did it, then so can you*, he told himself, aware as he thought it how ridiculous he was being. He allowed himself to feel nothing, neither hope nor despair, only each breath flowing in and out. But his mind refused to be silenced. What did they think he'd done? Surely they couldn't believe he was the killer. And where were Stewart and Simpson? He'd thought they were becoming friends. How could they not warn him what was going to happen? At least they could have had the courage to arrest him themselves.

The last dam of his self-restraint burst, yielding a flood of worries, large and small. He thought about his career, shaky enough as it was, and could only imagine the effect of such a scandal on his prospects of a permanent position. Even if he were not sacked as soon as he was released from gaol – he refused to consider the possibility that he might not be – how could he ever come back from this? How could he command respect from his students, all of whom would inevitably hear about his arrest from some 'concerned' source in the college gossip mill. No, it was hopeless. He might as well give up now.

He would have to resign his post before they could terminate his contract – pleading illness or some invented family crisis – and disappear. Go somewhere far away from Oxford and anyone he knew. Maybe even leave the country altogether – flee to somewhere warm and anonymous. Take a gig teaching English to students in Japan or Singapore. Somewhere he could start again.

Jonathan had almost begun to look forward to his imagined new life, revelling in the melodrama playing on the screen of his mind, when the door to his cell swung open.

The man across the table from Jonathan was incredibly handsome. His blond hair fell neatly across his forehead, and his dark-grey suit fit his form snugly. His full lips were parted in a smile, revealing two rows of even white teeth, but the smile did not reach as far as Turner's pale-blue eyes as he bombarded Jonathan with questions... so many pointless questions about tiny details... questions Jonathan had already answered over and over to other officers about his whereabouts and memories of the victims and even his personal life. After a couple of hours, Jonathan's head was reeling and he was in sore need of the painkillers now lying uselessly back at college. Not to mention, he'd been needing the loo for the past half hour and Turner showed no sign of running out of steam.

Then, without any warning, the man stood up and walked round behind Jonathan.

'So, Dr Reynolds,' he said, 'now that the formalities are out of the way, we can get on to the business at hand. Why have you been lying to us?'

'What do you mean?' Jonathan stammered, craning his neck

round to try and look at his interviewer. 'I've not been lying about anything.'

'Come on now, Dr Reynolds. It's no use pretending any longer. We've been through your room. We've found your diaries. And there's the letter confessing to the murders, of course.'

Jonathan's mind reeled. 'I don't – I don't know what you're talking about. What diaries? What letter?'

He looked for help from the solicitor he'd been assigned, a thin man who had so far barely made eye contact with him, but he just continued to rearrange the contents of the briefcase on the table in front of him.

'Really? You're going to play dumb?' The blond man's lip curled up at the corner. 'I thought you academic types were supposed to be intelligent.' He moved back round the table again to stare Jonathan in the eye. 'Don't deny this stuff – it won't wash. We've found too much evidence for that.' Then he held up his palms. 'I'm sure you had your reasons though – maybe they'd threatened you? Maybe someone else was forcing you to carry out the killings, blackmailing you? It's all right, you can tell us now.'

'B-but I couldn't have done – I couldn't have killed those men. You must know that. I was with Lawrence when the first two murders happened – he gave me an alibi and Detectives Stewart and Simpson confirmed I was no longer under suspicion.' Surely that had to carry some weight?

The man's sneer deepened. 'Ah yes, those two. You were lucky to get them working the case, weren't you? A DS who let herself get taken in by a sympathetic-sounding suspect – typical woman's reaction, of course – and her moron of a constable, who'd go along with anything she said for a chance to get inside her knickers. Well, unfortunately for you, a vaguely timed alibi from Professor Gresham is not enough to get you off the hook.

And your cover story for last night doesn't check out at all. Andrew Morris denies having been anywhere near your room. He spent the night working on a sermon.'

Jonathan's whole body went cold. Why would Andrew lie like that? Was he really that desperate to protect his own reputation? He tried to think of something to say, but came up blank.

The other man sighed, then flicked a sheaf of photocopies over the table towards Jonathan.

'What is this?' Jonathan asked, but the man just gestured to him to read.

As he scanned through the material, Jonathan's confusion deepened.

He looked up. 'I don't understand – what is this supposed to be?'

'That is your handwriting, is it not, Dr Reynolds?'

'It looks like it, but I've never seen this stuff before in my life!'

The man just sniffed contemptuously and indicated to keep on reading. As he did so, Jonathan felt the tops of his ears go hot. The things he was supposed to have written... things he would never say to anyone else in a million years. About Nicholas. Others. Then, as he turned the pages, his blood ran cold and he felt nausea in the pit of his stomach. Here the ideas expressed were quite different: disturbing, hate-filled rants, dark and hostile thoughts. Could he really have written such things?

He looked up again in perplexity. 'I – I don't... This isn't me. I'd never write this kind of thing.'

But there it all was in his own handwriting, in a notebook he remembered buying from the little shop on Turl Street the previous summer.

The blond man slid another photocopied sheet over the

table. 'And this letter, Dr Reynolds, I suppose you don't remember typing and signing this either?'

Jonathan shrugged helplessly. There it was, a comprehensive confession, all laid out under the college letterhead and with his signature clearly scrawled at the bottom.

'I put it to you, Dr Reynolds, that there are two possibilities here. One is that you are a very sick man, as our consultant psychologist believes. Like a lot of qu– homosexuals, you are deeply conflicted about your chosen lifestyle.' The man took on a look of distaste. 'But in you, this conflict pushed you into a pathological state, forcing you to externalise the guilt you felt inside, projecting it onto the men you felt attracted to and then punishing yourself in them. By killing them, you killed the part of yourself you despised, until it surfaced again and had to be dealt with. Again and again.'

Turner took a breath, flaring his nostrils. 'But that's what the psych types would say... they've always got some complicated bullshit to justify the ridiculous fees they charge. The other possibility, as I indicated earlier, is that you are just a weak man, come under the influence of some more dominant personality. Someone who was using you for his own purposes. Someone, perhaps, that you loved, or thought you did. So, come on then – which is it?'

Jonathan could feel the waves of hatred coming off the man. He struggled to rally himself. What could he say to exonerate himself? Then he thought of what his father used to say when he was growing up: 'If you can't think what to say, don't say anything.' And what was it Lawrence – oh, God, *Lawrence*! was he okay? – what was that Mark Twain quote he used to bandy around: 'Better to keep your mouth closed and be thought a fool, than to open it and remove all doubt.' He steeled himself, quelling the nausea he felt, and stared this furious Apollo down.

Maybe sometimes there was power in doing nothing. He twisted and untwisted a loose strand on his jacket.

The silence lengthened.

Finally, Turner shoved back his chair and stood up. 'Come on, Reynolds – look at how you're sweating, and blushing, and fiddling with your jacket. Classic signs of guilt. You may as well stop lying and confess,' he said, looming over him. 'I always get a confession in the end. Never missed yet.'

He leaned forward until Jonathan could feel his mint-scented breath on his face, so close Jonathan could have kissed him. Then he sat back down, adopting a more matter-of-fact tone. 'Besides, it's only a matter of time before Forensics comes up with something hard to confirm our other evidence. If you confess now,' he said, injecting a hint of warmth into his voice, 'the court's likely to go a bit easier on you in sentencing. You might even get to go home in the meantime. How would that be?'

Jonathan thought about his rooms, his bed, being able to take a shower, get some decent food. His stomach rumbled. For a moment, he thought about giving the man what he wanted. But then he shook his head.

'I'm sorry, but I c-can't,' Jonathan said. 'I don't know how you've got all this stuff, but I didn't commit those murders. I couldn't kill anyone. I just couldn't.'

The other man's expression hardened as he gathered the photocopies back up, slamming the folder down in front of him. 'Take the suspect back to the cells,' he said to the waiting guard. 'Maybe another twenty-four hours on ice will change his mind.'

The intervening hours were darker than Jonathan had ever imagined they could be. The isolation, the contempt from the guards, the gnawing worry that, somehow, he had committed these awful acts of which he was accused. All these things combined to bring Jonathan to such a pitch of anxiety and misery that part of him was glad his warders had removed anything from his cell he might have used to harm himself.

So it was with tears in his eyes that he found himself standing by the exit, with a small bag of his possessions and a strong sense of unmerited reprieve. The guards hadn't explained what was happening, only that he was being released on police bail and needed to report back to the local station every morning at 9am if he didn't want to be taken back into custody. What was going on?

As Jonathan emerged into the small car park outside, he looked around helplessly, not sure what he should do next or where he should go. Then he saw a familiar figure, telegraphing utter patrician disregard of their surroundings, accompanied by two other people, silhouetted black against the sunshine.

'Lawrence, thank God!' he said, rushing over to greet his colleague, then stopping short as he saw the haggard look on the older man's face.

'I'm so sorry, Jonathan. Not just for how I acted the other day, but that we didn't get here sooner. Locked up like a common criminal – it's simply awful! I had no idea what was going on till the police got in contact, then I had to persuade your... well, Andrew, to admit you were telling the truth about where you were. Even then this Turner fellow refused to listen. It was these two who pressed the matter and, of course, Turner couldn't hold you indefinitely without good cause.'

He paused, and Jonathan frowned as he recognised the other two figures standing beside Lawrence.

'What are you two doing here?'

The unexpected response came from Simpson, accompanied by Stewart's approving nod.

'Lawrence asked us to help him clear things up and expedite the process. Besides, we thought you might need help proving your innocence. We know you didn't type that letter or commit those murders. The only question is: who on earth did?'

Several hours later, Jonathan was showered, shaved, and dressed in fresh clothes, sitting back on the sofa in Lawrence's college rooms, no sign of the emotional scene that had played out there only a short time before. Lawrence had continued to beat himself up about the situation he'd put Jonathan in, insisting on taking him back to his house in North Oxford for some respite and 'a nice home-cooked meal'. This last had been more chilling than comforting, however, prepared and served by Lawrence's wife, Cynthia, who, now Jonathan had met her, proved to be an emaciated, expressionless woman who was clearly doped up to the eyeballs and who didn't once look at Lawrence the whole time they were there. It seemed there had been farther reaching consequences to the couple's loss than Jonathan had imagined.

He had no time to dwell on that now, however, as the two detectives began to fill him in on the events that lay behind his arrest. He listened, appalled, as Simpson and Stewart explained the theory about his divided psychological state, which seemed like the stuff of nightmares, or a film by Buñuel. It was only when she described the account of his supposed fight with DB that he stopped her.

'But that's not true,' he said, bemused. 'Why would anyone say that? I didn't have an argument with Stephen at all – Nicholas did.'

The detective froze, exchanging a glance with her partner.

'And this Nicholas would be?'

'Nicholas Rivers,' Jonathan said. 'One of my students.'

He described the altercation to the best of his memory.

'Well that *is* odd,' said Stewart, drawing out the words. 'Because that's precisely the opposite of what the witness said happened.'

'And who was that?' asked Jonathan, his indignation renewed.

'Oh, a certain student called Nicholas Rivers,' Simpson contributed, one eyebrow cocked.

'It seems,' Stewart continued, 'that Mr Rivers has some explaining to do.'

As Jonathan prepared for bed that evening, it was with a sense of deep gratitude for being back in his own quiet, ordered space, his own familiar things around him. When confronted back at college in his large tower room on West Quad, Nicholas immediately confessed that he had made everything up. Shamefaced and apparently contrite, he claimed he had been angry at Jonathan for not taking his side in the argument against DB, though Jonathan suspected something deeper was at work. When Stewart threatened to charge him with wasting police time, his expression turned to alarm.

'I just wanted to give him a scare,' he told the stern-faced woman. 'I thought he'd get taken in for questioning, get a bit of a shock, you know? Then the truth would come out and he'd be fine. I never dreamed they'd lock him up or anything like that. I'm really sorry.' He threw Jonathan a pleading look. 'I promise I had nothing to do with killing that poor man.'

The boy was overwrought, and for a moment Jonathan had felt a pang of sympathy as he saw the dark lashes that fringed those beautiful eyes were moist with unshed tears, even as he recognised the student's weakness of character. *Enough*, he thought, squashing his emotions, then turned and walked away.

As the detectives began to take down the rest of Nicholas's statement, he beckoned Lawrence to accompany him and they descended the flights of stairs and walked across the Quad to take a turn around the Gardens.

The flower beds around the Great Lawn were bursting with life. Begonias, petunias, delphiniums and phlox tumbled over each other in a riot of colour. Here and there, Jonathan could see the marks left by croquet hoops on one of the smaller lawns, and, as they continued along the curved path, he spotted a half-eaten sandwich left behind from some student picnic on the bench beneath the huge oak tree. There was no visible evidence of the existence of dozens of stressed Finalists, or indeed of a psychotic killer. Neither he nor Lawrence spoke as they circumnavigated the garden, simply enjoying the clean air and the quietness until they came to the gate that marked the entrance to Back Quad.

'Do you think that's it?' Jonathan asked Lawrence as they prepared to part ways. 'I mean, are there any more murders to come?'

'I don't know,' Lawrence said heavily. 'Perhaps not. We can but hope. Certainly, poor Stephen's death was suitably melodramatic. What spectacle could be greater than a conflagration that consumes the whole of a college building?' He lit a cigarette. 'Not just the madwoman in the attic, but the whole of Thornfield Hall. Poor drab Charlotte Brontë would be proud.'

'But what about the twentieth century?' Jonathan said. 'Isn't the killer going to want to bring his sequence up to date?'

'Perhaps he thinks that would be otiose,' Lawrence countered. 'After all, the twentieth century is the century of mass killings – murder on an industrial scale. The extermination of millions in concentration camps and Gulags. How could any one man rival genocide or the destruction of the atomic bomb?'

'I suppose you're right,' Jonathan said. 'And, of course, all of his own killings have taken place during the twentieth century. I guess collectively they could represent his statement on all that came before. No literary death could possibly constitute a suitable climax.'

Nevertheless, as Jonathan now slipped into bed, relishing the small luxury of freshly laundered sheets, he could not quell a sense of disquiet. A feeling that, somehow, the killer wasn't done with him quite yet.

# CHAPTER THREE

FRIDAY 29 MAY, FIFTH WEEK IN TRINITY

KATE

K ate's satisfaction at being reinstated on the case – and, she had to be honest, at Tom's public humiliation, the massive blot on his perfect record – was alloyed with frustration at the amount of time they'd lost. The Big Boss had promised to request more manpower and resources from the neighbouring forces in Gloucestershire and Northamptonshire, chagrined, she felt, by the fact that she'd been right and the flashy outside man he'd brought in had been so signally wrong. As it transpired, Tom, dear old *Tom*, had been under suspicion for quite some time of coercing confessions to up his conviction rate. Now he was out, pending an official enquiry, and Kate was back in. Under sufferance, of course. The Big Boss had made it abundantly clear she was on a short leash – 'You wouldn't be back in if I had any other options, let me tell you.' He was now under heavy scrutiny himself from the chief constable for the area, who was not a man to suffer fools gladly or forgive mistakes. He'd even begun a personal review of the investigation, hoping to catch something they'd missed. Kate was glad of the buzz she always got when under pressure. Still, there was so much ground yet to cover.

The problem at the start of the case had been too little material. Now the problem was that there was too much. Witness accounts, forensics and intelligence reports, victim family histories, alibis: everything had to be gone over again.

Kate blew the hair back from her forehead. It was way overdue for a cut. She sighed.

'Do you buy what the boy said?' Geoff asked her from across the room.

Kate gazed at him over the ever-growing mound of papers before her. 'Rivers' story? Not sure. I mean, I guess it's possible he didn't understand the consequences of what he did. But is anyone really that naïve – even an Oxbridge type?' She shook her head. 'Seems more likely he was pissed off with Reynolds and thought a night or two in the cells would be suitable punishment. Nasty piece of work.'

'You don't think he could have had anything to do with the murders themselves?'

'A boy like that? Please. Those killings took meticulous planning and nerves of steel. You saw the way he crumpled when he saw us. No, he hasn't got the temperament. I bet the only thing he's ever planned is the theme for his next birthday party. Snotty little shit.'

She was fresh out of fucks for these overprivileged public school boys with their trust funds and sense of entitlement.

'Yup,' said Geoff, sighing. 'Sort of kid who thinks he's Marky Mark just because he wears those overpriced boxer-shorts. But there was something I didn't like about him. And I don't think he was telling us the whole story.'

'People never do,' she reminded him. 'That doesn't mean they're killers, or even criminals. I'm not going to waste any more time on that kid.'

The man looked abashed, as though she'd rebuked him, and

she relented. Back on the case or not, she was still on thin ice and she needed his full support and confidence.

'Still,' she said, 'if it makes you any happier, why don't you do a search for his Oxford Romantics profile – see if anything suspicious turns up?'

Their long-standing legal request to force the dating agency's founder to grant them access to the user accounts had finally made its way through to a judge who had little patience with the privacy concerns the founder had raised and sternly ordered him to comply with the police investigation. For the past few days, their IT team had been trawling through hundreds of profiles – gay, straight, and bi – searching for anything that might link to the murders. So far, they had merely turned up a surprising number of highly sexualised conversations, eye-popping in their lurid detail, which had made their way swiftly around the station, occasioning much hilarity.

*So much for 'Romantics'*, Kate thought grimly. Did no one just want to meet up for a drink and a chat, then see where the evening took them? Then again, who had time for that nowadays? She found herself looking at Geoff again, who had turned back to his desk, one hand clutching the back of his neck. She noticed the wisps of fine reddish hair on the back of his hand, the light dusting of freckles down his pale neck. What would it be like to go on a date with him, she wondered, then she shook herself for even contemplating the ridiculous idea. Even if she had been willing to cross that professional line, with all the risks that entailed, he was far too young for her. What was he, twenty-six? And she was practically old enough to be his mother. He'd probably laugh at the thought of dating her, if it didn't disgust him.

Kate placed her hands on both temples and pulled the skin taut, then released it. *You sad, saggy spinster,* surprising herself with the viciousness of the thought. *Your mother was right:*

*you'll never get married again now. No man wants a woman who's too old to have kids.* She sucked in a deep breath. Why was she even contemplating this shit? Must be being confronted with bloody Tom again.

Did she even want to get remarried? To have children? It might make her parents happy, but she couldn't see herself settling down, giving up her chance of a decent career. I mean, it wasn't like women with children couldn't continue their careers, but you had to be realistic, she thought: all that time out didn't look good, and no one wanted to appoint a DI whose mind might be half on her kid's chickenpox or exam results. *Snap out of it*, she told herself. *No one's asking, so it's a moot point. Concentrate on the job in hand. You're good at that. At least you used to be.* Maybe she needed therapy as much as Reynolds clearly did.

The IT team had flagged several conversation logs in which one or more selected keywords relating to the murders had been mentioned, along with a few other profiles that seemed suspect for one reason or another and merited closer attention. She and Geoff had been making their way through the list whenever they could take time from processing the huge amount of other material thrown up by an investigation of this nature.

As the murders had made their way into the public sphere, the station had been inundated by communications both from the community in Oxford and further afield. There were the usual crackpots wanting to spread wild theories of government conspiracies or Russian involvement. Several confessions had been received from senders who turned out on investigation to be little old ladies who just wanted to be part of something, or social malcontents looking for a laugh at the police's expense. Then there were the ones that Kate found really disturbing. Letters from people – both men and women – begging to be put in touch with the killer if he were ever located. They spoke of a deep connection, a mysterious kinship across time and space. Said they were convinced they could save him, supply the missing love and understanding he needed. The level of rationalisation and fantasy was beyond Kate's comprehension.

She forced herself now to join Geoff in sifting through strangers' dirty laundry. Few of the profiles contained their users' real names, of course, and so each one had to be cross-checked against a list of identities reluctantly provided by the network's CEO, who'd provided the data in the form of masses of printouts and point-blank refused to help them analyse it.

After an hour, feeling the tension in her neck and shoulders, Kate pushed back her chair and gathered up the empty plastic cups littering her desk.

'Want some?' she asked Geoff.

She had to ask a second time before the man looked up from his batch of profiles.

'Huh?' he said, rubbing his eyes with a hand stained with printers' ink.

'Coffee. Want some?' She waggled her stack of cups at him.

'Er, sure,' he said distractedly. 'But then come and take a look at this.' He tapped a sheet of paper.

Her curiosity roused, Kate put down the cups and went over to him.

'What've you got?'

Geoff passed the sheet to her. 'I've tracked down Rivers' account.'

'Anything incriminating?'

'Not exactly. But look.'

Kate scanned the paragraph of text he indicated.

*You're weirding me out with this crap*, it read. *I don't want to "embrace the darkness." What I want you to do is to stop contacting me on here.*

Her gaze flicked up to meet Geoff's.

'Read the stuff before it,' he said quietly.

Kate turned over a couple of pages and began to skim the conversation threads. Rivers was a popular user, it seemed, and his profile had dozens of requests for a 'chat' or a 'meet', most of which had gone unheeded. She skipped past several anodyne exchanges.

[How's it going?

Not bad, and you?

Good, thanks – up to anything interesting this weekend?

Not really, just chilling.]

There were a couple of stark offers of sex.

[You sound hot – up for a shag? I'm bored and horny.]

*Charming. It's another world when you're young,* she thought fleetingly.

Kate homed in on the messages between Rivers and his interlocutor, a user with the unlikely screen-name of the Dark Knight. As she read, she felt that familiar tight feeling in her stomach. *This could be it.*

The user had started off the conversation with Rivers innocuously enough, discussing movies and novels. A bit pretentious to Kate's mind, but whatever. Quickly, though, the films and literature discussed took on a disturbing aspect: works featuring violence and death with unpleasant sexual undertones. Rivers had played along at first, even seeming turned on by the frisson of discussing such taboo topics under the cloak of anonymity. But as the other user's messages had taken on a more insistent, even aggressive tone – demanding Rivers meet with him, inviting him to participate in ever more disturbing scenarios – Rivers had clearly become alarmed. And when the Dark Knight had threatened to expose him to his friends and family, claiming he knew where he lived and all sorts of other things about him, Rivers had had enough and ended the conversation.

She looked up at Geoff. 'Pretty gross,' she said. 'I mean, I'm all for a bit of role play...' She blushed, seeing his raised eyebrow. 'That is, whatever people want to do in the privacy of their own home is fine by me. But this is all kinds of wrong, not to mention illegal.'

'And that's not all,' Geoff said. 'I've just scanned down the list of users by their real-life surnames, and guess what? Beatty, Greene, Berkeley – even Tudor and Bhatia – all of them had profiles. And I'm guessing all of them had one-on-one conversations with the Dark Knight.'

'Sounds like Rivers had a narrow escape,' she said, her skin crawling at the thought of what might have happened.

Geoff nodded, his expression grim. 'And he might not be out of the woods yet. Look at the Dark Knight's real-life identity.' He tapped the list in his hand.

'But that's one of Reynolds' students,' Kate said, as a chill shot through her. Suddenly the connections to the tutor made horrific sense. 'We've got to warn him.'

She reached for the phone, but when she put the call through, Reynolds' phone just carried on ringing.

'Come on,' she said, grabbing her coat. 'We need to get over to St Seb's. Now. Let's just hope we're not too late.'

*And now, at last, the endgame approaches. My long Work nears its end – its apotheosis – and when all is complete it will finally be seen and understood if the onlookers have learned how to read aright. Ah, but there's the rub... the lurking fear, the dread that they will not see. That they will refuse to see. But no. No, even then. Even if man is too far fallen and continues to hide in the darkness – for true enough he loves the darkness for his deeds are evil – even then there is one who sees. One who sees all.*

# CHAPTER FOUR



## JONATHAN

'Hey, let me take that for you, Dr R.'

Jonathan relinquished the heavy tray to Oliver gratefully and went back into the kitchenette to fetch the milk and sugar. Today's revision tutorial was for the optional paper on Medieval Romance, on which both students ought to perform well, but so far the session had been incredibly awkward. Nicholas had been uncharacteristically taciturn, refusing to make eye contact with either Jonathan or Oliver, and mumbling his replies to his fellow student. Jonathan had several times had occasion to be grateful to Oliver for breaking into a lengthening silence with a helpful observation or pertinent reference. In desperation, Jonathan had suggested a round of tea and coffee, as much to break the tension as to raise the energy in the room with caffeine. With the first of the students' Finals papers a mere day away, Jonathan hoped Nicholas managed to snap out of his current funk before then. It would be a waste if he achieved anything less than the First he deserved. He felt a sudden stab of sympathy for the two students: in only a few more hours they would be sitting behind a desk down at the examination schools, uncomfortably clad in subfusc in the summer heat. It had been bad enough sitting his own exams in that sweltering Liverpool exam hall in a tee-shirt and shorts. He couldn't imagine what it would be like trying to concentrate in a full black suit, white shirt and white tie, with a gown weighing down his shoulders. *Still*, he thought, *I suppose it provides a sense of occasion*.

Oliver took a sip of his tea, then resumed reading his prepared essay. He was developing what seemed to Jonathan a rather outlandish connection between King Arthur's Round Table and Fortune's Wheel in both Malory's *Le Morte D'Arthur* and the anonymous alliterative poem of the same name.

He shuddered as Oliver recounted Arthur's famous but disturbing dream: a vision of Fortune as a beautiful woman, dressed in luxurious furs and opulent jewels, turning a mysterious wheel upon which six kings were bound, hand and foot. Riches and success – misery and misfortune – all stemmed from the inexorable turning of the wheel.

'It's a familiar metaphor for the vicissitudes of life,' Oliver read from his prepared essay, as usual a thick sheaf of lined pages. 'And it's not original to this poem, of course, with parallels in the Classical tradition and elsewhere.'

So far, so standard. Jonathan took another gulp of coffee, grimacing at the bitter taste. Why had he made it so strong? He struggled to concentrate as Oliver outlined his theory that Arthur's Round Table represented the cosmic wheel overturned: a human attempt to stall the inevitability of entropy and change.

Jonathan yawned, mentally tracing the graceful curve of Nicholas's drooping neck, despite himself. He wished there were some way he could lift him out of his despondency. Tell him he didn't hold a grudge. That the Dean had already agreed to overlook the matter. But it was hard not to be drawn into the student's dismal mood, especially given what Oliver was saying.

'In the midst of life we are in death...' Oliver read. 'Not just a line from the Funeral Service, but a quotation from a Gregorian chant. Or think of the memento mori tradition, seen widely in medieval and Renaissance art. From the *danse macabre* to the image of the grinning skull, writers and artists were aware that death comes for us all. It is in *this* context that we must see the Round Table.'

Half a dozen objections occurred to Jonathan, and he jotted them down on the notepad on his knee, but for now he elected simply to listen and see where Oliver was headed. This wild argument seemed to actually mean something to him. Even Nicholas seemed jolted out of his gloom by his partner's increasing fervour, glancing at him from time to time, a strange look on his face.

*What's going on there?* Jonathan wondered. *Have they fallen out too?* It almost looked like Nicholas was disturbed by his peer's words.

'The Round Table is often seen as the ideal of human civilisation,' Oliver continued. 'An image of noble fraternity and equality. But it is a lie! A ridiculous hope.' The pages trembled in his hands. 'Camelot must fall – its ideals shattered – and Arthur must die. That is the one constant of the legend. Earthly things cannot last. Human structures and societies – friendship and love – all shall come to an end. And that end is Death, the ultimate Truth.'

He completed his peroration with flashing eyes, his chin raised as though defying anyone to contradict him. Jonathan searched for something to say that would not seem anticlimactic or, worse, cruel, but at that moment the telephone on his desk cut through the tense atmosphere with its shrill sound. Jonathan allowed it to ring out with a shrug of mute apology, but when the ringing stopped he quietly congratulated Oliver on a well-prepared thesis. Then, pretending to have forgotten an appointment, he suggested they schedule another tutorial for the following afternoon after their first paper.

He closed the door to his study with a sense of relief. The events of the past days and weeks were catching up on him. Mentally and physically exhausted, and with the signs of another migraine coming on, he lay down on the couch his students had just vacated. He would just take five minutes to recuperate, he thought, struggling to clear his head of the deluge of thoughts and emotions released by Oliver's speech. His eyelids were heavy. Against his will, they closed.

He jerked awake at a quiet tap on the door. He ignored the sound, hoping whoever it was would go away. He was not up to talking to anyone right now. He closed his eyes again. To his indignation, though, the handle turned and someone entered the room. Through half-open lashes, Jonathan could see it was Oliver, but he was now dressed all in black, a large bag over his shoulder. He closed the door and placed the bag on the carpet between them.

'So sorry to disturb you, Dr Reynolds.' The words were silky smooth. 'We have some unfinished business to attend to, if you'll pardon the hanging preposition...'

Jonathan tried to push himself upright, but his head reeled and he fell back against the sofa cushions. *So heavy*. He decided to let his head rest where it was. *So tired*. He forced himself to speak.

'F'you want feedback on your essay, have to wait 'til tomorr'... Busy.'

'I can see that,' Oliver said, eyebrow raised as he surveyed the rumpled cushions and the red marks on Jonathan's cheek and forehead where he had rested them against the side of the couch.

Jonathan flushed, detecting the sneer in Oliver's voice. He forced his eyes wider, fighting to clear his head. *What is the matter with you? Get it together.* The boy in front of him was a version of Oliver he hadn't encountered before. Bold, challenging, confident. Almost a different person.

'I'm going to have to ask you to leave, Mr Black,' Jonathan managed, forcing his lips to enunciate clearly. 'Otherwise I'll have to call the porters.'

He glanced quickly towards the phone.

'I don't think you'll be doing that, Jonathan,' Oliver said softly, stepping in front of the desk. Was it his imagination, or did the boy seem somehow taller? Stronger? What was going on? And why did Jonathan feel so weak?

'Look,' Jonathan stammered, 'if you're worried about Finals, or want some more tutorials, I'm sure I can arrange some more exam sessions. Would you like that?'

A disconcerting smile spread across Oliver's face. A smile that did not reach the impenetrable pools of black that were his eyes.

'You genuinely don't see, do you?' he said, taking another step towards Jonathan so that he loomed over him, blocking out the light from the window.

Jonathan desperately fought off his mind-fog, trying to work out what the boy's problem was. Had he been overcome by stress? He didn't seem the type, but you never could tell how the pressure of impending exams would take people. Whatever it was, he couldn't afford to have another student complaining about him to the Dean, not with everything else that was going on.

'It's important not to let anxiety or worry get in your way...' Jonathan wrenched his mind into gear. 'How about this?' he offered as a sop. 'I'll write a letter to the examiners, explaining that you're suffering from stress. They'll take it into account when they're marking your papers.'

But it was clear Oliver was not buying Jonathan's pose of concern.

'This has nothing to do with your ineptitude as a tutor, or my anxiety about the ridiculous hoops the university requires us to jump through. It has everything to do with your blindness to anything other than your own petty concerns. Your inability to see past a pretty face to the real talent in front of you. Or even to notice when someone puts something in your coffee. But, more important than any of this, it has to do with your hypocrisy and lies.'

Jonathan's skin crawled as he realised what Oliver was alluding to – he knew all about him and Nicholas. Was he going to threaten him with blackmail? Tell all to the college authorities? Was he secretly obsessed with Jonathan himself? Was this the Travis Greene nightmare all over again?

But as if divining the direction of his thoughts, Oliver snorted derisively. 'And still you do not see! Truly, if a blind man guides a blind man, both shall fall into a pit.' He stepped over to his bag and retrieved something from it, holding it behind his back.

'Look, if this is some kind of sick joke,' Jonathan began, trying to summon up anger, but only fear came rising from the depths of his stomach.

'No, Jonathan,' Oliver again cut in familiarly, with another cold smile. 'This is no joke. Merely a reckoning. For when the dark night cometh, then must the judgement fall. And all men's deeds shall be made plain. And the secrets they hide must come into the light.'

Jonathan had been mustering his strength to force himself up off the couch with a vague plan to rush at the student and try to overpower him. Now he froze again as the realisation of who Oliver really was hit him like a falling bookcase.

'And now you see. At last.' Oliver stared into Jonathan's eyes, not a shred of humanity behind his cold gaze. He brought out a length of rope from behind his back and advanced quickly. Jonathan opened his mouth to shout for help but only a croak came out. His limbs refused to aid him. With a strength and surety Jonathan could hardly believe, Oliver bound his hands and feet, and laid him upon the floor. He tried to call out, but managed only a hoarse whisper. Just what had been in that coffee?

Jonathan tried to see what Oliver was doing but could see only indistinct motions out of the corner of his eye and hear the sound of him rummaging through his bag. He tried to loosen his bonds enough to wriggle out of them, but the work was infinitesimally slow.

Oliver's head moved back into view. 'You know, this is really something of an honour, your being the last one.' That chilling smile again. 'Of course, it won't seem like that, when they find your body with the full account of your misdeeds lying on your desk. No, the press will have a field day with that. The tutor and his student lover, caught up in a *folie à deux*. United by their lust for murder.'

Jonathan's lack of comprehension must have been visible in his eyes, for Oliver continued.

'Don't you understand yet? You really do have a mediocre mind, don't you? I've set it all out in the confession, right there on the desk – not yours, this time, but Nicholas's. How you seduced Nicholas when he first came to St Seb's, using your modicum of power as his tutor, the illusion of authority. How you spent a year together planning a series of murders inspired by the texts Nicholas was studying. How you egged each other on to ever more vile and depraved deeds until at last Nicholas grew weary. How he planned one last murder before embarking on a new life on the Continent, free of any constraints, free of you. He's next on the list, by the way: I'm going to enjoy that one.' The boy's eyes shone with a disturbing light. 'By the time they find Nicholas's body, I'll be long gone.'

'But no one will believe it,' Jonathan said, struggling to think what else to say to dissuade Oliver from this madness. How to save himself – and Nicholas. 'There's no way anyone will think Nicholas capable of such a thing,' he tried.

The student's expression hardened. 'Sentimental to the last,' he sneered. 'You never could see beyond his pretty face to the shallow mediocrity beneath. Oh yes, his essays were clever enough – and they were clever three years ago when the student who wrote them did his undergraduate degree here. Nicholas's pose of erudition was a lie. Like so much else in this sorry affair. And all the time, the real intellect was right in front of you. A true scholar's mind. But you couldn't see it. You've never been able to see that.'

For a moment, Jonathan perceived a hint of sadness in the way the boy held his body and he castigated himself for not paying more attention to what had evidently been going on for the last three years, infatuated as he had been by the arrogance of youth and beauty, signally derelict in his academic and pastoral duties. In an instant he saw how he must appear to an outsider observer. As disgusting as January in Chaucer's *Merchant's Tale*. A lecher, lusting over a pretty young thing who cared nothing for him.

Suddenly the student's mood shifted again, and he struck Jonathan full in the face, drawing blood from the side of his mouth.

'You disgust me,' he hissed. 'But, you know, it's not your pathetic desire for Nicholas that really bothers me. This has never been about... sexuality.' He wrinkled his nose as he said the word. 'This is much bigger than that. And as for you, it is your intellectual simony that most cries out for punishment.'

'Wh-what do you mean?' said Jonathan.

'You know full well,' came the implacable reply. 'You, Lawrence, this college – all of you compromised by fraud and corruption. By lies upon lies. And *that* I cannot tolerate. For Truth is the only reality worth knowing.'

Jonathan's head began to spin.

'Must I spell it out to you like a feeble-minded child?' Oliver shouted.

He began to pace around the study, his movements increasingly agitated. Then, in a shift so sudden it was as though he had flicked a switch, his face and eyes went blank, expressionless. Jonathan's skin crawled.

'It was never about the all-hallowed canon of English literature,' Oliver said quietly, leaning against the arm of the sofa. 'Oh yes – I know what you thought. What you told those hapless detectives. And I knew that was what you would think, following the clues, the notes, your imbecilic nose. But a small part of me still hoped for more, I confess – that you would see beyond the surface, the most obvious interpretation of the signs, to the real truth.

'Even now, if you can tell me why I did what I did, there may be a chance for you. For, as it is written, *the truth shall set you free.*'

The boy stared at Jonathan, as if challenging him to pass the test – and hoping that he would. Jonathan cudgelled his brain, begging it to piece together whatever mad narrative his adversary had in mind. *Truth, lies, simony, corruption.* How did it all fit together?

'Yes, I begin to see it now,' he said cautiously, forcing himself to smile. 'How could I have been so blind to your true... genius?'

Oliver beckoned Jonathan to continue.

'The texts on which the murders were based never held the key to your plan in and of themselves,' Jonathan said. 'Clearly they follow the trajectory of the English canon, but, as you say, there must be some other factor that connects them. Something we have overlooked, blinded by the false trail so cunningly laid for us.'

Oliver said nothing in response to the blatant flattery, but Jonathan thought he detected a note of approval in his eyes. Emboldened, he went further, thinking back over the list of points on Simpson's whiteboard, searching for anomalies. As he did so he continued to work surreptitiously at the ropes holding him.

*Beatty, Greene, Berkeley, Tudor, Bhatia, Granville-Smith.* Such very different people, despite the lack of close family and friends that united them.

'The deaths have very little in common on the face of it,' Jonathan continued. 'Beheading, throat-slitting, plague, vampirism, fire. There must be something else that associates them, beyond their sexuality, of course.'

He risked another glance at Oliver and was rewarded with the hint of a nod. He felt like he was in a tutorial, but this time he was not the tutor and the stakes were higher than he could imagine.

'A variety of implements was used to wound or kill the victims. Knives, spears, syringes – but there were some oddities. Those pins found in Mike Tudor's body: they don't seem to have anything to do with Defoe's *Journal of the Plague Year*. That always puzzled me. And the first murder, based on *Beowulf*: you impaled Beatty on an iron spike. That doesn't happen in the poem. And the pictures on the note from the second murder included a spear as well as an axe and the holly branch. I didn't think it was relevant at the time, but the Green

Knight did *not* have a spear in the poem. Yes, the weapons must hold the key.'

He shook his head. 'But there was no spear in DB's killings... unless...' He recalled the little heap of charred wood and metal point at the base of DB's stretcher, a detail he'd seen and disregarded at the time.

Something nagged at Jonathan, sitting just out of reach at the back of his mind. He tried to calm himself, to allow it to surface. A picture materialised of a hedgehog, its spines glinting; the most incongruous image, but wait... He recalled *The Life of St Edmund*, an Old English saint's life he had been translating with the First Years only a few weeks previously. Every year the students were amused by the way the author characterised the murder of the eponymous saint, describing him as shot full of spears, 'as with a hedgehog's bristles, just as Sebastian was.' And then it all became clear.

'All the murders relate to the martyrdom of Saint Sebastian, don't they,' he pronounced triumphantly, momentarily forgetting his perilous position. 'The spears, the spikes – they represent the way Sebastian was killed by Roman soldiers, making the ultimate sacrifice for his faith. And the clues to the rest of his legend were there too – the Roman setting of *Titus Andronicus* and those mislaid props, Sebastian's efficacy as a defence against the bubonic plague, that's why you went to the trouble of recreating Defoe's description. The pins, too, alluding to Sebastian's popularity amongst early modern pinmakers. So many little details that we missed – that *I* missed. But the legend is central to what your sequence of killings means, isn't it? The victims represent a sacrifice – and a call on your college and me, your tutor, to make a sacrifice of our baser instincts. To call us back to God, the original centre of these colleges as monastic foundations, and the source of all truth, whether religious or intellectual. To call us back to our duty.'

But, again, Oliver smiled that disturbing smile.

'So close and yet so far, *Dr* Reynolds,' he said, placing an odd stress on Jonathan's title. 'I'd award that effort a beta-double-plus, perhaps. Saint Sebastian, so-called, is indeed central here, but his supposed sacrifice is not the issue. Like the other cretins in this benighted institution, you trot out the popular version of his death, stuck full of arrows or spears, as in that banal Botticelli print on the wall over there. But that is *not* how he died. The slightest research would tell you he survived that assault, was rescued and revived. Only later was he actually killed, clubbed to death on the orders of the emperor. The image on which this college was founded – which Hacker and his cronies proudly trot out ad nauseam – is an outright lie. And, as my mother always told me, lies are an affront against God.'

'But a lie that is easily remedied, surely?' Jonathan protested. 'Was it really necessary to perpetrate all those killings? For a harmless institutional myth? Those poor men.'

Oliver's eyes flashed. 'Those hypocrites deserved everything they got. Liars, all of them. Beatty, that insidious little snake, spreading malicious gossip, destroying reputations. Greene and Granville-Smith, both living a lie, pretending to be someone they were not – and of course, the college was only too happy to go along with it, covering up Greene's indiscretions, treating Granville-Smith like an aristocrat instead of the barrow boy he really was. Then there's Tudor – the pathological fantasist; Berkeley with his sordid affairs, worshipping the foolishness of the theatre; Bhatia, with his shady election campaign built on false promises. The righteous will feel no sympathy for them, merely disgust.'

'But everyone tells a lie from time to time,' Jonathan stammered. 'Most of the time it doesn't really hurt anyone. We must make allowances.'

'Just what I would expect from the hypocrite supreme, the

arch-liar,' Oliver snapped. Then, abruptly, he laughed. 'You know the sad thing is that I looked up to you when I first came here as an impressionable Fresher. This college stood for all my highest ideals – the pursuit of knowledge for its own sake, of truth – and you represented everything I aspired to be. And you seemed so genuine, so interested in us as your students.' He sneered. 'But the truth of what you were really interested in became quickly apparent. And, most egregious of all, the levels of deceit and corruption to which you would stoop. The hypocrisy of preaching to us about the importance of solid research and original insights, when your own career rested on fraud and lies.'

Jonathan gasped.

'Ah yes – I see you realise it now!' gloated Oliver. 'I know your other little secret, *Dr* Reynolds. In a moment of idle curiosity in the Bodleian, I called up your doctoral thesis, thinking I could impress you with my diligence, perhaps dropping a respectful reference or two into my essays. But as I read on in my snug library niche, warning bells began to ring. Whole sections of your thesis read like someone else had written them. There was something... Germanic about them. *Deutsch... Deutsch, alles Deutsch.* My mother tongue, as ever, came in handy. I followed up the references in your bibliography – days of dusty research it took – but I always find what I'm after in the end, and so it proved in this case. That obscure German work you'd tracked down and from which you lifted whole chunks... No one would ever find you out, because who but you would bother to consult such a forgotten, insignificant text? Or so you believed.

'At first I tried to excuse you, to consider the pressure you must have been under, but how can one excuse such blatant fraud? Even worse, the continuing hypocrisy as you used your bogus degree to gain a position teaching others – abusing a sacred position of trust. The more I thought about it, the more my wrath grew, as I saw that you represented only the most patent example of dishonesty and lies. There were so many others. So many. Lawrence Gresham, your mentor, culpably implicated in your fraud. Hacker and the Fellows, gluttons and fools, spouting pious lies about their institution's figurehead whilst covering up each other's misdeeds and putrid affairs. And those "poor men", as you call them. Over the months I saw my opportunity... the victims' weaknesses – each connected to you; each of them lying in his own way. About others, about themselves: who they were, what they'd done. Their lies – your lies – could not be tolerated anymore.

'No, the truth had to be told, for the truth will always out... And so your "confession" and that of Nicholas, will forever taint the precious reputation of St Sebastian's and its denizens. Reveal it for the nest of lies it is. Not only that, the deeds I have wrought will reverberate beyond these walls. For though I depart, others will follow me and take up my mantle, and my Work will continue, not just in this city but throughout the world. All the petty lies that men tell themselves and others accept – pretending like you that a little falsehood is nothing in the pursuit of a career, a relationship, a better life... All of that is supremely irrelevant besides the inescapable reality of Death. For Death is the only effective answer for such falsehood, such mendacity. Yes, Death is the undeniable fact – the only proof of our very existence: the ultimate Truth.'

Oliver was hissing into Jonathan's ear, flecks of spittle landing on his cheeks. His long hair brushed against Jonathan's neck and, mechanically, Jonathan thought of the attack on Bhatia, and realised what his mind had been trying to tell him. *Too late now.* The situation was hopeless – and, to his horror, Jonathan found something almost seductive in that. The other's passion, his fervour, was undeniable – was it so wrong to find a degree of pleasure in forming such a pivotal part of his grand plan? Would it be so terrible just to give in? Jonathan closed his eyes. But then something deep inside him rebelled. Fought back.

'How can you say that? How can you preach of truth, when all you've done throughout this chain of foul murders is to lie? Pretend you were someone you're not. Prey on people's emotions and manipulate them into your clutches against their better judgement. I'm not the real liar – you are!'

Jonathan's words had an immediate and startling effect. Oliver shuddered as if in shock and the mad gleam in his eyes seemed to fade.

'And there it is,' he said meditatively. 'The other interpretation of what I have done; the one I fear. For, like you, so few men know now how to read the world aright.' He stepped back from the couch and over towards Jonathan's bookcase.

'So many books,' he said. 'For of the making of many books there is no end. And so many ways of reading them. *For now we see as in a glass darkly*. The keys of the Spirit are not given to all, to unlock the meaning of things. Even I, even I did not at first comprehend.'

He turned back to face Jonathan and his tone became conversational. 'Caught up in my studies as a First Year, I did not even see the problem inherent in them. Not until one day in Trinity term, when Elias Richardson returned to deliver his visiting lecture on literary truth. Of course, the old fool prated on about relativism and other such nonsense. But one thing he said struck me: *Literature, by its very nature, is a lie*. Indeed, he saw this as one of its very virtues – to be able to imagine the world otherwise – but I saw through *that* ruse. I was devastated for a time. To think that all my hard work, all that time, had been wasted. Worse, had been devoted to venerating and perpetuating falsehoods: an affront to God Himself. I fell into a time of despair. Those long sleepless tracts of the night... But, as I turned it all over in my mind, I began to see beyond what Richardson had said to the reality he could not see.'

Oliver's eyes were gleaming again now as he reached the end of his peroration.

'Literature, like any lie, may *become* truth, nay it must. And that is what I have done – and all that I have done. I have turned literature's lies into truth and, in so doing, I have brought the lies of others into the light. You do see that, don't you?' he pleaded. 'I would like to think that you understand me at last, since it was you who set me on this path.'

'I do understand,' Jonathan said, hoping against hope to be believed. And in fact, there was a kind of twisted logic to what the boy was saying. 'I understand entirely. And I can protect you; keep you safe. I'll confess my guilt; make things right. Just spare my life and I'll help you explain what you've done to the police. They'll listen to me. And all this can have a happy ending.'

For a moment he thought Oliver was going to buy it. There was a flicker of uncertainty in the boy's eyes, a slight droop of the shoulders. But then the steel returned to his gaze.

'No. It's too late. I am too far along the path to give up now. You have to die for the Work to become complete. For the story to end and be transformed into history. I won't listen to you anymore.'

He stuffed a rag in Jonathan's mouth and stalked out of his view. Realising his time had run out, Jonathan wrenched desperately at his bonds, tearing at them with his fingernails. At last he managed to free his feet. Forcing his uncooperative body off the floor he tried to stagger towards the phone on his desk but his ankle, still weak from his fall a fortnight earlier, gave way and he slumped back down.

Out of his view, he heard Oliver grunt as though he were

lifting something heavy, and craned his neck round to see what was happening. As he watched, Oliver heaved a pig's head, fleshy and gross, over to the sofa, and Jonathan grimaced at the revolting sight of its coarse-bristled snout. Oliver raised a spear, point towards the ceiling, and rammed its wooden end through the soft cushions of the sofa so that it stuck upright, its shaft quivering. Then he heaved the pig's head onto the spike with another grunt of effort.

'Behold Beelzebub,' he said, panting. 'Lord of the Flies and Emperor of Falsehood. As disgusting as the society he governs. And you... prepare yourself for the final act.'

Jonathan's eyes widened as Oliver picked up another spear, hefting it in his hand, its metal point vicious in the last rays of sunlight from the window. As he raised the weapon high above his head in both hands, he looked for a moment like a pagan priest of old, preparing a ritual sacrifice. He plunged the spear into Jonathan's side, and, in an access of pain that was almost exquisite, everything went dark.

# EPILOGUE
## OXFORD, 1998, SUMMER VACATION

Jonathan sat on a stool in the Arrow and Quiver, nursing a gin and tonic. The consultant had warned him not to drink alcohol whilst taking the morphine tablets prescribed for his injured abdomen and cracked and bruised ribs. Still, just a single couldn't hurt, surely. He took quiet enjoyment in the sense that pain lurked somewhere just beneath the numbness, biding its time. The pain was a reminder that, despite the unreality of his recent experiences, nonetheless he himself was real, and what he said and did mattered. He'd long ago got over the embarrassment of having those diary entries read and analysed in all their hideous incoherence. He still couldn't remember writing them and hoped against hope that just maybe he hadn't – that Oliver had forged them, like he'd forged the signature on that letter. But he honestly couldn't be sure: there were so many things he couldn't remember. If he had written them, maybe he had more in common with Oliver than he'd thought. Something monstrous inside him, trying to get out. Maybe Dr Carter would help him discover what. When Lucia heard about what had happened, she had persuaded him finally to make an appointment to see a new therapist: 'to deal with the trauma, if nothing else.' No doubt she would have plenty to say. He shrugged, then winced at the movement.

'Are you feeling all right, Dr R?'

'How many times do I have to tell you, Geoff? Call me Jonathan!' He repaid the bigger man's solicitude with a smile. 'It's just a twinge. I'll be fine.'

He took a long, slow breath and listened as Kate and Geoff started to bicker amicably about some bureaucratic work matter. In the past weeks they'd met up several times, supporting Kate as the official review into her handling of the case progressed. She had been cleared of serious misconduct but given an official warning and would need to avoid any further infractions if she wanted to maintain her career progression. As they met up, they had also wrestled with their unanswered questions about the events in which they'd been caught up. And especially about the motivation behind Oliver's peculiar campaign.

As if she could read his mind, Kate patted him on the arm. 'So, what's your latest theory on our Dark Knight then?'

'Yeah,' Geoff added. 'Are we still thinking Norman Bates, or more Dennis Nilsen *Killing for Company...*?'

'Well, that's the million-dollar question, isn't it?' said Jonathan, frowning. 'Oliver certainly represented himself as a crusader for Truth, enraged by lies and hypocrisy, bent on revealing the webs of deception criss-crossing the university.'

'That's just some bullshit rationalisation,' Geoff said.

'Quite possibly. But there is some truth in what he was saying. I remember Lawrence telling me once that Oxford is a city of masks. The image it presents to the world rarely reflects what's really going on underneath, and the same is true of the people who inhabit it.'

'But that's the case with everyone,' Kate interjected. 'You can't spend much time as a police officer before learning that.'

Jonathan nodded. His experiences, if anything, had taught

him that the self was never truly knowable to another. People, like literary texts, needed to be interpreted, and their motivations were, in the end, unrecoverable. There was no singular, inalienable truth: *Now we see as in a glass darkly*. But, after his bruising experience with Andrew – now holed up in some religious retreat somewhere in the Home Counties – he'd met up with Reverend Little to talk things over, and slowly he'd started to believe that relationships of any sort, whether with God or lovers or friends, were ultimately based on faith. On trust that they were who they said they were, that they had your best interests at heart. And the truth was that you were always going to be disappointed somewhere along the way. Perhaps over and over again. But that was life. What other option was there other than to trust someone or something? Perhaps it was only the choice that mattered.

'You're absolutely right,' he told Kate. 'As usual. But you were telling me you'd finally received some information from the authorities in Germany. Did that shed any light on things?'

Kate made a face. 'Well it certainly would have encouraged us to look more closely at Black if it had got to us in time, instead of after we'd already captured him.' She went on to explain how she had requested that Interpol look into Oliver's past in Germany as part of the investigations. The slow-turning wheels of international bureaucracy had eventually elicited some interesting records on his family circumstances from Germany's Bundesamt für Justiz. The investigation had been hindered further by having to search under both Truman and Schwartz, but eventually the search had revealed Oliver's parents had split up acrimoniously when he was thirteen after his mother discovered her husband's decade-long affair with one of her closest male friends. Drunk and miserable one night, as Oliver slept in the next room, she'd taken an overdose. It got into the local papers and, racked with guilt and publicly shamed,

Oliver's father had been discovered in his garden shed some weeks later, having ingested rat poison. There had been no suggestion at the time that their surviving son might have had anything to do with it, but in the aftermath of the Oxford murders you had to wonder.

'It's all very interesting,' said Kate, looking earnest. 'And it certainly explains why he'd have an aversion to lies and deception. But my guess is there's some form of transference at work... an underlying crisis of sexuality. I mean, there's plenty of liars around Oxford who aren't gay. The fact that all the victims were... it's not just a coincidence! Maybe he was externalising some self-loathing part of himself – punishing what he couldn't tolerate in his or his father's identity.'

'Look who's been reading up on her crim. psych! Planning your next career move?' Geoff nudged his colleague playfully.

'No, I'm serious,' she replied, frowning. 'I've been thinking a lot about this. Looking back over the victims' profiles. Each of them, when you think about it, had some psychopathic traits of their own: grandiose sense of self-worth, superficial charm and a pathological need to deceive, lack of empathy, poor impulse control, a parasitic lifestyle, a tendency to blame others for their own problems. I mean, I guess we can all be like that at times – but, given that each of the targets had traits Oliver also embodied... maybe there was a dimension of narcissistic attraction too? He was both drawn to and repelled by the six victims.'

'Seven...' said Jonathan, 'or there would have been. And I hate to think what that says about me.'

'I didn't mean...' Kate looked mortified. 'Crap, I'm really sorry.'

'It's fine.' *She's probably right*, Jonathan thought. *I mean, look at those diary entries.*

'You know what I think?' said Geoff. 'I reckon it's a lot less complicated than that. I mean, maybe the kid had some self-loathing or whatever, but if that was enough motivation, then America's Bible Belt would be chock-full of psychopathic killers, wouldn't it?'

Kate rolled her eyes. 'No comment. What's your big suggestion then?'

Geoff shrugged. 'He was just wrong in the head. Frontal lobe damage or something. Brain chemistry out of whack. I don't know. You can't explain these things sometimes. Like your dress sense.' He shoved her playfully.

'Get off me, you big gorilla,' she snapped back. 'You've spent so much gym time on your traps and delts it'd have taken Oliver a month to saw through your neck!'

'Way too soon!'

As the two of them continued to bicker amicably, Jonathan slipped back into his reverie, reflecting on Oliver's possible motivations. The boy was, he knew currently, in a secure psychiatric hospital, heavily sedated and undergoing analysis, a special jury having deemed him unfit to plead following a forensic psychiatrist's report on the murders. Who knew whether they'd ever get to the bottom of what had been going on. It had to be more complicated than Geoff's theory, surely. After all, there was so much meticulous preparation involved. When searching Oliver's room, along with copies of his Scout, Maureen Jones's keys and various kinds of medical supplies, the police had found dozens of textbooks on everything from anatomy and physiology to poisons and forensic techniques. Books about Dahmer, Kemper, even Henry Lucas, sat on top of a well-thumbed copy of the Bible. Clearly, for Oliver, knowledge meant power. Chillingly, the investigators had also found several of Jonathan's request slips from the college library, all arranged neatly in a folder along with blown-up photocopies of his signature and page after page of imitation after painstaking imitation. Surely all that planning had to mean... Jonathan shook himself. No, he wasn't going down that particular rabbit hole. He should focus on his recovery and count his blessings.

He was very lucky indeed, he knew. First, that Oliver's thrust had slipped past his major organs, and secondly that Kate and Geoff had burst into his study at the critical moment, overpowering Oliver between them and then calling an ambulance. The paramedics had got through six bags of blood while Jonathan was being transported the short distance to the hospital. There, several more blood transfusions and the work of a skilled surgeon had saved Jonathan's life. He still had no memory of anything after Oliver stabbed him, but he was profoundly grateful to the two detectives. If they hadn't rushed across town to check on him... if they had arrived seconds later.

'Still with us?' Geoff said, patting him on the arm. 'You looked like you were miles away!'

'Sorry. Sorry.' Jonathan forced a smile.

'So, what are your plans,' Kate asked, 'once the docs have given you a clean bill of health?'

Jonathan considered. 'Do you know, I have no idea.' The long summer lay ahead, no tutorials or lectures to occupy him now the exam period was over. He should really try to make some progress on his long-neglected article, but somehow the whole project seemed trivial in the light of what had happened. There were far greater monsters in real life.

*Oliver was right about one thing*, he reflected. *Death comes for us all, and none of us knows the hour*. Jonathan had no sense of what he wanted to do with the life he had been granted on reprieve, but he was increasingly sure he did not want to spend it as one more earnest soldier, beavering away in Oxford's libraries, writing books and articles that few would ever read. Any research now, too, would surely be tainted by the knowledge of the intellectual fraud that had paved the way to his career. He had made a clean breast of it to Lawrence, not sure if he was hoping for redemption or punishment, but the old man had merely shaken his head sadly. 'What possible good could it do if that came to light now?' he had said. 'After all that has happened. After all that loss. No, try again – fail better.'

Hacker had been less forgiving. The man's lack of empathy was staggering. Lawrence had again tried to bring his influence to bear, but Hacker was having none of it. Jonathan knew the official complaint from Alistair's wealthy father hadn't helped. He was sure, too, the old shark blamed him for the college's poor showing in English Finals. Nicholas and Oliver's brilliance had not paid off. Nicholas had barely scraped a 2.1, and although, incredibly, Hacker had argued for Oliver's being allowed to sit his exams from the psychiatric hospital, his proposal had been rejected in no uncertain terms, and Hacker's legal reputation had suffered a significant blow in the process. In the end, it was sweet, determined Charlotte Rudman who defended the college's honour, with a solid First – built, Jonathan had to imagine, on long diligent nights in the library and a lucky run of exam questions. He rolled his eyes. It turned out it was she who'd sent him those treasured pigeon-post notes, as she'd tearfully confessed to him at the Leavers' Drinks. What could you do?

Jonathan looked ahead to the new term that would begin in a couple of months' time, bringing with it a new crop of Freshers. *And so it begins again. But not for me.* The only opening he'd found was a one-year lectureship at one of the posher colleges and he wasn't sure he could face the return to that kind of precarity. Maybe it was time to get out of Oxford. He sighed. Then he shook himself, seeing the indulgent looks on the detectives' faces, no doubt amused at his having drifted off once more. He noticed how close they were standing together, their hands almost touching.

'And how about you two then?' he said. 'Do the pair of you... have any plans?'

The not-so-subtle emphasis did not go unnoticed, and, as Stewart met his eye, she lacked her customary aplomb.

'Is it that obvious?' she said quietly, as though worried her colleagues might somehow overhear.

'Only to someone looking for it,' he reassured her.

Simpson frowned. 'I thought we talked about this?' he said to Stewart. 'There's no need to hide the fact we're together now you're no longer my superior officer. Unless you're ashamed of having a toy boy,' he added.

Meeting no response from Stewart, other than an indulgent smile, he answered Jonathan's enquiring look. 'Yes, there's been some more good news. Kate's been promoted to DI and been transferred to the Met. Apparently the Big Boss and his higher-ups were impressed by her work on the case. And saving your life didn't hurt either.' He flashed a mischievous grin. 'Anyway, I hadn't wanted to say anything while we were still working together, but I've had my eye on this one for quite some time now.'

He patted Stewart's shoulder familiarly, earning himself a scowl from the other detective. 'It's going to be tough at first, commuting between Oxford and London, but we'll make it work.' His voice radiated confidence, and the pair's patent happiness, evident in their body language and comfortable closeness, almost brought a tear to Jonathan's eye. *Careful*, he thought, *that drink on top of the painkillers is making you sloppy. Get it together.*

The three of them chatted about the flat Kate was renting in Kilburn, a short Tube-ride away from Paddington, where the

Oxford train terminated. After a while, Jonathan felt tired again and said he was going to go back to his rooms to rest.

'Yes, you take care of yourself,' Simpson urged him. 'We don't want any relapses, do we?'

Then he rummaged in his jacket pocket. 'Oh, I almost forgot.' He handed Jonathan a crumpled piece of paper. 'I spoke to my brother and checked it was okay to give you this. No pressure, of course. You don't have to use it.'

Jonathan unfolded the paper, which contained a phone number and a name: Gary.

'Gaz is a good guy,' Simpson said, 'and a lot cleverer than me. I'm betting if you met up for a drink, the two of you would get along. But, like I said, no pressure.' He placed one hand on Jonathan's shoulder with a firm, easy pressure. 'Whatever you decide, don't be a stranger.'

Jonathan shook hands with the pair, then made his way slowly back through college to his rooms. With all the students gone for the summer it was eerily quiet, and his footsteps echoed in the corridor as he passed the chapel and climbed the Buttery staircase.

Back in his study, he sat at his desk, feeling the relief in his legs and back. He was still building his strength back up after the prolonged stay in hospital. Even the short walk to and from the pub left him out of breath and weak. He glanced at the PC and monitor, now fully installed and set up where his VCR used to be, the orange standby light a subtle reminder of tasks not completed.

He picked through the items of post he had collected from the Lodge that morning but not yet opened. Amongst the junk there was a postcard from Lawrence, currently on holiday on one of the Greek islands with Cynthia. The picture on the front was of the head of a young man with luxuriant curls, smooth skin and full lips. The message on the back read, *Saw this and thought of you* and, not for the first time, Jonathan wondered precisely what message Lawrence meant to convey.

Beneath the postcard lay a thick cream envelope labelled in a familiar script. Jonathan reached for his letter opener. In the short note, Nicholas thanked him for his help throughout his studies and hoped he was recovering well. He professed to be content with the 2.1 he'd achieved instead of the First he'd been predicted. He spoke of his relief that Oliver had been stopped before he had had a chance to come for him too. The message ended with an unexpected sentence that set Jonathan's heart racing.

*I think often of the time you comforted me in your study when I was so upset, and, whilst I will always regret the chain of events that followed, I can never regret our kiss. Now that you're no longer my tutor, perhaps we could meet up again and see where things take us...?*

There was a phone number scribbled next to the flowing signature. Jonathan touched it with hesitant fingertips, then put the letter aside. Beneath a couple of circulars about upcoming concerts lay a message from the on-duty porter scrawled on the usual carbon paper. *Telephone call from Andrew. 271050. Back now. Please can we talk?*

Jonathan sat back in his chair, considering. Then he picked up the mobile phone Simpson had persuaded him to buy on the grounds of his personal safety. 'You never know when you might need a policeman on hand,' he had joked. So far, his was the only number in the phone's Contacts list. Jonathan typed in the numbers from Nicholas's letter and Andrew's note, finally adding the contact details for Simpson's brother.

For a long moment he stared at the three new numbers, his finger hovering over the edit button. Then, with a surge of confidence, he selected one of the numbers and pressed a button. An act of faith, of trust in himself.

*Contact Deleted*, read the message on the screen.

Jonathan put down the phone and walked over to the window. As he raised the sash, clean fresh air rushed in, cooling his cheeks. The scent of jasmine was intense. He rested his arms on the windowsill and looked out into the city. It was dusk and the street lamps were just turning on, illuminating the buildings and trees near to them with an orange glow. He directed his gaze further up into the clear sky, where he could already pick out a couple of stars twinkling in the dusk. As he watched, a wisp of cloud – or was it smoke? – drifted across the moon.

It was going to be a beautiful night.

*i look out of the narrow window the eye of my little room on the second floor its comfortable and they play nice music though the water is bitter*

*ill be seeing you. yes they play nice music. ill be seeing you*

*they think im mad of course and it suits me they think so but as the old charlatan said there is always some reason in madness and the truth is I see things plain things they are not ready to see and as the doctor said the truth is what the mind makes of things and i can wait i have time for fortunes wheel turns and all things come to those who wait*

*i see you looking as my window shows the darkening sky and the moon a pregnant sow and a tendril of smoke from some garden bonfire passes over it and heaven swallows the smoke*

*and ill be seeing you*

## THE END

# ACKNOWLEDGEMENTS

Thanks to Betsy, Tara, and the whole Bloodhound Books team, for believing in *Come the Dark Night* and working so hard to bring it to the public. I'd especially like to thank Ian for his editing suggestions, which have made this a much better and more streamlined novel. (Any errors and inconsistencies that remain are my own fault!)

Very grateful thanks for feedback, suggestions, and encouragement go to a whole host of friends and supporters. Particular thanks to those who read earlier drafts of the novel: Victoria (and for suggesting Bloodhound Books to me), Kate M (and for support both moral and material), Heather (just the latest in my series of debts over the years), Jon (and for a long and fascinating chat about Major Crimes), Felicity (Charlotte's number one fan!), Kate L, Matt, Stephen, and Anita. Heartfelt thanks, too, to Harry (who got me back into all this in the first place!), Jonathan, Cathleen, Holly, Simon, and my other friends and family.

Apologies to the City of Oxford for making up such terrible things about it, but thanks for the inspiration.

Finally, thanks to you the reader for buying or borrowing this book: if you enjoyed it, please consider leaving me a review on Amazon or Goodreads or recommending me to your friends, library, or book group. If you'd like to, you can follow me on Twitter @davidtregarthen

# A NOTE FROM THE PUBLISHER

**Thank you for reading this book**. If you enjoyed it please do consider leaving a review on Amazon to help others find it too.

**We hate typos.** All of our books have been rigorously edited and proofread, but sometimes mistakes do slip through. If you have spotted a typo, please do let us know and we can get it amended within hours.

**info@bloodhoundbooks.com**